THE SPEEDICUT MEMOIRS
Book 1 (1915–1918)

Also by Christopher Joll

Uniquely British: A Year in the Life of the Household Cavalry

The Speedicut Papers Book 1 (1821-1848): Flashman's Secret
The Speedicut Papers Book 2 (1848-1857): Love & Other Blood Sports
The Speedicut Papers Book 3 (1857-1865): Uncivil Wars
The Speedicut Papers Book 4 (1865-1871): Where Eagles Dare
The Speedicut Papers Book 5 (1871-1879): Suffering Bertie
The Speedicut Papers Book 6 (1879-1884): Vitai Lampada
The Speedicut Papers Book 7 (1884-1895): Royal Scandals
The Speedicut Papers Book 8 (1895-1900): At War with Churchill
The Speedicut Papers Book 9 (1900-1915): Boxing Icebergs

THE SPEEDICUT MEMOIRS
The Memoirs of Charles Speedicut

Book 1 (1915–1918)

Russian Relations

Edited
by
Christopher Joll

authorHOUSE

AuthorHouse™ UK
1663 Liberty Drive
Bloomington, IN 47403 USA
www.authorhouse.co.uk
Phone: 0800.197.4150

© *2018 Christopher Joll. All rights reserved.*

No part of this book may be reproduced, stored in a retrieval system, or transmitted by any means without the written permission of the author.

Published by AuthorHouse 05/24/2018

ISBN: 978-1-5462-9291-3 (sc)
ISBN: 978-1-5462-9292-0 (hc)
ISBN: 978-1-5462-9290-6 (e)

Print information available on the last page.

This book is printed on acid-free paper.

Because of the dynamic nature of the Internet, any web addresses or links contained in this book may have changed since publication and may no longer be valid. The views expressed in this work are solely those of the author and do not necessarily reflect the views of the publisher, and the publisher hereby disclaims any responsibility for them.

For

Jasper Speedicut

CONTENTS

Notes On The Editor ix
Introduction xi
The Speedicut Family Tree xiii
Foreword xv

Chapter One: Photographs Don't Lie 1
Chapter Two: In Trusts We Trust 14
Chapter Three: Promises, Promises 25
Chapter Four: The Splendours Of Frodsham 36
Chapter Five: Brotherhood 49
Chapter Six: The Three Monkeys 60
Chapter Seven: Death On The Ocean Wave 73
Chapter Eight: The Perils Of Heredity 85
Chapter Nine: Conspiracy To Murder 94
Chapter Ten: Stars In Their Eyes 104
Chapter Eleven: Base Thoughts Below Stairs 118
Chapter Twelve: A Gentlemanly Murder By The Moika 130
Chapter Thirteen: Operation Emerald 144
Chapter Fourteen: The Garden Of A Thousand Delights 158
Chapter Fifteen: To Lawrence In Arabia 171
Chapter Sixteen: Turkish Delights 182
Chapter Seventeen: A Camp Fire 196
Chapter Eighteen: In A Mess 207
Chapter Nineteen: Chimes Before Midnight 217
Chapter Twenty: The Pearly Pimpernel 231
Chapter Twenty-One: Aladdin's Cave 241
Chapter Twenty-Two: In The Bag 251
Chapter Twenty-Three: Out Of The Basket 261
Chapter Twenty-Four: On & Off The Job 273
Chapter Twenty-Five: End Game 284

NOTES ON THE EDITOR

After serving time at Oxford University and the Royal Military Academy Sandhurst, Christopher Joll spent his formative years as an officer in The Life Guards, an experience from which he has never really recovered.

On leaving the Army, Joll worked first in investment banking, but the boredom of City life led him to switch careers and become an arms salesman. After ten years of dealing with tin pot dictators in faraway countries, he moved perhaps appropriately into public relations where, in this new incarnation, he had to deal with dictators of an altogether different type.

From his earliest days, Joll has written articles, features, short stories and reportage. One such piece of writing led to an early brush with notoriety when an article he had penned anonymously in 1974 for a political journal ended up as front page national news and resulted in a Ministerial inquiry. In 2012 Joll wrote the text for *Uniquely British: A Year in the Life of the Household Cavalry*, an illustrated account of the Household Cavalry from the Royal Wedding to the Diamond Jubilee, and in 2018 he published *Bearskins & Helmets*, a book with illustrations about many of the heroes, villains and eccentrics who have guarded Britain's monarchs since 1660.

Since leaving the Army in 1975, Joll has been involved in devising and managing charity fund-raising events. This interest started in 1977 with The Silver Jubilee Royal Gifts Exhibition at St James's Palace and The Royal Cartoons Exhibition at the Press Club. In subsequent years, he co-produced 'José Carreras & Friends', a one-night Royal Gala Concert at the Theatre Royal Drury Lane; 'Serenade for a Princess', a Royal Gala Concert at the Banqueting House, Whitehall; and 'Concert for a Prince', a Royal Gala Concert staged at Windsor Castle (the first such event to be held there following the post-fire restoration).

More recently, Joll has focused on devising, writing, directing and sometimes producing events for military and other charities. These include the Household Cavalry Pageant (2007), the Chelsea Pageant (2008), the Diamond Jubilee Parade in the Park (2012), the British Military Tournament (2010-2013), the Gurkha Bicentenary Pageant (2015), the Waterloo Bicentenary National Service of Commemoration & Parade at St Paul's Cathedral (2015), the Shakespeare 400 Memorial Concert (2016), The Patron's Lunch (2016), the official London event to mark The Queen's 90th Birthday, and the premiere of *The Great War Symphony* at the Royal Albert Hall (2018).

When not writing and directing 'military theatre' or editing Speedicut family papers, Joll is a Trustee of The Great War Symphony and The Art Fund Prize for Museums and has written his yet to be published memoires, *Anecdotal Evidence*, an account which promises to cause considerable consternation in certain quarters.

INTRODUCTION

The chance discovery in 2010 of a cache of letters written during his lifetime by Colonel Sir Jasper Speedicut to his friend Harry Flashman, led to my having the privilege of editing and then publishing *The Speedicut Papers*.

When I sent the last manuscript of the series to my publishers, I thought that would be the end of my involvement with Speedicut. Imagine my surprise, therefore, when shortly afterwards I received through the post the following letter and a bulky, typed manuscript:

Villa Larmes des Russes, Cimier, France, 1st April 2016

Dear Mr Joll

It has come to my attention that you are the editor of the letters of my great-grandfather, Colonel Sir Jasper Speedicut. Consequently, I thought that you might be interested to have sight of the enclosed typescript which is a salacious, probably libellous and hitherto unpublished autobiography written by his late (and illegitimate) son, Charles Speedicut, who was, by coincidence, a close friend of my father.

I inherited the enclosed document on Charles' death in 1980 and, as he was something of a black sheep and not spoken of in my family, it has remained unread by me until recently. If you find that it is of interest to you, I might be willing to discuss the terms under which a <u>suitably expurgated</u> edition might be published.

Yours sincerely

Olga Lieven-Beaujambe, Duchess of Whitehall

A cursory glance at the manuscript was enough to show me that, despite the date on the letter, the covering note stated nothing less than the truth.

On further reading, it quickly became clear that Charles Speedicut had been involved in as many of the intrigues and scandals of the twentieth century as had his father in the nineteenth…

Despite the Duchess's strictures, I have limited my editing to the correction of Charles Speedicut's grammar and spelling, and the addition of historical or explanatory footnotes.

CHRISTOPHER JOLL
www.jasperspeedicut.com

THE SPEEDICUT FAMILY TREE

Colonel Sir Jasper Speedicut, 1st Baronet (1821-1915) m. (1) Lady Mary Steyne (1828-1855), only daughter of 3rd Marquess of Steyne; (2) Lady Charlotte-Georgina FitzCharles (1825-1917), younger daughter of the 8th Duke of Whitehall

had legitimate issue

Dorothea Charlotte Speedicut (1865-1919) m.
Prince Dimitri Lieven (1866-1919)

had legitimate issue

Princess Anastasia Lieven (1896-1919)
&
Princess Tatiana Lieven, 11th Duchess of Whitehall (1896-1955) m.
Lord Tertius Beaujambe (1898-1939)

had legitimate issue

Olga Lieven-Beaujambe, 12th Duchess of Whitehall (1938-)

…

Colonel Sir Jasper Speedicut, 1st Baronet (1821-1915)
&
Sibella Halwood (1875-1941) from 1898-1910, Mrs Lionel Holland

had illegitimate issue

Charles Lionel Jasper Holland (28th February 1899-1980)

from 28th February 1916 known as

Charles Lionel Jasper SPEEDICUT
later Major C L J Speedicut MC & Bar, Order of St Stanislaus (2nd Class), Order of Franz Josef (4th Class)

FOREWORD

I barely learned to read at Eton, which is why I'm not much of a books man. So, it's not surprising that I'd never heard of *The Flashman Papers* or *Tom Brown's School Days*. But there's bugger-all else to do in this dump except toss-off or read and as, at my age, the former holds few pleasures I asked the way to the library.

Once there I realised that I had a problem: where the hell was I going to start? Most of the library sections' labels looked as though the contents of their shelves would be better than a sleeping pill: who the fuck wants to read about Philosophy, Law, Economics, Geography, Needlework or Home Improvement? I was about to give up the whole idea of whiling away my time with an intellectual pursuit when my eye caught a sign saying Biography.

As there was a sporting chance that on these shelves there would be a book or two about some of the people I've known - such as Philip 'his baroque's worse than his bite' Sassoon, Dickie the upwardly mobile semi-royal Mountbatten, his millionaire bisexual wife Eddie, or David 'suck my dick' Windsor - I sauntered over for a closer look. What I found was shelf after shelf of unread tomes about people I'd never heard of who'd probably led worthy but infinitely dull lives: a bulky biography of someone called Benjamin Britten being a case in point.[1]

Then my eye caught a gaudy set of spines. I pulled out the first book on the left, which was entitled *Flashman*. I confess that I chose it because I assumed it was about a fellow who exposed himself: it wasn't, as I quickly discovered when I leafed through it. What it was, in fact, was the memoirs of an elderly Victorian General with a vivid imagination and a perpetually restless middle leg. I was about to put the book back on the shelf and head for the section that was sign-posted Adult Fiction when I tripped over the name Jack Speedicut.

---

[1] Benjamin Britten (1913-1976).

Well, I knew I didn't have any relations called Jack, but ours is an unusual surname so I started to read - and I carried on reading for the next half-dozen or so weeks until I'd finished the sixth and last book on the shelf.[2] It was good stuff and a lot of it had the ring of truth; it was even possible that the Jack Speedicut mentioned from time-to-time in the books was my Papa, thinly disguised with a new Christian name. This was a possibility that turned to a certainty when I glanced briefly through the utterly unreadable pages of *Tom Brown's School Days*. However, from what I have gleaned over the years about my Papa, many of the events Flashman credited to himself were actually those of my forebear.

With the six volumes of *The Flashman Papers* under my belt, so to speak, I then searched for something else to while away the time but, unless one enjoyed reading about hypocritical parlour-pink Socialists or transvestite Tories, which I don't, there was nothing further of interest under Biography. So, I turned to the Fiction section and there I found a series of books about carryings-on in high places called *Alms for Oblivion* by a disgraced ex-soldier called Simon Raven.[3] It was clearly fact disguised as fiction and I even recognised several of the coves in it.

Anyway, the whole experience set me to thinking that my own adult experiences might make interesting reading, so I started to write. God knows if what follows will ever be published or if I'll live to finish it. One thing is certain, however: thanks to the libel laws it won't reach the reading public whilst any of those I've portrayed remain 'above the sod' – and there's an appropriate turn of phrase if ever there was one...

Charles Speedicut
HM Prison Ford

---

[2] The first book in George MacDonald Fraser's *Flashman* series, *Flashman*, was published in 1969; the sixth book, *Flashman's Lady*, was published in 1978; the twelfth and last, *Flashman on the March*, was published in 2005.
[3] The *Alms for Oblivion* series was published between 1964 and 1976.

CHAPTER ONE: PHOTOGRAPHS DON'T LIE

So where should I start this account of my utterly disreputable life? To judge from some of the books I've flicked through recently, the current vogue is to start in the middle and then work both backwards and forwards at the same time. Bugger that. At heart I'm an old-fashioned sort of chap, so I'm going to start at the beginning and take it from there. But I'll spare you the nursery, nappies, my first erection and, indeed, my first fumbled emission. Instead, I'm going to start at the point when I found out who I really am.

So, sit back and let me transport you to London in the Year of the Bloke in the Skimpy Loincloth with the Gloomy Expression and the Long Beard, Nineteen Hundred and Fifteen. There was a war on, although as I was sixteen that didn't unduly bother me,[4] it was the end of the Lent Half, I was on holiday from Eton with my widowed mother, Sibella Holland, and living on the wrong side of the Park. Over breakfast on my first morning of freedom she'd announced that we'd been invited to lunch at the Cavendish Hotel. I groaned.

"Charles," she said severely, "put down that cover and pay attention." I reluctantly did as instructed. "Our host today is a friend of mine, Sir Jasper Speedicut. He's very rich, very old and, thanks to me, he has taken an interest in you."

"Oh, God," I sighed at the prospect of wasting valuable hours of my holiday with a senile old codger, who'd probably dribbled down Mama's ample cleavage at some point in the dim and distant past.

"Don't be blasphemous, Charles."

"No, Mama."

---

[4] Conscription at 18 was only introduced in 1916.

1

"As he can't have much longer to live – he is, after all, ninety-three or four," she went on, "and, as you could well benefit materially from him, it will pay you to be polite. Do you understand, Charles?"

"Yes, Mama," I said with a sigh, as I once again lifted the cover of the entrée dish on the sideboard and helped myself to a second portion of bacon and eggs.

Frankly, with newly sprouted hair on my upper lip and around my easily excited dick, the thought of having to spend time being polite to an ancient relic of the previous century when I could have been making a pass at Nellie the parlour maid was anathema; even if – as Mama said – he was 'taking an interest in me'. Having said that, I may have only been sixteen at the time but I already knew that a lack of money was a grievous sin; but sucking up to one of Mama's old flames for the sake of a half-crown and a pat on the head was about as appealing as learning Latin gerundives or Greek irregular verbs.

There was, however, a silver lining. For, if what I'd been told about the Cavendish by Tertius Beaujambe (pronounced 'Beecham') was true, then perhaps it would not be a wasted day after all: 'time spent in reconnaissance is seldom wasted', as a war-wounded, one-armed beak had told us the previous Half whilst holding forth on the balls up at Majuba Hill.

"It's a sink of iniquity, Charles," Tertius told me over tea in my rooms before – actually, I'll pass over that for now. "The proprietor is a Cockney cook called Mrs Lewis.[5] She's catered for half the crowned heads of Europe and the cream of Debrett's - and she's slept with most of them too, so dear Papa says, as a result of which she's given herself so many airs and graces that she's known as the Duchess of Jermyn Street."

"Really?" I asked, as I bit into a slice of chocolate cake.

"Papa also says that the late King bought her the Cavendish as a payment for services rendered."

---

[5] Mrs Rosa Lewis (1867-1952).

"No!" I exclaimed, passing Tertius a hot-buttered crumpet.

"Yes, and the best of it is that Ma Lewis is a keen supporter of young men from good families, even those who – like you - might be short of brass but still need a skin-full of fizz and a roger with, as she would put it, 'a nice clean tart'."

I think that I must have taken in a sharp breath at this point.

"Really, Charles, you shouldn't look so shocked after all that I've taught you: it's so middle class. Anyway, you'll be pleased to hear, given your impecunious state, that Papa says that she's not above cross-charging all such pleasures to her better-heeled clients."

Hmm, I'd thought, Tertius's papa, the Earl of Frodsham, was a prominent entry in Debrett's, so he should know.

So, it was that, whether I liked it or not, later that morning Mama bundled me into a taxi which took us to Jermyn Street in good time for our appointment with Sir Jasper. In those days, the Cavendish was still pretending to be smart, in a rather country-house-shabby sort of way and the food was reputed to be excellent (particularly the quail pudding). Mrs Lewis greeted us in the hall and Mama introduced herself.

"So 'ow can I 'elp you, Mrs 'olland?" she demanded imperiously, giving Mama the sort of look that she – Mama that is - normally reserves for tradesmen.

"We're meeting Sir Jasper Speedicut here for luncheon," said Mama rather stiffly.

"No, you breedin' ain't," replied the Duchess of Jermyn Street.[6]

---

[6] Editor's Note: Rosa Lewis's Cockney was, in the words of Pauline Massingham who knew her well, 'of a kind that is rarely heard today. Although she scattered H's wherever she went, her great peculiarity was that she [frequently] introduced an R between a consonant and a vowel. So, she said… bralcony for balcony. When she called for Moon, the faithful white-haired porter, she often shouted "Mroon!" ' *The Duchess of Jermyn Street* by Daphne Fielding, 1964, published by Eyre & Spottiswoode.

"I can assure you that we are," retorted Mama, "Sir Jasper wrote last week from Paris to invite us."

"Well, yer've bloody well been uninvited."

"What on earth do you mean?"

"Just that," Rosa sniffed. "That jailbird and counter-jumper wot calls 'imself the Druke of What's-'is-name, came in 'ere yesterday and said that I woz to cancel old Jasper's reservation as 'e'd been taken sick in Paree."

"Really?" gasped Mama.

"Fract," said Ma Lewis, with a firm set to her mouth.

"Well, as we are here," said Mama, "we might as well take luncheon anyway. Do you have a table in your dining room?"

"Certainly, dearie – if yer can affrord the meal." I thought that Mama would explode at this insult, but instead she turned to me.

"Charles, we are staying. Leave your hat and coat with the hall porter and follow me."

I did as she said and was about to follow her to the dining room, when I saw Mrs Lewis give me a very quizzical look.

"'old on a minute, young'un. Look me in the frace." Seeing no reason not to, I did as she asked. " 'ere," she said, "yer're a looker an' no mistake. 'fract, yer looks jest like the old roué 'imself. Younger, 'crourse, but I'd swear as yer woz a chip off his bleedin' cock." Had she said 'cock'? Surely, she meant 'block'?

"Whose block – my late father, Lionel Holland?"

"Never 'eard of 'im. Na, drearie, 'im oo yer woz goin' to 'ave lunch wiv."

"I'm sorry, Mrs Lewis but I…" At that moment, I felt a firm grip on my upper arm.

"You are to come with me *immediately*, Charles!"

It was my Mama. Before I could protest any further she'd dragged me away from Mrs Lewis and out of the hotel.

"What the devil's going on?" I exclaimed, hatless and coatless on a blustery Jermyn Street. "And what was all that about?"

"It's of no concern to you, Charles. Now follow me; we'll take luncheon at the Ritz and the expense be damned."

"Mother!" I cried, for she almost never swore, at least not in front of me. "What about my things?"

"Wait here and I'll fetch them for you." Despite her instruction I started to follow her. "If you set foot in that hotel without my permission before you're eighteen," she snarled with a steely look, "I'll confine you to the house when you're not at school. Do you understand?"

"Yes, Mother," I replied dutifully.

Mama's ban notwithstanding, I was determined to find out more. But over lunch I kept my own counsel. However, once we were back in Bayswater, I waited until Mama took her afternoon nap and then sneaked off to the local public library where I headed for the bound copies of the *Illustrated London News*. The most recent volumes were bereft of any mention of a Speedicut and it wasn't until I got to the one for January 1900 that my search was rewarded.

DARING ESCAPE FROM BOER CAPTIVITY
CHURCHILL & SPEEDICUT FREE

Below this headline was a story about how a certain Colonel Speedicut and the celebrated Mr Winston Churchill had escaped from a prison camp in Pretoria on successive nights.[7] Churchill I knew: who didn't? But could this Colonel Speedicut be the same man as the Sir Jasper who should have given us lunch? Below the jingoistic prose were two photographs side-by-side: the first was of a truculent-looking young man seated on a pony and dressed, somewhat incongruously, in a civilian suit. He was unmistakeably Churchill. The other photo was a studio portrait of a strikingly handsome, albeit elderly man in the elaborate uniform of a British cavalry regiment, his chest covered in foreign Orders and decorations. But the most remarkable thing about this photo was not the advanced age of the escapee but the uncanny feeling I had that I was looking at a portrait of myself some sixty years hence. I didn't need to see anymore. I glanced around to check that no one - particularly the librarian - was looking, tore out the page, folded it, put it into my inside breast pocket, closed the volume and left the library at speed.

"Where's my Mother?" I demanded of our housekeeper, Mrs Moody, who was fussing around in the hall with the afternoon post when I arrived home.

"I believe she's still asleep, Master Charles. Leastwise, that's what Miss Creeper said when I saw her in the kitchen a moment ago. Apparently, Mrs Holland said that she was to be woken at five with her usual cup of tea and Miss Creeper had come down to prepare…"

I didn't wait to hear any more: Mrs Moody bored for Wales and would have rabbited on for another half-hour if I'd let her. Instead, I took the stairs two at a time up to the first landing, off which was Mama's mauve boudoir – apparently, the Empress of Russia had had hers decorated in that ghastly colour, so, when our house had been done up before the war,

---

[7] The Rt Hon Winston Churchill (1874-1965); see *The Speedicut Papers: Book 8 (At War With Churchill)*.

Mama had decided that what was good enough for a Tsarina was good enough for her. I didn't bother to knock but barged straight in.

The old girl was laid out on a chaise longue with a camel hair rug over her lower half. She was clad in a silk and lace dressing gown, which matched the ghastly décor of the room, and had a lace handkerchief over her face. The curtains were drawn, but a heavily shaded and rather feeble electric lamp on her dressing table shed just enough light to ensure that the room was not in complete darkness.

"Mama!"

She lazily pulled away the hanky, turned her head and stared at me sleepily.

"What do you mean by disturbing me, Charles? You know I need my afternoon beauty sleep."

I couldn't think why, but I didn't say so: Mama was not a bad looking woman for someone the wrong side of forty, although she disguised with powder those wrinkles that were unmoved by her daily afternoon nap.

"I need to talk to you."

"Can't it wait, Charles?"

"No, it can't."

"Well, it will have to – at least until I've got dressed. Ring the bell and then wait for me in the drawing room."

"Mama…"

"The drawing room, Charles. I will be down in half-an-hour."

I was surprised that she'd agreed to break her rest, which was normally sacrosanct, but perhaps she had guessed what it was that I wanted to discuss with her and reckoned that there would be nothing further to be gained by trying to put it off. I yanked the bell pull for the crab-featured Creeper, slouched out of the room and headed back downstairs.

Nellie, the parlour maid, was kneeling by the fireplace in the drawing room in the act of lighting a fire. She was a pretty little thing, who'd given me a sly wink or two before the last Half, so – full in the knowledge that Mama would, despite what she'd said, be at least an hour – I decided to try my luck.

"Let me help you with that, Nellie," I said, as I dropped to my knees beside her. She mumbled something which I didn't catch, but whatever she'd said I reached over and covered her hand holding the spill with my own. I gave it a gentle squeeze and she didn't attempt to pull away. Instead, she turned her head towards me.

"Now, Master Charles, I don't need no help lighting a fire, leastwise not one as I laid earlier."

"What else have you laid recently?" I asked her, with a roguish grin.

"Ooh, Master Charles. You shouldn't speak like that to a poor serving girl like me. Besides which, I don't know what you're talking about."

"Don't you, Nellie?" I said, pulling her hand away from the fire and towards my flies. "So, you don't know what to do with this, then?" I asked, as I placed her paw over my bulging crotch.

"Really, Master Charles!" she said, yanking her hand out of my grasp and leaping to her feet. "What does you take me for?"

"A girl who know how to enjoy herself?"

"I'll have you know that I'm a good girl, I am," she replied, but without much conviction in her voice.

"Why don't we find out how good?" I leered, making a grab for her boobs that were hidden behind her pinafore.

"Master Charles, you're to stop that right away!"

But she didn't brush away my hands that were now grasping her tits, so I lowered my head towards her, moved my hands around to her firm rump and clamped my lips firmly over hers. They parted, as I guessed they might, and her tongue was as agile as a grass snake in a box of frogs. Tertius Beaujambe had taught me the basics, but this was the first time I'd had the chance to try out my technique on a girl: in my day, Etonians led sheltered lives at school, at least as far as the opposite sex was concerned. Anyway, I was making fine progress when, without warning, Nellie pulled away from me.

"I'd be on the streets if your mother or Mrs Moody was to walk in now," she gasped, whilst her boobs heaved up and down like a row boat at anchor in a heavy swell.

"You'll be on the streets for certain if you don't do as I ask," I said, as I walked towards the double doors that led to the hall. I think that, for a moment, she expected me to open it for her so that she could dash off back to the kitchen but, instead, I turned the key in the lock then strode over to the still-open curtains. Seconds later the only light in the room was the growing glow from the fire.

"Master Charles, whatever do you think you're..." Her voice died away as I advanced towards her, whilst at the same time unbuttoning. "Oh, my Gawd," she cried when I released my animal from its woollen cage. However, instead of bursting into a fit of hysterics and demanding to be let out of the room, she sank to her knees - and it wasn't in prayer. "Not in my mouth. Promise?" was all she said before she applied her lips. I nodded my agreement. Come to think of it, that was probably the only time in my life when I've kept that particular undertaking.

The next stage in my progress to adulthood didn't take long. Nellie clearly knew what to do and had done it before, as had I - although not with a parlour maid or a woman of any sort, for that matter - but the combination of my discovery earlier in the day, rampant pubescent lust, a lack of experience and the risk of discovery meant that a couple of minutes later

Nellie was wiping her face with my hanky whilst I buttoned up. When we were both composed, I escorted her to the door, unlocked it and gave her a playful pat on the bum as she scampered out into the hall.

"Same time tomorrow?" I called after her. She merely giggled in reply as I turned back into the room and headed for an easy chair next to the by-now blazing grate. I'd hardly settled myself into it when Mama swept into the room somewhat ahead of schedule. I silently thanked God that the business with Nellie had been dispatched as quickly as it had been.

"Now what's this all about?" demanded Mama, as she rang the bell then lowered herself into the chair opposite me.

"This," I said as I pulled out the article from the *ILN* which I'd purloined earlier and handed it across to her. She unfolded the paper and read it.

"This is an old article about the gentleman we were supposed to meet for luncheon, Charles. Why did you have to disturb my rest to show it to me?"

"Look at the photograph, Mama."

"I don't need to," she snapped, "I know perfectly well what Sir Jasper looked like fifteen years ago."

"But that's the point: he looks just like *me*, Mama."

"Nonsense, Charles. You're only sixteen and, in that photograph, Sir Jasper is in his late seventies. There's *no* resemblance at all and, anyway, his features are hidden behind that absurd cavalry moustache and those side-whiskers of his." I was clearly getting nowhere with this line of enquiry, so I decided to change my approach.

"You've never mentioned Sir Jasper before, Mama. How long have you known him?" I asked as innocently as I could.

"About fifteen or twenty years, I suppose," she said, staring wistfully into the fire.

"Where did you first meet him?"

"In Italy."[8]

"How frequently have you seen him since then?"

"Not often."

"And did he meet me as a baby?"

"Once."

"So why has he taken an interest in me if he doesn't know you that well and has only met me in the nursery?" Mama didn't immediately answer, for I think she sensed that this question was loaded.

"I'm not sure," she said at last. "Of course, his wife is the aunt of my childhood friend the Duke of Whitehall," she added hastily as an inspired after thought.

"Was that the person to whom Mrs Lewis was referring?"

"That insufferably rude woman! Just because, thanks to the snobbish behaviour of his mother's family, Charles had a humble start in life there was no reason for her to take the line she did. Charles Whitehall has *royal* blood in his veins!"

"Do I?"

"Good heavens, no – why do you ask?"

"I was only wondering and my name is Charles…"

"If you are suggesting what I think you're suggesting, Charles, then I would remind you that you were born almost nine months to the day after

---

[8] See *The Speedicut Papers: Book 8 (At War With Churchill)*.

your father and I returned from our honeymoon – and Charles Whitehall was *not* amongst our party in Italy."

"But the Colonel was - and Jasper is my third name."

"It doesn't signify and I never said…" But, before she could answer in full, Mama was quite literally saved by the bell.

"You rang, madam?" It was our compliant parlour maid.

"I did. We will take tea here, Nellie."

"Certainly, madam." Unfortunately, this unexpected and unwelcome interruption gave Mama the time to change the subject and move onto the offensive.

"What are you doing this evening, Charles?"

"Dining in, Mama, unless you have any other ideas," I said, without attempting to revert to the previous conversation – at least not yet.

"And tomorrow?"

"I haven't got a clue."

"Well, you should, Charles: you can't spend your holiday slouching around the house. You need to do something to improve your mind."

"Why?"

"Because it needs improving." Then she made a fatal error. "And so that when you do meet Sir Jasper, you'll be able to give a good account of yourself."

"I can't see why," I retorted. "We've already established that he hardly knows you or me. He might be sentimental enough to take a shine to me because we share the same Christian name but, even if he does, the most he'll probably tip me is a sovereign and that's if I'm lucky."

"Stranger things have happened, Charles."

"Indeed, they have, Mama," I retorted, "including the strange coincidence that you first met Sir Jasper in Italy on your honeymoon…"

"I never said that!" I ignored her and ploughed on.

"… I was born nine months later, we look like two peas out of the same pod – albeit that he's a deal older than me – and now he wants to meet me. There's more to this than meets the eye, Mama, and that's already a hell of a lot. Isn't it time that you told me the…" The door opened and Nellie reappeared with a salver on which were the tea things.

"Please leave the tray there, Nellie," said Mama, pointing to the table next to her, "and tell cook to come up."

"In half an hour," I added, for I was determined to bring my enquiries to a conclusion. As the door closed behind Nellie, I leant forward in my chair, fixed Mama with a gaze and gave her both barrels: "Mama, I'm old enough to fight. And if I'm old enough to do that then I'm old enough to be told the truth."

"The age of enlistment is eighteen, Charles, you're only sixteen."

"But I'm old enough to get married and, unless I'm very much mistaken, Mama, I think that Sir Jasper Speedicut is my father." She started once again to bluster, then clearly thought better of it.

"Very well, Charles, since you insist…"

CHAPTER TWO: IN TRUSTS WE TRUST

"… your father was Lionel Holland and that is my last word on the subject."

But it wasn't. A week later over breakfast I spotted an obituary in *The Times*:

> **Speedicut**, *Colonel Sir Jasper Jeffreys, Bart, KCVO, late husband of Lady Charlotte-Georgina Speedicut and father of Princess Dorothea Lieven, died in Paris on 1st April aged 94 whilst in the Service of his Country. Owing to the war his body was interred in France. There will be a Memorial Service on a date to be announced. Dulce et Decorum Est Pro Patria Mori.*

"This may explain why that lunch was cancelled, Mama," I said.

"What luncheon?"

"The one with your old boyfriend."

"Charles! You forget yourself - and what are you talking about?" I passed her the paper in silence.

"Oh, dear," she said when she'd read the obit, "that alters everything."

"How does the death of an old man in Paris - a man who you claim you hardly knew - alter anything and, even if it does, what does it alter?"

"I can't discuss it with you now, Charles, so don't press me. Anyway, I feel a headache coming on." She paused. "I think it may even be my neuralgia. I'm retiring to my boudoir. Tell Creeper to bring me the laudanum." She rose shakily from the table clutching her brow. "I'm not to be disturbed for the rest of the morning," she added, as she left the room,

I suspected that Mama's real reason for leaving the breakfast table so abruptly was not her neuralgia, real or invented, or to avoid any further enquiries from me but to use the telephone in her room without being overheard. Fortunately for me, my dear Mama wasn't very technical and I'm sure that she didn't realise that I could listen to her conversation simply by waiting for the bell in telephone on the hall table to ping once and then to lift the ear piece and put it to my ear. Five minutes later, having sent a message via Nellie to the Creeper woman, that is exactly what I did.

"Hello? Operator? Six-seven-eight-one, please." There were a series of clicks on the line and then a man's voice answered.

"The office of Sir Ernest Cassel,[9] how may I help you?"

"May I speak to Sir Ernest?" I heard Mama enquire.

"Who's calling?"

"Mrs Sibella Holland."

"May I enquire why you wish to speak to Sir Ernest?"

"It's a private matter."

"One moment, please, madam." There were some muffled words, then I heard a Germanic sounding voice on the line.

"Cassel speaking. How may I help you Mrs Holland?"

"It about the trust."

"The trust?"

"Yes, the one set up by Colonel Speedicut about fifteen years ago." There was a pause and some more muffled words.

"Of course, Mrs Holland, the one called the Black Jade Trust which Sir Jasper invested with Rothschild."

---

[9] Sir Ernest Cassel GCB GCMG GCVO (1852-1921).

"That's the one, Sir Ernest."

"What about it, dear lady?"

"I read in the newspapers this morning that Sir Jasper has died, in Paris..."

"Really? I will check." There were more muffled words: Cassel was doubtless telling his secretary to find *The Times*. "Yes, indeed, my condolences, Mrs Holland. But Sir Jasper's death does not affect the trust. If I remember rightly – just a moment, it's that file on the left – yes, the trust only vests..."

But before I could hear any more, I saw in the large looking glass over the hall table the wretched Creeper clutching a tray on which were a brown medicine bottle and a glass. She was Mama's spy below stairs. Worse still, she loathed me and took every opportunity to paint me in a bad a light with the old girl. If Creeper realised that I was listening in to Mama's conversation, she'd report me in double-quick time. So, I gently replaced the receiver, shuffled through some papers on the table and prayed that she hadn't seen what I was up to. Once the dratted woman had disappeared from view up the stairs I again lifted the telephone receiver.

"... I see. So, there will be no immediate change?"

"That is correct, Mrs Holland."

"May I enquire, Sir Ernest, the current value of the trust's funds?" There was a pause on the line.

"Under the terms of the trust I'm not permitted to tell you that, Mrs Holland. However, I can assure you that the funds are more than adequate to meet the trust's income obligations. Indeed, the capital has grown most satisfactorily thanks to Rothschild's wise investments and their ability to reinvest the major part of the income. By the way, Mrs Holland, there is something that I have been meaning to discuss with you. Do you have the time now?"

"What is that, Sir Ernest?"

"You will, I am sure, be aware that for the past three years, since the death of Sir Edward Sassoon,[10] I have been the sole trustee. I am no longer a young man and I think it would be prudent to appoint a second trustee. I hope you agree."

"I do, Sir Ernest," said Mama, "and I should be delighted to share the burden with you."

"That, Mrs Holland, is *not* permitted by Sir Jasper's settlement."

"Oh..." the disappointment in Mama's voice was clearly audible.

"No," went on Cassel, "the person I had in mind was Sir Philip Sassoon,[11] Sir Edward's son. He's a thoroughly sensible young man, a Member of Parliament and a Rothschild on his mother's side. He's back on leave from France and I'm dining with him tomorrow. He would, I am sure, agree to be a trustee if I were to ask him. Shall I do that?"

"That would be very kind of you, Sir Ernest."

"Is there anything else, dear lady?"

"No," said Mama and I heard her break the connection.

I too hung up the earpiece and returned to the dining room, poured myself a second cup of coffee and tried to work out the significance of what I had overheard.

Despite Mama's assertion that she hardly knew the late Colonel and that any resemblance I bore him was of no significance, nonetheless it appeared that he'd established a substantial trust fund to support her. Why would he have done that if she was a mere acquaintance? It didn't make sense – unless, that is, she had been the old boy's mistress and he

---

[10] Sir Edward Sassoon Bart MP (1856-1912).
[11] Sir Philip Sassoon Bart MP (1888-1939).

had provided for her. If that was the case, then the likelihood of my being his son increased exponentially.

I had to find out more, but it couldn't be from Mama: if she thought for one minute that I listened to her telephone calls I'd be gated until I was twenty-one. But I knew nothing about trusts. Then I remembered: Tertius Beaujambe had a trust. He would surely know all about them. Later that morning I posted him a letter to his home in Cheshire. I got a reply two days later.

> *Frodsham Splendens*
> *Frodsham*
> *Cheshire*
>
> *Dear old thing*
>
> *So, you want to know about trusts, do you? Well, I'm afraid I can't help beyond telling you that they aren't public documents. Your best bet is to tackle one of the trustees and get him to spill the beans. Who knows, you might be a residuary beneficiary (look it up in a dictionary) and, after you've pushed your sainted mater under a train, you will then be able to afford to buy me a meal.*
>
> *Meanwhile, life is hell here. The house is full of ravening beasts otherwise known as my relations. You'd have thought that with a hundred rooms there'd be space and to spare for everyone, but darling Papa has given over most of the house as an officer's convalescent home so we're all bottled up in the family wing. Thank God, I can take refuge with Nanny Lyons on the top floor.*
>
> *Love or whatever you like*
>
> *Tertius*

It was good advice but, having overheard the cautious Cassel on the telephone, I was sure that he would be no more forthcoming than Mama and probably less so. But Sassoon was a different matter. Assuming he'd agreed to be the second trustee – and that was soon confirmed by a letter from Cassel to Mama which I steamed open before she could read it – he would be unfamiliar with the background and might even tell me what I wanted to know, such as whether or not I was a residual beneficiary and what the trust was worth. I looked Sassoon up in *Who's Who* in the local library and then sent him a carefully worded letter. I got a reply by return inviting me to lunch at his house in Park Lane the following week.

Today the Sassoons aren't the family they used to be. But, before taxation and conspicuous consumption reduced them to the status of the merely rich, these ex-Baghdadi merchants were in the Croesus league. Not for nothing were they known as the 'Rothschilds of the East'. Prominent in Mesopotamia since the time of Nebuchadnezzar, they had for generations been the Viziers to the Caliph in Baghdad until David Sassoon had fallen foul of the Ottoman authorities in the early-to-mid-nineteenth century and had to flee for his life,[12] first to Persia and then to India. Re-established in Bombay, he'd built a vast fortune based on opium and cotton trading which was developed by his sons into two global businesses that embraced banking, real estate, docks, manufacturing and – as befitted their wealth - philanthropy.

In pursuit of this goal, David Sassoon had sent some of his sons to both England and China. The eldest son, Albert,[13] quickly established himself in London Society by reason of his riches, Semitic good looks, love of the turf and the then Prince of Wales's need for fully-funded entertainment and the occasional cheap loan.[14] Thanks to all of that, Albert received a Baronetcy which in due course passed to his son Edward, who had the common sense to bolster further his fortune by marrying a French Rothschild, Aline.[15] Their early married life was spent in Paris, where their children were born, but in 1897 the Sassoons moved back to London where they bought a grotesque, newly-built faux-French mansion at 25 Park Lane from the estate of the gold and diamond mining magnate, Barney Barnato.[16] This house, which was my destination for lunch, they

---

[12] David Sassoon (1792-1864).
[13] Sir Albert Sassoon Bart KCB CSI (1818-1896).
[14] HRH The Prince of Wales, later King Edward VII (1841-1910).
[15] Aline de Rothschild (1865-1909).
[16] Barney Barnato (1851-1897).

filled with a priceless art collection that passed on Edward's and Aline's early deaths to their son, Philip.

However, beyond Philip's biographical details which I'd culled from *Who's Who*, I knew none of this as I ambled from Bayswater across Hyde Park to the bottom end of Park Lane. I was, therefore, completely unprepared for the magnificence which confronted me when I was guided over the threshold of the Sassoon's London house – palace would have been a more appropriate description – by the butler, Garton, and into the vast marble hall with its great staircase which rose the entire height of the house. Whilst the exterior was grand but ugly, the interior was a riot of gilded plasterwork and furniture, priceless Brussels tapestries, Persian carpets, French and Italian porcelain and pictures, heaps of silver and, somewhat surprisingly, some excellent modern portraits of various Sassoons by Sargent, Orpen, Whistler and others.

Almost blinded by this dazzling display of wealth, I was led up to the first floor by the butler and into a large drawing room where Philip Sassoon was waiting for me. Dressed in an immaculately cut Yeomanry uniform, he was standing by a red marble fireplace with a greyhound at his feet. A very beautiful woman, who resembled an oriental odalisque by Ingres or David, sat in a chair by the window.

"Mr Charles Holland," intoned the butler. Sassoon strode forward to greet me, his hand outstretched and an appreciative gleam in his eyes.

"How *charmant* to meet you, Mr Holland," he lisped with a pronounced French accent as he shook my hand, "I don't believe you've met *ma soeur*, Lady Rocksavage."[17] The lady in question languorously extended a hand. I stepped forward, bent over and kissed it as it seemed, at the time, the only thing to do.

"I was about to leave, Mr Holland," she purred, "so that you can have my brother all to yourself." I mumbled something about that being a great pity, but she was gone before I could finish making an ass of myself.

---

[17] Sybil Sassoon, Lady Rocksavage later Marchioness of Cholmondeley (1894-1989).

"Now, Mr Holland, you must tell me what you would like *à boire* and then how I can help you."

"As I'm only just sixteen, I'm not really supposed to drink, Sir Philip, but…"

"Well, in that case, let's be *très Français* and both have a glass of white wine and seltzer. Since the war I haven't touched my stock of hock, so we use *un bon vin d'Alsace* instead - and you can have rather more seltzer than wine."

As he sauntered back to ring a bell on the wall, I took a good long look at my host, whose face was reflected in the vast gilt looking glass above the fireplace.

Philip Sassoon wasn't exactly handsome, at least not in the conventional English way. He had a high forehead, off which his dark hair was swept back; rather fine eyebrows which framed his somewhat hooded eyes between which an aquiline nose anchored his face; his lips were full and his chin line was chiselled and cleft. Had he been clad in an oriental robe rather than khaki he would have looked exactly like one of those romanticised Victorian pictures of Sinbad the Sailor or, a decade later, Valentino's portrayal of *The Sheikh*. As it was, he exuded charm and an exotic, sensual charisma which left me – to use one of his favourite phrases - *absolument bouleversé*.

"You are at Eton *n'est-ce pas*, Mr Holland?" he said indicating that I should sit in the chair recently vacated by his sister, whilst he remained standing by the chimney piece.

"Yes, sir, in Tatham's."

"Ah, my own house. And what are you going to do when you leave *chér* Eton?"

"I hadn't really thought, sir, what with the war and all that."

"Oh, it'll be over by the time you are ready. I'd advise a spell *chez* Oxford: I was at the House and had a splendid time. I didn't do any work, of course, but that's not really the point of Oxford, is it?"

"Err, no, sir."

"Ah, here's our drink and an *amuse gueule*," he said as a brace of footmen padded into the room bearing large silver salvers groaning under the weight of a wine bottle in a silver-gilt bucket full of ice, glasses, a soda syphon and a huge crystal bowl heaped high with caviar. "You do like Imperial Persian caviar, *j'espère?*"

"I do indeed, sir," I lied, as one footmen poured our drinks whilst the other heaped the golden caviar onto tiny pancakes. I'd never tasted millionaire's fish eggs before but, nonetheless, tucked in when handed a piled-up silver plate along with a fish-bowl full of the slightly diluted wine; we made small talk for several minutes.

"*Eh bien*, young Holland," Sassoon said at last. "How can I help you?"

"Well, sir, as I said in my letter, I believe you have recently become the trustee of a trust made by the late Sir Jasper Speedicut in which my family has an interest."

"*Vous avez raison*. My father was one of the original trustees of the Black Jade Trust and I have agreed to take his place, albeit it not for long."

"May I ask why, sir?"

"Why I have taken my father's place?"

"No, sir, why it won't be for long?"

"Because in a year the trust *sera résilié*."

"I'm sorry, I don't understand, sir?"

"Terminated – it will vest absolutely in the beneficiary."

"And who might that be, sir?" I asked tentatively. But before he could answer Garton the butler once more appeared.

"Luncheon is served, Sir Philip."

"Come, my dear Holland, we must not keep *les homards* waiting," said my host.

With one hand lightly clutching my upper arm he guided me out of the drawing room, along a corridor and into a conservatory overlooking Park Lane.

"As we are having an *intime déjeuner à deux*," he said, as we reached a small round table set amongst the lush vegetation, "I thought it would be more amusing for you to eat here rather than in the dining room, which is *un peu grand* just for the two of us."

The table was laid with a white linen cloth and covered in exquisite china, glass and *vermeil* eating irons. I was about to take my place when it sounded as though a Palm Court orchestra had struck up. Clearly my host had a gramophone conceal somewhere amongst the foliage.

"If the music disturbs you, *mon cher*, I will have the musicians dismissed. You only have to tell me," he said, showing me to my chair, which was close to his, and behind both of which were two more footmen who pulled them out for us. Once settled, the handsome fellows spread napkins over our laps whilst, from behind a group of potted palms, more servants appeared bearing wine and salvers on which were piled a veritable armada of split lobsters.

"I believe my chef has prepared our lobsters to suit all tastes – steamed, grilled, cold *avec mayonnaise*, or Thermidor if you are feeling really hungry. *Faites votre choix, mon brave...*" It was overwhelming. But that was Philip Sassoon: everything done to excess and bugger the expense. "This is not an observant house," he went on, inconsequentially, "although I draw the line at pork; otherwise how could I ever entertain or be entertained in Society?" I assumed that the question was rhetorical and anyway I didn't really understand what he had meant.

"Now, *mon cher*," he said, once I'd taken a brace of cold crustaceans and a good dollop of mayonnaise from a silver sauce boat that must have held a quart. "You were asking me about the trust."

"I was curious to know, sir…"

"Oh, do please call me *Philippe*," did I felt his knee press against mine? "and I will call you *Charles*," he said, once again placing his hand on my sleeve. "We are, after all, not *that* far apart in age and you calling me 'sir' makes me feel *si agée*."

"If you insist, sir – I mean, Philip."

"That's *beaucoup mieux*. So what, *précisément*, my dear *Charles* was it that you wanted to know?"

"Who, Philip, is the residual beneficiary of the Black Jade Trust and what is it worth?"

This time, before answering, he both clutched my arm and pressed his knee firmly into mine: was there, I wondered, a price tag for the information I so desperately wanted?

CHAPTER THREE: PROMISES, PROMISES

"*Mais, c'est toi, mon petit Charles.*"

"Me?" I gasped.

"*Certainement.*"

"And what is the trust worth?"

"I'm not sure to the nearest ten thousand pounds but I do know this: when it vests, you will be rich. Not as rich as me, *bien sûr*, but rich enough to do whatever you like."

I felt the room start to spin around me. I must be dreaming, I thought. This can't be true. Sassoon leant forward, dipped his napkin into a finger bowl full of iced water and applied it to my brow whilst I felt his other hand clasp my thigh.

"*Calme toi, petit Charles.* Money is not something to swoon over. Save your emotions for something more worthwhile."

"But why did Sir Jasper set up this trust for *me*?"

"*J'ai aucun idée, mon petit*, you will have to ask your mother."

"She won't tell me!" I said hotly.

"Then leave the question with me. Before I return to France, I will make some enquiries – and, when I have the answer, perhaps we can have a quiet *souper à deux*?"

"I would like that very much, Philip," I said

"In the meantime, *cher Charles*, I suggest that you keep this information entirely to yourself. It would not do if your Mama was to find out that I have been, how shall we say, *un peu indiscret?*"

"My lips are sealed, Philip," I replied, as I looked him squarely in the eye and gave him my most beguiling smile.

A couple of days later a letter addressed to me arrived from 25 Park Lane with an invitation to dine with Philip on the eve of his return to GHQ.[18] I was bidden for six pm 'to be followed by dinner here with a small group of friends. As it is war time, a dinner jacket will be sufficient.' You may be wondering, dear reader, what my Mama thought of all this. The answer is that she knew none of it. Indeed, I believe she assumed that I had obeyed her instructions not to 'loaf about the house' and to use the holiday to 'improve my mind'. So, I told her that a school chum had invited me to the theatre and supper afterwards. She didn't even ask me which play I was to see.

At the appointed hour two days later, I was once again on the doorstep of the Sassoon mansion. I rang the bell and, as before, I was met by Garton. However, instead of ushering me into the drawing room on the first floor, I was led across the hall and into a low-lit smallish, book-lined room on the ground floor in which there was a merry fire. Over the fireplace was a romanticised oil sketch of my host in uniform;[19] to one side of it was an inlaid French desk bearing a tray ladened with champagne and, to the other side, a large damask-covered sofa on which was draped the languid form of Sir Philip Sassoon. This time he was not in uniform. Instead, he was wearing gold-embroidered velvet slippers, black silk trousers, an elaborately frogged velvet smoking jacket, a soft shirt and a black bow tie. He sat up a bit on my arrival.

---

[18] Editor's Note: At this time, Sir Philip Sassoon worked on the Staff of the C-in-C, Field Marshal Sir John French (1852-1925). Later in 1915 he was transferred to the Staff of General Sir Henry Rawlinson (1864-1925), GOC IV Corps, and in December 1915 re-joined GHQ as Private Secretary to French's replacement as C-in-C, Field Marshal Sir Douglas Haig (1861-1928).

[19] The painting was by Philip de Lazlo (1869-1937).

"*Mon cher,*" he said, "*champagne?* You may be only sixteen – albeit a very grown up one - but I have some reasons for you to celebrate." I said that would be wonderful, Garton poured me a glass and then slid silently from the room, closing the door behind him.

"Come here and let me take a good look at you." He waved an elegant hand, which indicated that I should sit next to him on the sofa. As he sat up, I noticed that in his other he had a photograph. "Yes," he said more to himself than to me, "there can be *aucun doute. En fin, mon petit,* you want to know what I have discovered?"

"Yes, Philip."

"Even if it is shocking?"

"Yes, Philip," I said leaning towards him whilst wondering what could possibly be coming.

"Very well," he placed a hand on my knee, "your trust fund is even larger than I had thought."

"How large?" I asked eagerly. "Fifty thousand?" I added hopefully.

"No, *mon petit*: its value today is *two hundred* thousand pounds." I was speechless: two hundred thou' was a fortune in those days.[20]

"But there is more if you can stand it?"

"I can," I managed to say.

"Well, it seems that you are not the son of Mr Lionel Holland…"

"I thought as much," I murmured.

---

[20] Editor's Note: A rough equivalent today would be £40 million.

"You are, in fact," he went on, "the son of Colonel Sir Jasper Speedicut." He turned the photo for me to see: it was a younger version of the one I'd torn from the *ILN*. "I hope this does not shock you, *Charles*?"

"Thanks to Mrs Lewis at the Cavendish Hotel, and an article in the *Illustrated London News*, I had guessed as much," I said, "but when I confronted Mama she firmly denied it."

"*Mais naturellement, Charles*," he said giving my knee a squeeze, "she is, after all, a lady - and ladies do not willingly confirm *un scandale*, at least not their own. Anyway, I am pleased that this news does not come as a total surprise to you."

"It doesn't; but what else did you find out, Philip?"

"It would appear that, for obvious reasons, your father - your real father that is - was not keen to recognise *ton existence* during his lifetime. He had a family of his own and a very well-connected wife. However, he was induced by your mother to provide for your education and future – and to provide her with enough money to live in a style which her husband's bankruptcy and suicide had endangered. Her allowance is not large, but it is *suffisant*."

"So, when does the trust become mine?"

"On your seventeenth *anniversaire, mon brave*: in slightly less than a year's time." I involuntarily let out a low whistle. "There is, however, an additional clause which you may not like."

"What is that?" I asked placing a hand over his and encouraging its movement northwards. He didn't immediately answer.

"I'm not sure I can tell you that." I applied southerly pressure on his wandering digits. He still didn't answer so I lifted his hand and placed it back on his own leg.

"I see," he said, "*eh bien.*" His hand returned to my thigh. "Your natural father added a codicil to the trust of which your mother is unaware and which was also supposed to be kept secret from the trustees. Russell,[21] who drafted the trust, does a lot of work for me, so…"

"So?" I said moving his hand towards my crotch.

"So – for the trust funds to become yours absolutely - *tu sera obliger changer ton nom* to Speedicut."

"Is that all?" I sighed in relief.

"*C'est tout,*" he leaned forward and fixed his lips on mine whilst scrabbling with my flies.

It was in a state of sated lust and high elation that I sat through the dinner which followed. Half of what had been revealed earlier I had already guessed, but the facts about the trust, its obligation on me to change my name and – in particular - its size had left me feeling as though I had been reborn and won the Frankfurt lottery at the same time. But Sassoon again impressed upon me the wisdom of keeping the news to myself.

"There will be time enough to celebrate, *mon cher,* when you turn seventeen and become *Monsieur* Speedicut," said my host as he guided me into the drawing room, where a small group of men were gathered in front of the fire place, "now come and meet *mes amis…*

"Gentlemen, *je vous présente Monsieur Charles* Holland, whose trustee I have recently become… *Charles,* this is Mr Bertie Stopford,[22] *un de mes amis les plus amusants* and a pillar of London and St Petersburg Society." Stopford, stepped forward and extended his hand. He was quite angular, sported a thin moustache and must have been in his mid-fifties.

---

[21] The Rt Hon Sir Charles Russell, Bart KCVO (1863-1928).
[22] Albert Stopford (1860-1939).

"... Prince Ali Fahmy,[23] *qui est ton age* but is already an important associate of my family's in the Egyptian cotton industry." The young Gyppo also proffered his paw, gave me an appraising stare and a very soft hand shake. He may have been my age but he looked a lot older.

"... Mr Eddie Marsh,[24] who is Mr Churchill's quite *inseparable* private secretary." The middle-aged civil servant practically drooled as he clutched my hand with both of his.

"... Mr Harold Nicolson,[25] a rising star in the Foreign Office who has the unique distinction of being the man who handed our Declaration of War to the German Ambassador – and he's married," Philip arched a knowing eyebrow at this, "into *une des plus anciennes et les plus excentriques familles anglaises*." The handsome diplomat gave me an encouraging handshake.

"... and last, but by no means least, *le cher et puissant* Lord Esher,[26] who is the unofficial head of our military intelligence network on the continent and has, for years, been *le pouvoir véritable derrière le trône*. Regy, I have high hopes of this fatherless young man; I trust you will do what you can to guide his footsteps..."

"I should be delighted to do so," oozed the peer. "Come and tell me *all* about yourself, my dear," he said leading me off to one side.

It was a well-connected line up of men, all of whom (give or take) shared the same tastes and all of whom were, over the next few years, to play an important part in my life. But for that evening there was no agenda: only to chat, whilst Philip's staff plied us with the best food and wines that his money could buy which is to say, the very best. The talk around the sumptuously-laid table was, for the most part, gossip – Philip's preferred form of conversation - albeit that it was about matters of considerable seriousness such as the war in Flanders.

---

[23] Ali Fahmy Bey, also known as Prince Ali Fahmy (1900-1923).
[24] Edward (later Sir Edward) Marsh (1872-1953).
[25] Harold Nicolson (1886-1968) married the Hon Vita Sackville-West (1892-1962) the lesbian daughter of Lord Sackville.
[26] Reginal Brett, 2nd Viscount Esher GCVO KCB PC DL (1852-1930).

"You know this war is really *too* tiresome," said Esher. "Battles are supposed to be fluid, fast moving affairs. This stalemate in the trenches lacks any style or flair. Saving your presence, Philip, it's all French's fault of course."

"Why blame the French?" asked Stopford, who clearly hadn't heard him properly – or perhaps he was being witty.

"I don't," replied Esher. "As you very well know, my dear Bertie, I was referring to the esteemed Commander-in-Chief, our host's present employer, not our allies." There was general laughter at this.

"So, you're still gunning *pour notre pauvre* C-in-C, are you?" asked Philip.

"How can you even think such a thing, my dear Philip?" shot back Esher with a broad smile that revealed the truth.

"You know that if you succeed it will cost me my job - and then I won't be able to host *les petits soupers* like this one: I need the salary, you know," laughed Philip and everyone joined in.

"So how *will* you break the deadlock in France?" queried Fahmy. "Your troops in Egypt can't reach the Austrian's back door until they evict the Turks from Arabia and Mesopotamia."

"Churchill believes the answer is to bypass the Middle East," said Nicolson. "That's why he's trying to force the Dardanelles, knock out Turkey in her own backyard and then join forces with the Russians in the Balkans. I'm right aren't I, Eddie?"

"You are," replied Marsh, "but following the Navy's failure to silence the Turkish forts, not everyone thinks that is the answer, which may be a problem."

"Why?" I asked.

"Because, without full naval support, a landing on the beaches at Gallipoli will fail," stated Esher.

"But I thought Mr Churchill was First Lord of the Admiralty," I said, displaying my profound knowledge of public affairs.

"He is," said Nicolson, "but, as Eddie will confirm, that doesn't mean that he commands his Admirals." Marsh said nothing but looked at the ceiling.

"The Navy is reluctant to lose any more ships attempting to force the Straits," said Esher, "and so won't re-engage the forts. But Winston is determined to press ahead and that ass Kitchener has ordered Ian Hamilton to land his men even though the Turks hold the high ground."[27]

"Well," said Stopford, "I fear for Russia if we can't open a second front. It's nothing but bad news from St Petersburg – and I don't just mean military news. The Grand Duchess Vladimir has written to tell me that the political situation is highly volatile: the Tsar spends most of his time away from Court and the Tsarina, who's virtually running the country in his absence – God help the Russians – is totally in thrall to that lunatic peasant, Rasputin."[28]

"Unless someone removes that man – and Kitchener for good measure - it will end in tears," said Esher and those around the table nodded their heads in agreement.

"I'm sure it can be arranged," said Marsh. "After all, we don't just have your spies, Regy, we have the Brotherhood..."[29]

---

[27] Field Marshal Earl Kitchener KG KP GCB OM GCSI GCMG GCIE ADC PC 1850-1916) & General Sir Ian Hamilton GCB GCMG DSO TD (1853-1947).

[28] HIH Maria Pavlovna, Grand Duchess Vladimir Alexandrovich of Russia (1854-1920); TIM Tsar Nicholas II (1868-1918) & Tsarina Alexandra Feodorovna (1872-1918); Grigori Yefimovich Rasputin (1869-1916).

[29] Editor's Note: Readers of *The Speedicut Papers* will know that there existed, and possibly may still exist, a secret society at the heart of the British Establishment known as The Brotherhood of the Sons of Thunder. Charles Holland's natural father, Colonel Sir Jasper Speedicut, was a life-long member of the Brotherhood.

"The what?" asked Fahmy a micro-second before I could ask the same question.

"Nothing," snapped Esher, giving Marsh a stern look.

"Have you had any news of Felix, Bertie?" asked Philip, clearly trying to change the subject.

"As a matter of fact, I have," said Stopford, "his wife's just had a baby daughter and – rather surprisingly - he's talking about becoming an officer."

"You know," said Philip, "Felix Yusupov must be the only one of my friends who celebrated the outbreak of war whilst on his *lune de miel* – and in the land of the enemy for good **measure**."[30]

"The Yusupovs called on my family whilst passing through Cairo on their honeymoon," said Fahmy, "I thought them, him in particular, the most beautiful people I'd ever seen."

"Not as good looking as young Lawrence, surely?" asked Nicolson.

"Lawrence who?" queried Philip.

"Ned Lawrence,[31] the archaeologist," said Esher, "he's on the intelligence Staff in Cairo where I placed him at the start of the war. I have plans for him, particularly if Gallipoli fails…"

"Speaking of beauties, Regy, have you seen Mata Hari during your recent visits to Paris?"[32] asked Marsh, who seemed to have recovered his poise.

"No," said Esher, still tight lipped, "I gather she no longer performs, at least not *en publique*."

---

[30] Prince Felix Felixovich Yusupov, Count Sumarokov-Elston (1887-1967).
[31] Thomas Edward Lawrence (1888-1935).
[32] Margaretha Geertruida MacLeod, née Zelle (1876-1917), better known by the stage name Mata Hari.

"And has anyone yet introduced you to Miss Maggie Meller?"[33] asked Stopford.

"Miss who?" chimed in Fahmy.

"Marguerite Meller – a beautiful French tart who's set her heart on becoming Paris's latest *grande horizontale*," said Philip.

There was a lot more of a similar nature, but I don't recall the details now. In fact, I only remember the exchange I've just related because – well, you'll see… Meanwhile, school boys, even those with great expectations, need their sleep so, by midnight and despite a tempting offer from Philip Sassoon to stay for breakfast (I declined, as my absence from Bayswater overnight might have been difficult to explain to Mama) I was back home in my own bed. Sleep, however, was at first quite impossible; it was only in the early hours that I finally drifted off into a restless, dream filled snooze. As I'd been leaving Park Lane, Philip had held me back for a moment in the hall.

"*Charles*, I would like to give you a word of advice – and a promise."

"Please do, Philip."

"My advice is this: forgot the past few days, return to Eton, tell no one of your good fortune and apply yourself to your books. *Il sera difficile*, but it will repay you in the long run. Do you promise to do that?"

"I do," I said rather reluctantly, "and your promise?"

"I in return promise you *deux choses*: first, that as far as the war permits, I will continue and, indeed, deepen our new friendship - if that would be agreeable to you."

"It would," I said with complete honesty.

---

[33] Marie-Marguerite Meller, later Laurient (1890-1971).

"Second, again the war permitting, I will manage your transition to financial independence and a new identity on 28th February next year; I suspect that your mother may be more than a little difficult on a number of counts. *Et, si ce n'est pas possible à cause de la guerre*, I will arrange that Regy Esher stands in my place."

"That's very decent of you, Philip, but can I beg a small concession regarding my promise?"

"What is it?"

"If I don't share the news of my good fortune with someone I think I may burst. May I tell my best friend, Tertius Beaujambe?"

"Frodsham's younger boy?" I nodded. He thought for a moment. "His father's a level-headed sort of fellow, so the son's unlikely to be indiscreet." I was not sure that is how I would have described Tertius; he may have been a member of Pop, but… "Yes, I don't see why not - *mais personne d'autre. D'accord?*"

"*D'accord*," I promised him again; unfortunately, it was an undertaking that I was to break with profound consequences. But that lay in the future. I shook his hand, gave him a manly sort of hug and headed out onto the street.

CHAPTER FOUR: THE SPLENDOURS OF FRODSHAM

I really don't remember much about the rest of that holiday or the Half that followed it for, despite Philip Sassoon's advice, my entire attention was focused on 28th February 1916, a fact which – as I said I would - I shared with Tertius.

"That's splendid news, old thing. Now you won't have to scrounge off me for the rest of your life," laughed my friend when I told him about the trust.

"But there's more," I went on, "and I not sure how you're going to take it."

"Try me."

"Well, it seems that I'm not my Papa's son, which is why Colonel Speedicut established the trust for me in the first place."

"So what? Most of the chaps in Burke's Peerage have inherited via the wrong side of the blanket. There are heaps and heaps of examples in all the best families: Winston's brother Jack's father certainly wasn't the poxed-up Lord Randolph and even the late Prince Consort's father wasn't."

"Yes, I know all that, but how many of them have had to change their name?"

"What do you mean?"

"Only that, to get my hands on the loot, I have to become Charles Speedicut."

"I see," said Tertius looking pensive, "that might be a bit of a bummer here: you know how the chaps like to rag and some of them are dreadful snobs."

"That's what I'm worried about." He thought for a minute or two.

"The answer's simple: once you inherit, you call all the shots, yes?"

"Err, I suppose so."

"So, you tell your mater that you're not returning here at the end of the Easter holidays next year. You then take rooms at the Cavendish and have a full year of fun before you have to head for the trenches, assuming we haven't won or lost the war by then."

"You know, Tertius, that's a damned fine plan…"

Meanwhile, I didn't see Philip Sassoon as he was much pre-occupied with a power struggle within the War Office and the British Expeditionary Force. This eventually resulted in Haig becoming the new C-in-C in December, with Philip in permanent attendance as his Private Secretary. Quite how my new friend managed to switch allegiance from French to Haig without getting caught in the cross-fire was at the time (but not later) a mystery to me. Anyway, the politicking required to keep himself at GHQ meant that I saw nothing of Philip Sassoon during the rest of 1915. That is not to say that I disappeared off his radar or that he allowed himself to disappear off mine. He achieved this by the occasional letter and by delegating his self-appointed role as my guardian to the enigmatic figure of Lord Esher. It was a move that was to have serious repercussions for me.

Regy Esher is today a largely forgotten figure. This is partly because his heyday was during the late-Victorian and Edwardian eras and partly because he chose to operate in the shadows. That notwithstanding, in his day the 2nd Viscount Esher was an extremely powerful figure in the corridors of power and in the British Establishment: confidant to King Edward VII, Queen Alexandra and, later, Queen Mary, he was the chairman of the committee which reformed the War Office and he acted as an unofficial link between Buckingham Palace, Whitehall and the more important Courts on the continent. It's no exaggeration to say that he knew everyone and was, at least by his friends, liked and highly respected.

At the time, many people asked why Regy never accepted public office, including an offer of the Viceroyalty of India along with a Marquisate. I believe that the reason he chose to operate behind the scenes was because there were two dark secrets in his life. The dinner at Park Lane had exposed the first, although it was only later in the year that I came to realise that Regy's taste was for schoolboys and, later still, that his passions included his younger son, Maurice, with whom he had conducted an incestuous, emotional and possibly physical relationship whilst the lad was at Eton. The second only came to light during the long summer holiday of 1915.

My disclosure to Tertius Beaujambe of the prospective changes in my fortunes, didn't mean that I became any less close to him; quite the reverse in fact. He was a year ahead of me at Eton and destined to leave to join the Colours at around the same time that I would be transformed from the impecunious Mr Holland into the rich Mr Speedicut.

"You know, old thing," he said to me one idyllic early-summer afternoon, as we lazed in the shade of a waterside willow watching a crew of wet bobs straining from stroke to bow, whilst a dusky-hued cox yelled instructions at them.

"Isn't that your bridge partner, Ali the Sheikh of Araby?" I interjected.

"Yes, it is – but as I was about to say: early next year our happy partnership is going to be sundered by Kaiser Bill and his Jerry bravos. Whilst you're in Savile Row being fitted for life as a London loafer, I'll be donning His Majesty's khaki and heading off to the Shiny Tenth in France,[34] from whence I will not – in all probability – return."

"Don't say that, Tertius. From what I heard during the holidays the war may well be over by then."

---

[34] 'The Shiny Tenth' was a nickname for the 10th (The Prince of Wales's Own Royal) Hussars which, at that time, was the most fashionable regiment in the British Army.

"I doubt it," said my friend. "Thanks to the cock-up at Gallipoli and the bloodbath at Ypres, we're bogged down on both Fronts – and God-alone knows how many more *Lusitania* will have to be sunk before the Americans agree to come in on our side. No. I've just got to face the fact that my adult life is going to start – and may well end – in a trench on the Western Front."

"But there's still the summer holidays and Christmas to be enjoyed before then," I replied in a brave attempt to raise his spirits.

"I know," he sighed, "and I've been thinking about that. I wouldn't subject you to a family Christmas at Frodsham, but – other than the convalescing officers – the place will be largely uninhabited during the summer. Would you like to come and stay?"

"Would I!"

"Do you think your mater would release you?"

"To stay at Frodsham? She'll have packed my trunk before I can finish asking her!"

"Well, that settled then. As soon as this Half is over you return to London, dust off your summer suits and a dinner jacket, then jump on the train for Cheshire. With any luck, my Pater's under butler will give us the keys to the cellar and I'll be able to go to France next Easter bolstered by the best of memories."

And that's what happened – and much more besides.

As I'd predicted, when I returned to London at the end of that Half and proposed my summer plans to Mama she couldn't get me out of the house fast enough. So fast, in fact, that I scarcely had time to take a further lesson in *fellatio* from Nellie the parlour maid; the furtive session we did manage in the airing cupboard was so brief that it was scarcely worth the effort of unbuttoning or recording. But, I consoled myself, there was the whole summer holiday in Cheshire stretching in front of me, during which

I'd been promised by Tertius that all the pleasures of the flesh would be indulged to exhaustion.

I'd not heard a lot about Frodsham Splendens from my friend, who was generally tight-lipped about both his family and their possessions. I knew that it was a large house set in rolling countryside, whose ownership - as far as the eye could see from the front and rear steps of the house – had, since the time of the Conqueror, been exclusively Beaujambe. I knew too that a perfectly decent Jacobean house had been demolished to make way for the present building shortly after the parvenu Westminsters had unveiled Eaton Hall in the 1880s.[35] I was, however, wholly unprepared for the reality.

I'd persuaded Mama that I needed to travel First Class and so the journey from Euston to Chester, where I had to change trains and take the branch line to Frodsham Halt, was passed in comfort. Waiting for me outside the rather quaint Victorian station was Tertius at the wheel of a red two-seater Packard 30 with the hood down. He was clad in a white dust coat, helmet and goggles and looked like an aviator, albeit a grounded one, of the type that were featured regularly in the illustrated papers before the war.

"This is only the first time I've driven this," said Tertius as he directed a porter to put my bags in the boot, "so you'd better hang on tight... I almost put the brute into a ditch on the way here... I'll have to send a crate of beer to one of our tenants, who wasn't so lucky when I met him head-on at a rather tricky corner just down the road... How was the journey? I hope you haven't eaten as I've laid on something special to welcome you..."

He prattled on in a similar vein whilst we hurtled noisily along the narrow country lane that led from the station to the lodge, which heralded the entrance to Frodsham Park. How we got that far without killing at least some half-a-dozen yokels – several chickens and a brace of dozy pheasants

---

[35] Eaton Hall, Cheshire was an enormous Gothic revival palace built for Hugh Lupus Grosvenor, 1st Duke of Westminster (1825-1899), to a design by Alfred Waterhouse (1830-1905).

were not so lucky – I don't know, but I silently thanked God when we got to the relatively traffic-and-people-free drive to the main house.

Frodsham Splendens no longer exists; it was the victim of a German bomber which shed its load on the house in 1942 in the belief that it was Liverpool Town Hall. It was an understandable mistake. But in case you have never been to Liverpool, I will describe the house as I first saw it on that fine summer day in July 1915, when Tertius slewed the motor around a steep down-hill bend and Frodsham Splendens hove into view at the end of the drive.

Between us and its front steps, running down the steep hill into the valley below, was a dead straight, tree-lined avenue which crossed a hump-backed bridge over a weir that divided two ornamental lakes. At the end of this runway, which on the far side of the bridge was lined with chain-linked bollards, squatted the Beaujambes' mansion. It was a vast, four-square neo-classical pile built in a dark grey stone, arranged over two principal floors and surmounted by urn-bedecked balustrading, within and above which rose a huge lead-covered, four-sided pyramid supported by elephants. At the centre of each elaborately decorated façade of the house was a full-height portico, with steps leading down to a gravelled courtyard on the entrance front, a Tudor maze to the rear and, on the other two sides, the extensive formal parterres that were the only relics of the building's seventeenth-century predecessor. It looked like a cross between a Greek railway terminus and a Pharaoh's final resting place - and was probably the inspiration for one of Redmile's fantastical creations that were so in vogue a few years ago.[36]

"What do you think?" asked Tertius as he braked abruptly in a storm of dust and gravel to allow me to take in the house.

"Golly," I said. It was all I could say without being impolite or knowing what he thought.

---

[36] Editor's Note: Anthony Redmile was an eccentric 1960's designer who created 'fantastic' furniture and objets d'art by combining real skulls, shells, antlers and eggs with architectural and neo-classical forms.

"I think it's perfectly hideous. Consequently, it's the perfect setting for the people who live inside it – myself excepted, of course. Wait 'til you see the interior. 'Home, James, and don't spare the horses'!" he cried as he revved the engine, pulled down his flying goggles and released the handbrake.

Up until the moment that we hit the apex of the bridge, I'd never before been airborne. For one moment, as all four wheels left the drive, the sensation was quite serene. It was replaced a second later by a bone-crunching jolt as the motor landed, followed by a screech as it skidded and a loud bang as it hit a bollard and rolled over onto its side. We should have been killed but we had the good fortune to be thrown well clear of the Panhard before it flipped onto its back and exploded. We did not, however, escape unscathed.

I think I must have been temporarily knocked-out, for the first thing I remembered after I hit the ground was lying on my back and staring up at a cerulean blue sky, muddied by small clouds of acrid smoke. At first, I thought I was alright. With considerable care, I lifted first my left leg, then my right, then my right arm and, with even greater care, my head. All seemed to be in one piece. It was only when I tried to lift my left arm that I realised it seemed somewhat extended: my left hand, palm up, was below my knee. Then the pain hit me. As I discovered later, I had a full dislocation and it was agony until it was reduced. How much luckier was Tertius, who only had a broken head. But that is to anticipate.

The noise of the exploding car alerted the skeleton staff at the house and several severely traumatised convalescing officers who, as a result, had to be carted off to the military funny farm at Craiglockhart outside Edinburgh. Military mental malfunctions notwithstanding, it wasn't long before a good-looking footman in half livery and a vacuous-looking kitchen maid were staring down at us. Realising that we needed help, they turned and ran back to the house. But it was a while before two pairs of medical orderlies appeared with stretchers and carried us through the double height hall (I got a good look at the inside of the mosaic-lined pyramid above it as they did so and rather wished that I hadn't) and into a large room hung with gaudily gilt mirrors, hideous family portraits and populated with ugly iron bedsteads, on which lay or sat uniformed men, some bandaged and others in splints or with crutches.

"What have we got here, then?" asked a middle aged and moustachioed man wearing a white coat over his uniform.

"There been an accident just outside the house, sir," replied one of the stretcher bearers, "two civvies joy-riding by the looks of it."

"Hmm," said the doctor, "put them on those beds over there, get their clothes off and let's see how bad they are."

A couple of hours later, Tertius and I were sat on a bench to one side of the main entrance wearing draughty hospital gowns and surveying the smouldering wreckage of our arrival. Actually, to be more accurate, I was on the bench with my left arm in a sling and Tertius was in a wheelchair, with his head swathed in a white turban-like bandage. If we'd been in uniform, any visitors would have been forgiven for mistaking us for war wounded.

Fortunately, despite the fact that his face had been covered in his own gore, Tertius - or, thinking about it, possibly the remains of the car - had been recognised by the footman and so, instead of being confined to the drawing room ward and fed endless cup of tea, beds were made up for us in the family wing and the footman who'd been first to the crash, a fine figure of a young man called Percy, was assigned by the under butler to dance attendance upon us. My luggage, of course, had been consumed in the blazing wreckage.

"Worry not, old bean," Tertius said, "once you're able to get dressed, Percy will raid my father's wardrobe as you're more his size than mine. And, whilst you're about it, Percy," he called to the footman who was lurking by the steps, "please bring us a pile of sandwiches and a bottle of white wine. I'm most unaccountably hungry."

"I suppose we'll have to tell our parents about this," I ventured later, as I tucked-in to a wedge of brown bread and smoked salmon.

"I don't see why we should," replied Tertius. "Mine are pre-occupied with war work and what remains of the London Season - and your mater won't be at all happy to learn that you might be headed back in the direction of Bayswater. No, I think the sensible thing to do is to say nothing. We're in the best place to convalesce, what with the Army medics to look after our external injuries and my father's staff to attend to the rest of us. There's nothing we need that can't be provided right here and I, for one, certainly don't need my ghastly relations fussing around me, telling the cook that I need beef broth and builder's tea to get me back on my feet."

"But I think I ought to tell someone. My cheque book was in my luggage," I said pointing to the still smoking ruins of the Panhard, "and I can't wear your father's clothes for the whole of the summer."

"Well, who could you tell who might be able to help but who wouldn't interfere?" I thought about this whilst demolishing a roast beef sandwich. The obvious person would have been Philip Sassoon but I knew from his last letter that he was in France. Then I remembered Lord Esher.

"Can I send a telegram from the house?" I asked Tertius.

"Of course," he said, "just scribble a message then I'll get Percy to nip down to the village and send it from the Post Office. But who are you sending it to?"

"Lord Esher," I said as Percy appeared at my elbow with a salver on which was a blank telegram form and a pencil: the footman had clearly been well trained.

"Why him?"

"Because he's standing in for my one of trustees, he doesn't know my Mama and I'm sure he'll be discreet," I said.

"But he's also a notorious corridor creeper of the Oscar Wilde variety – my brother's Dame at Eton forbade him to be in the same room with Esher when the old pervert was visiting his son, Maurice."

"We'll have to lock our doors then," I countered as I dashed off the following telegraphic message:

> SERIOUS MOTOR ACCIDENT FRODSHAM STOP MINOR INJURY BUT LOST EVERYTHING IN WRECKAGE STOP CAN YOU HELP QUERY CHARLES HOLLAND

I didn't have to wait long for an answer. Tertius and I - he now in his own night clothes and with me in one of his father's coroneted dressing gowns - had been installed by the under butler, Mr Bowles, in the small family dining room. This was an octagonal chamber on the ground floor overlooking the drive. It was lined in fumed oak, hung with tartan curtains and bedecked with antlers, including a vast horned chandelier over the circular dining table: thank God, the food and wines at Frodsham Splendens were better than the decorations. We were about to start dinner when an aged telegraph 'boy' on a rickety bicycle arrived. Through the window we'd watched with amusement his headlong approach down the straight part of the drive.

"I'll lay you half-a-crown he collides with the front step," cried Tertius as the telegraph 'boy' did his unsuccessful best not to repeat our flight to destruction.

"Done," I said.

At first it looked as though I'd lost, for the brakes on the ancient machine had clearly seen better days and it was a miracle that the pensioner managed to stop before his front wheel buckled on the entrance steps. Barely had he skidded to a shuddering halt than Percy appeared under the portico to collect the telegram, which he brought to me seconds later as Tertius dipped into his dressing gown pocket and handed me a coin. I slit open the buff envelope and read the message aloud:

> MOST DISTRESSED BY NEWS STOP ARRIVING FRODSHAM HALT TOMORROW NOON STOP ESHER

"Shit!" said Tertius.

"Will there be an answer, sir, other than His Lordship's?" asked the footman, barely repressing a cheeky smile.

"No, Percy," I replied, "and can you please arrange for a motor to collect Lord Esher tomorrow?"

"Would the pony trap be in order, sir? His Lordship has, err, put out of commission the only serviceable motor car in the stables."

"I'm sure Lord Esher won't mind."

And he didn't, as he made clear when he arrived in time for lunch the following day. Tertius and I were enjoying the mid-morning sun and a glass of fizz under the east portico when my surrogate trustee appeared.

"Lord Esher," intoned Bowles the under butler.

"My dear Lord Tertius," Regy purred as he strode forward to my friend's wheel chair, limp hand outstretched, "thank you for sending your *charming* coachman to meet me. Such a *handsome* boy – I hoped that the journey would never end!" he burbled as he took Tertius's hand. "It is a *very* real pleasure to meet you, albeit it under *such* painful circumstances."

"Do please call me, Tertius, Lord Esher" said my friend, "and neither of us is really in any pain at all, thanks to this." Tertius held up his glass.

"I'm very pleased to hear it," said Esher as he took a glass proffered to him by Percy, "and *you* must both call me 'Uncle Regy'; I am, of course, acquainted with your delightful parents and old enough to be your father," Tertius pulled a face at this, but Esher had already turned to me as I rose to greet him.

"And, Charles, how *wonderful* to see you again, dear boy! My, my, you two really have been in the wars," he said as he surveyed my injuries, "and judging by the wreck opposite the front door you are both lucky to be alive. I had planned to return to London tomorrow but, under the circumstances, perhaps I should stay longer." Tertius threw me a look of despair.

"I'm sure that won't be necessary, err, Uncle Regy," I said as firmly as I could.

"We'll see about that. Now tell me how it happened."

But before either of us could recount the story, Bowles announced lunch. With the under butler in the lead, Percy the footman wheeled Tertius back to the family dining room, whilst Esher somewhat gratuitously took my undamaged arm, gave it a squeeze and guided me in their wake. During the meal, Esher ensured that the chat around the table was almost exclusively about the recent Half; the peer simply couldn't get enough detail about our activities out of the class room or off the field and river. Indeed, it was as much as Tertius and I could do to try to steer him away from talk of the communal bath in the changing rooms and back to the Furrow and the Wall. Eventually we gave up and started inventing salacious stories of illicit liaisons amongst his friends' Etonian offspring. We were only saved from having to talk about ourselves by the arrival of coffee.

"So, tell me, Charles," said Esher as Percy left the room and I wondered what new revelation he was going to demand, "*how* can I be of assistance?"

"For a start, sir – I mean, Uncle Regy - my cheque book's a charred stub and I'm completely out of funds. So, as I don't want my Mama to be alarmed, I'm in a bit of fix financially."

"Would twenty or even fifty pounds be sufficient to tide you over until you can get your bank to send you a replacement?" said Esher, reaching for his pocket book.

"Fifty should be more than enough," chipped in Tertius; Esher looked a touch miffed, but nonetheless counted out ten white fivers which he handed to me.

"And what else, Charles?"

"That's about it – unless you see Sir Philip Sassoon. In which case, could tell him what's happened and that we're alright? I don't want to alarm him with a telegram or a letter."

"Very sensible, my dear Charles. If you telegraph Philip that you've been in an accident, before you know it he'll have sent a team of top surgeons and nurses from London to look after you, emptied Fortnum & Mason of every delicacy they can supply in war time and sent enough exotic blooms for your bedside to stock the Chelsea Flower Show. Anything else?"

"As a matter of fact, there is – but perhaps you'd like a walk in the park after luncheon and we can discuss it?" Tertius arched an eyebrow but I ignored him. You see, my mention of Philip Sassoon had reminded me of my conversation with Tertius about school and had started a train of thought.

"What an utterly delightful idea," said Esher, "I can't wait to hear what you have to say." I bet you can't, I thought, but it won't be what you hope…

Half an hour later we were ambling around the maze – I wanted to keep his hopes up – when, despite my promise to Philip not to discuss my prospects with anyone except Tertius, I opened up.

"Uncle Regy, does the name Speedicut mean anything to you?"

CHAPTER FIVE: BROTHERHOOD

"Are you referring to the late Colonel Sir Jasper Speedicut?"

"I am," I replied.

"Hmm. Well, old Colonel Speedicut was an associate of mine for many years. Why do you ask?"

"Because," and I took a deep breath, "I have recently been told that he was my natural father and I'd very much like to know more about him."

"Has this got anything to do with the Black Jade Trust of which Philip has become a trustee?"

"Yes. It was Colonel Speedicut who established it for me."

"I see," said Esher. "Why don't we take advantage of that bench over there – this could take some time."

An hour later I knew more than I dared to hope about my real father. It emerged that Regy Esher had known him for about twenty years but, for some reason, also knew his life story long before they had met. As the tale unfolded, I lost count of the number of minor colonial, North American and European wars in which my Papa had been engaged and I noted with pride that he'd been at Balaclava, in the Mutiny and at both Isandalwana and Rorke's Drift. It appeared that he'd also been close to the Royal Family and had worked for Queen Victoria, The Duke of Clarence and King Edward VII. As to his personal life, Regy told me that Speedicut's first wife had died in childbirth and that he had then married the daughter of a Duke and produced one daughter, who was married to a Russian Prince and had twin daughters of her own.[37]

---

[37] Editor's Note: For a potted biography of Colonel Sir Jasper Speedicut go to www.jasperspeedicut.com.

"As you knew him so well, Uncle Regy, can I ask you one more question?"

"Certainly, my boy."

"When I inherit the trust next year I'm obliged to change my name. I think that could make life quite unpleasant at school and Tertius agrees. So, I've made up my mind to leave. Some people might say I was being a coward. What do you think my Papa would have done in my place?"

"Knowing Jasper as I did, I'm sure he'd have done the same. Indeed, I seem to remember him telling me that he had no time for school and left as soon as he could. He can't have been much more than seventeen when he joined the Tenth Hussars and the Bro..." He stopped in mid-word.

"The what, Uncle Regy?"

"Nothing, dear boy – nothing at all."

"Did you nearly say 'the Brotherhood', Uncle Regy?" he said nothing. "And wasn't a Brotherhood mentioned at Philip Sassoon's dinner party where I first met you?" Esher looked very uncomfortable. I put a hand on his thigh. "Come on, Uncle Regy," I said giving his leg a squeeze, "if my Papa was in this Brotherhood from an early age, why can't you tell me about it – and why can't I be in it too? It will give me something to do when I leave school and before I can join the Army."

"The organisation to which you refer is not a social club in which you can idle away your time, Charles, nor is it a Masonic or religious organisation given to good works..."

"So, what is it, Uncle Regy?" Despite increased pressure from my hand, he didn't respond and we sat in silence for what seemed like five minutes. Eventually, he gently removed my paw and looked me straight in the eye.

"You don't know what you are asking, Charles, and my heart tells me that I shouldn't give you an answer. However, my head tells me that you are, on the one hand, a sensible and trustworthy boy but, on the other hand, that you are inquisitive and won't rest until you've satisfied your curiosity. In the process of doing that you might, indeed you probably would, inadvertently create problems for me." He paused again. "If I do enlighten you it will be on the understanding that, once you know about it, you will already be fully committed to the organisation for life. You will, in effect, be 'buying a pig in a poke' and there will be no turning back. Do you understand?"

"You mean that if you tell me about this Brotherhood then I am automatically a member of it?"

"Yes, although you cannot be initiated as a member until you have left school."

"And this is the organisation to which my real father belonged for all his adult life?"

"It is."

"Then count me in!" I nearly shouted.

"Before I do, Charles, I need you to swear on pain of death - and I mean that literally - that you will not discuss what I am about to tell you with a living soul outside of the organisation. Not even Lord Tertius Beaujambe," he added giving me a very penetrating stare. "Do you so swear?"

"I do."

"Very well." He paused and took a deep breath whilst never breaking eye contact with me. "Since the reign of His Majesty King George III there has existed a secret society dedicated to upholding the best interests of this country by whatever means necessary. It is called The Brotherhood of the Sons of Thunder and, since the death last month of your father's oldest friend, Mr Henry Flashman, I have been the Great Boanerges or head of the Brotherhood."

"Who else is in it?" I asked.

"That you will learn once you have been initiated into the Brotherhood. All that you need to know for now is that most of our Brothers are in positions of authority and influence across a wide range of fields."

"But at least tell me if Philip is a member."

"I couldn't possibly comment," replied Esher - but in such a way that I thought I knew the answer. And that was it. Despite further persistent questioning, Esher would say no more. So, realising that I was on a hiding to nothing, I gave up and together, with me in a rather morose mood, we returned to the house.

After an alcohol-fuelled dinner, designed to ensure that Esher slept soundly (we locked our doors as a precaution anyway), the following morning the peer returned to London whilst Tertius and I settled into a happy and prolonged recovery.

Those of my readers who are familiar with the works of Mr Evelyn Waugh (a frightful shit and an appalling snob who's only redeeming feature is a talent for farcical fiction) will now expect me to relate a tale of a golden summer idyll spent, in a permanently pissed condition, lounging on the greensward at Frodsham Splendens in the company of my glamorous friend. In that they would be wrong for whilst, after a painful and explosive start, it was the best holiday of my teenage years, to relate the details would only be of interest to those who, like Regy Esher, derive pleasure from erotic tales of beautiful blond schoolboys fossicking 'midst the rustic (and rusticated) setting of one of England's ugliest houses.

For the same reason, I am omitting an account of my final months at Eton. As I discovered on the shelves of the library here, far and away the most tedious of Mr Powell's otherwise excellent *Dance to the Music of Time* is the first volume, which covers the schooldays of the principal characters: I do not intend to make the same mistake as Powell - and I do not have the comic wit of Waugh to leaven the tale. Besides which, I have observed that those who claim that their schooldays were the best days of their lives almost invariably have failed to achieve anything since then. I propose, therefore and without further ado, to move forward in time to Monday 28th February

1916, the date of my seventeenth birthday and the real start of my adult life, mentioning only in passing that Tertius had left school at the end of the Michaelmas Half *pro patria mori* with the Tenth Hussars and, in consequence, the place was a damned sight less entertaining than it had been.

Of course, the Lent Half was still in full, dismal swing as the momentous anniversary loomed, but I told my Dame that I had a frightful toothache and had to visit the family's Harley Street dentist. A month before that I'd arranged by letter with Philip that he would get Sir Ernest Cassel to contact Mama and ask her to meet with the two of them at the Cassel mansion on Park Lane on a 'matter related to your son's trust fund.' I'd assumed that she knew the trust came to an end when I reached seventeen, but Philip seemed to think that she knew neither the precise details nor the fact that her own allowance would stop.

> *She may not be very happy with that,*

Philip had written,

> *so, given the value of the fund, you may want to consider making a provision for her: an annuity that matches her present allowance might be one solution. In any event, it wouldn't be seemly for you to impoverish her.*

It was wise, albeit unwelcome advice.

> *There is also the question of your change of surname. That news will come as a complete surprise and probable embarrassment to your mother.*

He was right there too: the news would either bring on a tantrum or tears. In either event, both would be of epic proportions. However, the promise of a continuation of her allowance might just stem the tempest or the flood.

> *I assume, too,*

Philip's letter had continued,

> *that you have yet to tell her of your intention of leaving Eton.*

I'd written to Philip about this shortly after I'd seen Esher; I was sure that the latter would not be able to resist telling Philip and I wanted to get to him first with the news. I'd also taken the opportunity to tell him about the accident, although I had been careful not to mention the Brotherhood. But, despite making me promise to discuss it with no one, Esher must have told Philip and, thereby, confirmed my suspicions regarding his membership of the organisation.

You know my views on the subject of your schooling,

his letter went on: Philip thought I should stay at Eton until I was eighteen and then go up to Oxford or join the Colours if the war was still raging,

and your decision with regard to the Brotherhood,

he thought I should wait until the war was over,

but you are old enough to know your own mind so both matters are closed.

So it was that, on the morning of my seventeenth birthday, I boarded a train to London and then made my way by cab to Cassel's gloomy, marble-lined mansion a couple of blocks nearer to Marble Arch than the Sassoon palazzo. I arrived just after Mama; it was not a good start.

"What on earth are you doing here, Charles?" she demanded as I joined her in the sepulchral hall. "And why aren't you at school? You haven't been sacked, have you?" she asked suspiciously. Well, it was a reasonable assumption.

"No, Mama, I'm up here to visit the dentist," I replied with a modicum of truthfulness.

"In Park Lane, Charles? Don't be..." But before she could continue I was saved by Philip, clad in Service Dress, who at that moment glided in from the street in the wake of the Cassel butler, who a few minutes before had opened the door to Mama and then me.

"Mrs Holland? We haven't met. I'm Philip Sassoon - *et ce beau garçon?*" he arched an eyebrow in my direction.

"My son, Charles Holland, Sir Philip - although quite why he is here..."

But she was again interrupted, this time by the arrival of Sir Ernest, a forbidding-looking figure in a frock coat and a grey, manicured beard. Once more the introductions were made and the financier then led us into a cavernous, faux-Baroque room that made Frodsham Splendens seem a model of contemporary design and good taste. He positioned himself behind a vast desk and waved us into three chairs ranged in front of it. At this point Mama still appeared mystified by my presence; she didn't have long to find out the reason.

"Mrs Holland," growled the banker in his distinctive *mittel*-European accent, "you are I am sure aware that the Black Jade Trust, so generously established by the late Colonel Sir Jasper Speedicut, vests today." Mama nodded but said nothing. "Good," Sir Ernest continued, "but I suspect that you may not be aware of either its precise terms or of its value."

"That is correct, Sir Ernest," she said looking suspicious.

"Nor will you be aware of a secret codicil inserted by Sir Jasper."

Mama sat up at this announcement and her nostrils flared as though she'd just had a whiff of a rotting corpse. Despite this, the scene that followed was to some extent a disappointment, at least as far as hysterics went: Cassel read though the trust document, then gave a summary of its investments and their value and finally revealed the secret clause. To my intense surprise, Mama said nothing, although she looked as though she was now ankle deep in human putrefaction. Cassel paused, but when Mama remained silent he gave Philip a meaningful look.

"I hope you won't feel that the trustees have been dealing *derrière votre dos* - behind your back - Mrs Holland," lisped Philip. Mama sniffed but remained in a catatonic state. "But there is more..." and he proceeded to tell Mama of my financial intentions for her and my plans for myself (excluding, of course, any mention of the Brotherhood). Still she behaved like a well-trained Trappist monk to the obvious embarrassment of the two trustees. Hoping, I suppose, to break the silence, Sir Ernest rose and heaved on a bell pull behind his desk. Moments later a footman appeared, Cassel ordered that drinks be brought and it wasn't long before the servant returned sagging under the weight of a huge silver tray on which was a magnum of the Widow and four glasses.

"I don't normally drink before luncheon," said Sir Ernest, "but I think that at the very least we should raise a glass to celebrate young Charles's birthday." Quite why this seemingly innocent suggestion snapped Mama out of her self-imposed silence I don't know, but it did. Without any preamble, she rose to her feet.

"Gentlemen," she said giving the two men a withering look that said she thought they were not, "if you believe that there is anything to celebrate - *other* than your success in keeping me in the dark all these years - then *I don't*." Cassel started to protest but she cut across him. "You and the late Colonel Speedicut have conspired not only to make me superfluous to my son's future but have added insult to your injury by making me his pensioner. I should have expected nothing less from people like you." She then turned to me. "As for you, Charles, you always were a selfish and wilful child - quite like your real father in fact - and it's now plain to me that you will grow up to be the same as him. Unless I'm much mistaken, you will quickly squander every penny of the fortune he has left you - and when you have done so, *don't come crying to me*. From this moment on, I wash my hands of you." This time Philip tried unsuccessfully to intervene. "I have no regard for your opinion, Sir Philip, so save your breath to cool your *gefiltefisch*," she sneered; if Mama had slapped him, Philip could not have looked more affronted. Then, without giving either him, me or Cassel a second glance, she picked up her handbag, rose and sailed out of the room - and my life. As Mama slammed the door behind her there was an awkward pause whilst Philip looked at the gilded and frescoed ceiling and Sir Ernest inspected the expensive Persian rug beneath his well-shod feet.

"Could I have that drink you were offering, sir?" I asked in as steady a voice I could muster at short notice. "Then, perhaps, you could tell me how I can access my money for I rather suspect that, as a rather pressing priority, I am going to need to find a hotel and acquire a new wardrobe."

"As to a roof over your head," said Philip with a smile as he poured me a glass of fizz, "you can move in with me – until, that is, you can make *un arrangement plus permanent*. And I'll send a note to Huntsman telling them to open an account for you and kit you out, *aussi vite que possible*, with whatever you need."

"And I have already arranged for you to bank with Rothschild's," chipped in Cassel. "Here's a cheque book," he said handing me one that had been lying on his desk, "so that you can draw whatever funds you need. Once you have changed your name you will, of course, require a new one. I assume – indeed, I would advise – that you allow Rothschild to continue to manage your investments. They've done very well for you to date and I see no reason why they shouldn't do so in the future – unless, that is, you decided to fulfil your mother's prophesy."

"I have no intention of doing so, Sir Ernest," I said - and, at the time, I meant it.

During the lunch which followed, Philip expanded on his ideas for my immediate future.

"I think you should take rooms in Mayfair. There's a block I know of in Mount Street that has well-proportioned bachelor sets and good staff accommodation. Of course, *il n'y a pas de cuisine*, but then you wouldn't want *un chef* and they're equipped so that food can be sent up from the *rechauféé* kitchen in the basement. I will have us driven there *après le déjeuner* and, on the way, we can stop *chez* Huntsman and get your *trousseau* on order, then my car can take us to Jermyn Street and St James's Street where you can buy the rest of what you will need."

"Could we take tea at the Cavendish afterwards?" I asked hopefully.

"You can, but I'll not be joining you. Mrs Lewis is not exactly *ma tasse de thé*," said Philip whilst Cassel looked disapproving.

Despite this, by five o'clock Philip's chauffeur had left me at the Cavendish and I was safely ensconced in Rosa's parlour where she was, as usual, dispensing champagne. She reacted favourable to the news of my new-found wealth, independence and identity.

"What did I tell you, drearie? One butcher's 'ook at yer mug were enough to tell me yer woz Jasper's. So yer mrother's thrown yer out 'as she? Well, that's no 'ardship. She seemed like a right cow to me. Can't think what yer father saw in 'er. A nice clean tart off the 'dilly would 'ave been a lot less trouble - but we wouldn't 'ave 'ad you then, would we?" she added with a broad smile. "When d'yer get the keys to Mrount Street?"

"Next week, but Philip Sassoon says I should have it decorated before I move in. Meanwhile, I'm staying with him."

"That's no 'ardship neither," said Rosa. " 'e's rich as anything - although I can't says as I warm to 'im, but then 'e's not the marrying kind and I don't approve of waste. Pity, coz 'e's not bad looking for a breeding foreigner." She paused for a moment to down a glass of fizz and a calculating look crossed her face as she did so. "If yer setting up on yer own, young Charles, yer going to need a valet and a chauffeur ain't you?"

"I hadn't thought about it," I said - and I hadn't.

"Well, yer going to need someone to look after all those fancy clothes yer've just brought and yer not going to walk everywhere and spoil yer nice new shoes, now are yer?"

"Err, I suppose not," I answered truthfully.

"And yer going to need a good caterer to provide the vrittels for all them fancy parties yer going to be throwing, aren't yer?"

"I suppose so."

"Hmm. I might - just might - know of the right brokes to start orf yer 'ousehold."

"Who?" I asked.

"I'd rather not say 'til I've spoken to 'em. But when I've told 'em who yer are, they mright just be interested in coming outta retirement."

"You mean they're very old?"

"Na, dearie. They're not working coz when their last employer went to 'is Maker, Gawd rest 'is soul, 'e left 'em 'nuff to keep 'em out of the work'ouse for the rest of their breeding naturals. Come to think of it, I also know of a good caterer who'd be interested in supplying yer - unless, of course, yer'd prefer to set up an arrangement with my kitchens."

"Well, if you would ask them that would be splendid."

"Leave it wiv me, dearie. I'll 'ave a word wiv 'em and, if they're int'rested, arrange for 'em to me yer 'ere. Now 'ave another glass of frizz, afore you stagger off back to Babylon."

CHAPTER SIX: THE THREE MONKEYS

Over the next few days a number of things happened that were to have a lasting influence on the rest of my life. The first involved a visit to the offices of Sir Charles Russell, the same lawyer who had drawn up my trust, to start the process of changing my name by Deed Poll from Holland to Speedicut. Philip made the arrangements and sent me to the Temple in his run-about, a giant Hispano-Suiza.

On arrival, I was shown into Russell's wood-panelled office by an ancient clerk. Sir Charles was seated behind a large desk, dressed in a grey morning suit with a black silk topper perched on the back of his head (I found out later that he rarely removed his hat as it would have exposed his bald pate). He rose to greet me, waved me to a comfortable chair but remained standing.

"When your father drew up your trust, Mr Holland," intoned the lawyer to royalty and Society, "it was I who drafted it. However, when Sir Jasper later added the secret codicil about your change of name it was drafted by one of my clerks, who unfortunately overlooked the fact that you have to be eighteen to execute a Deed Poll."

"Does that mean that I have to retain the name Holland until my eighteenth birthday, Sir Charles, or – worse still – that the trust can't vest until then?"

"Technically, Mr Holland, the answer to both your questions is 'yes'. However, I have taken the liberty of consulting with your trustees and they have confirmed that they are willing for you to take control of your inheritance immediately – indeed, I understand that you have already drawn on it - but with one proviso."

"What's that?"

"That you change your name."

"But I thought you said that I couldn't do that until next year."

"*You* can't execute the necessary Deed Poll but, in English common law, it is possible for a minor's name to be changed by such means if it is executed by," he looked down at an open book on his desk and quoted, " 'everyone with parental responsibility for the child and providing that the child does not object to it'."

"Oh my God," I groaned, "that means I'll have to get my mother to agree to sign the Deed and, given the spiteful mood she's in, she certainly won't."

"So I understand," said Russell. "There is, however, a solution. The common law on the subject refers only to those with 'parental responsibility.' I understand that your mother made an explicit statement in front of witnesses that she had 'washed her hands' of you."

"She did."

"Fortunately for you, those two witnesses – Sir Philip and Sir Ernest - are willing to swear as much and, as your trustees, to assume the role of *in loco parentis* for the purposes of the Deed Poll. I assume that you have no objections to this arrangement or to your change of name?"

"None," I said with considerable relief.

"Excellent, well leave it all with me – and feel free to order yourself some new visiting cards."

The second event was my induction (using my new surname) into the Brotherhood; it was an experience which was as bizarre as it was, at times, frightening. Shortly after I'd returned from seeing Russell, Regy Esher got in touch via a letter which informed that I was to report to the Brotherhood's headquarters in Manchester Square at six pm the following Monday. I'm not going to tell you what happened, beyond saying that the Masons and the Jews have nothing on the Brotherhood when it comes to admitting new members. What I will put on the record, however, is that rolling up your trousers, bearing your left tit or having your foreskin sliced off are but trivial rituals when compared to the admission rites of the Brotherhood of the Sons of Thunder.[38]

Once the ceremony was over, and I had dried off and changed back into a suit, there was a rather jolly drinks party at which I met several members of the Brotherhood, in addition to those whom I already knew from Philip's dinner party the previous year.

"I have a couple of task in mind for you," said Esher looking serious, "although I will give you a couple of months or so to find your feet in London and move into your new flat, then I propose sending you to Russia."

"Marvellous! What I am to do?" I replied.

"Kitchener's making a visit to the Russian government in June and I want you to report back to me on his mood and opinions *en route* and whilst he's in St Petersburg."

"How on earth will I do that?"

"I'll arrange for you to be a temporary member of his Staff. He'll want to interview you of course but, after one look, he'll raise no objections. You're too young to be commissioned but there's no age limit for civil servants and, if you grow a moustache, there's no reason why he'll think you're not in your twenties. Brother Nicolson will have you appointed to a civilian job in the Foreign Office then second you to the War Office."

"But I haven't even been to university."

"Don't worry. It will be in a capacity low enough not to tax your skills but high enough that you can keep an eye on the Secretary of State for War. When Kitchener returns to London you will remain in St Petersburg to assist Brother Stopford, who is there representing the interests of the

---

[38] Editor's Note: For those readers who are interested, the ritual is described in detail by Colonel Sir Jasper Speedicut in *The Speedicut Papers: Book 1 (Flashman's Secret)*.

Brotherhood. He recently cabled to say that he could do with some help on a task we have assigned to him."

"What's that?" I asked.

"You'll find out in due course; all you need to know for now is that, by sending you to St Petersburg with Kitchener, I can kill two birds with one stone. Once you've completed your assignment in Russia you will be old enough to join the Colours and I'll get you a commission in your father's old regiment, the Tenth Hussars."

"And join Tertius Beaujambe in the mud of Flanders, of joy!" I said.

"I think not," said Esher. "I have something altogether sunnier in mind for you…" But he wouldn't be drawn on what that might be. Well, what he had already told me was challenge enough: I was being thrown in the deep end. I thanked God that, even at the age of seventeen, I was a powerful swimmer.

The third event happened shortly after the other two. I was enjoying a post-lunch snooze in Philip's comfortable library when Garton padded in with a letter on a salver. The words 'Cavendish Hotel' were embossed on the flap of the envelope so I didn't have to guess the identity of the sender. It was, of course, from Rosa Lewis, asking me if I could join her the following afternoon at the Cavendish 'to be interviewed by the gentlemen I mentioned at our last meeting'. I had to read that bit through twice because, as a potential employer, I had assumed that I would be interviewing them not the other way around.

Once more, Philip's enormous Hispano-Suiza conveyed me to the hotel. I was greeted by Scott, the hall porter, a moustached and rather lugubrious individual, who always had a fox terrier at his heels and was called 'Dirty Scott' by Rosa because he hated taking baths.

"Show 'im to the Elinor Gryn, Dirty Scrott," yelled Rosa from her parlour to the right of the front door.

The noisome porter duly led me across the hall into a white-panelled room with a classical marble fire surround, Georgian furniture and a vast, mauve chintz-covered sofa piled high with cushions in various shades of green and pink. Seated on the edge of this sofa were three middle-aged men. Together, they looked like the Three Monkeys: 'hear no evil', 'see no evil' and 'speak no evil'. It was, as it turned out, a highly misleading first impression. Two of them were dressed in Indian kurtas; hawk-nosed, bearded and with swarthy complexions, I immediately assumed were brothers. The third man was in a well-cut suit; clean shaven, blond and with high cheek bones he looked like an older version of the Russian dancer, Nijinsky, whose photograph had recently been in all the illustrated magazines following his release from house arrest in Hungary.[39]

As I entered the room they all leapt to their feet: the Russian executed a deep bow and murmured 'Excellency' whilst the two dusky types fell to their knees, lowered their foreheads to the floor and intoned something in what sounded like Persian or Hindustani. If I had been expecting anything it was certainly not this: it was the most extraordinary start to a job interview that I have ever experienced.

"Gentlemen," I managed to say, "please rise." They did as I asked but, when I told them to sit, they resolutely refused. Instead, they stood staring at me as though they were in the presence of a ghost. In order to break the silence, I walked forward with my right hand outstretched.

"We haven't met before. My name is Charles Speedicut and you are?"

"Atash Khazi, huzoor," the first man said, using a form of address I did not recognise or understand whilst grasping my hand with both of his and bowing low over it.

"Fahran Khazi, huzoor," said the second man and then did the same as his brother.

---

[39] Vaslav Nijinsky (1889-1950) was released from war-time internment on 1st February 1916

"Ivan Searcy, Excellency," said the oddly-named Russian, who not only took my hand but bent and kissed it.

"Do please sit, gentleman, this isn't a meeting of the Privy Council," I joked in an effort to break the ice. This time they did as I'd asked, but none of them cracked a smile.

An awkward silence followed as the three of them seemed to eat me with their eyes whilst I desperately tried to think of a way of starting the business of the meeting. After what seemed an age, I fell back on that old stalwart of royalty:

"Have you come far?" The silence deepened, so I tried again. "Err, Mrs Lewis seemed to think that you might be interested in working for me." Still there was no response from any of them. Then I suddenly realised that I was being incredibly thick; there was a logical explanation for their presence. "Are any of you acquainted with my late father, Colonel Speedicut?"

"We all are, huzoor," said the man called Atash Khazi.

"Might I ask how?"

"We, and our fathers before us, worked for His late Excellency," said the Russian. The other two nodded.

"I see," I said, "in that case you probably know a great deal more about him than I do."

"Huzoor?" queried Fahran Khazi.

"Well, you see, I only found out recently that he was my father."

"So, you never met him, Excellency?" asked the Russian.

"Only once, but I was too young to remember anything about him."

"That is sad, huzoor," said Atash Khazi, "for he was a burra sahib."

"And you do not know Her Ladyship, the begum sahiba, huzoor?" queried Fahran Khazi.

"Never met her," I replied, "although, of course, I know who she is. But, given my own circumstances, I'm not sure that she'd want to meet me."

"Even if she did, Excellency, it would be a meeting without point," said Ivan Searcy.

"Why?" I asked.

"Because when she received the news of our master's murder, huzoor," said Fahran. I interrupted him.

"Murder? I thought he died of old age in Paris."

"That is what they *want* you to think, Excellency," said Ivan.

"Who's 'they' and why do you think he was murdered?" I asked.

"We cannot be sure of the answer to either question, huzoor," said Atash, "but with your help we *will* find the answer."

"I see," I said, although I didn't and thought it wouldn't pay to linger on this momentous proposition – at least for the time being - so I changed the subject back to Lady Charlotte-Georgina Speedicut. "So, what's the matter with Her Ladyship?"

"She had a seizure after she read the telegram, huzoor. Since that dreadful day she has neither spoken nor moved. It is as though she too is dead, yet her great heart still beats." Fahran wiped a tear from his eye.

"She lives with a few servants at the Speedicut home in Wales, huzoor," added Atash. "The London house is closed up."

"Oh, dear, I am sorry to hear that – about Lady Speedicut, I mean," I said, although I privately thought that it was a blessing the old trot had been struck dumb and immobile by a stroke.

"And you do not know His late Excellency daughter, the Princess Lieven, and her two daughters, huzoor?"

"No. Are they with Lady Speedicut?"

"Unfortunately, not, Excellency," said Ivan. "Since the start of the war they have not left Russia." That was a relief, I thought.

"In that case, I may meet them," not if I could help it, I added to myself, "for I am being sent to Russia on government business in a few weeks' time?"

"Are you on a quest for the Brotherhood, huzoor?" asked Fahran.

"What do you know about the Brotherhood?" I demanded sharply and in considerable surprise.

"As His late Excellency's son, Excellency, we expected nothing else," said Ivan, "His late Excellency was much occupied with business for the Brotherhood for all of his long life. Our fathers, and we in our turn, helped His late Excellency with his tasks. Unfortunately, none of us were with him on his last assignment. Had we been..." He left the sentence unfinished but the implication was clear: the old boy would not have been murdered, if that indeed was the actuality.

"I see," I said, "well you are correct. I have recently joined and my assignment in Russia is, indeed, on Brotherhood business. But you are to tell no one."

"Our lips are, as always, sealed," said Atash. "Providing..."

"What?" I queried, scenting blackmail. There was an awkward pause and my suspicion of a demand for hush money increased.

"Providing that you agree that we can work for you, huzoor," said Fahran.

"And that you always take one of us with you wherever you go, Excellency," said Ivan.

"That doesn't sound unreasonable," I replied in relief, "although there is one thing we need to clarify. In what capacity, other than as bodyguards, do you propose that I should employ you?"

"We thought you might ask us that, huzoor," said Fahran. "My brother is an accomplished coachman, like our father before us, and he will run your stables."

"But I don't have a carriage and, anyway, I was planning to buy a motor."

"He is also an excellent chauffeur," said Ivan.

"I will be your valet and secretary," continued Fahran. "It is the job I did for your late father."

"And you, Mr Searcy?"

"Unlike my friends, Excellency, I have a business," he said handing me a card. It read:

Searcy's
Caterers to Society and the Gentry
Ivan Searcy
Managing Director

"However, despite this, I will look after your household needs and, whenever required, be available to accompany you. In that regard, it would make sense if I came with you to Russia: it is, after all, my homeland and you will find it helpful to have a Russian speaker by your side."

"Well, gentlemen," I said to all three of them, "you have it all worked out and it seems pointless to turn down your kind offers. So, I accept: the

Speedicut team is back in business!" They all applauded at this. "As you may know, for you seem to know everything," I went on when they had stopped clapping, "I have recently taken the lease on a flat in Mayfair, although I am currently staying with Sir Philip Sassoon. However, Sir Philip returns to France tomorrow, so, now that I have my own staff, I am going to move out of Park Lane and into this hotel, whilst my new flat in Mayfair is fitted out. You can all start working for me right away; is that acceptable?"

"It is, huzoor," they chorused.

"I also need to acquire a motor car. What make do you recommend, Atash?"

"Your late father always favoured Daimlers, huzoor."

"Then let's get one. If Daimlers were good enough for him then they're good enough for me." They all beamed at this.

"May I ask which tailor you use, huzoor?" asked Fahran.

"Sir Philip has introduced me to Huntsman and they are making an assortment of clothes for me. Why?"

"In recent years, huzoor, your late father used Henry Poole at 32 Savile Row."

"I see," I said. "Unfortunately, it's too late to do anything about the current order but, for the future, I will open an account with my father's tailor – and his shirt maker, boot maker, gunsmith and anyone else he used."

"That is a good idea, Excellency," said Ivan, whilst Fahran and Atash nodded their approval. "We will bid you goodnight now, but Mr Fahran will be at Park Lane tomorrow morning at ten o'clock – if that is not too early – in order to move you into the Cavendish Hotel, whilst Mr Atash arranges for you to acquire a Daimler and I take over the decoration and furnishing of your new apartment."

Without another word, they all got up and, in succession, took my hand and kissed it; I felt like an oriental potentate. It was only when the door closed behind Ivan, who'd turned and given me another deep bow before he disappeared, that I realised that I knew absolutely nothing about the three people whom I had just engaged and into whose hands I had placed my life. It also occurred to me that I had not settled on their remuneration. I set off in search of Rosa, who I hoped would have the answers. I found her alone, save for a jeroboam of fizz, in her parlour off the hall.

"'allo, young Speed. Wot d'yer want other than a large glass of brubbly," she said pouring me one before I could reply.

"I was wondering, Mrs Lewis…"

"Call me Rosa, dearie, like wot all me regulars does."

"I was wondering, Rosa, if you knew anything about the Khazi brothers and the Russian who calls himself Searcy. You see, I've hired them without asking them a single question about themselves. In hindsight, I feel a bit foolish…" I ended somewhat lamely.

"'course I does, drearie. I wouldn't have set up the meeting if I didn't know 'em from a bar of bleedin' soap, now would I?"

"I suppose not. So, what can you tell me about them?"

"I've known the two Khrazi brothers since they woz randy young whipper-snappers trying to get into me knickers. Me muvver woz the Speedicuts' cook and Masters Atash and Fahran were the eldest sons of the Crolonel's Afghan coachman, Muhamad Khazi, and Lady Charlotte-Georgina's black maid, Prissy. Old Mo had been in the Crolonel's service since the Afghan Wars, I think, and Prissy woz an ex-slave from the Deep South, oo the Crolonel and his missus pricked up on their travels. Both their boys - and there were a few other for Mo was never orf Prissy's nest - entered the Crolonel's service when they were of an age and took over from old Mo when 'e was killed on the Jameson Raid. Ivan's the adopted son – boyfriend if yer ask me - of Fred Searcy, who woz the Colonel's valet then private secretary. I'm not sure when old Fred first joined the Crolonel, but it woz very early on. The Colonel acquired Ivan in St Petersburg when 'e woz over there for 'is daughter Dorothea's wedding to Prince Lieven. When Fred retired 'e 'anded over 'is catering business, which the Crolonel 'ad financed, to Ivan and, when Fred popped 'is clogs, Ivan took over 'is duties with the Crolonel on a part-time basis. They're all good brokes and you couldn't be in safer nor more 'onest 'ands."[40]

"Phew, that's rather a relief. And what should I pay them?" I added as an afterthought.

"Well, thanks to old Speed, they've all got their own money so they don't really needs nuffing. 'owever, I thinks as yer should pay 'em sumfing. I'd offer the Khrazi boys ten bob a week each, with full broard, and Ivan half-a-crown for each day 'e works on yer business."

"I can easily afford that, Rosa," I said in relief, "now one last question. Can I move in here until my rooms are ready in Mayfair?"

"'course yer can, drearie. I thought yer'd never ask, but I 'oped yer would, so I've already reserved yer a suite on the second floor…"

And there's really nothing more to add. In the space of a few weeks I had been transformed, with the help of my father, Philip Sassoon, Ernest Cassel, Regy Esher, Rosa Lewis, the Khazis and Ivan Searcy, from a gawky schoolboy into a young man-about-town with more than adequate means, a smart flat, the finest staff to which a gentleman could aspire and my name on the shortlist for my father's old club, the Verulam. Such an instant apotheosis should have gone to my head but, before it could do so, I got my marching orders for Russia from Regy Esher in the form

---

[40] Editor's Note: Further details about the Khazis and the Searcys can be found in *The Speedicut Papers: Books 1-9*.

of a hand-delivered bulky package and a letter headed 'Secret – Destroy after Reading'.

>   *28th May 1916*
>
>   *TBOTSOT*
>   *Manchester Square*
>   *London W*
>
>   *Dear BS*
>
>   *There has been a change of plan. You are to assume the identity of Count Boris Zakrevsky (documents, biography & briefing papers enclosed), an English born and educated Russian aristocrat and a member of the Tsarina's inner circle who, at the request of the Tsar, will be attached to Lord Kitchener's Staff for the duration of his diplomatic visit to St Petersburg. You will travel with your Russian servant, Ivan Searcy (using his birth name of Ivan Ivanovitch Iglevsky) whose Russian papers are also enclosed.*
>
>   *You will report to Lord Kitchener at Scrabster on 4th June prior to embarkation aboard HMS Oak. On the 5th June Lord Kitchener's party, yourselves included, will transfer to HMS Hampshire anchored at Scapa Flow, which is scheduled to sail for St Petersburg at 4.45pm on that day.*
>
>   *At 7.30pm that evening, in order to confirm your presence on board, you will make your way onto the port side of the ship and use the electric battery powered torch provided with this letter to flash the attached Morse Code signal. You will then drop the torch and the code over the side of the ship.*
>
>   *In the name of TBOTSOT*
>
>   *TGB*

The Morse Code signal read: -.- --- ..- -.- [41]

---

[41] Editor's Note: This de-codes as 'KofK'

CHAPTER SEVEN: DEATH ON THE OCEAN WAVE

Had I received such a letter anytime in later years I would have chucked it in the bin, opened the safe, extracted my collection of passports and my emergency sovereigns, and bought a one-way ticket to Buenos Aires as fast as I could get to Thomas Cook. Why, I hear you ask? Because, as any aficionado of the thriller genre will recognise, it was a death warrant. However, despite my self-esteem at the time, I was a naive twerp with more arrogance than common sense. Did I for one moment suspect that I had been set up to encompass a political assassination? Of course not. In mitigation, I was only seventeen and this was my first assignment for the Brotherhood; that there was every chance it would be my last - indeed, had probably been planned as such - never crossed my mind. It should have done.

So it was that, in a state of blissful ignorance, on the 4th June Ivan and I caught the night train from King's Cross and headed to the most northerly part of the windswept land of the Picts. As I was in the guise of a Russian 'attached' to Kitchener's Staff rather than - as previously planned - a civil servant seconded from the FO, I had not yet met the great man (nor had I grown a moustache). The first was soon rectified when Ivan reported that he was on the train.

"Find his ADC, would you, Ivan, and give him my card?" These had been prepared hastily for me, in the name of my Russian alias, by Smythson's shortly before I'd left.

A few minutes later Ivan returned with an invitation to join Kitchener in his private carriage. I trundled down the corridor until I was intercepted by a brace of burly Grenadiers who stood guard at the entrance to the next coach. I explained my business and was told to wait whilst one of them went to fetch the ADC. A short while later a handsome Bengal Lancer hove into view.

"Count Zakrevsky?" I confirmed my false identity. "I'm Captain FitzGerald,[42] please follow me." I did as instructed and trailed after the latest in a long line of bachelor cavalrymen who had served - and in the case of 'Fitz' FitzGerald, lived with for twelve years - the porcelain-collecting, flower-arranging, poodle-loving Field Marshal. Despite these hobbies, and a penchant for buying life-size bronzes of nude boys to adorn his rose beds at Broome Park, Kitchener was the antithesis of the mincing, preening Lord Alfred Douglas-type of pansy. Tall, with a barrel chest large enough to carry a long row of medals and the stars of seven Orders, staring brilliant-blue eyes, and a walrus moustache, the Secretary of State for War looked in the flesh, seated behind a desk in a specially appointed mobile office, like an Old Testament prophet - and he was, in a very real sense, the Army's answer to God. As Margot Asquith later remarked,[43] 'if he was not a great man he was, at least, a great poster'.

"Count Zakrevsky," intoned the ADC.

"Who?" barked Kitchener, without looking up from the paper he was reading.

"The Russian liaison officer, sir." His boss made a sort of harrumphing sound and, still without raising his head, waved me to a chair in front of his desk. "Dinner will be in half an hour, sir."

"Good, I won't be long with this fellow." Did Kitchener think that I didn't speak English or was he just bloody rude? I decided to remain silent. At last he looked up at me with his piercing eyes and gave me an appraising almost curious examination. "Do - you - speak - English?" he asked in a way that indicated he expected an answer in the negative.

"Reasonably well, Field Marshal," I drawled in my most exaggerated Etonian accent. His eyes narrowed. Like many *arriviste* senior soldiers - and

---

[42] Captain Oswald FitzGerald (1875-1916), 18th Bengal Lancers.
[43] Margot Asquith (1864-1945), later Countess of Oxford & Asquith, was the barbed-tongued wife of the then Prime Minister, Herbert Asquith (1852-1928).

Sappers in particular - his bloated ego was easily pricked by the presence of someone he recognised (incorrectly in my case) as a social superior.

"Hmm. I believe," he said looking down again at the papers on his desk, "that you are acquainted with Her Imperial Majesty the Tsarina Alexandra."

"I understand that is the reason I have been attached to your suite, Field Marshal."

"My business is with *His* Imperial Majesty, so you're not going to be of much use to me..."

"I think you will find, Field Marshal, that the best way of influencing His Imperial Majesty is through *Her* Imperial Majesty, so you may find that I have my uses."

Thank God, I had read the Brotherhood's briefing notes before heading off for North Britain and had taken the opportunity to question Ivan on various points concerning the politics of the Imperial Russian Court and government. It never occurred to me, however, to question how I was to maintain my alias and make good on my 'official' assignment once I'd arrived in Russia. The Brotherhood's brief was silent on the subject; it was a large red flag waving in my face, but I failed to recognise it as such.

"Damned petticoat politics; bloody women should stick to the nursery!" Kitchener grumbled. "I suppose the next thing you'll be telling me is that I'll have to kiss the arse of that blighter Rasputin in order to get to the Tsarina."

"I'm not sure that you would have to go that far, Field Marshal, but it is certainly true that the *starets* wields considerable influence at Court, particularly with the Empress."

"We'll see about that, Count Zakrevsky. Well, you may yet have your uses - particularly if you can arrange for me to visit the Lomonosov Porcelain Factory whilst I'm in St Petersburg. Meanwhile, do you play bridge?"

"I'm afraid not, Field Marshal." It was the first truthful thing about myself that I'd said to him.

"Pity. Well, I'll see you on board tomorrow and you can sit next to me after dinner whilst we play. Who knows, you might learn something." To judge from the lascivious glint in his eye, that 'something' was probably not the rules of contract bridge. I was about to get up and leave when he shot a question at me out of deep cover. "You don't have any English relations do you, Count?"

"Not that I know of, Field Marshal.," I lied.

"Curious," he said. "You remind me very strongly of a damned Shiner I used to know. Frightful shit. He had a fuller set of whiskers, but otherwise you look like two peas out of the same pod. A curious coincidence... Good evening, Count."

The rest of the journey to the home of the Grand Fleet at Scrabster and then to its anchorage at Scapa Flow passed without incident, or any further contact with Kitchener, so I had plenty of time to muse on the undoubted fact that he knew my real Papa. Fortunately, it seemed that he had treated my resemblance to my forebear, as he had said, as a coincidence and I was not hauled back for questioning on my Russian credentials either on the train or later on His Majesty's Ships *Oak* and then *Hampshire*.

For those of you who have never been on a warship, you haven't missed much unless, that is, you have a perverted penchant for the pong of burning coal, axle grease, cordite and human reek bound together with brine. For some, but not me, this nautical cocktail is alleviated or enhanced by the presence of scores of tattooed tars in absurd trousers. Whether or not Kitchener felt that way was not clear, for he was far and away the coldest human being I had yet met; if he had any feelings, other than those for Fitz and his other poodles, he kept them to himself. He did, however, express himself quite forcibly over pre-dinner drinks in the *Hampshire*'s heaving wardroom - there was a Force 9 gale blowing outside - about the war situation in general and the Russians in particular.

"The Russian gold we're carrying from their deposits in the Bank of England may help them to buy more arms," he proclaimed, "but the real problem is the Russian soldier. Peasants mostly, they make poor fighting men and, to make matters worse, their officers are usually aristocrats of the chinless-wonder variety and..."

He droned on and on without interruption. We'd been taught at Eton that Gladstone bored for England when he spoke; after an hour or more I was in no doubt that Kitchener bored for Europe. Christ, I thought, if he goes on at this rate all the way to Archangel it will take me a month to write my report. Over Kitchener's endless, bombastic and dire prognostications I heard a clock chime and remembered that I had a duty on deck with the pocket torch. I slipped out of the wardroom, clawed my way in the teeth of the gale to the right-hand side of the plunging tub and did as instructed. I'd just dropped the lamp over the side when, with a shock, I felt a hand grip firmly my upper arm.

"What are you doing, Excellency?" I heaved a sigh of relief; it was Ivan. Without a second thought, I told him. "But you are on the wrong side of the ship, Excellency - and, anyway, why would you agree to signal to a German submarine even assuming that one could come to periscope depth in these conditions and launch a torpedo?"

"What the hell are you talking about? I agreed to no such..." But before I could say any more there was a huge explosion and the whole ship bucked like a Yankee bronco. Ivan and I were thrown into a heap in the scuppers, or whatever they call the drain that runs along the side of the deck: it was as though the Flying Scotsman had crashed head on with the *Hampshire*. Within seconds the tub started to tilt forwards and, even to a land lubber like me, it was clear that she was sinking fast by the head. Being the summer and given our location in northern climes it was still light; across the heaving sea I could see that we weren't far from land. All we needed to do was to get in a lifeboat and we would be safe. I yelled as much to Ivan.

"If the life boats can be launched, Excellency," he yelled back. "With this swell that could be difficult."

Unfortunately for all but a handful of the crew of HMS *Hampshire*, Ivan proved to be right. As the ship took a nose dive into the deep, the only survival vessels were a number of life rafts which broke loose as the *Hampshire* plunged towards Davy Jones's Locker. By good luck rather than good management, both Ivan and I managed to cling to one as we and it were swept off the deck by a great rolling tide of water. As it was, there was still the very real danger that we would be sucked under and drowned by the sinking ship had a further underwater explosion not blown our raft clear of her. As the *Hampshire*'s quarterdeck disappeared beneath the raging foam, and our life raft rose on the crest of a mighty wave, I am as certain as I can be that I saw the ramrod straight figure of Kitchener plant his moustaches firmly over the face of a Bengal Lancer. It was the last that I, or anyone else for that matter, ever saw of the arrogant bugger: with the sinking of the *Hampshire* England had lost her pin-up boy and I had lost the first half of my opening mission for the Brotherhood.[44]

At the time, this was the least of my problems, the greatest of which was to get to shore in one piece. But in a howling gale and with no oars we were at the mercy of wind, tide and Neptune - and the trident-wielding master of the mermaids decided that a happy landing on the coast of the Orkneys was not to be the fate of C Speedicut Esquire and his trusty Russian servant. So, instead of our pile of matchwood being dashed to pieces - and ourselves along with it - on the adjacent rocky shore line, as was to be the fate of all but twelve of the crew of the *Hampshire* who'd managed not to go down with the ship, our raft perversely headed out to sea.

Even in summer, the North Sea in the grip of a gale is no place for a young English gentleman and, since that day, I have never shared my better-heeled contemporaries' love for yachting. As Ivan and I realised that a mug of whisky-infused tea in a crofter's cottage was not to be our

---

[44] Editor's Note: Over the past 100 years, conspiracy theories concerning the death of Lord Kitchener have multiplied. However, recent examination of the wreck of HMS *Hampshire* has concluded that she almost certainly struck a mine laid by U-75. The presence on board of the mysterious Count Zakrevsky is now explained by Charles Speedicut's account, but it also begs several further questions – as yet unanswered - including the role and motives of the Brotherhood of the Sons of Thunder.

immediate fate, and that something even worse was in prospect, he very sensibly suggested that we should tie ourselves to our flimsy platform and huddle together for warmth. As we drifted further and further from land, and the light started to fail, I felt a curious glow start to steal over me that had nothing to do with Ivan's middle-aged charms. It was actually rather comforting and pleasant - a bit like a cuddle with nanny in a thunderstorm - and I surrendered myself to what I now know was the embrace of death.

"Wake up, Excellency!" I dimly heard Ivan yell in my ear. "Wake up!" And he started to shake me.

"Leave me alone, nanny," I murmured, "I'm having a lovely dream."

"No, you're not, Excellency!" and with a shock I felt him slap me hard on the face.

"What the...?" I cried, but instead of answering he pushed a flask between my lips and I took a pull on it. The gulp I took of neat vodka damned near choked me, but it also brought me back to the present. "What on earth did you do that for?" I managed to croak, once I'd recovered from the shock of the alcohol.

"You were drifting, Excellency."

"Drifting where?"

"To Eternity, Excellency."

"What? You mean I was dying?"

"You were surrendering to death, Excellency, when you should have been fighting him off. Now you know that, the danger is past."

"For the time being, Ivan. But unless someone finds us it can't be for too long: we're soaking wet, chilled to the bone, we have no cover and only your flask of spirits to keep us warm. Even if the storm abates, there's only a slim chance that anyone will find us..."

"Indeed, Excellency, but there is an old Russian proverb that states that the harvest is not in until the last sheaf of corn has been cut."

"You mean, 'where there's life, there's hope'?"

"Indeed, Excellency."

But what hope was there, adrift as we were in the North Sea at the mercy of wind and wave? As the sun dipped briefly below the horizon we drained Ivan's hip flask and I started to contemplate the prospect of the hereafter. It was so damned unfair, I thought, to be drowned before my life had really got underway. Then I realised that fair or unfair had nothing to do with it: life is a rolling of loaded dice and this time they had been loaded against me. As I realised that I would have no opportunity to enjoy my recent and unexpected good fortune, and that my wretched mother would, by default and the lack of a Will, inherit my inherited riches, I damned nearly blubbed in frustration at the injustice of the situation.

"I think the storm is slackening, Excellency," said Ivan as the sun started to rise a bare hour later.

"A fat lot of good that will do us, Ivan," I said, "unless someone spots us - and the likelihood of that happening is slight in the extreme."

"Remember the proverb, Excellency..." I refrained from answering as I didn't want to offend the fellow.

The hours wore on without any sign of rescue, although the storm finally passed over at around three in the morning. Despite Ivan's warning about 'drifting', I once again felt my eyelids starting to droop. But instead of the reassuring embrace of death, this time I found myself in a nightmare. We were still at sea on our raft but surging towards us through the waves was what looked like the head and neck of a one-eyed sea monster. As it got closer it receded below the surface and I heaved a sigh of relief that it had decided there was tastier prey in the deep below. Then, without warning, our raft rose in the air. I looked down in horror to find that we had been lifted out of the water on the back of a huge dull-grey creature from off whose flanks the sea was streaming. I dimly heard Ivan praising God, although why I couldn't think unless he was saying Grace ahead of being devoured...

In the past, when I'd had a nightmare, I would awake with a start. Not so on this occasion. Instead, the dream faded away and the next thing I knew I was staring up at a steel bulkhead from the relative comfort of a narrow cot on which I was lying, stark naked and covered in a rather scratchy blanket.

"Zo, you are avake?" I heard a heavily accented voice say next to me. I turned my head and found myself staring into a bearded face above a white roll neck sweater and below a naval cap. "Vould you like a cup of coffee?"

"Where am I - and where's my servant?" I demanded somewhat weakly.

"You are on His Imperial Majesty's U-boat 75, Count, and my name is Captain Beitzen.[45] Your valet - who told us who you were - is quite safe, although, as an enemy alien, he is locked in the brig."

"What are you going to do with us?" I asked rather feebly.

"A *zehr* good question, Count, vich I vill be leaving to our High Command vunce ve return to Kiel. In ze meantime, if you give me your parole and a promise of good conduct on behalf of yourself and your servant, I vill return your clothes and you vill be my guests aboard this boat - although as a submarine on active duty you may find ze opportunities for recreation zomewat limited."

That was the understatement of the year. I don't suffer from claustrophobia but I would not willingly submit myself to a repeat of the experience of life as a submariner under the North Sea, although it was - I suppose - preferable

---

[45] Kapitänleutnant Curt Beitzen (1885-1918).

to death by exposure upon it… It was with considerable relief, therefore, that after a further three days at sea, the U-boat returned to its home base and Ivan and I were handed over to the German Naval authorities. However, once back on dry land, the benefit of our rescue by the German Navy was soon more than offset by the problem of finding ourselves their guests at a time of war. Whilst we were treated with the consideration due to the survivors of a shipwreck, there was a combatant's iron fist inside the velvet glove of hospitality that wasn't long in starting to make itself felt.

I'm not sure what I expected would happened to us, although I had assumed we would be held captive, possibly for the duration of the war. It was a pleasant surprise, therefore, when we were lodged in adjoining rooms in the Officers Mess at German Naval Headquarters, albeit that there were bars on the windows and a brace of strapping Marines on guard outside our doors, and it was only a minor inconvenience that, other than a daily stroll around the grounds under an armed guard, we were obliged to eat and sleep in our quarters. The Germans had even been thoughtful enough to provide us with a change of clothing and the other bare necessities of human life such as toothbrushes and soap.

"This isn't too bad," I called through the inter-connecting door to Ivan. He didn't reply but, instead, put his finger to his lips and then pointed to the ceiling. His meaning was clear: our rooms were bound to be fitted with listening devices. He then made a walking gesture with his fingers by which I understood him to mean that we could talk more freely once outside the Mess.

"It is certain that we will be interrogated, Excellency," he whispered to me later that day on our first walk, "and they will want to know what we were doing on a British warship."

"What do we say to that?"

"Stick to the truth, Excellency, or at least as much of it as you need to. I have told the Germans that I am your valet, which is true, so they think I am of no significance. They believe that we are both Russians and that we were rescued following the sinking of the *Hampshire*. They will almost certainly also now know that Lord Kitchener was on the same ship and they will conclude, correctly, that he was on a mission to the Tsar. You should say that you were returning to your family in Russia at the conclusion of your English education and that, through their influence, you were attached to Lord Kitchener's Staff in order to make the journey home in the safety of a British warship."

"Some safety! But what will they do when they discover that I can't speak Russian? The Germans are a suspicious lot and are bound to conclude that I am a spy - then I'll be shot."

"Do you speak French, Excellency?"

"Ye-es, but it's very much of the schoolboy variety."

"No matter. If asked, you should hold to the story that you were English-educated and — yes - that, since you were eight, you have only returned to Russia for the school holidays. Consequently, your grasp of Russian is almost non-existent and that, anyway, like all Russian aristocrats, you speak French or English at home. Very few Germans speak Russian but most educated ones do speak either English or French."

So that's what I did. It could have worked; indeed, it should have worked. Had it done so, Ivan and I would have been sent to sit out the war in a prison camp in Bavaria or Baden. It was the damnedest bad luck that the shaven-headed fool in German Naval Intelligence who interrogated us over the next couple of days convinced himself that there was more to our mission than even I knew.

"I do not think you are telling me the whole truth, Count," he said. "Why would Lord Kitchener choose to cross the North Sea so soon after our glorious victory over the British Grand Fleet in the Skagerrak?"

"Where? Oh, you mean Jutland - I thought it was a British victory," I couldn't stop myself saying.

"Mere British propaganda, Count. It was a conclusive victory for our glorious High Seas Fleet. Why else would the British Grand Fleet slink back to Scapa Flow? And why else would Lord Kitchener be sent hurrying off to Russia to seek the assistance of the Russian Navy with the protection of the British sea lanes across the North Atlantic?"

"I'm sure that wasn't his mission."

"No? So why were you, the son and the grandson of an Admiral, attached to his Staff?" That was news to me - and might even have been a trap - so I ignored the question.

"Look," I said instead, "I've already told you that I was only on the blasted boat because I was returning to my family."

"So you keep saying, but it makes no sense. It is clear to me that you were on a secret mission - and, as you will not admit it, I have no choice but to send you to Berlin where you will be interrogated by the Secret Service. I am sorry to have to tell you that they have ways of making you talk..."

CHAPTER EIGHT: THE PERILS OF HEREDITY

Accordingly, Ivan and I were shipped off to the capital of the Imperial Reich, lodged in a military prison in the city and there we waited in isolation to be interrogated by the German Secret Service. From time to time the cover over the spy hole in the door to my cell would be lifted and the bare metal replaced with an eye; that, and a silent warder bringing me food three times a day, was the only human contact I had for a week. On the eighth morning of my imprisonment, by which time I was in a profound funk, I was frog-marched from my cell down a dank corridor and into a windowless interrogation room lit by a dim bulb hanging from the ceiling.

Before I knew what was happening to me, I was forced down and strapped into a wooden chair in the gloomy chamber. In front of me was a table on which was an angle-poise electric light, a box with a crank handle and coils of wire protruding from it and what looked like a large pair of pliers. Behind this table were two empty chairs. Once they'd secured me, one of the guards went over to the desk, switched on the lamp and tilted it so that it shone directly into my eyes, then he and his colleague unbuttoned my braces and dragged down my trousers and underwear, leaving them around my ankles; they then withdrew, slamming the door behind them. I freely admit that I was at this point in a state of abject terror, which only increased as the minutes ticked by. At last I heard a door open at the far end of the room but, as I was all but blinded by the glare of the lamp, I could only dimly discern that a figure had entered the room and had seated itself on one of the chairs opposite me.

"You claim that you are Count Zakrevsky, that you have recently completed your studies in England and that you were returning to your family in Russia when the *Hampshire* sank. Is that correct?" asked a man's voice in tolerably good English.

"Yes."

"I do not believe you," said the voice. "You also claim that you had no precise knowledge of Lord Kitchener's mission to the Tsar. Is that also correct?"

"Yes."

"Would it surprise you to know that I do not believe that either?" I decided to say nothing as there was really nothing I could say.

"Silence will not help you, Count," the man went on, "but perhaps this will..." He rose and walked over to me with something in his hand. "Do you know what these are?" he said holding a pair of pliers up to my face.

"Yes," I said.

"Good, so you are familiar with their usage in the removal of nails from wood?"

"Yes."

"But perhaps you are not so familiar with the effect they have when used for removing nails from a human hand," he said as he gripped the end of the little finger of my right hand with the carpenter's tool. I thought I would be sick with fear of the pain to come. "It's a crude way of extracting the truth," he said calmly as he started to pull on the nail, "and one that I prefer not to use. The blood makes *such* a mess, you know," he added.

The bile rose in my throat but I managed to choke it down. Then, to my astonishment, he released the pliers' grip and returned to the desk.

"You know," he said, "you can save yourself a lot of discomfort if you simply tell me the truth."

"But I *have* told you the truth," I managed to blurt out.

"I do not think so, Count," said the man, who once more got up, walked in front of table, reached behind him and then bore down on me with wires trailing behind him. "Are you familiar, Count, with the pain of an electric shock?"

"No," I practically jabbered, as he fixed the wires to my scrotum with small metal clamps that bit painfully into my skin.

"Well, you soon will be if you do not tell me what I want to know," he said as he moved back behind the desk. Then, without warning, he turned the handle on the box and I felt as though I'd been kicked savagely in the balls. I let out a yell that should have been audible at the Cavendish. "Really, Count, there is no need to make so much noise; I have this dynamo on the lowest setting - it delivered not much more than a tickle." He paused. "I'm going to leave you now to think about what the pain will be like when I turn up the dial – or if I decide to use the pliers…"

If, at that point, I could have given him any more information I would have done so without hesitating. But what I could tell him? That I was on a mission for the Brotherhood to spy on Kitchener, who in any event was now dead, and then to work for Bertie Stopford on some unspecified task? Even if I told him about the Brotherhood I doubted very much if he would believe me. It was an utterly hellish position in which to find myself and I wept at my predicament.

"Dwy your tears, Mr Speedicut," I heard a woman's voice lisp behind me. "Or, wather, I will as your hands are stwapped down." I felt a soft cloth being wiped across my face, then the glare of the lamp was extinguished and, once my eyes got accustomed to the lower light level, I saw that there was a woman perched on the edge of the table. She had blond hair swept back from her high cheek-boned face, her eyes were bordered by large lashes and, under her nose, a curious butterfly-shaped shadow had been thrown by the bulb above her. She was dressed in a tailored suit of mid-blue cloth, nipped in at her elegant waist. She was beautiful and - in that moment - she appeared to me to be an angel in blue. Then, with a terrible jolt, I realised that she had used my real name.

"I think you are mistaken, madam," I managed to croak. "My name is Count Zakrevsky."

"I think not, Mr Speedicut - unless, that is, your father sowed his wild oats in Wussia as well; come to think of it, he pwobably did... But the dates don't match. No, whoever was your mother there can be no doubt that your father was Jasper Speedicut. In fact, the only diffewence I can detect between you and him, other than you diffewence in age," she said giving my wired-up privates an appraising glance, "is that he was circumcised whilst you are not." I let out a gasp. "Don't be shocked, Mr Speedicut; I knew your father *intimately*..."

"Who are you?" I managed to ask.

"As I know we are going to have no secrets from each other, I will tell you: my name is Hilda von Einem. And, to complete the picture, I can tell you that your earlier intewogator was Colonel Ulwich von Stumm; he also knew your father. Needless to say, we are both members of the Pwussian Secwet Sewvice."[46]

"But how did you know my Papa?"

"It's a long stowy and will have to wait until another time." She came across towards me. Her heady perfume filled my nostrils whilst her right hand closed over my crotch. "Meanwhile," she said as she stroked my cock, "you *are* going to tell me why you were tvawelling to Wussia with your father's former servant and in the company of Lord Kitchener - unless, of course," and her hand moved from my tumescent prick to my balls where she pressed lightly on one of the electrodes, "you actually enjoy pain and pwefer to wait for Ulwich to weturn..."

The combination of fear and lust left me momentarily lost for words. The application of her lips to mine, swiftly followed by her tongue seeking out my tonsils, then made speech impossible - although I'm sure that my quivering rod, which she had started to stroke, spoke volumes on the subject of desire. I'd almost forgotten that I was strapped to a chair with an electric generator connected to my family jewels when, as swiftly as she'd started, the shameless hussy broke off the engagement.

---

[46] See *The Speedicut Papers: Book 9 (Boxing Icebergs)*.

"So why *were* you twavelling to Archangel disguised as a Wussian Count?"

"You promise that you won't let Colonel von Stumm hurt me?"

"If you tell me *everything* that I want to know, I can pwomise you that," she said as she reached forward and started once again to stroke my prick.

"I was travelling to Russia in order to assist a man – harder - called Bertie Stopford, although I don't know in what – not *too* hard - capacity."

"Herr Stopford?" she said. "How intewesting. He is known to us. And who sent you on this mission?" Her hand tightened its grip.

"An organisation based in London – it's a sort of private club – you – aah – you – won't – oh, that's good – have heard of it."

"The Bwotherhood of the Sons of Thunder?"

"Yes," I said in surprise (not for the first time), "that's the – ooh – one."

"Of course we know of it – it is affiliated to the Fwaternity of the Nibelungen."

"The what? Aah…"

"You do not need to know. All you do need to know is that in all pwobability you have been betwayed."

"Betrayed?" But before I could ask her any more, she increased not only the pressure but the movement on my throbbing member; her firm touch was too much for me to resist any longer, I let out a low moan and climaxed.

"I see that self-contwol is not your stwong suit, Mr Speedicut. Your father was the same," she said, using her free hand to extract from her jacket a hanky with which to remove the evidence. "Like father, like son."

"You said I'd been betrayed – what did you mean by that?" I asked once I'd recovered my breath.

"What were you to do for the Bwotherhood whilst you were with Lord Kitchener?"

"Report on his opinions," I admitted, for it could do no harm so to do.

"Is that all?"

"Well, I also had to flash a signal once we were underway."

"And you didn't think that was suspicious?"

"No." Then I remembered Ivan's words on deck. "My valet thought I was signalling to a submarine but I flashed the lamp towards the shore."

"You were supposed to flash it out to sea,"

"What? How do you know?"

"Never mind – and did it never occur to you that, in so doing, you were putting your life in danger?" she ploughed on.

"No. Besides which, why would the Brotherhood want me dead? I've only just started working for them."

"You are but a small pawn on a large chessboard, Mr Speedicut."

"Even if that's true, why would the Brotherhood conspire with our enemies to kill Lord Kitchener? It doesn't make sense – none of it does."

"I am not permitted to answer those questions, Mr Speedicut. All I can tell you is that nations may be at war with one another and still share common aims and objectives… Meanwhile, I repeat: you have been betwayed."

She reached down once again, but this time it was to undo the straps that held me to the chair. "Adjust your dwess, Mr Speedicut, before Ulwich returns."

I did so, having first carefully removed the wires from my genitals; a few moments later the Colonel reappeared as I wondered if he'd watched the preceding minutes from some concealed spot.

"I am so pleased you have come to your senses," said von Stumm, as he sat on one of the chairs behind the table whilst Hilda von E took the other, "but then Hilda is very persuasive, *nicht wahr*?" I mumbled something inane whilst concluding that he knew full well what Miss Hilda had just done to me. "Excellent. So, what are we going to do with you now?"

"Send me back to England?" I asked hopefully.

"I think not, Herr Speedicut. You were on your way to Russia, were you not?" I nodded. "Then we will enable you to complete your journey – subject, of course, to one condition."

"What's that?" I asked suspiciously

"Oh, nothing very stwessful – we merely want you to keep us informed of what you are doing with Mr Stopford for the Bwotherhood in St Petersburg," said Hilda.

"But if I agree, that would be to betray them."

"Have they not already betwayed you, Mr Speedicut?" replied Hilda quietly.

"Yes, but… Anyway, even if I agree, of what possible interest can my mission in Russia be to you?" I asked in bewilderment.

"That's our business, Herr Speedicut."

"And if I don't agree?"

"You will be shot as a spy – tomorrow, at dawn, just like Miss Edith Cavell,"[47] said von Stumm with considerable finality.

---

[47] Nurse Edith Cavell (1865-1915).

"I see," I said slowly. "And, if I agree," as if – under all the circumstances - I was going to do anything else, "how do you propose that I communicate with you?"

"A lady – a very experienced and beautiful lady," Hilda said giving me a knowing look, "will make contact with you."

"You do not, at this stage, need to know who, how or when," added von Stumm.

"But how will I know that I can trust this lady?" Von Stumm and von Einem put their heads together and conferred; then von Stumm picked up the dratted pliers.

"She will show you these," he said, holding out the instrument of torture.

"Alright. But how am I to get to Russia – and what about my valet, Ivan?"

"So many questions!" said von Stumm with evident irritation.

"So, you agree?" asked Hilda.

"I suppose so – anyway, what choice do I have?"

"None," said von Stumm.

"You will travel to Russia via Sweden along with your servant," said Hilda.

Then, suddenly, I realised there was a yawning flaw in this proposal.

"What am I going to tell Ivan?"

"Tell him everything," said Hilda. "As you now know, he already suspects that you have been betwayed by your fwiends. Because of your father, he is utterly loyal to *you* and, in consequence, he is completely twustworthy."

That I could believe, but what about Esher & Co in London, I wondered? If von Einem was right, they wouldn't be happy to hear that I had survived.

"The Brotherhood will have assumed that Ivan and I drowned along with Lord Kitchener. How are we going to explain our reappearance in Russia without disclosing that we were rescued by your U-boat? If they ever knew that, I would never be trusted and would probably be killed."

"We have already thought of that," said von Stumm.

"You will arrive in Stockholm on a Swedish fishing boat we have under our control," said Hilda. "Once you have landed you will make your way to the Bwitish Embassy and ask for the Ambassador. You will tell him that you were wescued by Swedish fishermen but that you had to remain on their boat until they weturned to their home port."

"Then what am I supposed to do?"

"The British Ambassador is a member of your Brotherhood and he will know of your existence if not your mission. All you will have to do is request that he sends you on to St Petersburg," said von Stumm.

"But won't he check with London?"

"Of course," said Hilda, "but as the first part of your assignment has, by default, been accomplished, Lord Esher will – unless we are much mistaken - have no hesitation in instwucting Mr Howard to help you on your way to your wandezvous with Mr Stopford."[48]

"Is there anything you don't know about the Brotherhood?" I asked at this latest revelation.

"Yes," said von Stumm. "We don't know what you and Mr Stopford are tasked with doing in Russia: once you are there, you will be able to tell us."

---

[48] Esme Howard, later Lord Howard of Penrith (1863-1939).

CHAPTER NINE: CONSPIRACY TO MURDER

A week later, Ivan and I found ourselves sitting in a café on the opposite side of the road from the British Embassy in Stockholm and ponging to high heaven of fish. Earlier, I'd tipped my hat to the limp-wristed cove on the Embassy's reception desk and sent in my name. A short while later, a rather superior-looking secretary had told us that it would be at least an hour before the Ambassador could see me, so we repaired across the road. For the first time since we'd been rescued I felt confident enough to confide in my trusty valet-cum-secretary without the danger of being overheard by Krauts or Krauts-posing-as-Swedish-fishermen. That someone in the café might be eavesdropping was a risk but, in a public place, it was not a great one particularly as our fellow coffee drinkers were giving us a wide berth for fairly obvious reasons. So, as Hilda von Einem had proposed, but keeping my voice down, I told Ivan everything – well, almost everything – about what had transpired back in Berlin.

"The long and the short of it, Ivan," I concluded, "is that I now simply don't know who to trust other than you. I *think* that the Germans believe that I am now working for them, which I have no intention of doing, and that I regard the Brotherhood as the enemy, which is true but only up to a point. What on earth I am to do?" Ivan said nothing for several minutes. When he did speak it was also in an undertone.

"Excellency, before I give you any advice let us review the facts. First, it is clear that the Brotherhood has been penetrated by the enemy, although that penetration may have arisen through its pre-war affiliation with the German organisation called the Fellowship of the Nibelungen.

"Second, even in a time of war, these organisations appear to be willing to work together when they have a common objective. In this case, that would appear to have been the death of Lord Kitchener.

"Lastly, the Brotherhood was willing to *risk* your life not necessarily to *take* it - for you always had a chance of survival, as proved to be the case – in order to encompass the death of Lord Kitchener. Do you agree with that so far?"

"I do," I said.

"Very well, Excellency. However, I hope you will also agree that it is unlikely that such co-operation – or the sacrifice of yourself – would be acceptable to many in the Brotherhood."

"Ye-es."

"So, it is probable that this plan was initiated at the very top of the organisation." He paused for a moment. "I would venture to suggest that the only person you need fear, therefore, is Lord Esher himself."

"That seems to make sense," I said, although I had no idea what motives Esher had for being a traitor or why he was willing to sacrifice me on my first assignment, "but can I rely on it?"

"Probably not, Excellency. You must tread very carefully, although I think that you can be reasonably certain that any close friends of Sir Philip Sassoon are friends of yours - Mr Stopford, for example."

"And the Ambassador here?"

"No, I think not, Excellency. The Germans seem to be altogether too familiar with him; he may be innocent of any treachery, but it is not worth the risk. Besides which, we only need him to hasten our safe delivery to St Petersburg."

"And then?"

"We do not yet know why Lord Esher wanted you in Russia, beyond his vague instruction that you were to help Mr Stopford. However, I think we can assume – given your instructions from the Germans - that your unspecified task in Russia for the Brotherhood has not been shared with the Fellowship of the Nibelungen and that, accordingly, it is probably not in the interests of Germany."

"My God," I groaned, "it's all so damned convoluted. So, who can I trust?"

"Once we are in St Petersburg, Excellency, I will arrange for you to get a letter to Sir Philip Sassoon in France in which you will spell out all you know and seek his advice."

"But what happens if the letter is intercepted?"

"Leave that problem with me, Excellency. I am sure that through the good offices of the Nehemiah I can find a secure route."

"The Nehe-what, Ivan?"

"The Society of the Mysteries of Nehemiah, Excellency. It is an international society of butlers, gentlemen's gentlemen and, a recent addition, the head concierges of the best hotels in Europe. It is an organisation to which my adopted father, the great Mr Frederick Searcy, belonged and of which I also have the honour to be a member. Its aims are much less strategic than those of the Brotherhood, but it has a long reach and powerful friends, as your late father knew to his benefit."

"All these secret organisations, Ivan! You'll be telling me next that our Government has no real control over public affairs."

"You may say that, Excellency, but I couldn't possible comment…"

When at last we got to see him, the Ambassador at first showed a surprising lack of interest in us beyond, that is, rather ostentatiously opening the window of his office. I had assumed that, as survivors of a naval disaster which had taken the life of the country's most celebrated and senior soldier, he would at the very least have hailed our safe return as a much-longed for piece of good news. Not a bit of it.

"Arrange new papers for you and your onward voyage to St Petersburg, Mr Speedicut? I think not. There is a war on, you know and it will be equally difficult to arrange passage for you to England. No, I'm afraid that you're going to have to sit out the war here. Stockholm's not a bad little place and, once you've had a bath, a change of clothes and arranged for funds to be sent to you, I'm sure that you will be tolerably comfortable. Bored, of course," he said giving a deep sigh that spoke volumes, "but comfortable."

It was only when I asked Ivan to leave the room and I addressed the diplomat as 'Brother' that his attitude turned from indifference to interest.

"Brother? My dear fellow, why didn't you say so at once?" I looked pointedly over my shoulder. "Yes, yes – how stupid of me. Well, this new information alters matters considerably. I will, of course, have to take instructions from the Great Boanerges, but once I know what he wants to do with you we can make it happen… In the meantime, I think it would be best if you lodged here in the Embassy and stayed indoors; as a neutral city, the place is simply crawling with spies. I'll tell my secretary to make the arrangements for you and your valet – some news clothes, funds and new papers - and, just as soon as I hear from London, we'll meet again. It shouldn't take too long for Manchester Square to respond to my signal."

To be precise, it was exactly four hours before I was summoned back to the Ambassador's office where he handed me a decoded telegram. It read:

> *BROTHER S TO PROCEED TO ST P WITHOUT DELAY STOP ASSIST IN ANY WAY YOU CAN STOP GB*

"I'll get my secretary onto it right away, Brother Speedicut," he said when I handed the flimsy back to him. "The quickest route will be by boat from here to Turku in Finland, then the railway to St Petersburg via Helsinki. With any luck, we'll have you in the Russian capital within the week."

"Do you know where Brother Stopford is staying?" I asked as I realised that, under the original arrangements, Bertie was going to make contact with me once I'd arrived in Russia with Kitchener.

"I've no idea, but Brother Buchanan at the Embassy will know.[49] I suggest that once you get to St Petersburg you head straight there; it's at 48 The English Embankment. I'll send Brother Buchanan a signal telling him to expect you and to make a reservation for you and your servant at whichever hotel Brother Bertie is lodged."

In the event, it was early July before we checked into St Petersburg's fashionable Grand Hotel Europe, a vast hostelry that had been remodelled before the war in a hideous Art Nouveau style and was located at the junction of the Nevsky Prospekt and Mikailovskaya Street. The concierge looked somewhat askance at our meagre luggage and ready-to-wear clothes and we were shown to a dingy pair of rooms on the top floor at the back of the hotel, which I'm reasonably sure were intended for hotel staff not guests.

"This won't do at all, Excellency," said Ivan wrinkling his nose at the utilitarian furnishings and thread-bare curtains. "I will go and speak to the head concierge." He returned five minutes later. "There's been a misunderstanding, Excellency, which will shortly be rectified. We've been asked to wait in the lounge whilst our bags are moved to new rooms - and there will be no problem with getting a letter to Sir Philip." Ah ha, I thought, so the Nehe-whatsit's reach was as extensive as that of the Brotherhood; and so it proved, in a way that was even more dramatic than the change in attitude of the British Ambassador in Stockholm. For, all of a sudden, we went from pariahs to honoured guests, our bags were moved to a suite on the first floor where we found a magnum of Roeder Crystal, a silver bucketful of caviar and enough flowers to fill a hothouse.

"That's better," I said to Ivan with a grin. "How did you achieve it?" He tapped the side of his nose, smiled and said nothing. "All we need now

---

[49] Sir George Buchanan GCB GCMG GCVO (1854-1924), British Ambassador in St Petersburg 1910-1919.

is to get some money, some decent clothes and to make contact with Mr Stopford."

"The first I have already arranged with the hotel, Excellency: the manager will extend you however much credit you need until you receive a transfer from Rothschild. The second we can do after luncheon: you will find everything you need in the shops on the Nevsky Prospekt. As for Mr Stopford, I understand that he is staying at Tsarskoye Selo until Monday, but I have left a message for him to contact you on his return. In the meantime, I need you to write that letter to Sir Philip Sassoon."

By the end of the day I had written to Philip, restocked my wardrobe and was ready to enjoy St Petersburg whilst waiting for guidance to arrive from Philip - and Bertie to return from Court. You know, even in July 1916, St Petersburg was not a bad place to be – excepting the damned mosquitos. The hospitality provided by the leading families was still lavish and every door swung open to a young Englishman with the right connections, as I discovered soon after Bertie Stopford had returned from dancing attendance upon the Tsarina. Yes, there were signs of privation and shortages in the shops and there was, certainly, a great deal of talk in the salons about the growing discontent amongst the labouring and peasant classes. However, the restaurants and theatres were still open, the assorted Grand Dukes, Princes, Counts and Barons were not yet looking for the exit door and revolution wasn't exactly in the air; but there were ominous wisps of dark cloud in the sky above the city which boded ill for the future, as Bertie told me over dinner on that first Monday night.

"I fear, my dear Charles, that many of my dearest friends here are living in a Fool's Paradise. The war is going badly, the Tsar, who spends much of his time at Mogilev, is out of touch with political opinion and he listens only to the Tsarina, who appears to have taken leave of her senses. You would have thought that, as a grand-daughter of Queen Victoria, she would know better than to listen to that ignorant peasant, Rasputin – although, come to think of it, the old Queen was obsessed with that Scotch oaf, Brown, and the damned Munshi.⁵⁰ If only the dear little Tsarevich were not…"⁵¹ He stopped abruptly

"Not what?" I asked.

Of course, with the benefit of hindsight, we now all know the answer to that question but it was not so in 1916. What we did know was that the Tsarina was utterly under the thumb of Rasputin and, accordingly, most educated Russians despised her for it.

"I fear, my dear Charles, that I cannot enlighten you. It is a close kept secret; not even the dear Grand Duchess Vladimir knows about it. What I can tell you, however, is that it explains the *starets* hold over the Empress – a hold that must be broken and which you are here to help me achieve.

"In the meantime, what can the dear Grand Duchess or the other members of *le gratin* do? Most are trapped here with their wealth in Russian land, mines or industry and all their cash repatriated since 1914 on the command of His Imperial Majesty. Even if they wanted to leave, the only thing they could take with them would be their jewellery.

"Of course, what we all hope for is a change in attitude by the Tsar, followed by an orderly change in policy and the introduction of more democracy. That is the only real hope for Russia – that, and victory over the Germans, which I have to say," he lowered his voice, "grows more unlikely by the day."

"But how can any of that be achieved?" I asked.

"The starting point is the removal of Rasputin, but it won't be easy," said Stopford with a grim look on his terrier-like face.

"Can't the government and the Grand Dukes gang up on the Tsar and demand that Rasputin be exiled?"

---

[50] John Brown (1826-1883), Queen Victoria's Highland Servant & Abdul Karin (1863-1909), Indian Secretary to Queen Victoria.
[51] HIH The Tsarevich Alexei Nikolaevich (1904 - 1918).

"You forget, my dear Charles, that Nicholas is an autocrat. Besides which, they tried it once before and he was shunted off to Tobolsk, but then there was a crisis at Spala and the Siberian *starets* returned," Stopford sighed.

"Can't he have an accident which so incapacitates him that he would have to stay away from Court?"

"That wouldn't work if he could still write to the Tsarina, such is his influence over her."

"Something more permanent then?"

"That, my dear Charles, is the reason why you are here."

"You mean I've got to kill the blighter?" I said as it dawned on me that once again the Brotherhood had lined me up for a very short life.

"Good heavens, no, Charles! Nothing as crude as that, my dear."

"What then?" I asked suspiciously.

"Your job is to ingratiate yourself with the people who could – and this is important - with *impunity* encompass the permanent removal of Rasputin: then encourage them so to do."

"Who are these people?"

"By the end of the summer you will know them all."

"But why do you need me? Surely you're already far better placed here than I could ever be?"

"That is the problem: I am *too* well placed. Were I to try to plot Rasputin's demise it would soon be known, the finger would be pointed at me and, through me, at the British government. The Tsar's relationship with the United Kingdom is delicate enough without our being accused of murdering the Tsarina's 'friend'."

"But if I'd drowned on the *Hampshire*," I nearly added 'as planned', "you would have had no choice but to act."

"True, but you didn't."

"So how am I to persuade someone whom I've yet to meet to carry out our dirty work?"

"With skill, my dear Charles, and the exercise of your youthful and not inconsiderable charms..." If he meant, by that, my body then – I thought - it would very much depend upon whom he had in mind as an assassin. "And, of course," he added, "the promise of a large sum of money in a Swiss bank account."

"For me?"

"No, Charles, for the man who does the job."

Later, I related all this to Ivan.

"Well, now at least we know the answer to the Germans' question, Excellency. But that begs another question: what are we going to do about it?"

"I'm not sure that I follow you, Ivan. I know I told you that I wouldn't help the Krauts, but what harm can there be in telling them that Rasputin is for the chop? And it will get me off the hook with them."

"That might be so, Excellency, *if* their interests were aligned with ours, but they are not. The last thing the Germans want is the removal of Rasputin."

"But why do they care if bugger lives or dies?"

"Because, Excellency, if Rasputin continues to control the Tsar, Russia will descend into revolution, which this time – with the army greatly weakened by the war - will result in the overthrow of the Romanovs, followed by a new government which will sue for peace with the Kaiser. Such an eventuality would allow the German High Command to concentrate all its forces on the Western Front, which would inevitably result in their victory."

"But how does that affect me?"

"Once you tell the Germans that Rasputin is to be removed, they will look to *you* to stop it happening."

"Oh, Lor'," I groaned.

"For a moment, Excellency, you sounded just like your late father."

"Is that supposed to be reassuring, Ivan?"

"That depends on what happens next, Excellency…"

CHAPTER TEN: STARS IN THEIR EYES

But, at first, nothing happened: I didn't inform the Germans of what was afoot and no one bearing pincers (or anything else for that matter) approached me on their behalf to ask. What did happen was that Bertie Stopford arranged that I attend an endless succession of lunches, teas, dinners, balls and outings at which I met the whole of St Petersburg Society.

Bertie told me that a Grand Duke had once joked that even London on a wet Sunday wasn't as boring as a room full of Romanovs. That may have been true before the war but, during the time I was there, St Petersburg Society's standards were increasingly undermined by the nagging worry that it was *fin de siècle* time. Whilst still superficially formal, below the surface life in and around the fashionable Nevsky Prospekt was a heaving mass of depravity – and the most depraved were the aristocrats and royalty who orbited around the drunken, smelly and utterly immoral figure of Gregory Rasputin.

Much has been written since the Revolution about this Siberian peasant, fake holy man and *soi disant* faith healer; I don't intend to add to the canon beyond relating my own experiences of him as required by this tale. I will, however, dwell on the three figures who were central to my story: Anna Vyrubova,[52] the Tsarina's porky Lady-in-Waiting and *confidante*, who was also the *starets*' cheer leader and mistress; and two of the grooms in Rasputin's Augean stable, Prince Felix Yusupov and the Grand Duke Dimitri Pavlovich.[53]

In a city with more than its fair share of handsome men and beautiful women, Felix and Dimitri stood out; added to which, Felix was the richest man is Russia, Dimitri was the favourite nephew of the Tsar and both had a taste for jewels, dressing-up and sodomy, although this didn't prevent Felix from being married to the Tsar's niece or – later – Dimitri restoring

---

[52] Anna Alexandrovna Vyrubova (1884-1964).
[53] HIH Grand Duke Dimitri Pavlovich of Russia (1891-1942).

some of his fortune after the Revolution by getting spliced to an American heiress.[54] Unfortunately, given my assignment for the Brotherhood, both of them were also excessively silly and not very bright. However, with their proximity to the throne and their position at the apex of Imperial Russian Society, they had the primary attribute which Stopford had specified: untouchability.

Thanks to Bertie's connections and my own youthful good looks, by the end of the summer I was an habitué of the vast Moika Palace, which Felix shared with his widowed mother when she wasn't staying at one of her other two St Petersburg mansions,[55] and Dimitri's hovel, the luxurious Belosselsky Belozersky Palace, which he'd inherited from his uncle and foster father, the Grand Duke Serge.[56] This Grand Duke, although married to a saintly German Princess,[57] preferred to share his bed with his stable boys and was consequently childless when he was blown to bits by an anarchist's bomb a few years before the war.

I first met Felix and Dimitri at Nevsky Prospekt 86, otherwise known as the Palais Zinaida Yusupova, when – a few weeks after I'd arrived in St P - Bertie arranged for us to take tea with Russia's richest woman. It was in more ways than one a life-changing moment. Unlike the Moika Palace, number 86 was large rather than vast and, like most of St Petersburg, had been built in the neo-Classical style with elaborate stone columns and yellow-ochre stucco. A butler ushered us up the central staircase and towards a large room on the *piano nobile*, the double doors into which were flanked by a brace of footmen; within, the furnishings made Philip Sassoon's Park Lane drawing room seem like the parlour of workman's cottage.

---

[54] HIH Princess Irina Alexandrovna of Russia (1895 – 1970); Audrey Emery (1904-1971).
[55] Princess Zinaida Nikolaevna Yusupova, (1861-1939).
[56] HIH Grand Duke Sergei Alexandrovich of Russia (1857 – 1905).
[57] HIH Grand Duchess Elisabeth of Russia (formerly Princess Elizabeth of Hesse and by Rhine and later canonized as Holy Martyr Yelizaveta Fyodorovna (1864 – 1918).

Under a chandelier the size of a waterfall and seated on a magnificent silk-covered gilt sofa, was the elegant figure of Princess Zinaida, swathed in black lace and swagged in ropes of quail egg-sized black pearls (Felix later told me that she was in permanent mourning for her eldest son, Nicholas, who'd got himself topped in a duel with a jealous husband in 1908). Ranged on equally grand chairs to either side of the Princess were Felix and his wife Irina; a middle-aged woman with two identically dressed girls of about my own age in tow; and Dimitri.

"*Le Chevalier Stopford et Monsieur Charles Speedicut…*" intoned the butler as Bertie, who must have awarded himself a 'knighthood' once he'd left Dover behind, oiled his way across a priceless Persian carpet towards our hostess. She didn't rise but, instead, lifted a jewel-encrusted paw for Bertie and me to kiss.

"Princess," he murmured in French, which was St Petersburg Society's *lingua franca*, as his moustache brushed the top of a steel-coloured, iceberg-sized diamond.[58] I swiftly followed suit as I prayed that my schoolboy French would stand the strain.

"You know my son, his wife and Grand Duke Dimitri Pavlovich, Sir Stopford," she stated, "but I am not sure if you have met Princess Lieven and her two daughters. I asked them to join us as the Princess is a fellow countryman of you both."

Christ, I thought, this must be my Papa's only daughter, Dorothea. I should have expected this meeting but, coming only a few short weeks after my arrival, I was momentarily floored. To make matters worse, it was clear from the expression on her face, which was icy enough to chill fizz, that she didn't need to know my name to know that we were related. Would she ask and what would I reply?

I shook hands with Felix, who gave me the sort of look I'd last seen at Philip Sassoon's Brotherhood dinner party, and then I took Irina's

---

[58] Editor's Note: This was probably the 35.67 carat 'Sultan of Morocco' purchased by the Yusupovs in 1840.

outstretched hand; she barely cracked a smile. Dimitri, on the other hand, gave me an enquiring stare and gripped my hand warmly; I thought for a moment that he wouldn't let it go.

"Princess Lieven," I said turning to my half-sister-from-the-right-side-of-the-blanket, "we haven't met although Bertie has told me all about you," I lied, "so I know that we share the same…" I paused, momentarily lost for the right words in French, "…family name. Your father was the distinguished soldier and courtier, the late Sir Jasper Speedicut, was he not?"

"He was," she said as she turned my bollocks to snowballs with her manner, "did you know him?"

"No," I said, "I never had that pleasure. Actually, I don't even know if we are related, although we share an unusual surname."

"Unless I'm much mistaken, Mr Speedicut," she said in English, in a menacing whisper edged with icicles, "you share rather more than that…" Then, without another word and without introducing her daughters, she turned to Bertie. This left me high and dry until the prettier of the two girls broke the permafrost.

"My name is Tatiana, Mr Speedicut, and this is my sister, Anastasia. People say we look like His Imperial Majesty's youngest daughters."

"Tatiana!" snarled her mother, who was clearly listening despite the fact that her back was turned to us.

"Whether or not that's so," Tatiana continued, "I must say that you do look awfully like dear old grand…"

"Tatiana, that is quite enough!" her mother barked as she turned back towards us; she looked daggers at my half-niece who ignored her.

"Do you think we could be distant cousins?"

Before I could answer, or Dorothea could intervene, Princess Zinaida commanded us to sit and, seconds later, a bevy of footmen entered bearing the tea things including a huge silver-gilt samovar, which was placed on a low table in front of our hostess.

"Your old friend Anna Alexandrovna is supposed to be joining us, Felix," Princess Z announced as she started filling glass cups in gilt filigree holders with a smoky-scented black tea, "but she's probably been delayed by the Tsarina, so we will start without her. I'm sure she won't mind."

What followed was fairly predictable. I found myself trapped between my two half-nieces, who chattered on about life in St Petersburg, the problems of the war and the loss of friends whilst their mother pointedly ignored me - and both Dimitri and Felix tried to catch my attention. I had resigned myself to a dull afternoon, leavened only by the fact that I had met the two most desirable men in Russia - men who might also be potential candidates for the Brotherhood's assignment - when the butler announced Miss Vyrubova.

"Princess," she gushed, "so many apologies! I simply couldn't get away. Her Imperial Majesty, you know - so insistent that only I can help her with her correspondence and other affairs of State. Then I was commanded to deliver a message to Father Gregory…"

Once again, introductions were made, Anastasia was told to move and the new arrival parked her enormous arse in the chair next to mine, leant across and gripped my arm confidentially.

"I hope you are enjoying St Petersburg, Mr Speedicut." I said that I liked what I'd seen thus far.

"So changed, so changed. You should have visited us before this dreadful war altered everything. I don't know how I would bear it without the dear Empress and the wonderful Father Gregory. Of course, you've met Father Gregory?" I said that I hadn't.

"But you *must*, Mr Speedicut, you *must*. He is a saint!" I saw Bertie, who was clearly ear-wigging our conversation, raise an eyebrow.

"And you know that the dear Empress relies upon him *utterly* – as does His Imperial Majesty - why, if it wasn't for Father Gregory's advice, I'm sure that this awful war would already be lost." I thought Bertie's eyebrows would take off.

"Where are you staying?" I told her. "I will speak to Father Gregory and tell him that he should meet you. I'm seeing him again later and I'm sure that he will agree – he is *so* fond of the young and they learn *so* much from him."

I bet they do, I thought, but I said: "That would be absolutely delightful." Then I added for good measure: "and a great privilege."

"You don't need Anna Alexandrovna to get you a meeting with Father Gregory, Mr Speedicut," Dimitri said before Miss Vyrubova could gush any further. "The door of the *starets'* apartment is permanently open to me…"

"And me," said Felix. Irina gave her husband a very old-fashioned look that was repeated on the faces of his mother and my half-sister.

"I would *never* allow my children to meet Rasputin," said Dorothea.

"But Mama," said Tatiana, "all our friends have met him and we would *so* love to."

"Well, you are not going to and that is that."

"Quite right," said our hostess, "and if Felix wasn't of age I would forbid him that sink of iniquity too."

"Really, Mama," said the doe-eyed Prince as Miss Vyrubova looked mortally offended, "what possible harm can there be in them meeting Father Gregory? You know how kind he is to young ladies of good family.

Tell her, Anna." Was there a hint of irony in his voice? I couldn't be sure as Miss Vyrubova, who had recovered her poise, launched into a panegyric on the subject of the benefits which the Siberian peasant could offer to the likes of the Princesses Lieven.

As the subject of Rasputin's social credentials were batted back and forth, one thing quickly became clear: although opinions were rigidly divided on the subject, in the febrile atmosphere of pre-Revolutionary Russia no one was going to fall out over it. Indeed, the universally debated subject of Rasputin in the salons of St Petersburg was a coded way of showing one's views on the Tsar: if you supported the *starets*, you supported the Tsar and vice versa. This situation, however, presented me with a very serious problem, for the people best placed to remove him were also those least likely to have a motive so to do. But that is to anticipate. By the time Bertie and I left the Palais Zinaida Yusupova, Felix and Dimitri had invited me – but not, to his chagrin, Bertie - out to dinner. Ivan helped me to change and, an hour later, I was spinning along the Nevsky Prospekt with Dimitri at the wheel of one of his fleet of expensive, open-topped sports cars with the richest man in Russia in the dicky seat behind.

"Where are we going?" I asked Felix, who had leaned forward and had his head close to mine in order to talk over the noise of the motor and the rushing wind.

"Surprise," was all he would say on the subject as we headed towards the docks, a part of St Petersburg with which I was not familiar.

Some minutes later, Dimitri slewed the car to a halt in front of a pier-side cafe. Judging from the display of mussels outside, its speciality was fish. To judge from the display inside of muscled matelots in tight trousers and skimpy tops, its specialities were wider than just the fruits of the sea. A very jolly evening ensued…

Over breakfast at the Moika Palace the following morning – an event that earned me a stern rebuke from Ivan on the subject of my safety etc etc when I eventually returned to the hotel - my new Russian friends made me two promises: first, that they intended to see a great deal more of me in the future and, second, that I would go with them the following evening to Rasputin's palace of varieties at Gorochovaia 64, conveniently located next to the railway station that served Tsarskoye Selo.

I've already said that I wouldn't be adding to the miles of guff that have been written about Rasputin, but I have to tell you of my first impressions of the man - and one or two facts that are not in the public domain.

As Felix told me on the way there in another of Dimitri's sports cars, Rasputin kept 'open house' every evening in the five-room flat which had been paid for by the Empress, who also paid for two housemaids and funded the St Petersburg school fees of the flat's other occupants, a niece and Rasputin's two daughters. Outwardly, the home of the *starets* was unremarkable: instead of a substantial town house of the type usually provided by royalty to their favourites, it was located in a modern, six-storey block no different to hundreds of other similar properties in the city. Leaving Dimitri's car in the care of the Secret Police, who had a permanent watch on the flat, we toiled up the stairs to the third floor and rang the bell of number 20. The door was opened by a maid who showed us across a small hall, through a pair of mottled glass-panelled doors and into a living room with some poor-quality paintings on the walls. In the centre of this parlour was a rectangular table, draped with a white cloth, with a large sofa and half-a-dozen rather lumpen chairs ranged around it. On the stained linen was a steaming samovar, a large number of half-empty bottles and glasses, and the remains of some cakes and pastries. In fact, the only notable object in the room was a wall-mounted telephone to one side of the double doors which had presumably been provided by the Empress so that she could chat with Rasputin whenever she wanted to. But if the setting was banal, its occupants were not.

Seated in the middle of the sofa and clearly drunk was Rasputin. Cuddled up next to him were Anna Vyrubova and a woman, who Dimitri whispered to me was another close chum of the Empress's called Lili Dehn,[59] both of whom were in

---

[59] Lili von Dehn (1888-1963).

nurses' uniforms. As we entered the room, I could see clearly that one of Rasputin's large hands was groping Miss Vyrubova's right tit whilst the other was up the skirt of Mrs Dehn, but both women appeared to be quite oblivious to their treatment and completely unconcerned by our presence.

Rasputin himself was dressed in a plain black cassock adorned with a pectoral cross which peeked out from below a long, straggly beard; his gaunt, white face was framed by lank hair, parted down the middle. But the most remarkable thing about him was his eyes, which were set under bushy brows in deep sockets on either side of his large nose; they appeared to have been rimmed with mascara. Whether or not they had been, the dark surrounds emphasised the brilliant blue colour of the eyes themselves. I have never seen anything quite like them, before or since. Felix introduced me:

"*Otets Grigoriy*," said Felix, "*my prinosim Vam angliyskiy posetitelya.*"[60]

Rasputin turned to look at me and I felt as though two searchlights were boring into my skull.

"*Sud'ba prikhodit ne kak d'yavola, no, kak angel.*"[61]

I'd been taking Russian lessons from Ivan, but I hadn't a clue what had been said so I smiled sweetly. They were the only words the priest spoke to me all evening – although he did stare at me for a time, as though he knew me but couldn't place me. Then, without another word, Rasputin re-engaged with the two nurses' principal assets.

Despite what has since been written about the man, I have no way of knowing whether or not the secret of the *starets*' power over men, women and sickness was hypnotism, but his eyes were certainly hypnotic.

Rasputin's fondling of his two acolytes continued uninterrupted and this behaviour set the tone for the rest of the evening, which saw the arrival

---

[60] "Father Gregory, we bring you an English visitor."
[61] "Fate does not come as a devil, but as an angel."

of several more women, a gypsy band and a great deal more wine and vodka. Yet the strange thing was that this was no bacchanalian orgy. In fact, the only person in the room who was behaving in a manner that would have been out of place at a cocktail party in St John's Wood was Rasputin, whose hands made free with his guests' nether regions as they cavorted with him to the wild folk music of the gypsies in the hall. From time to time, he would lead one of his dance partners out of the room and I assumed, rightly as it turned out, that it was to subject them to a 'fate worse than death'. I established this conclusively when, towards the end of the evening, I staggered past the musicians in search of a lavatory.

Thinking I had the right door, I turned the handle, pushed open the oak and found myself in a tiny study which was dominated by a broken-down leather sofa. Bent over one of the sofa's arms, her skirt pushed up over her back and with her knickers around her ankles, was the fleshy posterior of Miss Vyrubova, between the cheeks of which Rasputin's massively well-endowed manhood was plunging away. As I backed quietly out of the room, I couldn't help noticing that the peasant's monstrous dick was not in her tunnel of love but in the main drain above it. I tell you this not out of prurience but to explain why, the following year when she was arrested and examined by a police surgeon, Miss V was declared to be *virgo intacta*. Thanks to Bertie, I can also tell you why Rasputin preferred the ways of Sodom and why he was able to pleasure so many of his guests in one evening.

"It's one of the secret of his success," Bertie told me when I confided in him over lunch the following day. "You see, he tells his followers that the only way to salvation is through sinning with him. Once they are convinced of that, which doesn't take the poor fools long, he then gives them a taste of Siberian sin in the shape of a damned good rogering. Of course, he can't risk his female conquests getting pregnant - with the boys it's not a problem – as it would be social death for the unmarried ones and damned awkward for the rest, who probably haven't slept with their husbands in years. So, he subjects them all to Uranian practices - but he adds a refinement."

"What's that?" I asked in incredulity as the journey of a piece of Sole Véronique, a happy reminder of my fossicking in the port and the Moika Palace, halted mid-way to my mouth.

"He withdraws just before the critical moment, telling them that he can't, after all, give them his absolution. This *coitus interuptus*, at which Rasputin's an expert, ensures that he can service any number of his followers in one evening *and* the silly creatures keep coming back for more in the hope that they'll be the one to receive his redeeming fluid!"

"Actually," Bertie went on, "I'm fairly sure from all that I've heard and seen that Rasputin doesn't really like women – what he likes is the pursuit and the conquest. Once he's had them he rejects them, unless like Vyrubova and Dehn they serve another purpose. Anyway, my dear Charles, it's all moderately amusing providing you don't - as it were – get sucked in."

"You can be damned sure, Bertie," I said through a mouthful of peeled grapes, "that the last person in St Petersburg who is going to lay a finger on me is that smelly peasant."

"You haven't forgotten your assignment for the Brotherhood, I trust?"

"Of course not, Bertie. But I don't need to allow that bugger to have his way with me in order to complete the task. Besides which, I think I see a way..." I was about to lay out my thoughts when I heard a discrete cough behind me. I turned to find Ivan. Oh, Christ I thought, not another lecture.

"Can't it wait until after luncheon, Ivan?" I said rather testily. He looked pained.

"I bring you important news, Excellency." Bertie arched an eyebrow which I ignored. "When you hear it, you will be very pleased."

"Very well, Ivan, what is it?"

"Not here, Excellency."

"Will you excuse me, Bertie?" I asked putting my napkin on the table. As his mouth was full, he waved a knife to indicate his compliance. "This had better be good," I said to Ivan once I was in the hotel's lobby. Ivan said nothing but pointed me at a man with his back to me. As he did so, the figure turned. "Fahran!" I cried in surprise, "what the devil are you doing here and how on earth did you make the journey?"

"I am a messenger, huzoor," said my excellent valet. "I come from Sir Philip Sassoon, who facilitated my trip, and I bring you this." He reached into his inside pocket and produced a letter. Without thinking I tore it open but it was in a meaningless code.

"Look here, old chap, I terribly pleased to see you and all that but what the hell does it mean?" I said thrusting the missive at Fahran.

"Apologies, huzoor, I should also have given you this." From another pocket he withdrew a slim, soft-backed volume. It was headed 'Top Secret' and below that were the words 'Staff Duties in the Field: Volume 6 (Codes)'. "Would you like me to decrypt this letter for you, huzoor?"

"No, Excellency, that is my job," said Ivan intervening.

"I am your valet and private secretary, huzoor," said Fahran giving Ivan a dirty look.

"But I am also His Excellency's teacher," said Ivan snatching the letter from my hand.

"Boys, boys," I said soothingly. "Sort it out between you – I'm going back to finish my lunch."

An hour later, whilst Bertie went off to the Vladimir Palace on a mission to persuade his patroness, the Grand Duchess Maria Pavlovna aka the Grand Duchess Vladimir, to move to her house in the Caucasus, I settled down in my suite to read Philip's letter as decoded (in the event) by Ivan…

> *GHQ British Exponential Fart*
> *Montreuil-sur-Merde*
> *France*
>
> *My dead Charles*
>
> *I was deeply repelled to receive your letter, confirming as it did your survival. However, pointless to say, I was even more excited at its contents particularly with regard to the display concerning the Underwear.*
>
> *I have consulted with those Buggers whom I trust and we have concluded that the problem does not lie with the Little Thunder, who has treacled his powers and will have to resonate...*

At this point I stopped reading and rang the bell. Ivan appeared moments later with Fahran right behind him.

"Ivan," I said, in as kindly a manner as I could, "can I suggest that you have another attempt at decoding Sir Philip's letter and this time it might be an idea to ask Fahran for his help. Just a thought, of course, but..."

To say that Ivan looked crestfallen would be a considerable understatement. However, to my considerable relief - for I didn't want internecine warfare to break out in my household - Fahran resisted any temptation to an 'I told you so' moment and fifteen minutes later they returned to my suite with a new decode. It read:

> *GHQ British Expeditionary Force*
> *Montreuil-sur-Mer*
> *France*
>
> *My dear Charles*
>
> *I was deeply relieved to receive your letter, confirming as it did your survival. However, needless to say, I was equally if not more concerned at its contents particularly with regard to the disclosures concerning the Brotherhood.*

> *I have consulted with those Brothers whom I trust and we have concluded that the problem lies only with the Great Boanerges, who has treacherously exceeded his powers in an attempt to protect himself from the disclosure of certain personal information about himself which he believes you to possess and will have to resign.*

What could that be, I wondered: surely not the true facts about his relationship with his son Maurice? Everyone knew about that…

> *If he agrees to do this, without fuss or prevarication, he will be allowed to retire into private life retaining only his role as an unofficial advisor to Queen Mary. In the meantime, I have agreed reluctantly to assume 'the mantle', although my duties as the Commander-in-Chief's Private Secretary may somewhat constrain my powers to act until this war is over.*
>
> *With regard to your own situation, you are now safe from any decisions or directions from the Brotherhood that have deliberately sought to place you in harm's way.*

I let out a sigh of relief at this before I turned the page.

> *However, it is not in anyone's interest to terminate your assignment in Russia. Indeed, the successful completion of that mission is essential if we are to keep Russia in war. Unfortunately, that begs the question about your situation with regard to the Germans and on this I have thought long and hard. Here follow my instructions to you:*
>
> 1. *Short of telling the Germans the <u>real</u> reason why you are in Russia, once they have approached you in St Petersburg you are to comply with their requests and instructions.*
> 2. *You are to keep me fully informed, via coded signals sent from our Embassy, as to what are those requests and instructions.*
>
> *Please give my regards to Brother Bertie and to Brother Buchanan.*
>
> *Yours ever*
>
> *Philip*

CHAPTER ELEVEN: BASE THOUGHTS BELOW STAIRS

You will already have gathered that, by the end of the summer, I had - in addition to giving my relations a wide berth – identified a small group of Russians who were close to the Mad Monk and could, if they were so minded, have done the deed. At the forefront of my putative assassination team, which included a quack doctor, an immoral Guardee, a bent politician and a pair of Society popsies, were Felix and Dimitri. Identifying them all was the easy bit. Persuading them to conspire together to eliminate their 'friend' was a problem of an altogether different magnitude and one to which I didn't have a solution. At first, I withheld the problem from Ivan and Fahran because, with youthful pride, I was determined to solve it on my own. Eventually, as time marched on and the political situation in Russia deteriorated to crisis levels, I had no choice. So, after breakfast one day in mid-autumn, I presented them with the conundrum.

"You will have to bide your time, Excellency," said Ivan, "and wait for the right opportunity."

"But time is a luxury we don't have, Ivan. The Tsar could be overthrown at any moment," I said in despair.

"Something's bound to turn up," said Fahran, but with no real conviction, "it always…" There was a knock on the door.

"Can you see who that is?" I asked him. It was Bertie, who'd been out of town for a couple of weeks with one of his Grand Duchesses.

"How was Omsk, Tomsk or Chomsk – or wherever it was that you've been vamping with Mrs Vlad?" I asked as he lowered himself into a chair opposite me.

"That's no way to refer to the dear Grand Duchess Maria Pavlovna," he replied rather sniffily, "and since you ask, my dear Charles, I've been in Kislovodsk."

"Where's that?"

"It's a delightful spa in the northern Caucasus, where the Grand Duchess has a most comfortable house."

"So not on the front line?"

"By no means. But enough of this, my dear Charles, I have some news for you." He looked meaningfully at my two retainers, who took the hint and left. "We will shortly be welcoming a visitor…" It was a bit early in the morning to play along with Bertie's mystery game, so I cut to the chase by feigning indifference.

"Really?" I asked with a yawn.

"Don't you want to know who it is?" he asked somewhat peevishly.

"Not really – I've got my hands quite full enough trying to think of a way to get Felix and Dimitri into a murderous mood. Unless, that is, you've got any bright ideas?" He ignored my question.

"Mata Hari," he said as though he'd just pulled a plump rabbit out of his silk top hat.

"Mater Who?"

"Mata Hari. She's an exotic, oriental dancer of Dutch extraction who made something of a name for herself before the war, mostly in the horizontal position on a succession of royal and aristocratic sofas. We talked about her at Philip's the first time you and I met. Surely you remember?"

"Vaguely," I answered truthfully.

"What wasn't mentioned at the time – because you were not then in the Brotherhood – was that Mata Hari has done some work for us and, in the course of that work, learned something which she thought was to her financial advantage."

"So what?"

"With that information she tried, unsuccessfully, to blackmail the Brotherhood. In fact, it was your father whom she tried to use as a go-between."[62]

"Did she?" I said sitting up straight. "What happened?"

"Nothing," said Bertie looking a bit sheepish, "your father died and Mr Flashman, who was Great Boanerges at the time, decided that, after all, Mata Hari might still be of use to us. Her informant, Nurse Cavell, was not so lucky, but let that pass."

"What was Mata Hari doing for us?"

"She had privileged access to the German High Command and, as a neutral, her travel was initially not much constrained by the hostilities. By keeping her ear to the pillow in Berlin, The Hague and Lisbon she was able to pick up important information on the Germans' strategic plans which she passed back to us and we sent on to GHQ. However, when the conflict turned into a static slogging match her information on troop movements lost much of its usefulness as there weren't any. Of course, her principal value to us now is as a quadruple agent..."

"A what?"

"Well, she started off working for the Germans when she was the Crown Prince's night time comforter, but we persuaded her – don't ask me how but I believe your father was involved - that her best interests lay in working for us as well. Whilst keeping her on our books we allowed

---

[62] See *The Speedicut Papers: Book 9 (Boxing Icebergs)*.

her to take The King's sovereigns - her marketability, so she said, was in decline and she needed the funds - and more recently, she's also joined the Frogs' payroll. So, you see, she works for four of us and I wouldn't be at all surprised if she didn't try to add our hosts to her list whilst she's here."

"And where do her loyalties lie?"

"God only knows."

"So why does anyone trust her?"

"No one does, but she's a channel not only for information but for misinformation as well."

"But, if we know that she's working for the Germans and the French and they know that she's also working for us and them, then the only information that she's passing will be lies - and, as everyone knows that too, then surely her usefulness is zero."

"Ah, my dear Charles, how quickly you have spotted the fundamental flaw of all espionage and the double-cross."

"It's barking!" I said.

"Possibly, but it keeps a lot of people happily employed in snug offices far from the front line, when they could be up-to-their-crotches in Flanders mud. And, don't forget that there's always an outside chance the information might for once be correct. Each side includes the occasional truth as it's the thing that makes the lies believable."

"But what happens if she decides that she's backed the wrong horses and switches her primary allegiance back to the Huns?"

"Nothing – it's the price that intelligence has to pay - but if we found out, *and* she'd outlived her usefulness, then we'd expose her as a German spy and she'd be shot – just like Nurse Cavell."

"So, what's she going to be doing for us in St Petersburg?"

"The official reason, and the one which she has been told, is that she's here at the invitation of the Commander-in-Chief, Grand Duke Nicholas Nicholaievich,[63] who has long wished to, err, sample her wares."

"Has he actually expressed such a wish?"

"He has," said Bertie, "and, thanks to dear Maria Pavlovna, the letter of invitation is already on its way to Paris."

"And the real reason?"

"To give you a helping hand with your assignment."

"Does she know that?"

"Not yet."

"Oh, Christ!" I groaned.

"What's the matter, my dear Charles? I thought you wanted some help."

"I do," I said, but I couldn't tell Bertie that I too was - at least in theory - working for the Germans. The multi-layered, three-dimensional ramifications of the involvement of Mata Hari with me in a plot to kill Rasputin made my head spin. Then, suddenly, I spotted a way of escape. "I'm very grateful and all that for your proposal, Bertie, but what earthly use could a tart with a trick quim be in persuading two of the biggest poofters in Russia to do the deed?"

"There's an old Russian proverb which, roughly translated, says that the quickest way to tame a bull is to put a heifer in his byre."

---

[63] General HIH Grand Duke Nicholas Nicholaievich of Russia (1856 –1929).

"That may be so, but the proverb relies on the bull – in this case two bulls - not being as queer as 'Bosie' Douglas."[64]

"Really, Charles!" Bertie exclaimed in horror as he clutched his heart, which may have been touched by the exiled, mincing queen, "you go too far – besides which, my dear," he said recovering somewhat, "you underestimate Mata Hari's charms."

"And you, my dear Bertie, overestimate Felix and Dimitri's susceptibilities to the allure of an ageing, albeit very experienced, pussy."

The argument raged on, intermittently, until the day before Mata Hari arrived. However, which of us was right was never proved for, at the eleventh hour, Bertie and I agreed a strategy that did not require Margaretha, for such was her Christian name, to spend time between the sheets with our reluctant lotharios even if they could have been persuaded to break the habits of a lifetime.

We booked rooms for her in our hotel and, on the first night, gave her dinner in my suite. I couldn't decide how far we should go in briefing the ageing courtesan – Fahran and Ivan had both advised that we should hold back, particularly as it was certain that she would tell the Germans and I would then be compromised. But Bertie was determined.

"There's no point in beating about the bush, my dear Charles, particularly when the bush in question has provided a nest for more cock birds than either of us are likely to see in a lifetime." Speak for yourself, I thought. "Besides which, time is not on our side. No, I propose that we get straight to the point and put her to work without delay."

So, after Bertie had introduced me and she had failed to make the connection with my father, we did. After Bertie had given her, along with some rather good caviar, a concise overview of the state of Russia, the pernicious position of Rasputin and the importance to the Allies of

---

[64] Lord Alfred Douglas (1870-1945).

keeping Russia in the war, with some considerable (private) misgivings I laid our cards on the table.

"In short, Miss Zelle, Rasputin has to be permanently and irrevocably removed. We have identified the people to do it, all of whom are within his circle and have access, the problem is persuading them."

"How will you do that?" she purred in a voice that was as low as her ample *décolletage*.

"Because of the way that Russia works," said Bertie. "If we can convince our selected agents that they are acting in their own and the government's best interests, with immunity and – most importantly - with the sanction of a very senior member of the Romanov family, they will act."

"I see. And what is my role in all of this?"

"As you know," I said, "the ostensible reason for your visit is to 'attend upon' the Grand Duke Nicholas Nicholaievich at Mogilev. When you return to St Petersburg, no one will think to question you if you disclose – confidentially - that the Grand Duke is determined to preserve the Romanov dynasty by the permanent removal of Rasputin. Society's allegiance to the *status quo* is far greater than any personal loyalty to the Siberian peasant and, if it is believed that any action against the *starets* can be taken without risk and with the approval of the Commander-in-Chief and the Tsar's most respected near relation, then it will happen."

"Why can't you put that story about?" she asked quite reasonably.

"Because, my dear Margaretha," said Bertie, "neither Charles nor I have the necessary credentials.

"Which are?"

"To put not too fine a point on it," I said, "the ability to pleasure the Grand Duke into making the requisite pronouncement – or, rather, the belief by those that we seek to influence that he has."

"I see," she said. "And how do I benefit?"

"With a considerable amount of gold in a Swiss bank," I said.

"How much?" she queried.

"Enough to keep you in this delicious stuff for the rest of your life," said Bertie as he offered her more caviar.

"Then I agree," she said once again heaping fish eggs onto her plate.

The following day we packed her off to Stavka (the Russian GHQ) at Mogilev. She returned a week later with bags under her eyes and the need for additional upholstery whenever she sat: the Grand Duke Nicholas Nicholaievich might have been presiding by day over a retreat, but at night it appeared that withdrawal was no part of his strategy…

Once she'd recovered – well, the poor old trot wasn't exactly in the first flush - we put the next stage of our plan into operation. This involved my persuading Felix – not difficult if you knew (as I did) the most propitious circumstances in which to ask - to throw an intimate dinner in honour of Mata Hari at the Moika Palace in the new suite of oriental-style, informal rooms he'd recently had created in the basement. Needless to say, the guest list was my proposed group of conspirators comprising Felix, Dimitri and his step-sister, Marianne Pistohlkors. They were joined by a Society clap doctor called de Lazovert, who was best friends with another guest, Purishkevich, a millionaire politician who led the swivel-eyed monarchist faction in the Duma. In addition, there was a pretty ballet dancer called Karalli, who was reputedly sleeping with Dimitri (actually, she was fossicking with me when I wasn't overnighting at the Moika Palace) and a handsome Captain in the Preobrajensky Guard called Sukhotin, who – as I knew from several energetic threesomes and the fact that he like me reeked of the Prince's exclusive cologne - was sleeping with Felix.[65]

---

[65] Countess Marianne von Pistohlkors (1890-1976), Dr Stanislaus de Lazovert (1860-1920), Vladimir Mitrofanovich Purishkevich (1870-1920), Vera Alexeyevna Karalli (1889-1972) & Captain Sergei Mikhailovich Sukhotin (1887-1926).

Now, you may be wondering at this point whether or not Miss Hari had shown any signs of knowing of my relationship with the dreaded vons, Stumm and Einem. The short answer is 'no', although I had caught her giving me an enquiring – or was it appraising – look or two. You may also be wondering what role my two trusty lieutenants, Ivan and Fahran, were playing in this game. You'll have to wait and see…

What I will tell you is that we had debated at length exactly how Margaretha was to broach the topic of Rasputin's enforced demise and I had briefed the old trollop accordingly. I'll say this for her, she was a quick study and delivered her lines faultlessly. After the introductions and a magnum or two of fizz, during which the conversations - which were all in French - were inconsequential, we took our places at a round table. At this point, as directed by Fahran and agreed by Margaretha, I deliberately switched the talk to a debate about the stage versus the silver screen. It was led by Dimitri's niece, who had ambitions to tread the boards, and Miss Karalli, who was a budding movie star in addition to her existing stellar status at the Mariinsky.

"Do you think it's possible, Madam Zelle, that moving pictures will ever replace the stage?" asked Purishkevich.

"I think not," she replied throwing out her famous chest, "in my experience the paying public wants three-dimensional characters not the two dimensional one you see on the screen."

"But surely the two can co-exist," I said. "People like us will continue to enjoy the exclusivity of live performances whilst the masses will be able to watch silent reproductions." This was her cue and she took it.

"Possibly," she replied, "assuming of course that you continue to be in a position to attend the theatre…"

"Whatever do you mean?" asked Felix.

"Simply this, Prince, that in the short time I have been here I have seen significant evidence that you are all sitting on top of a pot that is about to boil over."

"I think you exaggerate, Madam Zelle," said Dimitri.

"If I do, Your Imperial Highness, then so too does the Grand Duke Nicholas Nicholaievich, with whom I have just passed a most agreeable few days at Mogilev."

"What does he say?" asked de Lazovert. She didn't reply immediately.

"It is his view," she paused again and you could have heard a kopek drop as the doomed aristos waited for her answer, "that the current situation is unsustainable."

"Anyone in politics knows that," said Purishkevich, "but what does he propose?"

"It is his belief that, since the pot can't be moved from the heat, the heat must be removed from the pot."

"He's talking in riddles!" Purishkevich replied with some heat. "Besides which the problem is insoluble: there must be reforms but, as the Tsar is an autocrat only he can implement them. Unfortunately, he listens only to the Tsarina, who is blind to the dangers, and who counsels him to resist all proposals. If only she could be banished to a nunnery the situation might be saved."

"His Imperial Highness disagrees," said Margaretha. "He thinks that anything which undermines the standing of the Romanov dynasty in the eyes of the masses, such as the removal of the Tsarina, would result in the house falling."

"So, what is he proposing?" asked Dimitri's half-sister.

"His preferred course of action," she paused again as though to martial her thoughts, "is – if I remember rightly - to neutralise the influence of Her Imperial Majesty with the Tsar. If that can be done, then other more beneficial influences can be brought to bear on His Imperial Majesty, the necessary constitutional reforms can be enacted, the peasants will go back to their hovels leaving the military free to concentrate on halting the Germans - and disaster will thereby be avoided."

"That all very well," said the dancer, "but how is the Empress to be 'neutralised' if she is not to be removed."

"Her Imperial Majesty is, so the Grand Duke thinks," Margaretha went on, "overly susceptible to…" we had reached the moment of truth, "primitive religious influences. If the present influencer were to be removed and replaced with one who gave progressive advice, then so would the advice that the Empress gives to His Imperial Majesty."

"Does he mean removing dear Father Gregory?" squeaked Miss Pistohlkors.

"He must do," said Miss Karalli.

There was a prolonged silence as those around the table, oblivious to the poached sturgeon in a lobster sauce in front of them, contemplated the implications.

"But even if anyone would do such a mad thing," said Dimitri, "they'd be hanged for murder at best – or, worse, sent to Siberia or the Front."

"That's not what the Grand Duke said," chipped in Margaretha.

"What *did* he say?" asked Felix.

"That whoever solved the problem would be a national hero."

No one reacted to this, so I changed the subject to the latest ballet at the Imperial Theatre and, five minutes later, it was as though it had never been raised. However, as events were to prove, the seed had been sown.

Later that evening, with Felix determined on some late-night drill with his Guardsman, I escorted Mata Hari back to our hotel where she invited me to sow a seed or two of my own. She may have been getting a bit long in the tooth, but I have always been open to a new experience and so I readily accepted her proposal that I have a night cap in her bedroom. The session which followed was the most challenging I had experienced to that date. It goes without saying that Mata Hari was a highly experienced professional and, after she'd dragged me over the line for the third time, I fell into a deep sleep, which was only interrupted late the following morning by a sharp rat-a-tat-tat on the door. I woke, bleary eyed, to find that I was on my own. As my eyes adjusted to the gloom, I realised that there was no trace of the ageing dancer in the room. The rap on the door resumed, so I pulled a blanket off the bed, wrapped it around me like a toga and staggered over to the oak.

"Who's there?" I demanded.

"It is Fahran and Ivan, huzoor." I let them in.

"Miss Zelle has left the hotel, Excellency," said Ivan. "We thought you ought to know."

"Really?" I replied, switching on the light.

"Yes, huzoor. She checked out an hour ago and took everything with her. Although she seems to have left something for you on the pillow," he said pointing over my shoulder." I turned and, sure enough, there was a parcel wrapped in brown paper and string where, several hours before, I had been wrapping my tongue around one of Mata Hari's still firm dugs.

"See what it is, would you, Fahran?"

He strode over to the bed, lifted the package, tore off the wrapping and revealed a note – and a pair of pincers.

CHAPTER TWELVE: A GENTLEMANLY MURDER BY THE MOIKA

I came to full consciousness with a jolt, for the message of the pincers couldn't have been clearer: 'I too am working with the vons and they will shortly know the double game you are playing', it said. The note itself was equally clear and considerably more explicit: 'For a young man you show promise – but your father was reputed to be better'. The two messages were bad enough; what was worse, as I told Ivan and Fahran once I was back in my own room, was the probability that – once they knew of our intentions and my perfidy - the Germans would move heaven and earth to prevent Rasputin being topped. The prospect of my potential assassination squad, along with myself, being the victims of an anarchist's (for which read German) bomb was all too real.

"The first thing that must be done, huzoor, is to prevent Miss Zelle from communicating with the Germans."

"But how?" I asked. "She's probably half way to the German Embassy as we speak."

"The German Embassy has been closed since 1914, Excellency," said Ivan giving me a slightly pitying look.

"Well, she's probably got a rendezvous with an agent on the train to Helsinki."

"Possibly, Excellency, but I think it unlikely. No, in all probability she will have to wait to send a letter from a neutral port or make contact there. Give me a couple of minutes and I'll get the sailings from here, Reval and Helsinki."

"How?" I asked.

"The Nehemiah, Excellency…" Ten minutes later Ivan returned looking, I thought, a touch smug.

"Well?"

"I have the answer, Excellency: Miss Zelle caught the train this morning - not to Helsinki but to Sevastopol. It seems that, thanks to a pass given to her by the Grand Duke, she was able to secure an officer's compartment on a troop train. I am also informed that he has given her a *laissez passer* which will, until we can get it revoked, make her untouchable. Apparently, she told the Grand Duke that she wanted to winter in the Crimea before returning to Paris via Persia."

"That's a smoke screen," said Fahran. "Even with the *laissez passer* she'd never linger in Russia knowing that we'll be on her tail. Her true intention must be to get from Sevastopol across the Black Sea to Constantinople, probably - to avoid detection - on a small fishing boat. Once she's in Turkey she'll be free to brief the Germans about everything she knows."

"Unless we can stop her, chaps," I said. "For that we need to consult with Mr Stopford. It's not just the Nehemiah that has a long reach."

"I know," said Bertie when I'd briefed him.

"What do you mean, you know?" I demanded.

"I know that Margaretha is on her way to the Crimea."

"How do you know?"

"Because I organised it."

"What? But her next stop after that will be a brisk row across the Black Sea followed by a briefing at the German Embassy in Constantinople – and that will be the end of my plan to eliminate Rasputin."

"I think not, my dear Charles. Remember, she is working for us too and she knows that the gold in that Zurich bank will only find its way to her vault once the Siberian is no more."

"That's assuming that we haven't been outbid by the Krauts."

"True, but she knows how any such double-dealing will end."

"Nonetheless, you can't be sure."

"Also true. We can but hope that she values her life higher than a sack of German Goldmarks."

"God, all this double-dealing! An illusionist's smoke and mirrors aren't in it. So, what are we going to do?"

"Nothing, my dear Charles, for there is nothing to be done. Either she will play us true or she will play us false. We'll find out soon enough. In the meantime, I suggest that you continue to encourage Felix and his friends as though nothing has happened."

So, I did and it didn't: which is to say that I duly watered the seed (and I use the term advisedly) that Margaretha had planted in the basement of the Moika Palace and no one attempted to blow up any of us as it germinated and grew into a full-blown plot. That said, there *were* signs of a possible betrayal. For, towards the end of November, Rasputin started talking – and then wouldn't stop - about not living to see the New Year. There was nothing particularly unusual in that, as the smelly peasant was forever making prophesies about his fate and that of Russia, which he always bound together as though they were one and the same thing (of course, in a sense they were, although he believed that Mother Russia's future prosperity was bound to his continued enjoyment of its myriad pleasures whilst we believed the diametric opposite). However, this time, in addition to forecasting his own demise along with that of the land from the Baltic to the Pacific, he refused to leave his apartment. Had he been warned by the Germans? None of us knew, but it posed the plotters with something of a problem.

"If he won't leave his apartment in Gorochovaia," said Felix over a planning meeting in his basement, "how on earth are we going to kill him? We can hardly shoot him dead on his own sofa surrounded by his children and staff."

"How about if we were to poison him?" asked Dimitri.

"How would you do that?" queried Purishkevich.

"We could bring him cakes laced with cyanide," said Vera Karalli, "that's how I murdered my faithless lover in my last film…"

"That might work," said de Lazovert, "and I have a plentiful supply of the poison in my dispensary."

"But won't it look a bit odd if we arrive with a box of cakes and then touch none of them ourselves," said Dimitri.

"It would," said Miss Pistohlkors, "but I believe that cyanide acts very quickly. So, we wouldn't have to touch the cakes providing Father Gregory ate his first."

"And if he didn't?" asked Felix: Dimitri's stepsister didn't have an answer to that. "No, it will have to be done here. That way, no one need know of our involvement. We poison the beast in this room, then carry his body up to the courtyard, put it in one of Dimitri Pavlovich's cars, weight it with chains and dump it in an ice-hole in the Nevka."

"And I'll put a bullet in his brain before you do so - for good measure," said Sukhotin, the brave Guardee.

"That's all very well," said Purishkevich, "but there remains the problem of how to lure him from his lair."

There was silence for several moments whilst they all applied their minimal brain cells to this important detail. In the end, no one had even a half-way sensible suggestion so, the following morning, I put the problem to Ivan and Fahran.

"The priest will need a powerful inducement to leave his flat, huzoor," said Fahran.

"Correct," I said.

"But he has a weakness, Excellency," said Ivan, "for the Imperial Family. If one of them were to invite him out he couldn't and he wouldn't refuse such a command."

"True," I said, "but about the only members of the Imperial Family that he trusts are the Tsar and the Tsarina – and we can hardly poison him in the Tsarina's mauve boudoir, now can we? And," I went on, "if any of the others were to ask him – and I'm sure that the Grand Duke Nicholas Nicholaievich, the Dowager Empress or the Grand Duchess Vladimir would all do as we asked – the monster would smell an Imperial-sized rat and barricade the front door of his flat."[66]

"There is one Imperial invitation that he couldn't resist and which could be easily arranged," said Ivan.

"Whose?"

"The Princess Irina Yusupova," replied Ivan, "she's His Imperial Majesty's niece and, as far as I know, has never even met Rasputin. If she were to invite him to the Moika Palace he'd be there like a shot."

"She'd never do it," I said, "according to Felix she can't abide the brute."

"But Rasputin doesn't know that – and, anyway, Princess Irina doesn't need to know that she's invited him," said Fahran.

"What on earth do you mean?" I asked.

---

[66] HIM Grand Duke Nicholas Nikolaevich of Russia (1856-1929) & HIM the Dowager Empress Maria Feodorovna (1847-1928).

"If Prince Felix were to say that his wife wished to meet Rasputin and then, once he'd arrived at the Moika Palace, the *starets* was told that she'd been delayed it would be too late… he would hardly bolt from the place on receipt of the news, now would he, huzoor? Besides which, he trusts Prince Felix."

"It might work," I said and, as everyone knows, it did.

What is not known, because each and every one of the subsequent accounts was deliberately false or misleading, is precisely what happened on the night of 16th-17th December 1916. I do, because I was there from start to finish.

As Team Speedicut had proposed, Felix duly told Rasputin that Mrs Y was simply gagging after all these years to meet him and that he was cordially invited to take after-dinner tea with her in the Moika Palace. At my suggestion, Felix had hinted that Irina was hoping to have some time alone with the bugger so that, he had added with a broad wink, she could 'make her confession'. Apparently, Rasputin had actually rubbed his crotch at this. Anyway, Felix had continued, in order that it shouldn't be a formal visit Father Gregory would be received away from the prying eyes of the staff in the new basement rather than in the absurdly grand rooms above.

On the night in question, I drove with Felix and the quack, de Lazovert disguised as a chauffeur, to Rasputin's apartment. We arrived there shortly after midnight, which may seem a bit late for a rendezvous with an Imperial Princess, but St Petersburgers habitually kept late hours. De Lazovert stayed in the car whilst Felix and I went to fetch our victim. Instead of using the main staircase, we ascended to the third floor via the communal fire escape in the inner courtyard. Felix rapped on Rasputin's back door. It was answered almost immediately by the man himself, already dressed in a heavy fur coat and carrying a small icon in his right hand. Thanks to Ivan's expert instruction, I was able to follow much of what was then said.

"See, Little One," Rasputin said using his pet name for Felix and waving the gilded image about, "look what the Little Mother has sent me. Anna Alexandrovna brought it this afternoon. And observe, it is signed on the back!" He turned the icon around and I could just make out in the dim light of the kitchen the signatures of the Tsarina and her four daughters. "I'm bringing it to show to your wife."

"That's nice," said Felix looking a bit uncomfortable: Russians of all classes are painfully superstitious and this was clearly not an auspicious start to the assassination.

The drive back to the Moika Palace, with de Lazovert at the wheel, was unremarkable. The doctor parked the car in the inner courtyard and then peeled off to join the other conspirators in a drawing room on the ground floor, where their role was to make a great deal of noise as though there was a party in progress, at the end of which Irina would meet Rasputin in the basement dining room. Meanwhile Felix led Rasputin and me down to the cellar rooms through a door in the corner of the yard. Contrary to popular belief, this new suite of rooms in the cellar had neither been especially sound-proofed nor refurbished specifically for the murder. As Felix had confided to me one evening when we had used the same entrance, the whole set-up had been built so that he could 'drag back' without the risk of bumping into Irina in the hall.

I'm now going to tell you next what *actually* happened, for it confounds all the fantastic stories put about later by Felix, Puriskevich and the others, presumably with the intention of establishing Rasputin's demonic powers and the sanctity, therefore, of his murder. Yes, it is true that Felix and I showed the *starets* into the small, vaulted dining room and that, laid on the round table, were *petits fours* – the pink ones laced with de Lazovert's cyanide and the brown ones, for Felix and me, poison free – and four bottles of sweet wine from Felix's vineyards in the Crimea two of which had been similarly spiked. However, it is not true that the Siberian wolfed down the cakes nor that he downed the wine in short order. What actually happened was this:

"Do take off your coat and hat, Father Gregory," said Felix. He did as my friend requested, revealing as he did so a blue silk peasant-style smock, embroidered with cornflowers and gathered at the waist with a belt; below this he wore baggy trousers tucked into soft leather boots. "Please sit here," he drew out a chair, "and help yourself to some food and wine. Irina will be down as soon as her guests have left." As he said this, we could all hear quite clearly the sound of men's and women's voices above – so much for the sound proofing and Felix's later claim that no women were involved – intermingled with American jazz on a gramophone.

"It sounds like a good party, Little One," said Rasputin as he poured himself half a glass of wine.

"Some pastries, Father Gregory?" I asked picking up one the salvers and handing it to him.

"You should know, Englishman," he said scowling at me, "that I never touch sweet food." What? This was news to me and, I presumed, the rest of the plotters, "and, as it is late, I shall drink but little of our host's wine."

Shit, I thought, de Lazovert had put enough cyanide in the pink cakes to kill a herd of oxen but in the bottles were only the last few crystals. If Rasputin sipped on but a single glass of wine he wouldn't even get indigestion. I threw a despairing look at Felix; he gave me a nod of understanding.

"Father Gregory," said Felix, "Mr Speedicut will go and find out when my wife's guests are leaving, so that she can come and join us. After all," he said giving me a meaningful stare, "we don't want your visit to be wasted."

Leaving Felix to look after the ghastly fellow I made my way out of the dining room, along the corridor and up an internal service staircase to the hall above. A pair of doors on the other side were open and I made for the sound.

"What's going on down there?" asked Dimitri.

"And what are you doing here," asked the pride of the Mariinsky.

"There's a problem," I said in as level a voice as I could.

"What problem?" demanded Purishkevich.

"He won't touch the cakes and he's hardly drinking."

"Damn!" said Sukhotin and the quack together.

"You'll have to shoot him," said Miss Pistohlkors, "take Dimitri Pavlovich's revolver."

"You shoot him if you want to," I said thinking furiously of a reason why I should not have to do the deed, "my – my government cannot be seen to be directly implicated in this affair."

"Well, then give my pistol to Felix Felixovich," said Dimitri as he drew the weapon from the holster on his hip. I took it, tucked it into the back of my trousers beneath my dinner jacket and headed back down stairs.

I found Rasputin looking absolutely none the worse for wear. The same could not be said of Felix, who looked as though he'd just had to fight off the randy bastard (I found out later that that is exactly what he'd had to do).

"May I have a word, Felix?" I said in French from the doorway of the dining room.

"Excuse me a moment, Father Gregory."

"Don't be long, Little One, we have unfinished business," the peasant said as he stroked through the fabric of his baggy trousers what looked like a large sausage and I stepped back into the corridor out of his sight

"You'll have to shoot him," I said in French handing Felix Dimitri's revolver, "and I suggest that you do it right now."

"But I can't," whispered Felix looking horrified, "I've never used a handgun in my life."

"Well, I can't do it either."

"What's going on out there?" growled a deep voice as I heard a chair being pushed back.

"For God's sake," I pleaded with Felix in an undertone, "if you don't do it now there'll never be another chance."

"But I can't," repeated our host.

I don't quite know what came over me at that point, but it's possible that I may have panicked. I know that the image of a stone-cold sober Rasputin finding the two of us with a loaded pistol was not a happy one.

"Give it to me you appalling coward," I said as I attempted to yank the gun out of his hand, but for some reason he wouldn't let go.

"How dare you call *me* a coward!" he cried.

"Little One," called out Rasputin, "what are you doing? Is the English pig trying to have his way with you, my darling? I will help you."

As I heard those words I made an extra effort to wrest the weapon from Felix, whose hand was frozen over the grip in a paroxysm of either fear or rage. In the ensuing tussle, we stumbled through the doorway, I saw Rasputin rise to his full height, the pistol went off - God only knows which of us pulled the trigger - I heard a low groan and watched as the *starets* slumped forward over the table cloth. Moments later, or so it seemed, the room was full of the party from upstairs. Felix just stood there, the smoking gun in his hand and a shocked expression on his face.

"You did it - thank God - well done - is he dead?" cried a chorus of voices, the last being our resident Doctor. Felix was still in deep shock so I answered for him.

"I suggest you find out," I said. De Lazovert stepped forward and, rather gingerly I thought, applied his fingers to the peasant's neck.

"There's no pulse," he said.

"So, he's dead?" asked Dimitri.

"Yes."

"Excellent," said Purishkevich, "let's go and finish off the champagne."

"Aren't you forgetting something?" I said as everyone headed for the door.

"What?" queried Sukhotin.

"The small matter of the *corpus delicti* or - to put it another way - that lump of festering meat over there whose life blood is currently staining one of Felix Felixovich's best damask tablecloths."

"We can't remove him until the coast is clear," said our budding film star, who had clearly been reading too many American detective novels, "give it an hour and the streets should be quiet by then."

It was actually a sensible suggestion – her first, if you don't include the poisoned cakes idea - which we followed and an hour or so later the party started to break up, but not before we'd agreed what had to be done. Dimitri summarised our duties as the clock struck two:

"I'll take Marianne and Vera Alexeyevna in my motor back to their apartment whilst Felix Felixovich, Charles, Sergei Mikhailovich and Stanislaus put the body in the sack, carry it up to the courtyard and dump it in the boot of the Felix Felixovich's car. Vladimir Mitrofanovich you go as planned to the station. Felix Felixovich, you will then drive your motor to the bridge over the Nevka, weight the sack with the chains and dump it through the ice hole. Agreed?" We all nodded as I thought I heard a groaning noise coming from the hall.

"What's that?" I asked

"I didn't hear anything," said de Lazovert as he passed Dimitri's pistol, which had been doing the rounds (a bit like its owner), to Purishkevich.

"I'll go and have a look," said Felix, who appeared to have recovered considerably thanks to several glasses of the Widow. He stumbled towards the double doors, opened one and disappeared from view.

The next thing we knew there was a ghastly, girlish scream from the hall. As one we rushed out of the drawing room to find Felix in an intimate embrace with the late faith healer. I say 'late' because that is what Rasputin was supposed to be, but as we could see, he was very much alive and kicking. We were all rooted to the spot in horror for a resurrection was taking place in front of our very eyes. Rasputin saw us, let out an inarticulate roar, pushed Felix away from him and lurched towards the door to the courtyard.

"Quick," shouted Dimitri, "shoot him, Vladimir Mitrofanovich!" Purishkevich raised the pistol and loosed off two shots at the departing corpse. Both missed.

"Give it to me," snarled the Grand Duke as he legged it after the Siberian, whose exit path was marked by a trail of blood on the marble floor and in the snow in the courtyard. As I emerged into the open, a third shot rang out, I saw Rasputin fall and then Dimitri walked over to the fallen man and shot him in the base of the skull.

"That should do it," he said holstering the gun. At that moment Felix reappeared brandishing a bronze nude in his right hand. Without a word, he went over to the dead man and started beating his body with the statue.

"Get him off!" Dimitri ordered Sukhotin and Purishkevich. "He's hysterical: Stanislaus, can you give him something to calm him down?" The doctor turned and went back into the palace. Meanwhile, by the time the soldier and the politician had dragged Felix off Rasputin, the richest man in Russia was covered in Siberian gore and looked as though he'd been working inexpertly in an abattoir.

"There must be a change of plan: Felix Felixovich, you stay behind and, once you composed yourself," I saw the quack return, pull up one of Felix's sleeves and jab him with a small syringe, "get yourself a change of clothes and order your servants to clear up the mess. Girls, you'll have to make your own way home - not you, Charles," my heart sank, "you, Stanislaus, Sergei Mikhailovich, Vladimir Mitrofanovich and I must dispose of the body."

But before any of us could move the doorbell rang. My heart leapt in fear.

"Go and see who it is, Vera Alexeyevna," said Dimitri. She turned and walked back through the hall to the front door; I followed at a distance.

"Excuse me, Your Excellency," a man said, "I heard pistol shots. Is everything alright?" Thank God Vera held her nerve.

"Quite alright, thank you, Constable, the men were shooting at champagne bottles. Just high spirits, you know!"

"That's alright then," said the policeman, "but in these times, you can't be too careful."

"Indeed not – well, goodnight, Constable."

"Goodnight, Your Excellency." Vera closed the door and sank onto the marble floor; then she spotted me. "Get me a glass of brandy would you, Charles?" I did and then returned to the courtyard to tell the others what had happened.

"Hmm," said Dimitri, "if the policeman has second thoughts he'll be back. We'd better get rid of this," he pointed to Rasputin's body.

After a lot of cursing, eventually we managed to get the bloody corpse into the sack, bound it with ropes, stuffed it behind the back seat and, with Dimitri at the wheel and with de Lazovert's feet holding down the sack, drove off to the pre-determined ice hole in the Nevka.

It was a hellish journey, for the road was rough and the wretched motor kept breaking down, but eventually we got to the right spot where, whilst Dimitri stood guard over the car with the bonnet open, the four of us dragged the bloody sack to the parapet and pitched it over into the hole in the ice below. With a great splash, it plunged into the freezing water. At this point Rasputin should have disappeared beneath the frozen surface of the river never to be seen again. Unfortunately, which is a word that has and will lurk in the pages of this book like an evil fairy, in our haste to dispose of the mad monk, I'd forgotten to attach the chains to his ankles. We only discovered this omission when, moments later, the hessian reappeared.

"Oh God!" groaned de Lazovert.

"What are we to do?" I asked.

"Get down there and push it under the ice," said Dimitri, who'd come over to see what was happening. We eventually managed this with the help of the motor's crank handle, although we were all soaked and frozen by the time the makeshift shroud had finally disappeared under the ice sheet.[67]

And that should have been the end of Rasputin. We drove Purishkevich, Sukhotin and de Lazovert to the Warsaw Station where they boarded a hospital train bound that afternoon for the Front, Dimitri returned to the Grand Duchess Elizabeth Feodorovna's palace, where for some reason he was staying, and from there I walked back to my hotel, where I decided to spend the rest of the morning in bed. I was woken around 2 pm by Ivan and Fahran.

"Excellency," said Ivan, "I think you had better get dressed. A letter from the Grand Duke has arrived for you marked 'urgent' - it looks as though there's a serious problem."

---

[67] Editor's Note: There are several conflicting accounts of the murder of Rasputin. Speedicut's story, as related above, explains many but not all of the inconsistencies in those reports.

CHAPTER THIRTEEN: OPERATION EMERALD

As I found out when I met up with Dimitri and Felix at the former's temporary residence, a 'serious problem' was something of an understatement. The two of them were seated either side of a roaring fire in a cosy study, alternately sluicing down copious quantities of brandy and strong black coffee, an activity which didn't bode well.

"That bloody German bitch who calls herself the Tsarina has reported Rasputin missing," Dimitri opened up as I appeared.

"So what? She was bound to," I said helping myself to a glass of the French restorative and pulling up a chair.

"It's worse than that. She's written to Dimitri Pavlovich accusing him and me of murdering the bugger," said Felix

"Well, you did," I said quite reasonably.

"But she's not supposed to know that," said Dimitri.

"Everyone else does," I replied.

"Yes – but no one else would tell the Tsar that we were to be arrested for murder."

"She's done what?" I gasped, "but you're both supposed to be heroes."

"What are we going to do?" moaned Felix.

"I've absolutely no idea but give me an hour and I'll find a solution," I said, as I reckoned that I could be on a train to Helsinki within that time.

"Make it thirty minutes, Charles," said Dimitri, "any longer than that and we'll all – and that includes you - be in the Fortress of Peter & Paul."

Ten minutes later I was back at the Grand Hotel Europe where I rang for Ivan and Fahran.

"Pack!" I said. "We're leaving town now."

"That's not a good idea, Excellency," said Ivan, "a hurried departure from the city would excite suspicion and at the moment only the Grand Duke and Prince Yusupov are implicated in the murder."

"How the hell do you know that?" Ivan said nothing but tapped the side of his nose. "I see," I said, "so what do you advise?"

"Two things, Excellency: first, you should tell the Grand Duke to write to the Tsarina refuting the outrageous accusation and speculating that Rasputin is probably on his way to Siberia - without a body there can't be a murder; second, you should consult with Mr Stopford before you do anything precipitate."

"Very well, but I'm not going back to Dimitri's place, particularly if he's in imminent danger of arrest. I'll send him a note with your advice and you, Ivan, can deliver it. In the meantime, Fahran, can you please find Mr Stopford? I haven't seen him for a couple of days: let's hope he's not fossicking with a Grand Duchess in the Caucasus or the Crimea."

The note was duly delivered and Ivan returned with a reply saying that Dimitri would do as I had suggested. Meanwhile, Fahran had found out that Bertie was once again at Tsarskoe Selo, where he'd been with the Empress for a week, but was expected back at the hotel that evening. Over the next couple of days, a number of things then happened.

First, Bertie told me over dinner on his return for dancing attendance on the Tsarina that I was to sit tight in the hotel and avoid the other conspirators until the fuss had died down, then – as my job in Russia had been successfully completed - he would arrange for me to return to London.

Second, early on the morning of the nineteenth, Rasputin's frozen body was found floating on the Malaya Nevka river. So now the murder was official, which was bloody awkward to say the least.

As Bertie reported, after a visit to Tsarskoe Selo to keep the utterly distraught Empress Consort of All the Russias supplied with black lace-edged hankies, the secret post mortem carried out on the brute showed that he had died of drowning. Given the number of times he had been shot, I found this very hard to believe. However, Bertie was adamant – after all, he'd had it first hand from the Tsarina - that water had been found in Rasputin's lungs, which meant that he must have been alive when we pushed him under the ice. Further, to judge from the state of his hands when he was found, he had tried to claw his way out from under the frozen surface of the river before succumbing to the cold. It was incredible: perhaps the man did have supernatural powers after all. One thing was for certain, however, no one would ever find out as, so Bertie said, in double quick time Rasputin had been embalmed and buried in an unmarked grave at Tsarskoe Selo with – incredibly, given his humble birth - the Tsar, the Tsarina and their four daughters as mourners.

I spent a very dull Christmas confined to the hotel, although not nearly as dull as the Christmases suffered by Felix, who'd been banished by the Tsar with Irina to the Yusupov estates in the Crimea, and Dimitri, who'd demanded a Court Martial but, instead, had been posted to the Russian Army in Persia. Actually, both orders saved their lives, but that is to anticipate. Christmas presents were also in short supply, but nonetheless valuable. Fahran and Ivan clubbed together to buy me a pair of silver candlesticks from Fabergé for the dining room at Mount Street. Unsurprisingly, there was nothing from any of my Russian friends, but Bertie gave me the best present of all: one First and two Second Class tickets for the train to Helsinki and a warrant from the British Ambassador giving me, Fahran and Ivan passage back to England on a British warship.

Unlike the voyage out, the return trip was unremarkable and by late January 1917 I was back at my apartment in Mayfair. Atash met us at the station in a gleaming Daimler and Ivan bade me a tearful farewell on the platform saying that he had to (temporarily) leave my service and attend to his business. Fahran looked rather pleased by this news, although I knew that there wasn't a hint of animosity between the two of them. Back at the flat I found a note from Philip Sassoon informing me that he was on leave from France and asking me to call on him at my 'earliest convenience', which I did the following morning.

"*Mon cher* Brother Charles," said Philip as I was shown into his study by Garton, "I gather from Brother Bertie that you have done particularly well on your first assignment – although whether it will be enough to stop *la deluge en Russie* remains to be seen. The question is what are we going to do with you now?"

"I had rather hoped for a spot of holiday, Great Boanerges…"

"Well how about *un court séjour à Paris*?"

"Paris? In war time?"

"*Bien sûr*, Brother Charles – and, *naturellement,* at the Brotherhood's expense."

"So more in the way of a working holiday, then?"

"Russia has sharpened your senses, *mon brave*. Yes, there is *une petite tâche* that we need you to do whilst enjoying the fleshpots of Pigalle and Montmartre."

"How small?"

"Do you recall that at our first dinner together we discussed a certain Marguerite Meller?"

"Ye-es," I said rather hesitantly. "Didn't Brother Bertie mention her? Isn't she a pretty tart on the make?"

"Correct. You may also recall that I said that this *poule* had ambitions to be a *poule de luxe*."

"I remember something of the sort – but Brother Bertie never mentioned her the whole time we were in St Petersburg."

"He wouldn't have done for, *comme tu le savez*, he has no interest in her sex – unless, of course, she was a Grand Duchess," he added with a laugh. "But we do."

"In what role?"

"As a member of the Brotherhood."

"I didn't know that women could be members."

"There's nothing against it in *les règles*, although she would be the first and she may be the last, but she is necessary to our purpose."

"Which is?"

"To establish once and for all where your friend Mata Hari's ultimate loyalty lies."

"But, as we are reasonably certain that she didn't try and prevent the assassination of Rasputin, I thought we now knew."

"On that affair, she is *en clair*, but there have been other issues where her ultimate *fidélité* is less certain. In particular, we have reason to believe that she has been passing secrets to the Germans learned in the course of her 'duties', *entre les draps*, with the French High Command."

"So, what has Miss Meller got to do with it?"

"Like many of their kind," said Philip, looking a bit as though he was passing an ostrich egg-sized dump, "she and Mata Hari share a *tendresse* for their own sex. It's a form of *vacances* from their day-to-day business on their backs, I suppose. However, these two ladies don't know each other. I need you to engage Miss Meller on our business by giving her a glimpse of the privileges and contacts she will enjoy in the Brotherhood, then, if she agrees, introduce her to Mata Hari – who's staying at Hotel Elysée Palace on the Champs Elysées – and, finally, get her to find out the truth about Mata Hari."

"How on earth will she do that?"

"Where all secrets are freely exchanged, *mon cher Frère Charles* - on the pillow... You will stay for *le déjeuner*, I trust."

So that was it. No sooner had Fahran unpacked my togs in Mount Street than I had to bugger off to Paris to enrol a Parisian hooker into the Brotherhood, introduce her to an ageing Dutch exotic dancer-cum-spy, then get the Pride of the Place Vendôme to seduce the Dutchwoman and thereby induce her to confess to blabbing to the Huns about the secrets that she (Mata Hari) had screwed out of a bunch of Johnny Crapaud Generals. No small task I think you will agree. Well, at least I got to stay (all expenses paid) at the Meurice and Philip said that I could (no, should) take Atash with me (Fahran wanted to come but his elder brother said that it was his turn - and who was I to argue?)

Somewhat to my surprise it all went like a dream. So much so, in fact, that there's no point in relating much of it, beyond noting that Miss Meller was an expert with her lips (a skill that I found out from personal experience and which was to earn her a place in history, as I will in due course relate) and that the Head Porter at the Meurice behaved as though he'd seen a ghost when I checked in. On the latter score, I assumed that my father, who I understood had died in the Ritz, had been a regular at the Meurice before the war, a fact confirmed by Atash with a tear in his eye.

Consequently, I was back in London in time for my eighteenth birthday on 28th February, a day which poor old Mata Hari spent in a Paris prison cell awaiting her trial for treason. She'd been arrested two weeks earlier by the French police on evidence I'd provided to the Deuxième Bureau. This tale of treachery had been sucked out of Mata Hari by Mistress Meller and was then related to me whilst the upwardly mobile French tart serviced my principal asset: how she managed to ingest it up to my pubic hairs without choking I'll never know. Anyway, Margaretha's arrest was an event which, in my view, served her damned-well right for the bitchy note on my performance which she'd left for me on her pillow in the Grand Hotel Europe... You don't cross a Speedicut with impunity.

To celebrate my arrival at the age at which I could be conscripted, Ivan laid on a waist-expanding breakfast in my dining room at Mount Street (catered by his company, Searcy's) and - over coffee - he, Fahran and Atash presented me with a silver porringer to go with my Christmas present. What it was to have rich servants! Needless to say, there wasn't so much as a card from my estranged Mama but there was a large Louis Vuitton trunk, tied around with a red, white and blue bow, from Philip. When I opened it, I found that it contained a complete set of the uniforms required by a Tenth Hussar subaltern (they had been made by Huntsman and fitted me like a glove), The King's Commission appointing me a Second Lieutenant in The Shiners and a letter from Philip wishing me Many Happy Returns etc and telling me to get my arse to Cairo, no later than the end of March, where I was to report to Brother Murray, the Commander-in-Chief of the Egyptian Expeditionary Force.[68]

Murray, so the letter said, would then second me to work with Brother Lawrence, who – so I'd read in *The Times* - was engaged in getting the Arab desert tribes to raid the Hejaz railway, which ran from Damascus to Medina, and so keep tens of thousands of Turkish troops, who might have been deployed fighting us, busy scurrying around Arabia chasing Bedouin shadows. The letter went on:

> *I think you will find it all quite fun and certainly better than the mud of Flanders, which is where you would otherwise have to serve.*
>
> *Brother Murray is a dry old stick and will shortly be replaced, so The Chief tells me, by Allenby who isn't in the Brotherhood but should be.[69] Brother Lawrence is a curious individual, but Operation Emerald (see attached briefing note), is vital to our covert strategy for defeating the Ottomans.*
>
> *Finally, I enclose travel warrants for you and your servant, wish you every good fortune and trust that you will stay in touch.*

---

[68] General Sir Archibald Murray GCB, GCMG, CVO, DSO (1860 –1945)
[69] General (later Field Marshal) Sir Edmund (later 1st Viscount) Allenby GCB, GCMG, GCVO (1861-1936)

You know, in the past sixty or so years more nonsense has been written and said about Ned Lawrence than any other wartime leader whom I can recall. Of slight stature, with a head that was a bit too large for his body, straw-coloured hair, piercing blue eyes, a deceptively self-effacing manner and a pronounced taste for Arab boys and flagellation, Thomas Edward Lawrence, the grammar school-educated bastard son of a Baronet, was first romanticised by the Yankee scribbler, Lowell Thomas, then deliberately self-mythologized in his own book, *The Seven Pillars of Wisdom*. Lawrence went on to be beatified by his supposed withdrawal from public life: Saki's epigram 'If you're going to hide your light under a bushel, make sure people know exactly which bushel it's under', is a perfect description of this phase of Ned's life. To complete the legend, he was sanctified by service in the ranks of the Tank Corps and the RAF, deified by a conveniently early death and then immortalised by my old friend David 'Shagger' Lean, who stole some of *my* best anecdotes for his epic film, *Lawrence of Arabia*.[70]

Although every account of this remarkable and enigmatic poseur carries elements of the truth, no one has ever managed to see all the way through Lawrence's own bullshit or reveal the real reason why he had been inserted into Arabia in the first place. I am now going to do so as it's something I feel well qualified to do - but you must be the judge of that when I have finished.

So, let's go back to the beginning and the briefing note on Operation Emerald, which I read in the First Class compartment of a train to Portsmouth as it trundled away from London with me and Fahran, who was in the role of my orderly, beardless and clad in the guise of a Tenth Hussar Corporal (a detail thoughtfully arranged by Philip).

---

[70] Lowell Thomas (1892-1981), American journalist; *The Seven Pillars of Wisdom* was first published in 1922; H H Munro (1870-1916), aka the satirical author 'Saki'; David (later Sir David) Lean, CBE (1908-1991) English film-maker. His epic biopic, *Lawrence of Arabia*, was first screened in 1962.

TOP SECRET

*BRIEFING NOTE
FOR
BROTHER CHARLES SPEEDICUT, 2ND LIEUTENANT,
XRH
RE
OPERATION EMERALD*

1. *Background:* Before the war your late father uncovered a German plot to raise the Arab tribes of the Ottoman Empire in a Muslim Jihad or Holy War against the Infidel (i.e. the British) and thereby oust us from control of Egypt, the Suez Canal and India. The plot required the leadership of a mythical Islamic figure known variously as 'Kasredin, 'the Chosen One', 'Greenmantle' or 'the Emerald' (see para 2 below). The Germans believed, incorrectly, that your father, who had spent some time as a captive of Muhammad Ahmad a.k.a. The Mahdi (the last man to claim to be the 'Chosen One'),[71] knew of the existence of The Mahdi's only son whom the Germans believed could be the man to declare the requisite Jihad. Your father's advanced years precluded him from any further active engagement in uncovering and defeating this German plot and the task was passed to Brother Arbuthnot, who recently disappeared (presumed killed) whilst on undercover duties in the Levant. Importantly, up to the moment we lost contact with Brother Arbuthnot he had not, over a period of four years, been able to substantiate the existence of The Mahdi's son nor had he found any evidence that the Germans had been able to advance their plans in respect of initiating a Jihad against us in the region.

2. *The Legend of the Kasredin:* To explain the legend, we can do no better than reproduce an extract of a report written for the Brotherhood by your late father, in his customarily robust style, concerning a conversation he had with a senior member of the Prussian Secret Service in 1912:

    "I told Major von Stumm

---

[71] Muhammad Ahmad bin Abd Allah (1844-1885). See *The Speedicut Papers: Book 7 (Royal Scandals) & Book 9 (Boxing Icebergs).*

My heart lurched at the mention of a name that was all too familiar to me, but I read on:

> *that the legend of Kasredin is a Turkish folk tale which states that a great leader, known as 'the Emerald' or 'Greenmantle', will rise out of the desert and lead the faithful in a holy war to drive the infidel – which, surprisingly given that they are all Mussulmen, includes the Ottomans - from the face of the earth. It's the same twaddle as the Jews' belief in a Messiah or the rubbish proclaimed by Muhammad Ahmad, of late but unlamented memory, who told me that he would reveal himself as the Emerald once he'd slaughtered every Turk between Khartoum and Constantinople.*
>
> *The legend of Kasredin is, of course, religious moonshine but the arse-scratching fellaheen believe it. However, it's worth noting that they also believe that the earth is flat, that banking, tobacco and alcohol are a sin and that women are neither to be seen nor heard (thinking about it, they could be right on that last one). Of course, if the legend could be made reality and then harnessed by Europeans – as I believe the Germans plan - it might be used to great effect in the affairs of the Ottoman and our own Mussulmen-infected Empires. However, in my experience, you would have an easier job herding cats or getting the Irish to stop talking."*

3. *The Arab Revolt: Last June, thanks to a treaty negotiated by a Turkish deserter,[72] we managed to persuade Sherif Hussein bin Ali, Emir & Grand Sherif of Mecca,[73] to raise the flag of revolt against Ottoman rule in Arabia. To date, the so-called Arab Revolt has enjoyed a distinct lack of success. This is partly because Sherif Hussein's Bedouin forces, under the leadership of his son Emir Faisal,[74] are ill-equipped and, more importantly, because only a limited number of the tribes of the region have thrown in their lot with the Revolt. In fact, the majority of the tribes have remained loyal to the Ottomans, who pay them handsomely for so doing. Consequently, whilst Arabia, the Levant & the northern half of Mesopotamia remain under Ottoman control, the*

---

[72] Lieutenant Muhammed Sharif al-Faruqi (1891-1920).
[73] Sherif Hussein bin Ali (1854-1931).
[74] Emir (later King) Faisal bin Hussein bin Ali al-Hashimi, (1885-1933)

Egyptian Expeditionary Force ('EEF') is unable, with the EEF's right flank and rear held by the enemy, to advance from Gaza to take Jerusalem and Damascus and so roll-up the Levant, open the back door to Constantinople and a second British Front in eastern Europe, thereby relieving pressure on our embattled Russian and French allies.

4. *Operation Emerald: Although it seems clear that the Germans have failed in their attempt to set the Middle East ablaze by finding (if indeed he ever existed) and then using the son of The Mahdi in the guise of the Emerald, it is nonetheless a sound plan. Indeed, in the Brotherhood's hands, it could be used as the means of making the Arab Revolt effective. The objective of Operation Emerald is, therefore, to find or create our own Kasredin and use him to unite the Arab tribes against the Ottoman Empire. This initiative is being led by Brother Lawrence, who is in possession of £30,000 of the Brotherhood's gold to bribe the Bedouin as necessary, is a hugely experienced Arabist and knows his way around the Bedouin tribes; the latter fact being the principal reason why he was placed by the Brotherhood with Brother Clayton's Arab Bureau (since 1916 part of the Intelligence Staff in Cairo) and is now attached,[75] in the field, to the forces of the Emir Faisal although he continues to report for operational purposes to the Arab Bureau.*

5. *Your role: Brother Clayton reports that Brother Lawrence is something of a maverick, which is both a strength and a weakness when it comes to the successful execution of Operation Emerald and is lax in his reporting to Cairo on both operational and Brotherhood business. We are concerned, for example, that Brother Lawrence has lost sight of the <u>means</u> of implementing the objectives of Operation Emerald, although - for the time being - we remain confident that he has not lost sight of the <u>ends</u>. Your role is, therefore: (1) whilst acting as Brother Lawrence's deputy, to send the Brotherhood in London confidential reports on his motives, actions and future plans as they relate to Operation Emerald in particular and Arabia & the Levant in general; and (2) to encourage Brother Lawrence to identify (or appoint covertly) from amongst the Arab tribal leaders a man who would be credible as the Emerald and then so promote him.*

---

[75] Brigadier General (later Sir) Gilbert Clayton CB (1875-1929).

For those of you who haven't visited Cairo, particularly in wartime, I wouldn't recommend it: the pyramids and the Sphinx are impressive enough but the rest of it reeks. As we approached Alexandria on a Royal Navy destroyer, Fahran told me that my father liked Cairo and Alexandria, although he did qualify that by saying that the old boy had had the advantage of being the honoured guest of the then Khedive's youngest brother, which probably made a difference; unfortunately, Fahran wouldn't elaborate on what that difference was. I had no such advantage, although the GHQ Mess in the capital of the Sultanate (we'd annexed Egypt when the Turks came into the war, kicked out the Khedive and installed another brother of my Papa's chum on the throne as the first Sultan)[76] was comfortable enough in a colonial sort of way. Beyond its gates, however, lay a sprawling, stinking city crawling with diseased beggars and filthy light-fingered urchins; it was a bit like Glasgow on a sunny day. You know, I can't think why we bother with the place - Scotland that is - it's a land of appalling weather populated by whinging benefit scroungers and its sole exports are a revolting drink and even more revolting politicians. Well, how else would you describe Drambuie and Ramsay MacDonald? If the heathen Jocks ever ask for independence we should give it to them in a flash. Come to think of it, we should give it to them anyway; at the very least it would allow Howe to cut income tax by ten percent.[77] But back to Cairo.

As instructed, I reported to the HQ of the Egyptian Expeditionary Force in Cairo, where General Murray was still – just - in the saddle (Allenby didn't arrive until mid-June 1917). He was holed up in a grand office and looked distinctly grumpy when I presented myself for duty.

"Ah, Brother Speedicut," he said once his ADC, a Captain in the Royal Inniskilling Fusiliers, had left the room, "any relation to that turd in the Shiners who I served with in South Africa?"

---

[76] Editor's Note: Speedicut *père*'s friend was Prince Ali, youngest brother of Khedive Tewfik Pasha (1852-1892). Tewfik was succeeded by his eldest son, Khedive Abbas II (1874-1944). Abbas II was deposed by the British in 1914 in favour of his uncle, Hussein Kamel (1853-1917), who remained on the Egyptian throne until he died in October 1917.

[77] The Rt Hon Geoffrey (later Lord) Howe (born 1926). This reference indicates that this memoir was written after the General Election of 4th May 1979.

"If you are referring to my late father, Brother Murray, then the answer is yes." I said through pursed lips; it was not a good start. Murray harrumphed and changed the subject.

"I gather from the Great Boanerges that you have recently been useful to the Brotherhood in Russia and that he has arranged for you to be posted here as a reward." I said nothing as my family pride was still hurt. "Hmm. Young fellows like you should be on the Western Front, not poodle-faking out here – but let that be," he said waving his hand dismissively. "So, the Great Boanerges wants you to join Brother Lawrence in the desert, does he?"

"I believe that is correct."

"Hmm," he said again, "well, you'll have to find him first." He rang a bell on his desk and the ADC sloped back in. "Where is Captain Lawrence, O'Gorman?"

"In Arabia, sir."

"I know that, you bloody fool: but *where* in Arabia?"

"The last we heard from him, sir, he was heading for Abu el-Naam," said O'Gorman after he'd leafed through a folder.

"Where in God's name is that?" barked Murray.

"It is, I believe, sir," he consulted his notes again, "a station on the Hejaz railway some hundred and fifty miles north of Medina."

"There you are, Speedicut: Abu el-Naam's your destination. Well, trot along then – Medina's a thousand miles from here, so you should find Lawrence this side of Christmas - although why you or anyone else would want to bother I can't think. This whole bloody theatre's a side show and Lawrence's Boy Scout antics with the Arabs are a side show of a side show..."

"But how am I to get to Abu el-Naam, General?" I said.

"Don't call me 'General', Speedicut: I am accustomed to being addressed as 'sir'."

"Certainly, General," I replied.

I may have been only recently commissioned but I knew that no self-respecting Shiner used the 's' word, besides which I was still smarting from his insult to my father. Nonetheless, it looked for a moment as though the C-in-C would explode, as the colour in his mottled cheeks changed from pink to purple. O'Gorman shuffled his feet whilst Murray gave my cavalry boots and britches a withering glance. Then, reflecting perhaps on the superiority of *l'arme blanche* to the PBI or, more likely, realising that I was close to Philip Sassoon, he decided not to pursue the subject of my impertinence.

"I haven't the faintest idea how you'll get there," he said at last whilst picking up some papers off his desk. When I didn't move he spoke again, this time rather testily to his ADC. "Oh, very well. O'Gorman, make the arrangements for Mr Speedicut to join up with Captain Lawrence, would you? Then bring me the latest cargo manifest for that arms shipment which has just docked in Alexandria - I'm trying to fight a war here, not arrange bloody holiday outings for teenagers." O'Gorman touched my elbow and I dutifully followed him out of the C-in-C's office.

"Sorry about that, Speedicut," he said once he'd sat me down in his own office and offered me a cup of tea. "It wasn't wise to rile him, no matter what the provocation: the General's never been much fun but, since he heard that he's to be recalled, he's been like a bear with a sore head. Now, how the hell *are* we going to get you to Lawrence?" He thought for a moment. "Can you ride a camel?"

CHAPTER FOURTEEN: THE GARDEN OF A THOUSAND DELIGHTS

"Do you know how to ride a camel, Fahran?" I asked my valet when I got back to my room in the Mess.

"I do, huzoor. I had to learn when I accompanied your father on the late Lord Kitchener's Nile Expedition in 1898."[78]

"How difficult is it?"

"Not *too* difficult, huzoor, it just takes a bit of practice."

"Could I master it in a week?"

"Possibly, huzoor, but why only a week?"

"Because that's all we've got before we set off to join Captain Lawrence in Arabia."

"And how are we going to get there, huzoor?"

"Emir Faisal's Bedouin army – which the chaps here don't much rate since it got a bloody nose trying to take Medina - has recently managed to secure Yenbo on the coast of the Red Sea, due west of Medina. We're to take the train to Suez and from there the Navy will ferry us to the port, where we'll be met by an Arab guide with camels. From there we ride to Captain Lawrence's camp which, so the Staff here understands, is somewhere to the north of a railway station called Abu el-Naam, which Lawrence is due to attack. No one seems to know if we'll meet up with him before he does, but..." I trailed off rather lamely.

---

[78] See: *The Speedicut Papers: Book 8 (At War with Churchill)*.

"If you can give me some gold, huzoor, I'll go down to the market and see if I can buy us a couple of good camels for you to learn on - and some clothes."

I should have asked Fahran why we needed clothes, as we'd arrived from England with a couple of steamer trunks full of uniforms and civvies. It was only when, the following morning, he woke me with a cup of tea in one hand, a heap of strange clothes over his other arm and the news that my camel awaited me by the front steps of the Mess that I thought to ask.

"What are you doing with all those?" I asked pointing at the linen.

"They are your new robes, huzoor."

"What do I want with robes, Fahran?" He put down the tea by my bed and held up what looked like a pair of substantial pyjama trousers, a nightshirt and a dressing gown made of a heavy white fabric edged with gold lace, a coil of black and gold rope, a fancy checked and fringed dishcloth, an elaborate belt, a long riding whip and a pair of short, soft leather boots.

"These are the wedding robes of a Sherif of the Beni Sakhr, huzoor. They were the only ones I could find in the market that are suitable for you to wear."

"I wouldn't be seen dead in them, Fahran, besides which I'll be drummed out of the Mess if I'm caught wearing them."

"Be that as it may, huzoor, you will find – as did your father - that they are much more comfortable to wear than British Army uniform when you are riding a camel in the desert and a lot safer when you are behind enemy lines."

"And what will you be wearing?"

"Need you ask, huzoor? My father's Afghan robes, of course!"

Half an hour later I went down the back stairs of the Mess to the kitchen entrance, whence I had directed Fahran to take the camels – well, I wasn't going to risk a ribbing from my fellow Subalterns when they saw me dressed up as Ali Baba, nor was I going to make a public display of myself trying to mount a camel.

In the event, my first camel-riding lesson was a disaster. I'd only ever encountered the animals as a child, at the Zoological Gardens in Regent's Park with my Mama, and then only from a safe distance. Up close they were unappealing to say the least. The two that Fahran had acquired, along with a Nubian handler who couldn't have been more than twelve and apparently came as part of the purchase, were reasonably well groomed and lavishly saddled. However, the haughty look in my mount's heavily lashed eyes, and a curled lip that exposed long, ribbed and dirty fangs, was not encouraging.

"A word of caution, huzoor," said Fahran as the little black boy brought forward my beast. "Camels have vile tempers and are prone to spitting, biting and kicking when out of sorts, which is most of the time. The best way to avoid injury is to allow your handler to make the camel kneel, then mount and take control of the animal with the reins and your whip. Should the camel start to swing his head around, correct it with the whip before he removes your knee cap with his teeth. In fact, as you will see, you use the whip on his neck for all commands – kneeling, rising, walking, trotting and galloping."

"What about stopping?" I asked.

"For that – and for turning – you use the reins, huzoor."

"And how am I supposed to sit on that?" I said pointing at the blanket-covered, doubled-pommelled footstool that was strapped atop my beast's hump.

"There are two ways, huzoor. The Army sit astride the saddle as though riding a horse, but the locals prefer to crook the right leg around the front saddle post and lock it under the left leg – a bit like the way an English lady rides side-saddle. It's a more comfortable and secure way to ride, providing one is wearing robes."

Light started to dawn on why Fahran had insisted I wear fancy dress.

"So, if you would like to mount, huzoor, we can start the lesson."

By this time my camel was collapsed on the dusty cobbles of the kitchen yard, with his legs folded under him and his head held high on a curved neck. Getting into the recommended riding position was easy, although I saw a nasty gleam in the ungulate's eyes as I clambered aboard.

"To make your camel stand, huzoor, tap it lightly once on the neck, but take care, the camel will raise its rear end first and it will tip you... Too late, huzoor! Dust yourself down and try again, but this time hold on to the pommel."

As I spat dirt out of my mouth and swallowed my wounded pride, the little Nubian boy who'd clung-on to the reins as I'd mounted, tapped the beast on the neck with his own whip and the camel once again lowered itself back to the ground with a surly grump.

"Now try again, huzoor," said Fahran patiently. "Get a good grip with your leg, hold on to the post – that's right - now tap *gently* with your whip."

This time I was prepared for the fore and aft lurch and managed to stay in the saddle.

"Good, huzoor," said Fahran encouragingly as his own camel rose to the upright. "Now follow me – and remember to use the reins for turning and stopping and the whip for pace and dismounting."

"But how will it know if I want to dismount or speed up?" I asked.

"Another good question, huzoor – by the way, go with the swaying motion of the camel as it moves – it's much more comfortable that way. Watch me." He tapped his camel on the neck and it started moving forward with a rolling kind of gait and Fahran rolled with it. As he moved away from me I realised that he hadn't answered my earlier question.

"So how do I make it move?" I shouted to his retreating back. He craned around and shouted back:

"Hit it on the neck with your whip and say 'hut, hut, hut'…"

I did as he instructed. Thank God, my right leg was firmly locked around the saddle post. Had it not been I would have shot out of the back door and probably broken my back on the cobbles ten feet below. As it was, I remained in the saddle as I flew past Fahran at a gallop. Mud houses flashed by me on either side as the bloody camel headed down the road towards a bridge over a canal; on the other side, and coming towards me fast, I could see a large, opened-back lorry full of British soldiers. It was immediately clear to me that there was insufficient room for us to pass each other in safety and, as the distance between us closed, I was faced with a head on collision and certain death. I vaguely heard shouting behind me as I hauled on both reins to try and slow the camel's forward momentum. Nothing happened except that a short trip to Eternity got closer and closer. Desperately, I hauled on the right rein to the point where both of the beast's eyes were looking at me. Fortunately, this had the effect of making it swerve to the right towards the banks of the canal.

They say that, in moments of danger, your life flashes before you. Mine didn't, but it did occur to me to wonder if camels could swim. However, before I could find out, the bugger applied its brakes so suddenly that I was ejected forwards out of the saddle, sailed over its head, described a gentle arc through the air and, with my robes billowing behind me, plunged head-first into the murky depths of the waterway. As my head broke back though the surface the only thing of which I was conscious was the raucous laughter and obscene language of the Tommies in the truck.

"Enjoyin' yer fuckin' swim, Mustapha?" jeered one.

"Nah," said another, "those fucking Gyppos can't even do the fucking doggy-paddle."

"It's the first fucking bath the fucker's had this fucking year," yelled another.

"Are you alright, huzoor?" I heard Fahran call to me as I swam towards the bank, where my camel was grazing on some shrivelled grass which it washed down with great sucks of water from the canal.

"Yes," I managed to call back as he approached at a trot, "but that's the end of the lesson for today, Fahran."

I walked back to the Mess in a bedraggled state and managed to slip up to my room without being seen. A short while later, as I towelled myself dry and then pulled on a cotton dressing gown, Fahran appeared looking distinctly sheepish.

"It could have been worse, huzoor..."

"You mean I could have collided with the lorry?"

"Err, yes, huzoor – or fallen onto the road. As it is, there is no damage done and your robes will soon dry."

"If you think for one moment, Fahran, that I'm ever again climbing aboard one of those smelly brutes then you must be mad."

"But, huzoor, how will we get to Captain Lawrence's camp?"

"Frankly, Fahran, I don't know and I don't care – but I will tell you this: if it comes to it, I'd rather crawl across the Empty Quarter than sit on one more camel."

But, of course, I did get back on the beast later that day, although I prepared myself for the ordeal with a liquid lunch. By the time Fahran traded the camels and our Nubian back into hard cash in the Cairo camel market a week later, I was a sore but reasonably proficient jockey.

On the morning of our departure, Fahran stowed our surplus kit in the trunks, which he lodged for safekeeping with the Mess Sergeant, and we set off for Cairo Central in a rickety carosse. The journey by rail to Suez was hot but unremarkable, Suez itself was an even hotter dump and it was with some relief that we boarded a Royal Navy patrol boat which whisked us down the Red Sea towards our destination. There was nothing much to do on board, so I loafed off to the Wardroom where I found and then leafed through a couple of dull tomes. One was an unreadable treatise on metaphysics, whatever they were, and the other an obscure dissertation on something called the paranormal. After a couple of minutes, I returned them both to the shelf and picked up a well-thumbed copy of *The Illustrated London News* instead. God-only knows how the two books had found their way onto HMS *Ignoramus*: in my experience, as evidenced by the over-used state of the *ILN*, most sailors can't even read.

If Suez was a dump, Yenbo was dump *de luxe*. The Lieutenant in command of our tub, a handsome fellow in his twenties with an unfortunate German moniker that sounded like the name of a marzipan-covered, multi-coloured sponge cake,[79] had warned us that he would linger only long enough to drop Fahran and me on what passed for a quay before shooting off back to the safety of Suez. Quite how we were to meet up with our guide he didn't say and then I realised that no one had seen fit to tell us back in Cairo. Actually, I'd forgotten to ask. I assumed, I suppose, that someone looking not unlike a representative of Thomas Cook would be there to meet us, clip board in hand and with an envelope containing a map and a route card...

Unfortunately, as the sun set like a ripe orange over the limpid waters of the Red Sea, no such figure appeared to greet Fahran and me as we stood, feeling somewhat foolish, on a rotten wooden pier in our Shiners' shorts, shirts and pith helmets with our Arab robes in the bags at our

---

[79] Editor's Note: The Royal Navy officer in question must have been His Serene Highness Lieutenant Prince George of Battenberg (later 2nd Marquess of Milford Haven) (1892-1938). Speedicut's post-World War I friend, Lord Louis Mountbatten (formerly HSH Prince Louis of Battenberg and later Earl Mountbatten of Burma) (1900-1979) was serving as a Midshipman with the Grand Fleet at the time.

feet. Since I could only speak the most basic Arabic, and Fahran's was terribly rusty, we couldn't even ask for directions and anyway what would we have said: 'please show me the way to the guide who is to take us to Captain Lawrence'? Even if Fahran had managed that, I doubt he would have understood the reply.

I was beginning to think that the only solution would be to take a seat in the waterside hovel fifty yards away that looked like Yenbo's only cafe (and that was stretching the imagination) in the hope that our uniforms would attract the attention of our guide. I was about to propose this to Fahran when a beggar in filthy robes, with a grizzled beard and a patch over one eye, rose from a coil of rope on the dockside and slowly dragged himself over towards us with the obvious intention of soliciting some small change.

"*Imshi!*" growled Fahran.

"No, wait a moment, Fahran," I said as a distant memory suddenly came flooding back to me. If I remembered rightly, from what little reading I'd done at Eton, the one-eyed beggar was always the undercover agent in the works of Strider Hagrid or was it John Buckup? Perhaps both. Yes, I thought, it was just such a person who had been the vital contact in *The King of Sheba's Mineshaft* or was it *Buster John*?[80] I couldn't remember. Anyway, I was damned sure that our Military Intelligence knew those stories back to front, assumed that I did and that this evil-looking sub-specie limping his way towards us was our man. I said as much to Fahran and added: "Let's see what he wants."

When he reached us, the reek from his rags, made worse by the intense humidity of the evening, was almost too much to bear and I nearly joined Fahran in telling the man to fuck off. But he was our only hope, so instead I gave him an enquiring look.

---

[80] Editor's Note: I think Speedicut is referring to *King Solomon's Mines* by H Rider Haggard (1856-1925), published in 1885 or *Prester John* by John Buchan (1875-1940) published in 1910.

"Engl-eesh?" he whined. Well, that was a good start, so I nodded. "Jigjig?" Was that, I wondered, the password which Cairo had forgotten to give me? It seemed likely, so I nodded again. He turned and gestured that we should follow him.

"Come on Fahran," I said to my valet, "get the bags. He's obviously our guide or, please God, he's not but he's going to lead us to him."

Fahran looked doubtful and started to protest, but I was having none of his doubts and set off in pursuit of the beggar who was, rather surprisingly, now setting a cracking pace. Fahran had no choice but to sling his rifle, pick up our bags and tag along behind me.

In no time at all we were in the town, which was a maze of tiny, unpaved streets dimly lit at intervals by reeking oil lamps. But where the pavements should have been there were open sewers beyond which were mud brick houses with overhanging wooden balconies that almost touched each other across the uneven road. Had it not been for the appalling pong, it would have been quaint - pretty even - like a scene of Bethlehem from one of those illustrated texts one was given at Sunday School. However, as we walked deeper and deeper into this stinking labyrinth, I started to worry that I was wrong and Fahran's doubts were justified. So, I surreptitiously unfastened the loop that held my Service revolver in place in its leather holster. Thank God, I thought to myself, that I'd had the foresight to load the shooter before we'd disembarked.

We'd just turned the hundredth corner, and I was about to tell Fahran that I had made a mistake and that we should ditch the beggar and make our way back to the port, when the bundle of rags in front of me stopped abruptly and a filthy hand poked out from the tattered robes, pointed at a hanging carpet over a door on our left and was then poked itself in our direction, palm upwards. The meaning was clear: we were at our destination and the bugger wanted to be paid. I flipped him a small coin and he disappeared like shit down a crapper.

From within the house I could hear strange, wailing music, which was actually quite inviting. I turned to consult with Fahran but, before I could do so, there was the sound of a woman's laughter from above me and I caught a most welcome whiff of an exotic perfume. We both looked up and there was a busty bint clad in baggy pyjama trousers made from a brightly coloured material, above which she had a bare midriff, topped by a large pair of bristols barely held in place by a silver scarf that was tied around her like a cross-over halter. The lower half of her face was hidden behind a skimpy bit of gauze, indeed the only bits of her face which were visible below a low hanging, coin-hung head-band were her eyes, which were large and rimmed with kohl. She gave us a long hard look, stretched down her right arm in our direction, crooked and un-crooked her index finger then disappeared back into the house. It was an obvious invitation to enter.

"What do you think, Fahran?"

"I don't know, huzoor. Is it likely that our guide would be in such a place?"

"What sort of place?"

"Well, it's obviously a brothel, huzoor."

"A brothel? Is that right? Gosh, it might be fun…" At this point, you should remember that I was only eighteen and, although I knew my way around, I'd never before been to a whore house.

"And dangerous, huzoor – to your health if not to your life."

"You mean it's probably staffed by poxed-up tarts of the sort that hang around Seven Dials?"

"Something like that, huzoor."

"But we don't have to screw them, Fahran. Perhaps the madam speaks English and can direct us to a hotel."

"In this town, huzoor?"

"No, you're probably right, but she might get someone to lead us back to the port and we can hang around there until our guide shows up."

"Or, more likely, we pay a fisherman to take us back to Suez."

"Well, we won't make any progress to Lawrence or Cairo by standing here."

"No, huzoor."

"In that case, forrard on..."

With a show of reluctance, Fahran picked up our bags, pushed aside the carpet curtain with his elbow, shouldered open the door and walked in with me behind him. We found ourselves in what I can only describe as a scene from the Russian ballet. On the floor in front of us was a large Persian carpet on which were placed, at angles, a series of silk covered oriental-style sofas covered in tasselled cushions, all of which had seen better days. Draped across two of these divans were women dressed virtually identically to the one we'd seen on the balcony outside; neither looked up as we entered, instead they continued to draw on hookahs, which bubbled pleasantly and from whose burners curled a bluish and very fragrant smoke. Behind the divans, on a wooden table, I could see an old-fashioned gramophone, with a large horn, on which a record of native music bumped along under a large stylus holder. The walls were all hung with carpets and from the low ceiling was suspended a cluster of coloured-glass lanterns which threw rainbow-coloured light around the room. As my eyes became accustomed to the gloom, the woman from the balcony reappeared at the back of the room.

"Welcome, Engl-eesh - to the Garden of a Thousand Delights."

"You speak English?"

"A lee-tle. What is it that you seek? Girls? Boys? Both? Or perhaps our donkey?"

"Well, actually..." What the hell was I going to say next? I could hardly say that I was looking for a guide to take us to Lawrence. "Err, only a bed for the night."

"Then you have come to the right place, Engl-eesh," she purred. "Follow me." I threw a glance at Fahran who merely raised his eyebrows, so I did as instructed and trailed after the madam's swaying rump to the back of the room, through a beaded curtain and up a rickety flight of stairs. "Together or separate?" I look again at Fahran who mouthed 'together'.

"One room for the two of us will be just fine," I said as the lady of the house pushed open a door. Inside there were no beds, but another carpet and yet more piles of cushions. On a table between the pillows were a washbasin, a jug and a tall, lit candle. "Sleep well, Engl-eesh," our hostess said as she closed the door behind her.

"It could be worse, Fahran," I said, without much conviction, "And in the morning, we can make our way back to the port, find the British Consulate and arrange a passage back to Suez."

"I think you'll find, huzoor, that there isn't a consulate of any description in this tip."

"Perhaps you're right," I said somewhat crestfallen at this obvious rebuke, "but let's get our heads down and we can review the situation in the morning."

Within thirty minutes Fahran was snoring gently, but loud enough to keep me half-awake. At some point, however, I must have drifted off and I found myself in a rather confusing sort of dream in which Fahran was crawling around the room on all-fours wearing soaking wet robes. He had a camel saddle on his back and was telling me to climb aboard, but I couldn't as I was being indecently engaged by one of the veiled girls from the room below. Although we were both fully dressed, she was kneeling over my prone form, her well-filled bodice dangling over my face whilst she fumbled with my flies. I reached up one hand to give her boobies a good fondling but she brushed it away, so with my other I went on a quest between the well-muscled thighs I could feel under her loose silk trousers, whilst she flipped out my by now rather over-excited dick.

Given the girl's obvious profession, I had been taken aback somewhat by her not allowing me free rein with her tits and, despite what she was doing to me with both her hands, I decided not to take anything for granted. So, instead of making a headlong assault on her Aladdin's cave, I allowed my hand to slide up slowly between her legs. Imagine my surprise when I reached their junction and, instead of feeling beneath the soft fabric the entrance to her pleasure garden, I encountered what was undoubtedly a pair of large balls. The shock was so great that I woke up.

Kneeling over me was the girl in my dream. She disengaged with my middle leg, put a finger to her veiled lips, appeared to write something on a piece of paper, dropped the note on the cushion beside me and vanished from the room.

CHAPTER FIFTEEN: TO LAWRENCE IN ARABIA

In the dim light from the candle I unfolded the note and read:

I will send you to Lawrence in the morning. Arbuthnot. MI6.

I read the note again, for its brief contents were so astonishing that for a moment or two I thought I might still be dreaming. But I wasn't. I adjusted my dress and then gave Fahran a nudge; he woke up somewhat groggily.

"What is it, huzoor?"

"Read this," I said passing him the paper without further explanation. He held it up to the candle and read.

"How did you get it, huzoor?"

"No idea," I lied, "I heard a noise, woke up, saw one of the tarts we passed earlier leaving our room and then I found it."

"I should have bolted the door – my father would never forgive me if we had been murdered in our beds."

"Well, fortunately we weren't and your father is no longer here to chastise you."

"I wouldn't be so sure about that, huzoor."

"Let's not get hung up on metaphysical speculation, Fahran."

"What's metaphysics got to do with anything, huzoor?"

"Do you know, I've absolutely no idea. In fact, I don't even know what metawhatsits are. It must be something I read somewhere. Anyway, enough of this pointy-headed nonsense: it looks as though we have, after all, stumbled on our man."

"I thought you said that it was a woman who left you the note, huzoor?"

"I did, but…" I could hardly tell him what had actually happened, "but…" and then the answer came to me, "I, err, know from the Brotherhood's briefing note that Arbuthnot is a man. So, she must have been running an errand for him. Anyway, it doesn't matter. The fact is that this Arbuthnot fellow is going to get us to Captain Lawrence and that's the main thing."

Fahran once again adopted his doubtful look, this time tinged with scepticism. Did he guess that I had not told him the entire truth? If so, he didn't say. Instead, he got up, piled some cushions in front of the door, borrowed my revolver and then slumped back down at the base of the door with the weapon clutched in his hand.

"There will be no more intruders this evening, huzoor. Sleep well." I did, although the dream which followed was quite unprintable.

The following morning, we were woken by the plangent wail of a *muezzin* calling the Faithful to their dawn prayers. My wrist watch, a Christmas gift from Philip, confirmed that it was six o'clock. Fahran, ever the attentive servant, poured some water from the jug into the bowl and offered to shave me.

"In cold water, Fahran? I think not. Besides which, shouldn't we be growing beards to go with our robes?"

"A good idea, huzoor – and we should change into them. But you will still want to wash your face and brush your teeth, surely?"

So, I splashed water on my face, rubbed some tooth powder around my gums with the tip of my index finger and then exchanged my uniform for my guise as an Arab Sheikh. Fahran did the same.

"That will have to do, Fahran. How do I look?"

"You will pass, huzoor, providing you keep your lower face covered with the *keffiyeh*."

"Like this?"

"Excellent, huzoor."

"Good. We can brush up properly once we get to Lawrence's camp."

"Assuming that they have a bathroom, huzoor, which I think is unlikely..."

Before he could make any further comments on the probable lack of the usual trappings of civilization chez Lawrence there was a sharp rap on the door. Without thinking, I drew the pistol which I'd just recovered from Fahran and pointed it at the oak.

"Open it," I whispered. He did so. Standing silhouetted there was the veiled woman of my dreams. No, let me re-phrase that: it was the woman who had visited me during the night, at least I thought it was although it might have been the brothel keeper, assuming that they weren't one and the same person. I then noticed that she was holding a tray on which there was an oriental coffee pot, two handle-less cups and a pile of *baklava* on a glass plate.

"Break your fast want you, effendi?" she asked without any preamble or the trace of a Scotch accent. She didn't sound like the madam who'd met us the night before, so was it Arbuthnot? There was no way of telling without making a grab for her crotch. Whoever she was, she certainly didn't seem surprised by our dress or the sight of my pistol pointed at her guts; at least it didn't show it in her eyes, which were all of her face that I could see.

"Err, that would be good. Thank you. Take the tray would you, Fahran?" He did as I asked but the bint remained where she was.

"El Aurens you seek?" was it a question or a statement? I couldn't be sure.

"Who?" I asked.

"The officer Engl-eesh the Bedu who leads." Did she mean Lawrence? Her strangely inverted English was not easy to understand but who else could she be talking about?

"We do," I said, keeping my gun levelled at her slightly hairy belly button.

"Camels and your Bedu guide behind this house there are. Ride you can?" I nodded. "Good. Food and water are there for days four. To El Aurens the guide you will take."

"Thank you," I said. "Can our guide English be speaking?" Damn, her quaint phrasing was catching. "I mean, does he speak English?"

"Enough," she said. Then, without a further word, she turned on her heel and left.

"What do you think, Fahran? Is it a trap?"

"There's only one way to find out, huzoor. Besides which, what choice do we have?"

"None," I said, "but let's at least meet our fate on a full stomach. We didn't eat last night and I'm starving." It didn't take long for us to polish off everything on the tray before we were ready to go. "Well, Fahran, once more unto the beach..."

"I think you mean 'breach', huzoor."

"No, Fahran, I mean *beach* – sandy things just like the desert we're off to..."

"There weren't any beaches at Agincourt, huzoor."

"Who said anything about Agincourt?"

"I assumed you are quoting from *Henry V*, huzoor..."

"Why would I do that? I was making a joke. Anyway, if you want me to quote from *Henry V* – 'lead on, Macduff'!"

"It was 'Lay on, Macduff,' huzoor – and it's from *Macbeth*," he said quietly and with a hint of exasperation, but he picked up our bags and left the room nonetheless. Was I the only gentleman in Arabia to have a well-heeled valet who was also well-educated? I made a mental note to ask Fahran, if we survived the day, where, how and why he'd learnt all this stuff.

In the event there were no problems, at least not initially. As room service had promised, a Bedouin with three moth-eaten camels was waiting for us in the dusty alleyway that ran behind the knocking shop. He was a handsome, dark-skinned cut-throat, probably not much older than me, clad entirely in rough brown robes with a hooked nose, a tightly-cropped beard and a hawk-like gleam in his eyes. Over his shoulder was slung a British Lee-Enfield rifle, criss-crossed over his *thobe* were a pair of ammunition bandoliers and around his waist was a leather belt into which was secured a curved dagger. He looked as though he had stepped straight out of the *Thousand & One Nights*.

"Greetings, effendi, I am thy servant, Soadad al-Obeid," he said as he touched his forehead, lips and heart with his right hand in the traditional Arab greeting. "Thou wishes me, *insha'Allah*, to take thee and thine," he said nodding towards Fahran whom he looked at leerily, "to the camp of El Aurens."

"I do," I said.

"Then mount, effendi, and prepare thyself to ride north."

I'd looked at the map before we'd left Cairo and reckoned that we would find Lawrence after a couple of days... Four days later, and despite a number of rather spirited camel races with our guide, we had not arrived and I had started to question whether or not Master Soadad knew what he was doing or where he was going. When I questioned Fahran on the subject he, however, had been reassuring.

"We must be going north, huzoor, for we keep the sun on our backs."

That was true enough, but with nothing but flat sand stretching endlessly to our front I was beginning to wonder if that was sufficient navigational data.

"Surely, we should have picked up the tracks of the Hejaz railway line by now, Fahran?"

"Patience, huzoor. The desert is a big place."

"You can say that again, Fahran." But he didn't.

The time it was taking to connect with the British-led Bedouin raiding party was, however, less of a worry than the state of our rations which, although virtually inedible, were running low: a diet of dried camel meat is only slightly more appealing than one of toasted camel dung. Worse still, we had only a few drops of water left in our goat bladder water containers. I raised this problem with Soadad.

"Worry not, effendi. We will reach a well long before nightfall."

And, somewhat to my surprise, we did; although how the hell he found it I'll never know, for there was only a small pile of stones in the seemingly endless sand to mark the wellhead.

We downed the camels and, whilst I got out my Army issue compass to check that we were still headed north, Fahran and Soadad took the skins over to the well and, using some rope which our guide had thoughtfully brought with him, dropped them into the depths. I had the prismatic compass to one eye when, out of the corner of the other, I saw that Fahran had returned with a tin cup, full to the brim with clear water.

"Drink, huzoor. The water is good."

I was about to put down the compass and take the cup from him when I noticed through the narrow aiming prism something strange at the furthest extent of my line of sight: it looked like a faint plume of smoke.

"What's that, Fahran?" I said pointing at the phenomenon I'd observed.

"What's what, huzoor?"

"Smoke – on the horizon. Do you see it now?" He squinted in the direction I was pointing.

"No, huzoor, but lend me your binoculars and I will take a closer look." I un-looped the glasses from around my neck, passed them to him and he scanned the horizon. "Ah, now I see what you mean."

"Could it be coming from a locomotive on the railway, do you think?"

"I'm not sure, huzoor. It might be a sand whirlwind, in which case we'll need to shelter in the lee of the camels. I'll ask Soadad," he said handing me back the binoculars.

Whilst the two of them conferred, I watched through the glasses the column of smoke getting closer as it headed straight for us. By the time the two of them joined me I'd already worked out that it couldn't be a train as there was no track in its path.

"It must be a sandstorm," I said to Soadad.

"No, effendi, it is a camel. Look again."

"My God, it's Turks!" I exclaimed, putting down the binos and reaching for my pistol.

"No, effendi - Bedu."

"Well, that's alright then," I said with considerable relief. I once again exchanged the pistol for the binos and refocused them. This time I could make out a robed rider atop a gaily-caparisoned camel rapidly closing the distance between us. "Perhaps it's Lawrence," I added happily as I lowered the glasses.

"No, effendi, it will be..."

But he broke off before saying any more and ran to his prone camel, against which his rifle was resting. Before he got there a shot rang out, Soadad spun on the spot, his *keffiyeh* flew off and he collapsed in the sand, blood and brains pumping from a large hole in the back of his head. I was too shocked to move, but Fahran already has his rifle up into his shoulder as the armed rider approached.

"Hold your fire, Fahran," I whispered to him. "With Soadad dead this fellow's our only hope of finding Lawrence."

At about ten yards distance from us, the Bedouin reigned up and got the camel to sit. He then slid from the saddle and approached us with his rifle at the trail. Of diminutive size, Soadad's killer was dressed identically to our late guide, although his robes were black, appeared to be of better quality and were richly decorated with gold lace.

"What are you two fellows doing here?" he demanded in faultless English.

You could have knocked me down with a camel whisk at this extraordinary turn of events. Good God, I thought, perhaps it's Lawrence; then I remembered that he'd been to a grammar school in Oxford and probably spoke with a shop keeper's accent. But before I could ask the man, Fahran spoke.

"What's that to you?" he snarled, whilst keeping a bead on our guide's killer.

"Only that you are drinking at my well, old boy, and – as your friend over there has just discovered to his cost - I'd rather you'd asked before you'd done so."

"So why don't you kill us too?" I demanded.

"Oh, it wouldn't do to kill a chap from the good old *alma mater*, now would it? Even if he is dressed up like an extra from a silent picture and has a Music Hall Afghan in tow."

"*Alma mater*?" I gasped. "Eton?"

"The very same, old bean. Surely you remember me?" he said pulling his *keffiyeh* away from his face. "Sherif Ali. We weren't in the same house but I met you several times with your chum, Tertius Beaujambe."

"Of course!" I said. "You coxed the winning Eight at Henley in '15."

"The very same," he said, "although I've grown a 'tash and put on a bit of weight since then."

"And didn't you and Tertius win the Eton & Harrow contract bridge match the same year?"

"As a matter of fact, we did..."

"Excuse me, huzoor," Fahran broke in, "you may have been at school with this gentleman, but I feel bound to point out that he's just shot and killed our guide."

"Yes," Ali stated rather matter-of-factly, "I'm sorry about that. But he knew perfectly well that he was not permitted to drink here. Now, turning to more important things, what brings you to Arabia, Holland?"

"Actually, I'm now known as Speedicut – Second Lieutenant Charles Speedicut, Tenth Hussars – and we're on our way to join Captain Lawrence," I replied rather stiffly, for Fahran's comments had reminded me that we'd just witnessed a cold-blooded murder.

"I thought as much," Ali said breezily. "The Scout Master and his boys are about twenty miles north of here getting ready to biff the Turks at Abu el-Naam. If you're ready, and you can stand my company, get your chap to fetch that gun, knife and camel," he said pointing to the late Soadad, "and I'll take you both to Lawrence." I thought for a moment, but as we hadn't a clue as to the whereabouts of our destination and were, frankly, in a bit of a hole, the decision was an easy one.

"Lead on, Macd..." I gave Fahran a stern glance, which I followed up, once we were mounted and trotting along behind Ali, with the question I'd been meaning to ask him since we'd left Yenbo: "Tell me, Fahran, how is it that you know so much about the works of the Bard? I didn't even know you'd been to school – not that that makes much of a difference: look at me - four years at Eton and I can hardly spell..."

"I didn't have much schooling, huzoor – neither my father nor my mother had any and so didn't see the point – but old Mr Searcy thought that we children should at least have a knowledge of the classics. So, as we could all read, he gave us books. I couldn't get on with Aristotle, Chaucer or Jane Austen, but I really liked Shakespeare's dramas."

"Why?"

"All the murder and mayhem, I suppose, huzoor. It appealed to the Afghan in me, although it's really Atash who's the bloodthirsty one. Give him half a chance and he'd slit a throat as soon as ask a question: just like our old dad, in fact."

"And you?"

"Me, I'm more the thinking type – I usually leave the rough stuff to Atash. But that doesn't mean I couldn't use this," he said whilst looking at Ali's swaying back and fingering Soadad's dagger that was now in his belt, "if I had to..." which was, I supposed, reassuring – even though it seemed probable that I had brought the wrong brother on my first (and I sincerely hoped last) mission behind enemy lines. Well, time would tell.

Over the next couple of hours there was little chat as we trailed after Ali: the desert has that sort of effect on one I've found. It was dark long before we breasted yet another moon-lit sand dune and found ourselves looking down into a depression in which a ring of camels circled a rather jolly bonfire.

"Welcome to the camp of El Aurens," said Ali quietly over his shoulder.

Lawrence must have had look-outs posted but I saw none. However, Ali slowed our little caravanserai from a trot to a walk as we approached the camp and he signed for us to dismount before we reached the first couched camel. It was only when we got closer that I saw the barrel ends of several rifles pointed at us over the tops of a number of saddles.

"*Salaam alaikum*," murmured Ali as he led his camel inside the ring of rifles. I heard a voice answer back, '*alaikum salaam, Sherif*', as Fahran and I followed him. Ahead of us a small group of Arabs and a uniformed British officer were seated around the fire.

"Greetings, Aurens! See who I have found wandering in the desert," cried Ali. "They may look like comic strip Bedu but they are in fact Second Lieutenant Speedicut and his orderly come to join your gang of ruffians..."

"Really?" queried Lawrence, "I wasn't expecting anyone. Who sent you, Speedicut?"

"Manchester Square, Brother Ned," I said giving him as much of a clue as I dared to our true identity and purpose.

"Aa-ah, yes, well - take a pew next to me. We only got back about an hour ago from el-Naam, where we've laid mines under the tracks to the north and south of the station and cut the telegraph in preparation for tomorrow's show. Have you eaten? There's some really good goat stew in the pot. Then you can tell me why you have been bowled in my direction, how you got here – and why you're togged out for a fancy-dress party on Boar's Hill. And don't worry about Ali; he knows all about the Brotherhood and its plans for a second Front on the Hellespont."

CHAPTER SIXTEEN: TURKISH DELIGHTS

Whilst Lawrence and Sherif Ali sat listening in silence, over the next hour – with the occasional prompt from Fahran - I did as he'd asked. In between the various episodes of the tale, from which I omitted my covert role for the Brotherhood and the more salacious aspects of the incident in the Yenbo brothel, I tried to swallow down a few mouthfuls of rice and rancid goat *à la mode*.

"You know," Lawrence said when I'd finished (the story not the goat stew, which tasted even worse than camel), "there are some things that I don't understand. The first is this business with Arbuthnot. I'm as certain as I can be that the wretched fellow had his throat slit in Damascus. Do you know any different, Ali?"

"That was the story being told in the bazaars, Aurens - along with a number of other stories about him which I don't care to repeat..."

"Really?" queried Lawrence; but Ali clammed up on any discreditable disclosures about the man from MI6. "Well, nothing about Arbuthnot would surprise me. Anyway," Lawrence continued, "the note that was left with you, Speedicut, can only have come from Brother Arbuthnot and he did, one way or the other," he said giving Ali a sharp look, "get you here. So, I think we can assume that he is still alive. I'll let Cairo know the next time we are in touch with them, probably after el-Naam."

"What else?" I asked.

"Well, for a start, this whole wretched business of the Emerald. Anyone with even half a brain knows that there's no such person and never will be, unless, unless..." Lawrence stared into the fire looking thoughtful

"But I thought, Brother Ned," I said, as I vaguely recalled the Brotherhood's briefing paper, "that the plan was to create our own Emerald; whether or not he's the real thing is immaterial if he succeeds in uniting the tribes in a *jihad* against the Turks." Lawrence chose to avoid answering this question and instead turned to Ali.

"What do you think, Ali? Could we invent an Emerald?" he asked our old-Etonian Bedouin.

"I think that you should forget this Emerald nonsense, Aurens. With one or two exceptions, myself included, the Bedouin may be uneducated but they're not stupid; they would spot a fake emerald as quickly as your Queen Mary acquires them."[81]

"Not if he was a mighty warrior who emerged from the desert sweeping all before him..." Lawrence mused quietly.

"What *will* unite the tribes is gold," Ali continued, as though Lawrence had not spoken, "and the realisation that the Turks are on the losing side."

"But at the moment they're not; hence the need for the Emerald," I chipped in. "It's a classic 'chicken and egg' situation."

"Unless," said Lawrence, "whilst we polish an Emerald, the chicken starts laying golden eggs at the same time as giving the turkey a series of nasty pecks."

"The tribes will happily take the gold, Aurens, but mere 'pecks' won't impress them enough to change sides," said Ali. "Attacking railway stations, blowing up track and destroying the occasional train are good fun and all that – and they are certainly tying down Turkish troops in Arabia – but they are not sufficient to convince the tribes that they're backing the wrong side, particularly when the EEF is bogged down at Gaza. In fact,

---

[81] Editor's Note: I assume that this is a reference to HM Queen Mary's (1867-1953) repossession of the famous Cambridge emeralds, which were left by her mother, HRH Princess Mary-Adelaide of Teck (1833-1897), to Queen Mary's younger brother, the feckless Prince Francis of Teck (1870-1910), who bequeathed them to his mistress, the Countess of Kilmorey. On the death of Prince Francis in 1910, Queen Mary 'obliged' Lady Kilmorey to accept £80,000 for their return to the Royal Family.

the deployment by the Turks of additional troops to guard the Hejaz railway has actually made the situation worse rather than better."

"What on earth do you mean, Ali?" asked Lawrence sounding more than a little miffed at this implied criticism of his desert marauding.

"I mean, my dear Aurens, that the presence of additional Turkish troops on the EEF's right and rear flanks makes it *more* not less difficult for your chums to advance from Gaza to capture Jerusalem, Damascus and Constantinople. It's a fact which rather discourages the tribes from switching allegiance."

"So, what would convince them?" I asked.

"Something big," said Ali.

"Such as the Emerald?" said Lawrence.

"Forget the Emerald, Aurens and focus on staging an event that will make the Bedu sit up and take notice."

"What for instance?"

"Seizing Aqaba," said a voice behind me: it was Fahran.

"Where?" I asked, as Lawrence and Sherif Ali looked deeply sceptical.

"Aqaba," said Fahran. "It's a small port at the top of the Red Sea. If we took it - and held it - not only would it shake the Turks rigid but it would give us a base from which to cut permanently the Hejaz railway at Mudawarra and thereby isolate the Turkish troops in Arabia, which in turn would allow the EEF to advance north through the Levant to Constantinople."

"It couldn't be done," said Lawrence. "It's too heavily defended. I'd need a small army to take Aqaba and for that we need the Bedouin to unite. We're back to your roast chicken and boiled eggs, Speedicut."

"As I understand it, sir," said Fahran, "it's only heavily fortified on the seaward side."

"That's because it's guarded on the landward side by the Nefud desert," said Ali.

"And the Howeitat," added Lawrence. "Auda's yet another treacherous Bedouin who's deep in the pay of the Turks.[82] No. This is all pie-in-the-sky stuff. Until the Emerald raises the banner of Holy War," Ali made a tut-tutting sound at this, "I intend to go on raiding the railway - starting tomorrow morning with el-Naam." It seemed as though tempers would fray at any moment so I decided that it would be prudent to change the subject.

"What else puzzles you, Brother Ned?" He thought for a moment whilst he poked the fire with his cane.

"Your party rig," he said giving me an appraising glance. "I wear a *kiffiyeh* when riding, but I've never thought to wear full Arab dress before. I assume it's a sight more comfortable than boots and britches?"

"It is," I said, "and it also means that you can ride like the Bedouin rather than as though you're on a horse."

"Hmm, 'like the Bedouin', eh? Like a mighty Bedouin warrior..." Lawrence said, staring once again at the base of the fire and giving it another prod. "Your robes are too big for me but, Ali, do you have a spare set I could try on?"

"I do, Aurens, although they are probably not very clean," he said.

"Full of your lice, eh?" said our leader: Ali the old-Etonian looked considerably affronted at this. "But that doesn't matter. We can get a Turkish washerwoman to give them a scrub once we've taken el-Naam."

---

[82] Auda abu Tayi (1874-1924).

Despite all the rubbish you've seen at the movies about the Arabs giving Lawrence a set of Sherifal robes after he'd ridden across the Nefud desert, you now know the truth about his iconic dress (and a great deal more besides). He was a vain little man and – as I thought at the time – he realised that not only was the outfit quite flattering but that it would add a touch of romantic glamour to his exploits. Little did I realise that he had something much bigger in mind. Shortly after this conversation, Lawrence said that we should turn in as he planned an early start for the raid on el-Naam.

I'd hardly shut my eyes, or so it seemed, when Fahran was shaking me awake with a tin mug of tea and camel milk; I held my nose and drank it. A short while later Lawrence, robed as an arse-, crotch- and armpit-scratching Arab (and I use the phrase in its absolutely literal sense) mounted his camel and ordered his motley crew of about thirty assorted Bedouin, a small mountain gun and a Lewis machine gun (both of which had been dismantled and strapped to the sides of baggage camels) to march on the strategically insignificant railway station at el-Naam.

If you want a detailed account of the tactics Lawrence employed in this attack, or a blow-by-blow tale of the fighting that followed it (or indeed of any other fighting in which I've been involved over the years), then I must refer you to the vast bibliography covering the Revolt in the Desert, as it came to be known. My purpose in these scribblings – as you should by now have gathered - is to reveal the real facts, motives and scandals behind the published history of events in which I've participated or of which I've been an observer. What I will tell you, however, is that we dismounted just short of a sand dune that over-looked el-Naam station, a halt on the Hejaz railway comprising a stone-built water tower and a fortified blockhouse, both of which looked vaguely like scaled-down Crusader castles; alongside these buildings ran the track on which was a stationary engine and carriages with an assortment of uniformed Turks milling about. Judging by the smoke and steam coming from the engine, the train was about to depart in the direction of Medina.

Lawrence had the two guns dismounted, re-assembled and carried to the edge of the dune from where, just in time, he brought down a reasonably accurate artillery fire on the train, out of which dozens of Turkish troops were soon scrambling whilst others started to return our fire. One lucky round from our mountain gun struck the lead carriage and in, I suppose, a desperate attempt to save the engine, I watched through my binoculars as the tender was uncoupled from the wreckage of the carriage and the engine started to move off south.

"That won't help them," said Lawrence, who was lying next to me. "There's a mine about fifty yards down the track."

No sooner had he said it than there was a large explosion and the engine bucked like a bronco in a cloud of smoke and sand but, unfortunately for the raid, it fell back onto a section of undamaged track and a short while later, with about a Company's worth of Turkish infantry trotting beside it, was chugging its way south.

"Damn!" I heard Lawrence swear. "Say your prayers, Turks…" and he then ordered his men and the machine gunner to rake the remaining infantry, the stranded carriages and the station buildings with a hail of bullets.

By the time the returning fire had died out there were Turkish corpses everywhere, although only one of Lawrence's boys had been injured. Our leader rose to his feet, waved his pistol over his head and ordered his men forward. We found a scene of utter carnage around the station buildings. I counted at least seventy dead, but there were probably more, and those Turks that weren't already dead were quickly finished off by the sword-wielding Bedouin. To say that the station at el-Naam was not a pretty sight would be a considerable understatement and, when no one was looking, I threw up the entire contents of my stomach.

So much for the attack on el-Naam. It was my first action in Arabia and the only one during which I didn't fire a shot. Over the following weeks we continued to raid the railway as we worked our way slowly north. For most of the time it was like shooting ducks in a barrel and I quickly tired of it, for there was no sport in the slaughter and – as far as I could see – little point to it, except to bolster Lawrence's growing reputation as a successful guerrilla leader. As we saw on the posters in the stations which we raided, the bounty on the blond head of the British Army Captain in the flowing Arab robes was mounting by the week.

But it was not only Lawrence's value, dead or alive, that was growing. As Ali had predicted, our success – with or without the Emerald - was attracting more and more followers; Ali himself had 'persuaded' (for which read: 'used most of the Brotherhood's remaining gold') the fearsome Auda abu Tayi to bring over to us the Howeitat, his tribe of smelly cut-throats. So, by the time we reached Wadi Sirhan towards the middle of June, Lawrence's purse was virtually empty but our ranks had been swelled by the arrival of several hundred more Bedouin with the result that El Aurens, the academic archaeologist turned military intelligence officer turned romantically robed revolutionary, was commanding an army of five hundred bearded desperados rather than just a raiding party of thirty. With this force at Lawrence's command, Fahran's proposal for the capture of Aqaba was turning from an impossible dream into a real opportunity. It was also, by the day, becoming more and more of an obsession with our leader.

However, the build-up of Lawrence's forces had not gone un-noticed by the Ottomans, as we discovered from a middle-ranking Turkish officer who, somewhat unluckily for him, we captured alive on our last raid before arriving at Wadi Sirhan. At first, he was reluctant to talk, so Auda had him stripped and staked out in the midday sun. Even this grilling was insufficient to make the man blab and he fainted in the heat without disclosing anything. At this point, Auda said it was time to get serious, so he had one of his men tip a bucket of camel piss over the poor unfortunate to revive him, which it did most effectively, then Auda knelt by the man, flashed his dagger in the poor bugger's face and seized the Turk's not insignificantly-sized wedding tackle.

"If, son of a syphilitic whore," he snarled in the man's ear, "thou dost not tell me all that thou knowest, thou wilt shortly be fit only to work in the Ottoman Sultan's harem." Needless to say, the Turk quickly spilled the beans as Fahran, whose Arabic was improving by the day, translated for me.

"We believe that you are massing to attack Aqaba, Aleppo or Damascus," the Turk squealed as Auda tightened his grip.

"And what else?" demanded the Howeitat's chief.

"Our General has a Brigade of cavalry on stand-by," croaked the Turk. "When your destination is clear, the cavalry will be dispatched to bolster the defences of your target. Aaagh!"

Unfortunately for the Turk, his confession didn't stop Auda, who was a vicious sod, from emasculating the fellow anyway. But the Bedouin chief must have had a trace of compassion for, as his victim writhed on his bindings and yelled in agony, Auda nodded to one of his thugs who unsheathed a rusty scimitar and separated the Turk's head from his body with a single blow. At least, that's what Fahran told me happened; I'd already legged it behind a palm tree to park my lunch in the sand. That evening Lawrence called a council of war around the cooking fire: Ali, Auda, Fahran and I were in attendance.

"If we are to take Aqaba, the Turks must believe that our target lies elsewhere. What does anyone propose?"

"A series of small raids northwards towards Damascus," proposed Ali. "That should convince them."

"But it would involve dividing our force and I don't like the idea of doing that," said Lawrence.

"We move immediately and hit them before they can reinforce Aqaba," said Fahran.

"Not a bad idea. What do you think, Auda?"

"I like it not, Aurens. Thou hast yet to secure the tribes at Wadi Rum from whence thou wilt launch the attack."

"Good point. How long do you think that will take?"

"It's a question of gold, Aurens. Hast thou enough remaining?"

"No," he replied with a sigh, "but there's plenty of Turkish gold in Aqaba. If the tribes join us, it shall be theirs. Would they agree to such a promise?"

"Possibly, Aurens," said Ali, "but it will take time to convince them – and they will want something on account."

"Why not raid the Ottoman Bank in Ma'an and use the proceeds to buy the tribes at Wadi Rum?" I asked.

"It's hardly heading in the right direction," said Ali.

"But it's the only vulnerable Turkish-held town this side of Aqaba where we can be certain that there is a stash of the shiny stuff sufficient for our purposes," I replied, "and, before the Turks realise what we are up to, we ride hard for Wadi Rum, hand over the sovs to Auda's cousins and press on to Aqaba."

"With a Turkish cavalry brigade hard on our heels," said Ali.

"Lawrence could always throw the Turks off the scent by leaving that fat-arsed Ottoman Governor a note saying that he needed the rhino to start his *jihad* - and sign it 'with love from Kasredin'..."[83] I replied.

"That's madness," said Ali. "Anyway, I thought we'd agreed long ago to forget all this Emerald nonsense."

---

[83] Editor's Note: Speedicut is presumably referring to Hajim Muhtittin Bey (d. 1965), who was the regional Governor based in Deraa. Hajim Bey was the man whom Lawrence would later claim had him beaten and raped, an allegation which is now much disputed by historians.

"*You* may have done, Ali," said Lawrence giving the hem of his latest robe a twitch, "but I haven't: I think that Speedicut's idea has merit – real merit."

And that, dear reader, is exactly what happened although all the accounts of the battle of Aqaba seems to have conveniently overlooked my proposal and its implementation or, as in the case of Lean's film, reinvented the story entirely. And whilst we're on the subject of fiction, the actual battle for Aqaba didn't take place there but – and this is undisputedly a fact - at a fortified blockhouse midway between Ma'an and the port.

This blockhouse, an unremarkable piece of contemporary Ottoman architecture at a fly-blown dump called Abu al Larsan, had already been seized at the end of June by a bunch of Bedouin based at Wadi Rum who were so overjoyed at being bribed by Ali with the Turks' gold from Ma'an that, without so much as a 'by your leave, Aurens', they charged off and seized the first Ottoman outpost they could find. Unfortunately for them, the Turks decided that they wanted it back and dispatched a Battalion of infantry to recover it and then, for good measure, annihilated a peaceful (and completely innocent) Arab encampment nearby. This was a bad move on the part of the men from Constantinople, for the slaughtered villagers happened to be yet more cousins of Auda who, when he heard the fell news, galloped off with half Lawrence's force and slaughtered three hundred of the buggers for the loss of only two of his own men. Auda would have topped the other three hundred if Lawrence and the rest of the 'Bedouin Field Force' hadn't arrived in time to stop him. Actually, it would be more accurate to say that it was Ali and me who stopped Auda, for Lawrence was out cold for much of the time. It happened thus.

I'd just finished what passed for breakfast (don't ask) and was wondering how I could stay out of trouble for the rest of the day, when a horseman came galloping into our camp with the news of the slaughter of the innocents. Auda let out a roar and, before we knew it, had disappeared with his chums in a cloud of sand as I've already described.

"Quick!" yelled Lawrence to Ali and me, "get the boys mounted."

"Why, Aurens?" asked Ali.

"Because Auda hasn't got a hope of re-taking Abu al Larsen on his own."

However, by the time we arrived Auda had very nearly proved Lawrence wrong and, although there was still some brisk fighting to be done, had already sent half the Turkish Battalion to the hereafter and was just starting on the other half.

Despite Ali's proven ability to pot someone at fifty yards from the back of a trotting camel, this was not a skill given to most men (myself included), so it was just as well that in all our prior engagements – as at el-Naam - we had dismounted before engaging the enemy with small arms fire. The charge at Abu al Larsan was different: we were in hot pursuit of Auda and so had no opportunity to dismount before we collided with the Turkish *sangars*. I was, as usual, armed with my trusty Webley and found myself in the lead as we galloped through the enemy positions.

"Rein back, Speedicut!" yelled Lawrence over the sound of battle, "I'm in command here."

"Have it your own way," I said to myself, hauling back on my camel's head rope as I loosed off shots to the left and right of me. Now I admit that it might have been wiser to have stopped shooting at that point, but my blood was up and it was the first charge I'd ever been in, so it was an unfortunate accident that I pulled the trigger on the last chamber of my revolver at the very moment the head of Lawrence's mount passed in front of the barrel... The camel did the nearest thing to a cartwheel that I've ever seen such a large beast perform and Lawrence went flying. I turned in the saddle to watch his flight and, although – fortunately - the camel didn't fall on him, his head collided on landing with an inconveniently placed boulder. The result was that he was unconscious for most of the rest of the day.[84]

---

[84] Editor's Note: Lawrence and his biographers have previously believed that it was Lawrence himself who shot his own camel in the head during the action at Abu al Larsan.

Whilst our leader was out for the count, and once Ali and I had stopped Auda from turning the surrounding sand red with Turkish blood, we got in a huddle to decide what to do next. It didn't take us long to agree that the logical thing was to press on to Aqaba, towards which were fleeing those Turks who hadn't been captured or who had escaped Auda's righteous vengeance.

"Give them time to tell their friends what's happened," said Ali wisely, "then we'll send a scout forward with a flag of truce to inform the garrison that we'll spare them if they surrender." Auda growled at this but, as Ali was a descendant of the Prophet and so outranked him, he grudgingly agreed. "We should then be able to walk in unopposed." And that is precisely what we did a couple of hours later as the blood red orb of the sun sank over the western horizon. When Lawrence eventually came around it was to discover that he had captured Aqaba.

"To think that no one knows about this in Cairo – and who there would believe it even if they did know?" said Ali jokingly whilst Lawrence took a restorative pull on my hip flask.

"You make a very good point, Ali," he said looking pensive. "We must get the news to them. It's vital that our position here is reinforced from the sea before the Turks try to push us into it."

"What about using the Turkish telegraph system to send Cairo a message?" I proposed. "We know that your old friends in Military Intelligence have tapped into it."

"I'm afraid that's not going to be possible, huzoor," said Fahran, "Sheikh Auda's men have destroyed it." Auda made his usual growling noise at this embarrassing news.

"I could commandeer one of the fishing boats in the harbour and sail around the Sinai Peninsula, up to Suez and on to Cairo," said Ali, "I do, after all, know how to steer a boat."

"I don't suppose there's an 'Eight' in the harbour, Ali. Besides which, that would take too long," said Lawrence. "Anyway, no one in Cairo would believe you: you may be an old-Etonian, but..." He paused, rubbed his bruised head and took another pull on my flask. "There's only one thing for it. I'll have to ride across Sinai and take the news to Murray myself. I can do it in forty hours."

Sensible decision, I thought, and whilst you're in Cairo, I added silently, I can put my feet up in Aqaba and get some much-needed rest.

"It took the Children of Israel forty *years* to cross Sinai," Auda said in a subdued voice.

"Yes, but Moses didn't have a compass, Auda," quipped Lawrence

"Within two risings of the sun? Test not the patience of Allah, Aurens, thou hast only one life."

"And I can only lose it once, Auda, but I don't intend to do so – for it is not yet written..."

"Blaspheme not, Aurens," said Auda; but he could see that whatever he said would make no difference, so he changed tack. "Very well, if thou art to cross the desert thou must at the least take two warriors with thee. The sands are as treacherous as the Turks."

It didn't need Auda to warn Lawrence about the dangers that lurk above and below the surface of the yellow, gritty stuff as, after months already spent in the desert, we all knew full well that the sands of Sinai would certainly not be the beaches at Bournemouth.

"And what would I do with your men in Cairo, Auda? But you are right – Sinai's a damned dangerous place and it would be foolish to try it on my own. So, who can I take? The boys are too young..."

I should have mentioned earlier that Lawrence was served (or should that be serviced?) by a brace of handsome young camel handlers, neither of whom (D Lean please note) was called Farhaj or Dahoum.

"Whoever it is, must be competent on a camel... I know..." he said, looking first at Auda then at Ali, "I'll take..."

CHAPTER SEVENTEEN: A CAMP FIRE

"... you, Speedicut."

What? Not bloody likely! The Nefud was bad enough - but Sinai had a worse reputation than Blackpool: it's all in *Exodus* if you doubt me.

"Not without me you won't, sir," said Fahran.

"Very well," said Lawrence, as I tried desperately to think of a good reason why I had to stay put in Aqaba, "I'll take both of you. Satisfied, Auda?" Auda grunted noncommittally whilst I prayed that he would say that the choice was entirely unsuitable.

"As thou wishest, Aurens." I looked pleadingly at Ali but failed to catch his eye.

An hour later we were on our way for what turned out to be the roughest ride of my life. Lawrence had boasted to Auda that we would cross Sinai in forty hours and he later claimed that we did it in forty-nine. The truth is that we took nearly three days, arriving in Suez on the evening of the 9th July. Could we have ridden the one hundred and seventy-odd miles as the crow flies (camels don't), over some of the worst terrain on earth, in two days? It's possible but, because of Lawrence's bump on the head, we were obliged – thank God - to take two longish breaks for rest. We were also slowed by a hitherto unpublished incident of profound significance which I will now reveal.

It's quite easy to lose track of time when you are on a helter-skelter dash across mountain and desert, but I'm reasonably sure that it was towards dusk on the second day that we rounded a large spur of rock and saw, in the middle distance, a lone cameleer coming towards us across a flat stretch of sand.

"Bedu?" asked Fahran, who had been the first to spot the man.

"I think not," said Lawrence.

"A lone Turk out for a stroll?" I ventured.

"Unlikely," said Lawrence, giving me a stern look for my levity. "In any event, there's only one way to find out," he added as he whipped his camel into a trot then a lolloping gallop. Having no choice, Fahran and I followed on behind, although I took the precaution of drawing my pistol. The man must have seen our dust cloud for he halted and waited. As we drew closer I could see that he was, like us, dressed in Arab robes with his *keffiyeh* drawn across all but his eyes. We were about twenty paces away from him when he drew a handgun and, in Arabic, ordered us to halt.

"Declare yourselves!" he shouted as we ground to a dusty stop.

"My name is Captain Lawrence," said our leader, "and these are Mr Speedicut and his servant."

"What are you doing in Sinai?"

"We are making our way as quickly as we can to Suez."

"Why?"

"That is our business."

"Show your faces." We did as he ordered. "Well, you're a sight for sore eyes and no mistake, dear," the man suddenly said in camp, theatrical English as he pulled his headdress away from his face.

"Brother Arbuthnot?"

"The very same, duckie."

"But you're supposed to be dead."

"Didn't young Speedicut here tell you that I'd pointed him in your direction in Yenbo, dear?"

"Yes," I broke in, "but it was an Arab woman who left me the note and possibly the same woman who directed us to the guide the following morning."

"True that is," said Arbuthnot, adopting a voice and phraseology that I remembered all too well, "and to Lawrence took you he did."

"So, it was you all along?" I said as I nearly fell out of the saddle at this disclosure.

"Fooled you, didn't I, dear?"

"And the beggar who led us to the brother, was that you too?"

"It was," he said with considerable smugness.

"Well, I'll be buggered," I said, and then immediately regretted it, "that was a better performance than Henry Irving." Or Sarah Bernhardt, I added to myself.

"Glad to know that my time in provincial rep wasn't wasted, dear," said Arbuthnot giving me a lascivious wink as I remembered the feel of his balls.

"Enough of all this," said Lawrence, "what *are* you doing here, Sandy? And, anyway, why aren't you dead?"

"As to the second, dear, it was me who put that story about. You see, I needed to go deeper undercover for this Brotherhood business you've found me on."

"What business?" demanded Lawrence. But before he answered, Arbuthnot looked at me and Fahran, then raised a plucked eyebrow.

"Don't worry," said Lawrence, "Speedicut's in the Brotherhood and his man's in the know."

"Tell you what, Ned, dear," said Arbuthnot, "let's stop for a cuppa and I'll let you know all about it." Lawrence said that we couldn't halt for long as we had to get to Suez but, nonetheless, he made his camel kneel. Ten minutes later we were sitting around a small fire that Fahran had laid, sipping the sweet mint tea that he'd swiftly prepared.

"So, what *are* you doing here?" asked Lawrence.

"Have you heard of the Convent of St Catherine?" he answered somewhat inconsequentially.

"Of course I have," replied Lawrence but, as I hadn't, I said so.

"Well, for your information, Miss Charles, it's a mid-First Century Greek Orthodox monastery way to the south of here, full of well-hung Greek monks who spend all day chanting and... well, you're too young to understand."

"That's as maybe," I said, "but other than the obvious, of what interest is it to you?"

"Within the walls of the monastery, and closely guarded by Miss Monk and her friends, is one of the oldest libraries in the world."

"So what?"

"For your further information, Miss Ignorant, it contains a unique collection of early Jewish, Christian and Islamic documents, many of which have never been seen by anyone other than the dear old Mother Abbot who runs the place."

"Fascinating," I replied sceptically, "but of what possible interest to the Brotherhood is a pile of dusty old books?"

"Because, Miss Curious, as I found out after I'd used my charms, there is in the library – or rather there was - a document the possession of which will allow me to complete my current assignment for the Brotherhood."

"What's that?" asked Lawrence.

"To emerge from Sinai like old Mother Moses, dear, declare a Holy War on Miss Turk and sweep her and all her girls from the region. It's what I'm on my way to do now..."

"But that's the task that I've been given!" said Lawrence looking considerably affronted. "Anyway, what document would give you the ability to do any better than I've done already?"

"The Scroll of Kasredin, dear," he said tapping his chest.

"Never heard of it," said Lawrence dismissively.

"Few people have," Fahran said unexpectedly.

"What do you know about it?" I asked in astonishment.

"As children, we were told the tale by my father: I've always assumed that it was just folk lore."

"We all know the Legend of the Emerald or Kasredin or Greenmantle as he's variously called," said Lawrence rather dismissively, "but I've never heard of the Scroll of Kasredin."

"As the story was told to me, sir," Fahran went on, "the true Emerald would be identified by the possession of a sacred scroll, written and then hidden by Moses. It's a bit like the legend of King Arthur and Excalibur or the coming of the Jews' Messiah; with the cross-over between the Semitic religions, these stories are really all one and the same thing anyway."

"And you've found it, Sandy?" demanded Lawrence of Arbuthnot.

"That's right, dear," he lisped.

"Show me."

With considerable reluctance Arbuthnot reached inside his robe and drew out a plain tin tube with a screw top, which he undid. He then inserted two fingers and used them to remove a ragged piece of brown papyrus which he unrolled and held up for us to look at in the light of the fire. I could make out what looked like Hebrew script but I'm no scholar and so I couldn't be sure. Not so Lawrence, whose eyes widened as he read it.

"Fascinating," he said at last. Then he put out a hand to take the scroll.

"Sorry, dear," said Arbuthnot, rolling up the paper, putting it back in the tin and pushing the tube out of sight within his robe, "this little darling is never going to leave mother's loving embrace. Anyway, you'll have to excuse me, dears. I'm going to have a piddle and then I must be on my way for my date with Miss Destiny, Dame Fame and old Mother Fortune."

I thought Lawrence would try and stop him, for it was clear as a pikestaff that our leader realised that his own date with Destiny was about to join Arbuthnot's piddle in the sand, but he didn't. Instead, he stared into the dying embers of the fire as though they foretold his fate. Meanwhile, Arbuthnot got up, minced away from us and disappeared behind a rock.

"Time to pack up and get on our way, gentleman," said Lawrence wearily, as he clambered to his feet.

A couple of minutes later I was about to throw a leg over the saddle of my couched camel when I heard a cry from the general direction in which Arbuthnot had gone to relieve himself.

"What's that?" I asked as, this time, I could distinctly hear the word 'help' being shouted.

"Wait here," commanded Lawrence, giving Fahran and me a steely look. Then he strode off, following the man from MI6's footprints in the sand whilst Fahran and I mounted our camels, got them off their haunches and waited as ordered.

I'm not sure how long we sat there, but it can't have been more than a minute or two before we both heard a shot ring out, followed moments later by the figure of Lawrence marching back towards us on his own, a grim look on his puckish face, his *keffiyeh* trailing from one hand and a still smoking pistol in his other.

"I was too late," he said quietly as he reached his camel.

"A scorpion?" I asked.

"Or a snake?" asked Fahran.

"Neither - quicksand. By the time I got to him, only his head and shoulders were showing. I tried to pull him out with my *kiffiyeh* but it wouldn't reach. So, I put the poor chap out of his misery – better that than a slow death by drowning..."

"And the Scroll?" I asked.

"What? Oh, the Scroll. Unfortunately, that went down with him," said Lawrence rather too quickly. Did he involuntarily touch his chest in a religious gesture of the type made by Arabs and left-footers? In the failing light, I couldn't be sure. "Time to be going," he ordered as he clambered aboard his camel.

Twenty-four extremely uncomfortable hours later we arrived at the outskirts of Suez. I was sore, dirty and damnably tired but the sight of the arse end of civilisation was as welcome as the Ritz. At first our presence in the town was unremarked - just three more scruffy Arabs to add to the port's low life - but as we got closer to the administrative heart of the dung heap, where Lawrence hoped to find a telephone with a line to Cairo, heads started to turn and, with the Port Authority's office in view, we were stopped by an officious Tommy in the uniform of the Military Police.

"Where the bleedin' 'ell d'ya think you're goin', Abdul?"

"To use the telephone, *effendi*," Lawrence said in a fake Arab accent.

"No, you're bleedin' not. *Imshi*!"

"That's no way to address an officer in Military Intelligence," I responded in my most pompous voice, "unless you want to spend the rest of the war under close arrest."

"And oo the bloody 'ell d'ya think you are, Mustapha?"

"Mr Charles Speedicut of His Majesty's Tenth Hussars."

"And I suppose you're the bleedin' Arkand of fuckin' Swat," the Military Policeman said to Fahran.

"As a matter of fact, my father was a Kizilbashi Kahn, but that won't mean anything to you. I am a Corporal in the same Regiment as Mr Speedicut and, therefore, outrank you."

"You can fuck me sideways if you think I'm goin' to believe any of that fuckin' crap. Now fuck off the lot of you - or I'll put all three of yer hunder fuckin' harrest."

I'm not sure what would have happened next, and we never got to find out, for at that moment a large and red-faced matelot, in Navy whites with three gold rings on his shoulder, ambled out of the Port Authority office.

"Commander?" Lawrence called over to him, "could we trouble you for a moment?" The sailor looked up in surprise, his eyes widening as he tried to reconcile Lawrence's soft Oxford tones with the sight of three filthy dirty camel-borne Bedouin.

"We'd be most awfully obliged," I added for good measure. More out of curiosity than anything else, I presume, he walked over towards us.

"What's going on?" he demanded of the soldier.

"These fuckin' A-rabs, sir, not only claim that they are British soldiers but that two of 'em are fuckin' hofficers."

"Ridiculous," exclaimed the heir of Nelson. "Anyway, what do they want?"

"To use a telephone," said Lawrence in a measured manner before the policeman could reply. I could tell from his voice that he was having trouble keeping his temper under control.

"What the devil would *you* want with a telephone?" barked the sailor in his best quarterdeck manner.

"To speak to the Commander-in-Chief," said Lawrence as though it was an everyday matter.

"Absurd," the sailor spluttered, "even if you are who you say you are - which I very much doubt - why would Allenby want to speak to a pair of junior officers like you?"

"Allenby, did you say?"

"Yes," he replied.

"So, Murray's gone: well that's a step in the right direction."

The pride of the Mediterranean Fleet was so taken aback at this that he was temporarily speechless. By the time he'd recovered, Lawrence had couched his camel, slipped out of the saddle and approached the naval type. Unfortunately, this somewhat diminished Lawrence's height advantage for the top of his head now barely came up to the Commander's shoulder. Nonetheless, he looked up into the fellow's face with his piercing blue eyes and spoke in a low voice:

"I want you to listen very carefully, Commander Whatever-your-name-is, to what I am about to say." The matelot remained silent, transfixed by

Lawrence's intense gaze. "My name is Captain Thomas Edward Lawrence. I am attached to Prince Faisal's Arab Army as an advisor. I have spent most of this year behind enemy lines in Arabia leading raiding parties on the Hejaz Railway. Three days ago, we captured the strategically important port of Aqaba. Now, whether you believe me on not, it is vital that I communicate this information to the Commander-in-Chief as soon as possible and I have ridden across Sinai, without rest, expressly for that purpose. If you do not allow me to use your telephone and speak to GHQ in Cairo I will, I promise you, find someone who will. When that happens, I will tell General Allenby of this conversation and my guess is that, by the time I've finished, you will be lucky to be in command of a row boat on the Serpentine. Your future lies, as never before, in your own hands. Help me or suffer the consequences."

The upshot was that, twenty minutes later, Lawrence was yelling down the line to Allenby in Cairo, who - once he'd digested the news - ordered Lawrence to get to Cairo as fast as he could.

"Certainly, sir, we will depart immediately. What's that? Put the Commander on? A moment, sir." Lawrence handed the apparatus to the sailor who braced up visibly as he took it and then, as Allenby barked orders at him, held the receiver away from his ear.

"Top priority, sir? ... of course, sir... the Admiral's motor car to take Captain Lawrence to the station? ... certainly, sir... and a special train to take him to Cairo? ... consider it done, sir... I will have Captain Lawrence in Cairo before the morning." He replaced the receiver on the hook, let out a low whistle and then, despite their differences in rank, gave Lawrence a salute which I'm sure the Commander usually reserved for sea-going royalty.

We actually arrived in Cairo shortly before midnight. Lawrence was whisked off for a late-night rendezvous with the C-in-C, without having the opportunity to change, whilst Fahran and I made our way to the HQ Mess under our own steam. You won't be surprised to learn that, dressed as we were, we had some difficulty gaining admittance and only did so when I demanded to see the Orderly Officer who, to my delight and surprise, turned out to be none other than Tertius Beaujambe, recently arrived from France and about to join Allenby's Staff as an ADC.

"What on earth are you doing here dressed up like Sinbad and ponging worse than a Guardsman's feet?"

"It's a long story, Tertius..."

"Well, the bar's still open and some of the chaps are playing backgammon and bezique, so come along and tell me over a glass of fizz."

"Shouldn't I have a bath first?"

"I should say not, old fruit. When you walk into the bar in that rig you'll create a sensation – and we could do with some excitement around here."

So, I packed Fahran off to find the Mess Sergeant and get me a room, him a bed and to find our trunks. I then followed Tertius through the deserted ante room and on into the bar where an assortment of uniformed types was drowning their boredom or fleecing their brother officers. Everyone looked up as I walked in.

"What in God's name, Beaujambe, do you mean by bringing a filthy wog into the Mess?" demanded a portly infantry Major whom I seemed to remember was the PMC.

CHAPTER EIGHTEEN: IN A MESS

I decided on the instant that it was time for a bit of fun.

"Excuse me, *effendi*," I said in a fake Arab accent, which I tried to make as convincing as Lawrence's, "but I look for *hammam*. No here?"

"What?" screamed the dyspeptic PMC. "You think this is a Turkish bathhouse? Get out!"

"Excuse, excuse, *effendi* – all these young men. I assumed..." The Major grabbed me by the arm whilst Tertius, who had immediately guessed what I was up to, stood aside as the apoplectic footslogger tried to drag me out. As he manhandled me towards the door my *kiffiyeh* fell off.

"Hang on a moment, Freddy," said a Captain in Cherrypicker uniform, "isn't that the young Shiner who went off to help Lawrence in Arabia?"

"Good God," the PMC said, stopped dead in his tracks and gave me a long, hard look. "I suppose that under that sun tan and beard it might be... Are you?" he demanded of me.

"Speedicut of the Tenth at your service, Major – gentlemen," I said greeting the room in the Arab fashion.

"So, what the hell are you doing here?" demanded a Gunner, the state of whose backgammon board looked as though he could do with a distraction.

"And what the blazes do you think you're wearing in the Mess?" said a pompous idiot in Staff tabs, whom I recalled from my previous stay in Cairo.

"I've just crossed Sinai on a camel," I said nonchalantly in answer to both questions, "and Beaujambe suggested that I should have a drink before going up for a bath and some much-needed shut-eye."

"Sinai? But you can't have – and even if you have, why would you have taken the risk?" said the Cherrypicker.

"To bring you the news that we've taken Aqaba."

"Aqaba?" spluttered a bucolic looking Sapper, "but that's held by the Turks."

"Not any longer," I said dismissively as I turned and asked the barman for a pint of fizz.

"It's not possible," said another Sapper, along with most of the rest of the officers in the room.

"It is," I said. "We did it – or rather, the wogs did it - under the leadership of Ned Lawrence and, because Ned was unconscious for most of the assault, myself."

"I don't believe it," chimed back the chorus of doubters.

"Don't take it from me," I said, taking a long pull on the tankard of bubbly I'd been handed by a wry-faced Mess barman, "ask the C-in-C in the morning. Ned's with him now telling him all about it." There was total silence in the bar as they all digested my momentous news; then, without warning, the room seemed to erupt.

I finally got to bed at about three AM, blind drunk and riding a wave of popular acclaim. Fahran sensibly didn't wake me until mid-way through the morning.

"Major Lawrence's complements, huzoor, but he would be grateful if you could join him at the offices of the Arab Bureau at your earliest convenience."

"*Major* Lawrence - the Arab Bureau? What's all this, Fahran?"

"Captain Lawrence was promoted last evening, huzoor, in recognition of his work in Arabia. You will, I am sure, recall from the Brotherhood's briefing paper that the Arab Bureau is the organisation which has taken overall responsibility for the direction of the Arab Revolt. It's headed by Brigadier General Clayton, who is a member of the Brotherhood and both Major Lawrence's superior officer and his local controller." I knew better than to ask Fahran how he knew any of this, instead I let him shave me and, after a bath, help me dress in uniform.

"So, I'm no longer the Sheikh of Araby, eh, Fahran?" I said looking in a mirror on the back of the door.

"No, huzoor – but still the handsome and dashing Mr Speedicut."

"Flattery will get you everywhere, Fahran," I said giving him a broad grin, "and you look somewhat less like a cut-throat from the bazaar now that you too have changed and shaved."

"I miss the beard, huzoor, for it always reminds me of my late father - and I far prefer his robes to this dreary khaki... By the way, a Staff car will be here for you in ten minutes: time enough for a quick breakfast, huzoor."

My stomach wasn't up to a 'full English', so I grabbed a coffee in the ante room before joining Fahran at the entrance to the Mess where a khaki-coloured motor was waiting for me.

"Good luck, huzoor," he said giving me a snappy salute as he closed the door, "Whilst you're at the Arab Bureau I'll get the trunks packed."

Before I could ask him what he meant by that, the motor was driven away from the steps. A few minutes later it pulled up at GHQ Cairo where I was greeted by a smartly dressed Captain on the Staff who swept me through security, up a broad flight of stairs and along a corridor to a pair of frosted-glass panelled doors from behind which I could hear muffled voices, including what sounded like a woman's.

"Wait here would you, Speedicut?" said my guide. "General Clayton should be finished in the next five minutes, then he'll see you."

I parked myself on a chair, besides which, face down, was a small stack of back copies of *The Illustrated London News*. With nothing else to do, and realising that I hadn't read any news since I'd set off for Yenbo, I picked up the one on the top and turned it over. 'TSAR ABDICATES' screamed the headline over a picture of the hapless monarch, his hatched-faced wife and attractive children. In the article which followed I learned that, a few weeks after my birthday, the Tsar had been obliged to step aside in favour of his brother, who had promptly declined the dubious honour. Meanwhile, Mr Nicholas Romanov and his family had been place under house arrest at Tsarskoe Selo whilst a Provisional Government, under the leadership of a certain Prince Lvov,[85] was running the country in place of the Tsarina. So, it seemed that the Brotherhood-inspired murder of Rasputin hadn't done the trick after all and that I'd risked my neck for nothing.

I then leafed through the remaining magazines but they were all of an earlier date, so I was none the wiser as to how matters currently stood in St Petersburg. My thoughts about Felix, Dimitri and my other Russian friends – not forgetting my relations and Bertie Stopford – were interrupted by raised voices coming from Clayton's office.

"I tell you, Gertrude, we have no choice. Esher says that if he tells anyone what he knows the whole plan could fail." It sounded like Lawrence but I couldn't be sure.

"But he's only a youngster," said a woman's voice, "and he's given valuable service."

"That's as may be," said an older voice that I also didn't recognise, "but he knows the truth about Aqaba - and a whole lot more besides." I wondered who they could be talking about and, anyway, what was 'the truth about Aqaba'? We'd taken it and that was that. Far from being a secret I was

---

[85] Prince Georgy Yevgenyevich Lvov (1861-1925).

sure that, at that very moment, Allenby was briefing *The Times* stringer in Cairo on the subject.

"And what's one life compared to the success of the Arab Revolt?" asked the voice that sounded like Lawrence. "I had no compunction last January executing that rascal, Gasim, in order to stop a blood feud that would have ended the Revolt before it ever crossed the starting line."

"It's hardly the same thing, Ned," said the woman, "and there's a much better way to ensure his silence."

"What's that?" asked the older man.

"Get the boy a gong, Gilbert, and tell Allenby to puff him in the press. Then get him posted immediately to Maude in Baghdad,[86] where I can keep an eye on him: that will keep him quiet, away from the Revolt and out of harm's way. Anyway, I won't be a party to a murder, not even if it is to save your precious Brotherhood's Operation Kasredin."

Oh, so this was Brotherhood business, was it, I thought, *and* that old chestnut, the blessed Kasredin. Knowing my luck, I would be the poor sod who, given my success in dispatching Rasputin to a watery grave, would have to push whoever they were talking about into the Suez Canal.

"Murder, Gertrude?" said the older voice, probably that of Gilbert, "I hardly think that a posting to do one's duty for King and Country in Flanders constitutes murder."

"When the life expectancy in the trenches is less than two weeks," said the woman called Gertrude, "it's the next best thing." That was a relief, I thought. You see, assassination was not and never has been my bag: better by far – and a sight more certain - to leave the job to the barbed wire in No Man's Land and a Hun machine gunner. "Besides which, you know full well that it's precisely the reason you propose sending..." She

---

[86] Lieutenant General Sir Frederick Maude KCB, CMG, DSO (1864-1917) was GOC III Indian Army Corps also known as the Tigris Corps.

was interrupted by the ringing of a telephone before she could identify the unlucky sod.

"Clayton here... yes... outside you say... very well... thank you." A few seconds later the door opened and I heard the same voice say: "Mr Speedicut, do come in."

I did as bidden and marched into a sparsely furnished office where the voice introduced himself as Brigadier General Gilbert Clayton. I gave him a crisp salute.

"Of course, Mr Speedicut, you know Major Lawrence." Ned gave me a rather tight-lipped smile when I congratulated him on his promotion; somewhat to my surprise, I saw that he was still rigged out in Arab robes although they were clearly a fresh set. "But I don't think you've met Miss Gertrude Bell,[87] who's been the Bureau's Oriental Secretary in Baghdad since we captured it in March."

An attractive middle-aged woman, with fair, curly hair piled on top of her head but with a rather school-marmish air, advanced to shake my hand. I couldn't help noticing that she had a cracker of a figure beneath her mannish dress and I assumed that the particular groves of academe which she obviously frequented were planted on the isle of Lesbos.

"A great pleasure to meet you, Mr Speedicut," she said in a cut-crystal accent as she gave my hand a firm shake. "Your exploits with Major Lawrence in Arabia will shortly become the stuff of legend. All being well," she gave her companions a rather stern glance, "I believe we will be hearing a great deal more of you in the future." Clayton interrupted Miss Bell with a rather forced cough.

"Yes, yes, Gertrude, that's all as may be. But my reason for asking Mr Speedicut to join us is to thank him for his *past* service. Well done, m'boy," he said to me, "I'm extremely grateful to you for your help and all that, but the 'powers that be' seem to think it's time you did some *proper* soldiering.

---

[87] Gertrude Bell (1868 – 1926).

So, no more scampering around sand dunes for you," he said with a rather stiff laugh. "You'll get your Orders in a day or two, in the meantime have a bit of a rest, take a look at the sights – the pyramids are well worth a visit – and enjoy Cairo."

"Thank you, General," I said with some relief, for I was dreading having to venture once more into the Land of Sand with Lawrence - although I equally dreaded having to join the Shiners in France. Maybe, I thought, I would be rewarded with a Staff posting somewhere, perhaps with Philip and his Chief at their comfortable chateau outside Paris. "Do you have any idea where I'm to be posted, General?" Clayton looked a bit shifty.

"Posting? No, no, that's not my responsibility, I'm afraid, Speedicut. That will be down to General Allenby or, more likely, the War Office. But I'm sure that wherever it is you'll wear your MC with pride."

"I'm sorry, General," I said, "but what MC?"

"The Military Cross, m'boy. Didn't I tell you? I'm going to send Allenby a memo saying that your action at Aqaba deserves no less. It should be gazetted by the end of the month if the dunces in London don't block it and I can't see why they should: heroes are in rather short supply at the moment. Well, be off with you then – and give my love to the Sphinx." I saluted and was half way to the door when Gertrude Bell spoke.

"Mr Speedicut, are you by any chance free for an early dinner at Shepheard's this evening?" I said that I was. "Excellent, my motor will collect you from the Mess at six."

"Now look here, Gertrude..." I heard Clayton say as I closed the door, but I didn't linger to hear the rest as I couldn't wait to get back to my room and tell Fahran of my good fortune.

"Congratulations, huzoor," he said with a beaming smile when I told him. "It's not many Second Lieutenants who have an MC without having served in the trenches; which reminds me, huzoor."

"Reminds you of what, Fahran?"

"To tell you that our trunks are packed and we'll be able to catch the SS *Omrah* sailing for Marseilles at midnight tonight."

"Why would we want to do that?"

"Because you will shortly be receiving Orders to report to the regiment in France, huzoor."

"How on earth do you…" Then, with a clang like the chiming of a great funeral bell, the penny dropped. I sat down and held my head in my hands.

"What's the matter, huzoor?" I told him of the conversation I'd overhead outside Clayton's office. "I see," he said when I'd finished.

"It's not that I mind doing my bit, Fahran. Dammit, why should I be exempted when all the chaps I was at school with are out there? But when you realise *why* I'm being sent to France – well, then it's puts a different complexion on it."

"Indeed, huzoor," Fahran said sympathetically.

"And it's not just that. I've once already been lined up by the Brotherhood for a one-way ticket to the hereafter and I don't fancy my chances a second time. Why on earth I ever asked to join the wretched organisation in the first place, I can't think…"

"Because like me, huzoor, you choose to follow in your illustrious father's footsteps."

"But he made it to over ninety, Fahran. If the Brotherhood has anything to do with it, I'm not going to see nineteen."

"If it *is* the Brotherhood's doing, huzoor. If it's not - and it could well be that Major Lawrence and General Clayton are acting on their own initiative and for their own reasons - then I'm sure that Sir Philip will intervene."

"How can we find out?"

"Ask him, huzoor."

"But there isn't time, Fahran. He's in France."

"There is if you send him a telegram, huzoor."

An hour later, Fahran was on his way to the nearest civilian telegraph office with a telegram we'd concocted for Philip Sassoon, which I hoped he would be able to decode without too much difficulty. It read:

> RETURNED TO CITY OF ENIGMATIC CAT STOP INFORMED SIBLING SERVICES NO LONGER REQUIRED STOP REWARD IS FROG MUD BATH STOP IS THIS YOUR INTENTION QUERY SPEED

The answer wasn't long in coming:

> DEFINITELY NOT STOP EMBARK TOMORROW SS ORSOVA FOR SACRED KEY HOLDER CITY VIA MOUNT STOP YOUR BROTHER NEEDS HELP WITH REVOLTING BEAR STOP FURTHER ORDERS TO FOLLOW STOP GB

"Key holder – mount – revolting bear? What on earth can Sir Philip mean, Fahran? Am I to go to Rome via Mount Athos? And why does he think I have a brother with a bear? Can you make any sense of it?"

"The easy bit is the SS *Orsova*, huzoor, which leaves Alexandria tomorrow afternoon for – I believe - Southampton."

"I had worked that much out for myself," I said testily.

"I think, huzoor," said Fahran looking mildly pained at my petulance, "that 'sacred key holder city' is St Petersburg – it's St Peter who holds the keys of Heaven - via 'mount', which must mean your flat in London, huzoor. The 'revolting bear' is Russia which is, as you know, in the grip of revolution, which means that 'Brother' must be Mr Stopford…."

"You know, I believe you're right, Fahran. Well done." Then I suddenly remembered the article in the *ILN*, which I'd read earlier, and another penny crashed into the bucket. "Oh, Lord!"

"Huzoor?"

"This telegram must mean that I've got to help Mr Stopford rescue the Russian Royal Family. Why the hell didn't I let General Clayton have me sent to the Western Front?"

"That's a *very* good question, huzoor."

CHAPTER NINETEEN: CHIMES BEFORE MIDNIGHT

Philip must have sent at least one more telegram for, within the hour, I received a brown envelope from GHQ containing instructions for our embarkation on the *Orsova*, the news that I was being temporarily seconded to the Foreign Office and the instruction to report to Mr Harold Nicolson at the FO on my return to London. However, before all of that I had the somewhat dreary prospect of dinner with the Arab Bureau's very own bluestocking, Miss Gertrude Bell. I had no idea why she had invited me to dine, unless she had been instantly *bouleversé* (as Philip would have said) by my blue eyes and cavalry bearing; that, however, seemed unlikely. Whatever the reason, I could think of a lot of better ways of spending my last evening in Cairo and for one moment I considered chucking. However, I've always been a polite sort of chap not given to gratuitous rudeness or defying social conventions one of which was dress, on which subject I sought out Tertius.

"Standards have been allowed to slip since the Krauts and the Turks got uppity," opined Tertius, "and Service Dress will do for dinner at an hotel with a lady. Of course, you could put on that Arab frock of yours and *épatez les bourgeois de Caire* but you'd probably asphyxiate Miss Bell in the process, which – thinking about it - might not be such a bad thing, as you could then come and join us at the casino."

Now, in the fiction of Mr Buchan, I would have spent the evening that followed being inveigled by Miss B into hunting down Fifth Columnists in the backstreets of Cairo after coffee or, in the case of Mr MacDonald Fraser, giving her a sound rogering under the billiard table in Shepheard's whilst Allenby and his pals miscued the pills above. On that score, it is true that over the sherry trifle and lumpy custard in the hotel's Moorish dining room I established that Miss B was no follower of Sappho. Indeed, so it emerged, she had for many years nurtured an unrequited passion for a married Welch Fusilier Lieutenant Colonel with a VC;[88] he'd bought it at Gallipoli and, ever since, Miss B had sublimated her passion into her work.

However, over the Brown Windsor glop – it did not merit the appellation 'soup' – and the main course which followed it she and I discussed things much more historically significant than the aforementioned fictional storylines and, as truth is often stranger and much more interesting than fiction, I think they are worth recording for posterity. This is particularly so because, if France and Britain had implemented my off-the-cuff answers to her questions, the Middle East would be a very different place than it is today.

"You know," she said, as a waiter swept away the half-full soup bowls and presented us with plates of over-done horse masquerading as beef, accompanied by pale-hued roast spuds, sickly-looking greens and a Gyppo chef's idea as to what constituted Yorkshire pudding, "the food here is supposed to be the best in Cairo. In reality, it's dreadful, for which I apologise. Quite why the hotel management think that, wherever we happen to be in the world, the British always want to eat *à l'anglaise* has always been a mystery to me."

"I don't have a great deal of experience on that front," I replied. "You see, before I was sent on this caper I'd only ever been to Paris and St Petersburg, where the cooking is anything but à *l'anglaise.*"

"So, you've come to the Middle East with a fresh and open mind?"

"I'm not sure about 'fresh and open'," I replied. "Blissfully ignorant might be a better description. Before I arrived here, and setting aside a briefing paper I was given on the subject of the Revolt, the sum total of my knowledge of the region amounted to a reasonable understanding of events in the Holy Land, as described in the Bible, and a vague memory from my history lessons that a lot of time and energy was expended in the Middle Ages trying to get the Holy Places back from the Saracens, whoever they might have been. Oh, yes," I added as I dredged back

---

[88] Lieutenant Colonel Charles Doughty-Wylie VC CB CMG (1868-1915).

through memories of my time spent dozing through history classes at Eton, "I also knew about Byron swimming the Hellespont to liberate Greece and the Charge of the Light Brigade, all of which had something to do with the 'Sick Man of Europe' although I can't now remember what. If, last Christmas, you'd asked me for a geo-political analysis of the region or a dissertation on the virtues and vices of the Ottoman Empire, I would have had to disappoint you."

"And now?"

"Now I think I have a better understanding of what's going on in the region, albeit that I've only had a worm's eye view."

"That's very interesting, Mr Speedicut. No, I won't have the horseradish, thank you," this to the over-diligent waiter who then dumped the sauceboat in front of me. "All too many of my colleagues have preconceived notions: they're either ardent Arabists, like Lawrence, Ottoman apologists or Zionist zealots. I very much fear that our plans for the region are more informed by prejudice than by common sense."

"What plans?" I asked. "I thought that the region was only of interest to us as a means of biffing Kaiser Bill's backside."

"In some quarters that is the view but it ignores the fact that, if we are successful in opening a Second British Front with Germany, we will - in the process – have destroyed an Empire which has controlled the Middle East, and protected its highly important archaeological sites, for more than six hundred years. What then?"

"Who cares?" I said, helping myself to the horseradish sauce to disguise the flavour of the meat.

"For a start, we do." The waiter returned and proffered more condiments. "No, I really don't want mint sauce or cranberry, *thank* you. Really – do they have no idea?"

"Why does anyone, other than the archaeologists, give a fig for what happens?" I asked, picking up the conversation which the waiter had interrupted.

"Because of the Suez Canal: it is not only part-owned by us but it is also the strategic route to India and our Empire in the East. To keep the Canal open and secure, we need a stable and friendly government in Egypt."

"But I thought we'd got that. Surely we effectively annexed Egypt at the outset of the war?"

"You are better informed than you claim, Mr Speedicut. However, our control of Egypt only secures the west bank of the Canal. To the east there lies the potential for chaos. If the Arabian Peninsula is in turmoil, not only is the Canal vulnerable but so too are the sea lanes through the Red Sea and our coaling station at Aden. If Mesopotamia falls into the hands of a hostile power then the Persian Gulf is also at risk."

"I understand about the Canal and Aden," I said trying to look interested in the subject as the waiter slopped red wine into our glasses, "but why does the Persian Gulf matter?"

"Oil, Mr Speedicut. We have reason to believe that the Gulf region is rich in it."

"So what? The Navy and our industries run on coal from Wales and our motor cars run on American petrol, don't they?"

"Both statements are true, Mr Speedicut, at least as matters stand today, but there are some of us who think that in the post-war world the demand for oil will increase exponentially. If we are right, then it is essential that Britain is in control of a source that is far closer to home than Texas, Mexico, or California."

"I see," I said, "and what about the Levant; is there oil there too?"

"Probably not," she said, "the issue with the Levant is the French – and the Jews."

"What has either of them got to do with it?" I said as the waiter splashed more red wine into my glass.

"As far as the French are concerned, the disintegration or the forced dismemberment of the Ottoman Empire, which has moved materially closer thanks to the exploits of Ned Lawrence in Arabia, General Maude in Mesopotamia and – we hope – General Allenby in Palestine, presents them with an opportunity to expand their Empire."

"But they don't have one."

"Not on the scale of ours, that's true, but they control a large swathe of north Africa and they want to secure a foothold on the eastern Mediterranean littoral."

"Why – if there's no oil?"

"That's a very good question, Mr Speedicut. Let me answer it with another: why do the French do anything?"

"I've absolutely no idea," I said with a laugh. "And what about the Jews?" I added, as I tried to steer the conversation onto securer ground – well, I knew Philip Sassoon, I'd met Ernest Cassel and I'd read my Bible, albeit not since I'd left Sunday School.

"Ah, the Jews," she said heaving a deep sigh. "That is an altogether different issue: in return for further financial support for the war they, it seems, want a homeland or – if you listen to the Zionists – they want their homeland back."

"Where exactly?"

"Jerusalem and the Jordan Valley or, to give the places their Biblical names, Judea and Samaria."

"So why can't they have them? From what I've seen of the area as far north as Petra it's barren, barely occupied by nomadic Bedouin, of no significant strategic importance once the Turks have gone and if, as you say, it doesn't have oil, then I would have thought that we were getting the better half of the bargain: we get bags of much needed cash and the Jews get a load of ancient monuments and tons of useless sand."

"I never said they couldn't have a homeland in Palestine. They can. Providing, that is, that someone can convince the Grand Mufti, the Roman Catholic and Coptic Popes, the Greek and Russian Orthodox Synods, the Archbishop of Canterbury and the peoples currently in occupation of the land, that Jerusalem and its environs should be given to unbelieving foreigners who were last in control of the area before Roman times."

"Surely, it's just a matter of telling them?"

"Would that it was that easy… And even if it were, it – and the rest of agreed Anglo-French policy for the region - leaves out one very important factor."

"What's that?"

"The Arabs – or rather the nationalistic ambitions of the principal tribal families in the region."

"What ambitions?"

"Are you aware of the promises that have been made by the Arab Bureau to Sherif Hussein in return for him initiating the Arab Revolt, Mr Speedicut."[89]

"You mean sack-loads of British - or should that be Jewish - gold?"

"No. Sovereignty over the region once the Turks have gone."

---

[89] Sherif Hussein bin Ali (1854-1931), Emir and Grand Sherif of Mecca.

"Ah," I said trying to sound knowledgeable, "a carve up of the old Ottoman Empire into new, independent Arab kingdoms for Hussein's family rather than adding them, one way or another, to the French and British empires?"

"Precisely. What better way to secure the tribes' support to both oust the Turks *and* to protect our post-war interests."

"The second part will never work."

"Why not?"

"Because, leaving aside what the British and French governments have planned, it pre-supposes that the tribal leaders, and more importantly the tribesmen themselves, could possibly agree for more than five minutes to control anything other than the land on which their tents and camels happen to be squatting at that particular moment. In my recent experience on the ground that's an impossibility."

"But that is to forget or to ignore the significant settled populations which already exist in places like Jerusalem, Damascus, Basra and Baghdad."

"If you are saying, Miss Bell, that a bunch of - for the most part - ill-educated, arse-scratching nomads, with archaic not to say barbaric religious beliefs and murderous inter-tribal enmities stretching back generations, are capable of getting their heads around the concept of arbitrary national borders, urban populations and constitutional government then, in my limited, albeit first-hand, experience, I think – and please forgive me for being blunt – that you are living in cloud-cuckoo land."

"So, what would be your solution?"

My analysis thus far was nothing more than common sense based on four months of living with the Bedouin. What Miss B was now asking for required considerably more than that. As I didn't want to make a fool of myself, and to buy some thinking time, I signalled to the lurking waiter to refill my glass. In his enthusiasm to comply, he poured half a bottle of the very decent claret into my lap: fortunately, most of it was caught in my napkin.

"You can sponge yourself off in my suite after dinner," said Miss Bell in a no-nonsense voice than reminded me strongly of my Dame at school. As the Chateau Petrus seeped into my underwear, I remembered snatches of a conversation I'd had with Fahran whilst changing for dinner. Thank heaven that he, at least, had a grasp of strategic issues in the Middle East.

"You ask a very tricky question, Miss Bell, but here's what I think might work: garrison the bits that matter to us and the French, give the historic sites to Thomas Cook, place the control of Jerusalem in the hands of an ecumenical board of clerics, let the Jews have the rest of the Holy Land in exchange for the Lombard and Wall Street rhino, and leave everything else to the Bedouin to sort out amongst themselves."

"Interesting, if unconventional, Mr Speedicut. Unfortunately, that's not what Sykes and Picot have agreed will be done to protect British and French interests, although the establishment of a Jewish homeland is what Balfour plans to announce in order to secure the Jews' support," she said, as much to herself as to me. "However, it completely ignores what we've already promised the Arabs."

"You mean self-government after the war?"

"Precisely; and to an Englishman, 'my word is my bond'. Neither Ned nor I will be moved on that…"[90] Once again the waiter hove into view, clutching a fresh napkin and a brace of menus, and she changed the subject. "Would you like some cheese and pudding, Mr Speedicut? It might help you to forget the taste of what we've just eaten?"

---

[90] Editor's Note: The Sykes-Picot Agreement of May 1916 allocated spheres of influence and control to France, Britain and Russia in a post-Ottoman world; the Balfour Declaration of November 1917 establish Britain's commitment to the establishment of a Jewish homeland in Palestine; and Gertrude Bell lobbied tirelessly at the post-war Peace Conference for the creation of the Kingdoms of Greater Syria (Syria & Iraq), Transjordan and Hejaz for Sherif Hussein and his sons Faisal and Abdullah.

Over the mousetrap which followed, we talked mostly about Lawrence, with whom Bell was clearly smitten albeit on an un-requited basis. She was also worried that he had 'gone native' and lost his objectivity.

"If that weren't bad enough," she went on, "he's utterly obsessed with the Legend of Kasredin and talks about almost nothing else. It's clouding his judgment. It's absurd given that he's achieved every goal he's been set, and more, *without* such a figure."

"I know," I said.

"He won't admit it, but I'm sure that he thinks he has found this mythical person. Do you know who it might be?"

"Possibly," I said, "although it's just a hunch; I have no hard evidence."

"Do tell me," she said as, for the first time, she leaned forward and placed a hand over one of mine and gave it a warm squeeze.

"I think that it's – it's the person Ned sees when he has the need to use a shaving mirror."

"You mean that Ned thinks that *he* is Kasredin?" Her grip tightened.

"Yes."

"Good Lord," she exclaimed, "that explains everything…"

But as to what 'everything' was she wouldn't say and, over the tasteless trifle, she switched the subject to herself as I've already mentioned. I turned down the sickly-sweet coffee that was then offered and Miss B said that in that case, and as my time was limited, we should go up to her set of rooms so that she could repair the damage to my uniform. With hindsight, despite the fact that she ordered me to, it was reckless to have removed my trousers so that she could swab them clean. However, her manner was business-like and contained not a hint of any impropriety. Feeling rather ridiculous, I stood in my shirt, tie, underwear, suspenders and socks in her sitting room whilst she took my tunic and bags off to the bathroom and then hung them on the balcony to dry. As she came back into the room she must have noticed that my shorts had been drenched as well.

"You can hardly go to Alexandria with your underpants in that condition," she opined in a brisk, no-nonsense voice, "take them off too and I'll rinse them out for you. Then I'll put them on the balcony with your trousers and jacket. In this heat, they'll be dry in no time."

"But I've nothing else to wear whilst they do."

"I'll get you a bath towel to wrap around your middle then you can give me your, err, things…"

And, of course, you can guess what happened. I did as she'd instructed but, half way through the operation, the towel fell off revealing rather more of me than I thought, wrongly at it turned out, she could stand. From that moment on the end game was inevitable as one thing led to another and we ended up on the double bed. Now don't complain: I only stated at the start of this chapter that we hadn't had a romp *under the billiard table*. I made no mention of anywhere else and, what with her unrequited passion and my pent-up lust, my youth and her approaching maturity and the moral laxity which wartime seems to encourage… Anyway, God only knows what she'd learnt at Lady Margaret Hall but, whatever it was, her behaviour was most un-ladylike in virtually every department - although she did draw the line at conventional penetration. For the rest of her and me, it was open season and by that I mean exactly what I have just written.

Prior to that night on the second floor of Shepheard's Hotel, if asked I'd have been dismissive of unmarried academics of the female variety, summarily condemning them as tight-arsed dykes (and in the cases of the haughty Vita Sackville West and the neurotic Virginia Woolf I was, as you will in due course read, right) but that night made me more open minded. The things that Miss Bell did to me with her lips, teeth, tongue, fingers and an un-lit candle from the bedside table, as we bounced around naked – save for her corset and stockings and my service dress cap which we'd exchanged at the start of the bout - were nothing short of an education.

By the time we'd finished, I'd progressed from a Higher School Certificate in fornication to a PhD.

When I staggered out of the hotel an hour later to be met by Fahran in a fiacre piled high with our trunks, I was barely in a fit state to climb in, let alone board the train to Alexandria or even, the following afternoon, mount the gangway to the waiting troopship. The voyage back to Blighty, as the lower decks insisted on referring to the land of hope and glory, was uneventful: a boatload of odoriferous Tommies and tattooed tars not being conducive to fun and frolics of any but the most basic variety of which, thanks to Miss Gertrude Bell, I had no immediate need.

Atash and Ivan, whom Fahran had telegraphed from Gibraltar, met us off the train at Waterloo and the four of us drove back to Mount Street in the comfort of my Daimler.

"So, you are *en route* to Russia, Excellency," said Ivan once I had brought the home team up to speed.

"It looks like it, but I won't know more until I've seen Mr Nicolson tomorrow."

"Assuming that is your next destination, Excellency, I will accompany you as – despite the war - my business is running well and I can certainly spare the time."

"What about me, huzoor?" said Atash from behind the wheel of the motor as we swung into Berkeley Square.

"And me," said Fahran.

"Gentlemen, gentlemen," I replied soothingly, "I will certainly be allowed to take one of you, possibly two but certainly not three. For obvious reasons, I will take Ivan. Fahran, you need a break and any way it's not your turn so, Atash, if Her Majesty's government will agree, you may come too. We will all know our fate tomorrow morning."

Waiting for me at Mount Street was a letter from Nicolson. Instead of meeting him at the Foreign Office he proposed a lunch at the Travellers Club in Pall Mall so that is where I met him.

"My dear Brother Speedicut," he said quietly as he gripped my hand rather too warmly in the club's somewhat cramped entrance hall. "Congratulations on your Military Cross; it was gazetted this morning. Your late father would have been so proud of you. He had many decorations, you know, but never one for gallantry… I suggest that we go straight into lunch, if that is agreeable with you?" Unlike Shepheard's and despite the war the food wasn't too bad, which is more than can be said for my instructions. "The Great Boanerges has asked me to tell you that he is very concerned about your recent treatment and to reassure you that it was not the Brotherhood's doing. It would appear that Brother Esher, or ex-Brother Esher as I should now call him, not only exceeded his duty to the Brotherhood in his capacity as Great Boanerges but has continued from the side-lines to try to, err, bury certain personally damaging facts of which he believed you to be in possession."

"So, to keep the secret of his activities in his son's bedroom he plotted to send me to the sea bed and, when that failed, to have me blown to pieces on the Western Front?" Nicolson feigned shock at this but didn't attempt to deny it.

"Unfortunately, it would appear so. But put all that behind you. The new GB has also asked me to tell you that, although you should be on leave, he has a pressing need for you to join Brother Stopford in Petrograd, as we must now call it."

"That much I know," I said as I tucked into some pretty decent cold poached salmon, "but what is my assignment? I assume it's to help Brother Bertie extract the Imperial Family."

"No, I'm afraid it's not that. Despite the close family ties with our own Royal Family, the government deems that it would not be expedient at the present time to offer the Tsar and his family sanctuary in this country."

"Why ever not?"

"Politics, my dear Brother Charles – if I may? And do please call me Brother Harold."

"Well, they'll be safe enough until the place settles down. Prince Lvov will hardly want to harm them."

"So, you haven't heard?"

"Heard what?"

"That Lvov's government has fallen and Russia is now in the hands of a socialist republican firebrand called Kerensky."[91]

"If he's a republican, he'll want to be shot of the Imperial Family as quickly as he can, surely?"

"Let's hope not literally, Brother Charles," Nicolson simpered.

"I shouldn't worry," I reposted, "before the Tsarina can say 'fetch my tiara' they'll all be in a *pensione* in Monte Carlo sponging off the Grimaldis."

"One can only hope so."

"So, if I'm not to rescue the Romanovs what is my task? Not my half-sister and her brood?"

"You will be relieved to hear, Brother Charles, that as your half-sister is still a British national our Embassy has taken an interest in her and we believe the Lievens are safe on their estate in the Crimea." I heaved a sigh of relief, as the prospect of acting in the role of the Scarlet Pimpernel to my Russian relations was only slightly more appealing than trying to snatch the Romanovs. "However," he went on, "your remark just then about tiaras was percipient: you are to help Brother Stopford recover the jewellery of the Grand Duchess Vladimir."

---

[91] Alexander Fyodorovich Kerensky (1881-1970).

"You're not serious?"

"I fear that I am. You see, unfortunately for you and Brother Bertie, the Grand Duchess left her jewellery behind in Petrograd when she retired to her country estate at Kislovodsk earlier this year."

"But why should the Brotherhood have any interest in rescuing a handful of baubles belonging to a German Princess who happens to be the widow of a Romanov Grand Duke?"

"I think you will find that it is rather more than a handful – and the Brotherhood is acting at the request of a *very* important person."

"Who?"

Rather late in the day, Nicolson looked around the half-empty dining room to make sure that we weren't being overheard, then he leant forward and whispered:

"The Queen."

CHAPTER TWENTY: THE PEARLY PIMPERNEL

"Miserly Mary? You'd think she had enough jewels, what with the Cullinan chips and the Cambridge loot," I couldn't help saying.

"Brother Charles, you forget yourself. It is the wife of our sovereign to whom you refer. I am sure that Her Majesty is motivated only by the desire to keep the Grand Duchess's priceless collection out of the hands of the revolutionaries."

"So, have I also got to secure the Dowager Empress's trinkets as well?"

"No. It would appear that she has most of them with her in the Crimea, unlike the unfortunate Yusupovs."

"What did or didn't they do?"

"I understand from Felix, who writes to me occasionally that, despite his exile following that unfortunate business with Rasputin, he has been able to return to Petrograd two or three times and has secured the Rembrandts, along with a handful of important stones, which he's taken to Yalta. However, he has bricked up the bulk of Zinaida's and Irina's jewels in his palace in Moscow."

"Why on earth didn't Felix and the Grand Duchess Vlad take everything with them? It's not as though even the largest collection of rocks would fill more than a couple of Gladstone bags."

"Unfortunately, as with so many other Russians - the Dowager Empress excepted – it seems they thought that the revolution was just a temporary aberration and that they would be able to return to their palaces, unbrick their jewels and resume their lives after a few weeks. With the rise to power of Kerensky – and who knows what might follow him - that would now seem to be highly unlikely."

"So, when do I have to pack my bags?"

"I have booked you a passage in a convoy that leaves from Harwich for Helsinki next Monday. On arrival in Helsinki you will be met by our *Chargé d'Affaires* who will see you onto a train to Petrograd. Brother Bertie, who has been on an errand to the Grand Duchess and her family in the Caucasus, will collect you from the Finland Station and take you to his hotel, although he has told me to warn you that the city is not what it was and that food of almost any sort is in very short supply. Consequently, he has asked that you take with you a couple of trunks packed with tinned goods…" Searcy's would oblige, I thought, particularly as I was planning to take Ivan with me.

"So, it won't be a holiday then?" I said with as much irony as I could get into my voice.

"Anything but, I would have thought," said Nicolson, "and probably not without it dangers."

"In which case may I take my secretary, my valet and my chauffeur as bodyguards?"

"I'm afraid not, Brother Charles. The Foreign Office will allow you to take one servant but that is all." Fahran and Atash won't like that, I thought, but there was a firm set to Nicolson's chin which told me that the decision would not be subject to review. "On a more cheerful subject, my wife and I are giving a dinner party tomorrow evening and, despite the late notice, very much hope that you will join us."

"I should be delighted," I replied.

"It will just be a small gathering to entertain *Maître* Diaghilev, who is passing through London, and dear Winnie Polignac, who also happens to be in town. Do you know either of them?"

"No," I said, although I'd read about both the Russian impresario and the fabulously rich Singer sewing machine heiress – and I seemed to remember Tertius saying that the former was not safe with handsome boys and the latter with pretty girls.[92]

"The Woolfs and the Bells will also be there," continued Nicolson, "as will the Morrells and a young artist they've befriended called Miss Carrington, whom I hope you will take in to dinner.[93] Now do tell me about how you got on with young Brother Ned in Arabia…"

I won't trouble you with an account of that dinner party, beyond telling you that our hostess, Mrs N, aka the Hon V Sackville-West, looked like a man in drag and for the entire evening kept her rising-star diplomat husband firmly under her thumb. Collectively, the guests represented an impressive cross-section of the twentieth-century's intellectual, artistic and sexually deviant *gratin* (Diaghilev addressed not a word to me during the evening but gave me several very queer looks)[94] and the big money which supported them. Almost everyone around that table was to play a role, of one sort or another, in my life in the post-war world. However, before I recount any of that, I need to set down the quite extraordinary few months I was about to undertake in revolutionary Russia. I should start this tale of larceny, imprisonment, murder and general derring-do by giving you a more detailed description of the two principal players in the first act of the drama: the Grand Duchess Maria Pavlovna of Russia, more usually referred to as the Grand Duchess Vladimir, and Mr Albert Stopford, the Brotherhood's man in Petrograd. Both have, of course, already featured frequently in my narrative thus far but, given the importance of what was to follow, I think they both deserve a bit more 'colour' before the curtain rises.

---

[92] Sergei Pavlovich de Diaghilev (1872-1929) and Winnaretta Singer, Princess Edmond de Polignac (1865-1943.)
[93] Leonard Woolf (1880-1969), Virginia Woolf (1882-1941), Clive Bell (1881-1964), Vanessa Bell (1879-1961), Philip Morrell (1870-1943), Lady Ottoline Morrell (1873-1938) & Dora Carrington (1893-1932).
[94] Editor's Note: This may have been because Diaghilev recalled Speedicut's father (see *The Speedicut Papers: Book 9 (Boxing Icebergs)*) rather than for any sexual reason – or, maybe, for both.

Mrs Vlad, as I always like to think of her, had the reputation in Petersburg Society of being the grandest of the Grand Duchesses which, considering that she wasn't a Romanov by birth (unless you count her being the great-great-grand daughter of the barking-mad Tsar Paul I), was a tribute to the fear she instilled in her peers and those lesser mortals who strayed into her orbit. Born merely Her Highness Duchess Marie of Mecklenburg-Schwerin, a minor north German Grand Duchy about the size of Yorkshire, she was known within family circles as 'Miechen'. Originally, she'd been lined up as a brood mare for a middle-aged minor German Princeling, Prince George of Schwarzburg,[95] until - that is – the rather younger Grand Duke Vladimir Alexandrovich of Russia hove into Schwerin on the Grand Tour.[96]

As the son, brother and uncle of successive Tsars he was a much better catch than a mere Prince of Schwarzburg and catch him Marie did. In due course, the marriage produced four boys and a girl so,[97] despite the fact that pretty is not a word one would have used to describe her, Mrs Vlad must have had something going for her. Whatever it was, until the day he died in 1909 at the relatively early age of fifty-six, Vladimir Alexandrovich encouraged her to establish, and then supported at considerable cost, the most fashionable, cosmopolitan and glamorous Court in St Petersburg. The glittering gatherings at the Vladimir Palace were rivalled only by those of the Dowager Empress and far outshone the dreary bourgeois set-up at Tsarskoe Selo presided over by that other German Princess, the crabby, deadly dull and religious-neurotic, Tsarina Alexandra.

In addition to giving Mrs Vald a blank cheque for entertaining, Vladimir Alexandrovich also smothered his wife's not insignificant top hamper with enormous and historically important jewels, mostly set by Cartier. This considerable collection was housed in five large glass-fronted display

---

[95] His Serene Highness Prince George of Schwarzburg-Rudolfstadt (1838-1890)
[96] His Imperial Highness Grand Duke Vladimir Alexandrovich of Russia (1847-1909).
[97] TIH the Grand Dukes Alexander Vladimirovich, Kirill Vladimirovich (1876-1938), Boris Vladimirovich (1877-1943) & Andrei Vladimirovich (1879-1956) and the Grand Duchess Elena Vladimirovna (1882-1957).

cabinets in her bedroom in the Vladimir Palace – one each for her suites of diamonds, rubies, sapphires, emeralds and pearls – and included a necklace of emeralds the size of matchboxes, one of which had belonged to Catherine the Great and weighed more than a hundred carats, a one hundred and thirty-seven carat sapphire, a ruby that had belonged to Napoleon's first squeeze, Josephine, and a pair of huge and perfectly round pearl earrings. In addition to all of this, Mrs Vlad was one of Fabergé best customers and acquired an extensive collection of his trinkets and bibelots.

As I've already recounted, when the going got rough in Petersburg, Mrs Vlad, who'd been plotting and scheming to have her eldest son Kiril Vladimirovich replace the Tsar, popped most of her swag into a hidden safe in the Vladimir Palace, deposited two suitcases full of Fabergé cigarette cases and the like with the Swedish Embassy and legged it off to her country estate in the Caucasus with her two younger sons and a crocodile-skin case containing her 'country jewellery'.

Given all of the above, it is curious that Bertie Stopford should have become such a stuffy of Mrs Vlad. Born the son of a country parson, whose modest living was at Titchmarsh in Northamptonshire, Bertie claimed that his great-grandfather was the Anglo-Irish Earl of Courtown,[98] a claim which I have since verified. Bertie also asserted that his papa was chums with three occupants of the British throne: Victoria, Edward VII and George V and that he, Bertie, was both an 'Honourable' and a 'Knight of the Realm' - assertions he was careful to make only once he was well clear of Dover. This was all complete tosh, although Philip had told me that, as a result of her obsession with, and his involvement in, the fine art world, Bertie was indeed on some sort of terms with Queen Mary.

However, in addition to his remote connection to the Peerage and his dealings with May of Teck, Bertie had two other important personal attributes: he was a great charmer and a rampant poof. These two characteristics had undoubtedly brought him into the pink-hued circles of Philip Sassoon and Felix Yusupov. What I haven't been able to establish

---

[98] James Stopford, 3rd Earl of Courtown (1765-1835).

is how he got into those circles (and the Brotherhood) in the first place or how he supported the extravagant life style in London, Paris and St Petersburg that went with them – an expense that was way beyond the means of a rural Rector's son. I know that he dealt in antiques and he probably acted as a commission salesman for Cartier and Fabergé, which is what may have brought him to the attention of Mrs V, who could never purchase enough beautiful *objets* in white silk-lined leather cases. It's equally possible that he met her through Felix for whom, I know for a fact, Bertie procured equally beautiful 'objects of desire' encased in trousers. What I also know is that he was the most discreet and obliging man who ever trolled down Bond Street, the Faubourg St Honoré or the Nevsky Prospekt; nothing (as you will see) was too much trouble for him to do on behalf of his friends and acquaintances *providing* they were royal, rich or aristocratic.

After an uneventful crossing of the North Sea and a dismal train ride from Helsinki, Bertie met Ivan and me at St Petersburg's Finland Station, as promised by Harold, and took us off to the Grand Hotel Europe indicating, as we got into a rickety taxi, that we should not talk. Deprived of conversation, I spent the journey from the terminus to the hotel looking out of the open window of the cab. It was plain as a pikestaff that all was not well in Russia. Virtually every shop on the Nevsky Prospekt was boarded up, the streets were patrolled by armoured cars and the pavements seemed to be populated by a rag-tag-and-bobtail assortment of shifty-looking strikers and unkempt soldiery, all of whom loafed around aimlessly. The hotel, where the staff was on strike and the lobby had been turned into a makeshift canteen for the revolutionaries, wasn't much better. It was only when we got up to Bertie's room, which Ivan and I were obliged to share with him, that he spoke.

"Did you manage to bring any food?" I pointed to our trunks. "Thank God," he said as Ivan handed him the keys, "I've been living off stale rye bread ever since I got back from Kislovodsk."

"Are things that bad?" I asked.

"Worse," he replied as he prised open a tin of Dundee cake and a jar of Wensleydale, which he started to eat with his fingers, "this dear country is in a state of chaos. I got a letter this morning from the Grand Duchess saying that, the day after I left her house, it was turned upside down by the local Committee of Workmen and Soldiers looking for food, jewels and money."

"But I thought that Kerensky was now in charge."

"That's what he thinks," he said washing down the fruit cake and cheese with vodka straight from a bottle on his bedside table. "But the truth is that the cities are largely in the hands of the different Red factions and their military committees. Once they sort out their differences, Kerensky will be blown away and then who knows what will happen. What is certain is that any hope there was of a restoration of the monarchy is now a distant dream. When Kerensky goes, those Romanovs and other members of prominent families who are in the hands of the socialist revolutionaries are likely to end up dangling from lamp posts – and that's if they're lucky."

"You make it sound like the French Revolution," I said.

"It is worse, my dear Charles. Massacres of senior officers by their soldiers – usually with the utmost barbarity - are now almost a daily occurrence. And it's not just officers: poor, dear Prince Viazemsky was first blinded and then slowly tortured to death by his own peasants, who forced his wife to watch. You mark my words: the Reds' leaders will make Robespierre and Danton seem like Tweedledum and Tweedledee."

"So how long do you think Kerensky has got?" I asked, which was a roundabout way of enquiring how long it was safe for us to remain in Petrograd.

"A few weeks at most," he said opening a tin of sweet biscuits from Fortnum & Mason. "Every day the situation worsens and another army unit goes over to the Reds. Why, last night soldiers of the Preobrajensky Guards - of all regiments - broke into Donon's and stole all the wine from the restaurant's cellar! At the point at which Kerensky ceases to command any military support it will all be over for him – and that day can't be far off. After that it will be open season on our Russian friends and us, too, in all likelihood."

"And is there no opposition to these Reds?"

"None in Moscow or St Petersburg, although parts of the Caucasus, Ukraine, Siberia and the Crimea have yet to fall to under the control of the *soviets*, as the workers committees are called. It means that we will have to move fast if we are to complete our assignment. It can't be long before the *moujiks* break into the palaces and use them to house workers co-operatives. When that happens, our chance to recover the Grand Duchess's jewels will be lost…"

"… and Queen Mary won't be pleased."

"What's she got to do with it?"

"I thought that we were acting on her command to recover the jewels into her safe keeping: that's what Brother Harold told me."

"Did he, indeed? Well, I'm acting on the orders of dear Maria Pavlovna and they do *not* include delivering her collection to the British Royal Family. She would be horrified at the very thought after the way King George refused sanctuary to his cousins."

"I wonder why it is, then, that Brother Harold, the Great Boanerges and the Foreign Secretary all think that we're acting on behalf of the Queen, Bertie? Dammit, I'm here at the expense of the Foreign Office to whom I've been seconded for the duration."

"The reason that the Brotherhood and the Foreign Office believe that I am acting for the Queen, and so providing me with assistance, is because that is what I told them when I was in London last month."

"What? And they believed you?"

"Brother Harold, the Great Boanerges and the Foreign Secretary all knew that I'd been to Buckingham Palace and that my visit was to talk about Romanov jewellery with the Queen. What they didn't know was that I had been tasked by Queen Mary to find out what had happened to the Imperial Crown Jewels. I had the sad task of informing Her Majesty that the Tsarina's jewels and the Imperial Crown Jewels are in the hands of the revolutionaries - but I had the happy task of telling her that most of the Dowager Empress's jewels are safe in Yalta. In consequence, I think we can be reasonably sure that Queen Mary will convince King George to see that his aunt *and* her jewels are rescued."

"But what about the Vladimir collection?"

"I didn't mention it and Her Majesty didn't ask."

"So, what the hell am I doing here?"

"I knew, dear Charles, that rescuing Maria Pavlovna's most treasured possessions was a job that I couldn't do on my own and that, once it was done, I would need the Embassy to help me get them out of the country. So, I'm afraid that I was somewhat economical with the truth and, knowing that our friends in the Brotherhood and the FO will never ask her, I said that it was Her Majesty's command and that I needed you to help me to carry it out."

"… And thereby you've embroiled me in a highly dangerous adventure, when I could have been on a much-deserved leave after months up to my arse in sand, stinking camels, murderous Turks, Arabs and Ned Lawrence!"

"Aren't you flattered that I asked specifically for you, dear Charles?"

"No, I'm bloody well not, Bertie." There was an awkward silence after this outburst, during which Bertie scoffed an entire box of Terry's chocolate truffles and I came to the conclusion that it was useless to fart against thunder. "So, what's the plan? Have you got the keys to the Vladimir Palace?"

"Unfortunately not and they would be no use even if I had. The main door on the Embankment is guarded by the Reds and the side doors and the back entrances are bolted from the inside. The only things that dear Maria Pavlovna were able to give me was a clear set of instructions for finding the jewellery – and this." He pulled a small safe key out of his waistcoat pocket.

"So how the hell are we supposed to get into the Palace?"

"That's a problem I've yet to solve…" I was about to explode again when Ivan coughed.

"There is a way in, Excellency," he said.

"How on earth do you know?" I asked.

"I was brought up in the Palace, Excellency. My father was one of the Grand Duke's coachmen and my mother was a kitchen maid."

"But I thought you told me that you worked for the Yusupovs and that is where you first met my father."

"That is correct, Excellency. My first job, when I was just fourteen, was as a trainee under-footman in the Yusupov Palace but before that I lived at the Vladimir Palace with my parents."

"So how do we get in?" asked Bertie.

"Through the sewers, Excellency."

CHAPTER TWENTY-ONE: ALADDIN'S CAVE

"You're joking?"

"I was never more serious, Excellency. We will be able to enter the Palace through a maintenance manhole in the scullery. Below the cover there is an iron ladder that goes down into the sewers which drain into the Neva. If Mr Stopford can tell me in which room the safe is hidden, I will be able to lead you there from the scullery."

"But how do we get into the sewers in the first place?" I asked "And are they big enough to allow us to use them?"

"As to the first question, Excellency, I have an idea that I will confirm tomorrow. As to the second, the answer is 'yes' – although the sewers are not wide enough to walk in."

Bertie's hollow cheeks adopted a rather greenish tinge either at the prospect of crawling through raw sewage or because of the combination of fruit cake, cheese, biscuits, chocolates and vodka which he'd indiscriminately wolfed down since we arrived; I couldn't be sure which. Ivan must have noticed this too for he added:

"But as the Palace is not in use, Excellency, the sewers should be reasonably clear of…"

"Yes, yes, I get the picture," I said hurriedly before Bertie could be sick.

The next morning, Ivan slipped out of the hotel on his mission to find the way into the drains of the Vladimir Palace. He didn't return for hours and Bertie and I started to fret that he'd been arrested or worse. But towards four there was a knock on the door and Ivan reappeared.

"Well?" Bertie demanded.

"We cannot use the sewers, Excellency."

"Why ever not?" I asked.

"I managed to get a boatman to take me down the Neva, Excellency; it was not easy but eventually I found someone who would do as I asked. When we got to where the Palace's sewers drain into the river, I could see that the outlet pipe had been barred. I found out later that it was a precaution ordered by the Grand Duke Boris Vladimirovich when the troubles started earlier this year."

"Damn. So how are going to get in?" asked Bertie, looking somewhat relieved that he was not going to have to crawl through piles of old turds.

"After I left the boatman, Excellency, I didn't know what to do and for a couple of hours I wandered the streets racking my brains trying to remember if there was any other way in to the Palace. I had almost given up and was about to return here, when I met an old man whom I had known when I was a boy and who, until he retired last year, had worked all his life for the Grand Duke and then, when His Imperial Highness died, the Grand Duchess. The old man had been a very close friend of my mother's, if you know what I mean, Excellency, and he was extremely pleased to see me. Once I had assured myself that he had no sympathy for the revolutionaries, I told him that I needed to get into the building without being seen and I asked him if there was a way."

"What did he say?" Bertie and I demanded in unison.

"He said that there was."

"And?"

"It seems that when the Palace was built for the Grand Duke in the early 1870s, just before his marriage to the Grand Duchess, he ordered that the construction should include a concealed doorway with a secret staircase leading from the street directly up to both his bedroom and his study on the first floor. My mother's friend had been the Grand Duke's most trusted page and had acted in, err, a confidential capacity for His Imperial Highness. He said that these arrangements had been made to allow the Grand Duke to 'entertain' his lady friends without disturbing Her Imperial Highness."

"And?"

"Unfortunately for His Imperial Highness, after their marriage the Grand Duchess decided that she would like that particular corner of the first floor for her own suite of rooms.

"And?"

"So, the Grand Duke had the doors that led from the small lobby at the top of the spiral staircase concealed, although one of them still opened into the back of the wardrobes that the Grand Duchess had installed in her bedroom. However, according to my mother's friend, Her Imperial Highness never knew of the door's existence."

"But is the door on the ground floor still there or did the Grand Duke have it blocked up as well?" asked Bertie.

"It would seem not, Excellency. As Her Imperial Highness did not know of its existence, the Grand Duke did not consider it necessary... but I know where it is and how to open it."

"How on earth did you get the key?" asked Bertie.

"There is no key, Excellency. The door is concealed in the portico of the side door at the right-hand end of the Palace and opens when a certain stone is pushed."

"You are certain of that, Ivan?" I said.

"I am, Excellency, for you see I have returned here directly from Her Imperial Highness's wardrobe."

"So where is the safe, Bertie?"

"Give me a moment and I'll check," he said, getting up and going over to a briefcase on a table by the window. He fished around in it and then pulled out a rather crumpled looking note. "I hid it in my shoes on the way back from Kislovodsk," he said in answer to my unasked question. "Now let's see: yes, the safe is behind a painting of Aladdin's Cave in the Moorish boudoir, which overlooks the Neva and is accessible only from her study which leads off her bedroom."

"In which is located her wardrobe, Excellency," added Ivan, looking – with some justification - just a touch smug.

"All we have to do, then," I said, "is wait until it gets dark, slip into the Palace with a couple of bags, open the safe, remove the jewels and bring them back here. Then tomorrow we can catch the first train to Helsinki and from there the next boat for Blighty."

"I'm afraid it won't be quite as simple as that, Excellency. For a start, the guards at the main entrance to the Palace, who fortunately paid no attention to me earlier this afternoon, may be more alert this evening. There is then the danger of being stopped in the street by soldiers or revolutionaries on our way back from the Palace. Lastly, there is the problem of keeping the jewels here, even overnight: the head concierge tells me that the police have taken to raiding the guests' rooms."

"Is that true, Bertie?"

"I believe so," he said, "they were clearly in here whilst I was away, judging from the state of it when I got back."

"So, what are we going to do?"

"If I may be permitted, Excellency, I believe that I have a workable plan…"

In late-August in St Petersburg the sun sets around eight and rises around five. However, Ivan was concerned that, with the virtually lawless condition of the city, it would not be wise for three well-dressed men carrying suitcases to be out late on the streets. So, he proposed that, as soon as darkness fell the following evening, we would leave the hotel by the kitchen entrance, disguised as a team of plumbers carrying holdalls containing our tools and that, on completion of the rescue, we would return not to the hotel but to the British Embassy where we would lodge the swag in the Ambassador's safe, then change into evening dress before returning later to the Grand Hotel Europe, as though from an Embassy dinner. As plans go, it was a good plan

"The head concierge will get us the necessary disguises, Excellency. He is a member of…"

"… the Nehemiah," I completed the sentence for him. Bertie looked puzzled at this reference to the butlers' and concierges' international network but neither of us enlightened him.

"And I will pre-position your evening dress and my suit at the Embassy tomorrow," he continued, "providing only that you, Excellency, or Mr Stopford, can make the necessary arrangements with the Ambassador."

"That won't be a problem," said Bertie, "Sir George is a good friend of mine."

"But if we succeed in getting the jewels to the Embassy, Ivan, how will we ever get them out of there?"

"There is an old Russian proverb, Excellency: a wise man who wishes to cross the Volga safely engages only one boatman at a time."

Twenty-four or so hours later, had you been standing by the back entrance to the Grand Hotel Europe, you would have seen a scruffy plumber and his two mates slouching away from the kitchens and, had you then been standing on the Palace Embankment twenty minutes hence, you would have seen the same group stopping for a fag break by the right-hand side door of the vast Vladimir Palace. A group of Red Guards were gossiping around a brazier under the Palace's main portico some fifty feet away, but they paid us no attention. I lit up a gasper for Bertie whilst Ivan slid into the shadow of the doorway. There was a clonk followed by a grinding sound, which was so loud I was certain it would attract the attention of the Reds and, for one dreadful moment, I thought that it had when one of them called over something in an incomprehensible Russian dialect.

"Say '*niet, spasibo*', Excellency," I heard Ivan whisper. I did so and the answer seemed to satisfy the fellow, who went back to jawing with his pals. Then I heard Ivan whisper: "When they're not looking, come in."

I glanced over at the Reds, who were now engaged in making tea, and gave Bertie a shove towards the doorway, pulling the cigarette out of his fingers as I did so. He was only a slight man and he stumbled down the short flight of steps with me hard on his heels, minus the Woodbines. Ivan must have then pushed the door back into place, cutting off the feeble light from the gas lamps on the Embankment. With the entrance closed, it was black as pitch in what I assumed was a lobby, until Ivan switched on an electric torch he'd acquired along with our disguises.

"Please follow me, Excellencies."

Immediately to his front I could see, in the feeble beam of the torch, a cobweb encrusted iron spiral staircase which Ivan proceeded to climb followed by Bertie and me. As promised, the staircase ended on the floor above in a windowless space barely large enough for the three of us with our bags. I heard the creak of hinges as Ivan pulled a narrow door towards us and, in the lamp's flickering light, realised that we were – to judge from a faint aroma of a heavy perfume - in the back of a woman's clothes cupboard that was hung with an assortment of full-length fur coats. Ivan switched off the torch, pushed through the coats, opened the door on the other side and stepped out into a large, lavishly furnished bedroom illuminated by moonlight which flooded in from a window overlooking an inner courtyard.

It looked as though everything was as Maria Pavlovna had left it, except that five tall, glass-fronted display cabinets ranged along one side of the room were empty. From Mrs Vlad's bedroom Ivan led us first into her study, a cream and gilt room of neo-Classical design, and then he turned left through an open doorway into her boudoir. I'd never seen anything like it before. Facing us, immediately opposite the door from the study, was a grotesquely ugly *faux*-Moorish carved and pierced white marble and gilt fire surround surmounted by a clock set in matching pierced marble and gilt. To our right was a tall, arched window covered in oriental fretwork through which I could see the Neva flowing in the moonlight on the other side of the Embankment. Either side of the window sill, sitting on a beautiful Persian carpet that covered the whole floor, was an ivory inlaid table of the sort I'd last seen in Cairo, a small round gilded chess table and four footstools. The walls were exotically tiled up to the dado and then papered above in an elaborate red and blue Arabic-pattern design ending in a high-relief ceramic cornice. At the opposite end of the room from the window was a semi-circular alcove, which filled the full width of the room and was fitted with a deep banquette upholstered in what looked like purple silk.[99] To top-off this ghastly decoration, the *pièce de résistance* was the domed and coved ceiling above the cornice which comprised a mass of mosaics and gilding; it would not have looked out of place in the Topkapi seraglio. Above the awful fireplace clock facing us was the only painting in the room, a fanciful depiction of a craggy cave lit with lanterns and piled high with treasure. It was framed in dark, heavily carved wood. Ivan stepped forward, reached up and pulled on the lower right corner of the picture. It didn't move. He then tried the lower left corner, but the picture still didn't budge.

"Do you think it could be locked?" asked Bertie.

---

[99] Editor's Note: Speedicut had appended his own footnote here: 'Some years ago, at Cliveden, I was told by my good friend, Genya Ivanov, to whom I'd related this story, that on the left side of the alcove was a jib door, which must have opened onto the spiral staircase from which we'd just emerged, but it had been papered over and was invisible to us and also, presumably, to Maria Pavlovna'. Readers may be interested to learn that 'Genya Ivanov' was Captain Yevgeny Ivanov (1926-1994) the Soviet Naval Attaché who was at the heart of the Profumo Scandal.

"I don't know without looking, Excellency and for that I'll need to stand on something." I dragged over one of the footstools but it wasn't tall enough for the purpose, so then, with Bertie's help, we carried over the rickety ivory inlaid table. Using the footstool as a stepping stone, Ivan climbed up rather gingerly as the table creaked ominously. Ivan then ran his right hand up the side of the frame. "Not a lock, Excellency, but a catch." I heard a click and the picture swung away from the wall. Behind it was the promised safe measuring about three feet by two. "Please pass me the key, Excellency." Bertie did so, there was the sound of a turning lock and Ivan pulled open the door of the safe. It was filled from top to bottom with morocco-leather boxes.

"My God!" I said rather too loudly. Bertie and Ivan both hushed me to silence as I heard the measured tread of soldiers pacing the pavement below the window. It seemed that we'd found the Grand Duchess's treasure but, if the Red Guards had moved to a position in front of the side door, how were we ever to get it to the Embassy? I whispered as much to my companions.

"Remember the Volga, Excellency." Ivan whispered back. "I'll pass the boxes down to you if you are ready."

"But we don't have nearly enough room for all of them in our bags," I said.

"We'll empty the cases and leave them behind," said Bertie. "Dear Maria Pavlovna, will just have to order new ones. If she gets her jewels, I'm sure she won't mind."

Box-by-box (I lost count at two hundred) Ivan started to empty the safe passing them to Bertie who handed them to me and I stacked them up on the carpet. The safe was about half-empty when, with a great crash, the table on which Ivan was standing collapsed without warning, pitching him back onto my neat stack of boxes, many of which burst open spewing diamond necklaces, ruby earrings, sapphire brooches and a huge emerald encrusted tiara onto the rug. The noise of the breaking table and Ivan's fall reverberated around the room and must have been clearly audible from the pavement outside. We all froze and listened out for shouts from below.

There were none, but it was possible that was because the Reds had halted in their tracks at the sounds from above. Scarcely daring to breathe, we must have remained immobile for about five minutes. At last, we heard the sound of iron shod feet once more reverberating off the pavement. Ivan, who hadn't said a word up to that point, let out a low groan.

"I think I have hurt my leg, Excellency." I took a look and, in the moonlight, could find nothing amiss until I tried to rotate his right foot. He groaned again.

"Bother," I said, "you have either twisted or broken your ankle. Lie still until we've emptied the safe and then we'll see what's to be done."

"I can empty the boxes, Excellency," he said through gritted teeth.

"Good idea. Bertie, let's bring over that other table. It will never take my weight so you're going to have to empty the rest of the safe."

At last the job was done and I had the chance to look at our haul. It was extraordinary: the sheer quantity, size and variety of Mrs Vlad's collection defied description. Even out of their boxes, it was doubtful if we would be able to cram everything into our three workmen's bags without damaging the tiaras, of which there must have been a dozen and a half.

"There's nothing for it," I whispered to Bertie, "I hate to do it but if we're to take the lot…"

I reached forward and folded a huge sapphire kokoshnik-style tiara flat; a few of the stones dropped from their settings so I slipped them into my pocket for safekeeping. This time it was Bertie who groaned. But he saw the sense of what I was doing and it wasn't long before almost everything had been packed away in the bags or, in the case of the loose stones of which there was a fistful, in my pocket. All that remained was a cardboard shoe box to which none of us had paid any attention. Assuming that it didn't contain any rocks, I tossed it onto the pile of empty jewellery boxes; as it landed, the lid fell off revealing fat bundles of high denomination Russian bank notes secured by paper sleeves. It didn't take Bertie long to count them: the shoe box contained two million roubles.[100] There was no room in our bags so he stuffed the bundles inside his shirt. However, there still remained the problem of what to do with Ivan.

"Can you walk?" I asked him.

"I don't think so, Excellency, but if you could help me up I will try." The upshot was that he was just about mobile, providing we supported him and he didn't put any weight on his ankle. "You must leave me here, Excellency."

"Out of the question, old chap," I said in a robust undertone. "One way or another we'll get you back to hotel. Here, Bertie, give me a hand…"

It took us until past midnight – I know because a nearby church clock chimed the hour – to get Ivan and the swag down the spiral stairs and back to street level. At which point we realised the previously unseen flaw in our plan: how were we to know if there were Red Guards lurking on the other side of the concealed door? The muffled sound of raucous singing confirmed that in all probability we would not be able to exit un-noticed. That was enough of a problem on its own, but added to it was the fact that, even if the coast was clear, how were we to get to the Embassy with the jewels as well as an injured Ivan?

We were debating these thorny issues in whispers when we heard an ominous clonk followed by a grinding noise; I froze as the concealed door slowly opened towards us and two uniformed and armed figures were silhouetted by the lamplight from the pavement.

---

[100] Editor's Note: Before the collapse of the rouble after the October Revolution of 1917, 2 million roubles was worth approximately £100,000 which equates to £20 million at 2015 values. It is impossible to calculate today's value of the Grand Duchess's jewellery as it was sold-off or broken up and disposed of piecemeal in the 1920s. We do know, however, that Queen Mary paid £28,000 for a pearl and diamond tiara (known today as the Vladimir Tiara) which is still in the Royal Collection, giving it a 2015 value (without accounting for the value of the provenance) in excess of £5 million. The Grand Duchess's collection of Fabergé cufflinks and cigarette cases, which she deposited with the Swedish Embassy in 1917 and was only discovered in 2008, were sold in 2009 for £7 million.

CHAPTER TWENTY-TWO: IN THE BAG

If I'd had a gun I would have used it and risked the consequences, but none of us was armed. A surprise physical assault was also out of the question, burdened down as we were with Ivan and Mrs Vlad's baubles. As fear coursed through my body, we shrank back a few paces towards the spiral stairs.

"*Ferme la porte, Seryozha,*" said one of the figures in an undertone, "*alors donnez-moi la lampe.*"

There was a click, but no illumination.

"*Merde! Qu'allons-nous faire maintenant, Borya?*"

I'm not sure which of us was the first to realise that the brutal and licentious Russian soldiery rarely speak French, but it was Bertie who spoke.

"*Sergei Platonovich? Boris Vladimirovich?*" In the pitch darkness, all I could hear was a horrified intake of breath. "*C'est Bertie...*" he continued, switching on our torch and pointing the feeble beam in the direction of the door.

Standing in front of us, and looking utterly horrified, were two men dressed as soldiers with rifles over their shoulders, knapsacks on their backs and red scarves tied around their upper left arms.

"My God, Bertie," said one of them in English, "what are *you* doing here?"

"I could ask you the same question, Boris Vladimirovich."

"Seryozha and I have come to get my mother's jewels," said the man called Boris, "and who are these people with you?"

"So have we," said Bertie, "and I don't think you know Charles Speedicut and his servant, Ivan. Charles, may I present His Imperial Highness

251

the Grand Duke Boris Vladimirovich and Prince Sergei Platonovich Obolensky."[101]

Dear God, did Bertie think that we were upstairs in the vestibule at some Grand Ducal reception? I cut across him.

"Gentlemen," I said, "the task is accomplished: we have the jewels and a considerable amount of money. It only remains for us to get out of here and make our way without detection to the British Embassy. We would have done so before you arrived, had we not been uncertain as to what was out there on the pavement."

"You needn't worry about that," said the Grand Duke, "Sergei Platonovich and I took the precaution of giving those louts a crate of vodka about an hour ago. They should be out cold by now."

"Well, that's a relief," I went on, "but how are we to get from here to our Embassy without being stopped? We didn't reckon on Ivan injuring his ankle or there being so many jewels."

"We have a truck parked around the back. We will escort you to it and then drive you to the Embassy. But before we do so, may I ask you, Bertie, how you knew about this entrance?" Bertie told him and then asked how he knew about it. "My father told me of its existence shortly before he died. He thought the knowledge might come in useful."

"So, who sent you here?" I couldn't help asking.

---

[101] Editor's Note: Unlikely as it may sound, the concealed entrances and the staircase, identified rather coyly on extant architectural drawings as the 'marital staircase', are located exactly as Speedicut describes them – a fact I was able to verify by checking the plans of the Vladimir Palace which are freely available on Google. In 1920, when the Vladimir Palace became the House of Scientists, the ground floor entrance was sealed. Albert Stopford himself never recorded the details of the rescue of the Grand Duchess's jewels and it is stated in some sources that he gained access to the Palace through the sewers. However, the contemporary account of Prince Serge Obolensky (1890-1978) states that Stopford and an accomplice – variously identified as the Grand Duke Boris Vladimirovich or Prince Obolensky himself - used the 'marital staircase' to enter and leave the Palace. We now know the full facts.

"No one, Mr Speedicut. I knew that my mother had asked Bertie to rescue the collection but when the Reds took to guarding the front entrance I assumed that you would find the task impossible, so that's why I asked Sergei Platonovich to give me a hand…"

"And what were you going to do with the jewels once you had secured them, Excellency?" asked Ivan.

"We hadn't thought that far ahead. What were *you* going to do with them, Bertie?"

"I…" Bertie started to say but I interjected as I'd had an inspiration that would, I hoped, get me away from Bertie and out of the damned country.

"I'm accredited to the Foreign Office," I said, "so I am going to take them out in the Diplomatic Bag and lodge them in your mother's bank in London until she decides what's to be done with them. It's the only safe way. Bertie is going to take the cash we've found to Her Imperial Highness to tide her over until she decides to leave Russia."

I thought Bertie might object to all of this, as we certainly hadn't discussed any of it, but he remained silent. Perhaps he thought that it would be easier to take a cut from the roubles rather than the stones: I know it was an unworthy thought, but he was certainly due a commission as was I… For the rest, there's not much to relate. Thanks to the Grand Duke's vodka, the Red Guards were comatose under the Palace's main portico, Boris's plan to get us safely to the Embassy in a military truck worked like a dream, the jewels were stowed in the Embassy's largest safe and we returned to the hotel as planned.

The following morning a quack was called to attend to Ivan, Bertie went off to see the Ambassador and recover the cash, prior to setting off immediately for Kislovodsk with the loot stashed in his trousers, and I bought a brace of capacious leather bags in which I proposed to transport the swag once Ivan was fit to hobble. Thus far everything was working – more or less – exactly to our improvised plan and I assumed that Ivan and I would soon be able to travel out of Russia under the immunity provided by my diplomatic status. My optimism took no account of three unforeseen factors: Ivan's ankle, which was actually broken and took two months to mend, the Bolshevik Revolution, which took place at the start of November – and my Russian relations.

The first of these eventualities meant that Bertie had returned from delivering Mrs Vlad's petty cash long before I was able to leave St Petersburg. So, we agreed that he would take the Vlad trinkets to London much as I'd planned to do: using a hastily arranged diplomatic passport (thanks to his membership of the Brotherhood) and exiting Russia via Helsinki in mid-September. Regrettably for my bank balance, but perhaps not for my conscience, I was unable to liberate the loose stones from the Ambassador's safe before Bertie hoofed off back home with the rest of the swag. On arrival in London he deposited the collection in a bank vault and then paid a visit to the Palace (please note the order of events). No one knows what transpired at his meeting with Queen Mary, but a few weeks later he was arrested in Hyde Park in mid-grapple with a Guardsman. It was snowing at the time, a fact which elicited a typically wry comment from the Minister of Munitions when told of the incident: '… in this weather? It makes you proud to be British!'[102] Anyway, for pleasuring His Majesty's property Bertie was sentenced to spend twelve months picking oakum at His Majesty's pleasure in Wormwood Scrubs. Now far be it from me to cast aspersions on our sainted Royal Family, but the fact that none of Mrs Vlad's *bijoux* appeared above the Royal fringe, or on the substantial Royal *balcon* under it, until their rightful owner was beneath the sod three years later begs a question or two on the subject of coincidence, don't you think? Why, for example, should a well-known sod be arrested and charged for an illicit grope in bushes that His Majesty's Metropolitan Constabulary knew he'd taken his pleasures in all his life but on which, until that moment, they had turned a Nelsonian eye?[103]

---

[102] Winston S Churchill (1874-1965).

[103] Editor's Note: It is not often that Speedicut plays fast-and-loose with the truth. However, the actual facts are that Stopford was not arrested, charged and convicted for an act of gross indecency with a Scots Guardsman, Robert Anderson, until September 1918 and Churchill's remark was made about a different incident many years later when he was Prime Minister. Readers may think I should have deleted or amended this story, but I have chosen instead – since the account is not entirely inaccurate - to let it stand, albeit with a footnoted correction.

Anyway, that was the last I saw of Mrs Vlad's priceless collection, which I'd risked so much to liberate, until a few years later I was flicking through the *ILN* at the club. In a large photograph of a State Banquet at Buckingham Palace for some dusky wog, I spotted Mrs Windsor sporting one of the better Vladimir tiaras which I remembered squashing flat. It was a confection comprising overlapping, diamond-set circles from which had hung some rather pretty pearls. As far as I could judge from the black and white photograph, Mrs W had swapped the pearls for emerald drops, presumably to match those Cambridge stones around her neck which she commandeered from her late brother's mistress. This, and Bertie's incarceration, proved in spades the proverbs that 'it's a brave man who crosses a determined woman' and 'everything come to she who waits'.

In the meantime, I was stuck in Russia, which was spiralling rapidly into dangerous chaos. Revolutions are unpredictable events and, therefore, all the riskier. One common factor they all seem to possess, however, is that they tend to be started by those who are on the fringes of power and merely want to get their own hands on its levers: Mrs Vlad's plan to oust Tsar Nicky and replace him with her son Cyril being a case in point. Unfortunately, in the process of unseating the powers-that-be, the aristocratic revolutionaries invariably lose control of the affair, which ends up in the hands of the petty bourgeoisie who masquerade as the downtrodden peasantry whilst ruthlessly exploiting them for their own selfish ends. That's when the trouble starts and the blood begins to run in the gutters. Don't imagine for one moment that Robespierre, Lenin or Mao could have stepped straight into the driving seat if the toffs hadn't first so destabilised the state that the army and the police could no longer be relied upon to defend the status quo.

But that's enough philosophising. The plain facts of the matter were that, as predicted, whilst Ivan's ankle was getting stronger Kerensky's grasp on the Russian tiller was getting weaker. By late-September an ineptly managed army coup to restore the monarchy, led by a slit-eyed Cossack General called Kornilov,[104] who was secretly supported by Kerensky, proved to be a damp squib; its only tangible result was the

---

[104] General Lavr Georgiyevich Kornilov (1870 – 1918) was a Cossack by birth.

arrest, incarceration in the Peter & Paul Fortress and, later, murder of a clutch of Grand Dukes. More significantly, and in a move that sounded the death knell of Kerensky's government, this military flop led directly to the arming by the Soviets of sixty thousand of the great unwashed to form the new Red Army. By the end of October, Lenin's Bolsheviks had ousted the moderates in the Soviets, Kerensky was booking a one-way ticket out of Muscovy and St Petersburg was a damnably dangerous place to be, even under the 'protection' of diplomatic immunity. The shortest route to safety lay to the west, but travel was no longer simply a matter of turning up at the Finland Station and buying a ticket. Nonetheless, that is what Ivan and I would have done had it not been for a chance encounter of my still lame secretary-cum-valet, who was taking his daily remedial walk on the Nevsky Prospekt on the day the Red flag was hoisted over the Duma.

"Excellency," he said as he limped into our room, "I have some very bad news."

"Don't tell me there was no food in the market."

The situation on that front had deteriorated as fast as those on the military and political front lines and our trunks had long since been emptied of what little of our imported provisions had been left by Bertie.

"No, Excellency, I have just seen your half-niece, the Princess Tatiana, and she told me that her mother, father and sister have all been arrested."

"What? The last I heard of the Lievens they were safe on their estate in the Crimea along with the Yusupovs and the Dowager Empress."

"It seems, Excellency, that they recently returned to Petrograd with Prince Yusupov to try and retrieve some of their possessions."

"They must have been mad. What happened?"

"They were arrested by Red Guards when they tried to enter the Lieven Palace through the kitchens."

"My God, that's awful. My half-sister may be a haughty cow but I wouldn't wish imprisonment in a Soviet dungeon on my worst enemy - Lord Esher excepted - so where are they being held and why wasn't Tatiana caught as well?"

"Princess Tatiana remained in hiding whilst the entry to the family's palace was attempted, Excellency. She told me that she believed they are now in the Bolsheviks' headquarters in the Smolny Institute where they are also holding His Imperial Majesty's brother."[105]

"Do you think there is any chance we can save them, Ivan?"

"From the Institute, Excellency, I would think not. But it is probable that they will be transferred at some point to join members of the Imperial Family and that might present an opportunity."

"So, what can we do?"

"First we need to confirm that they are still in Petrograd. That will probably require quite a lot of money."

"I'll leave the sleuthing to you, Ivan, whilst I try and sort out some gold. In the meantime, do you know where to contact my half-niece?"

"I do, Excellency. Thanks to the Head Porter…"

"… who's a member of the Nehemiah…"

"… she is hidden in the hotel's laundry room. I thought that I'd better ask you before I brought her up here. Besides which, there might be questions from the staff, none of whom, except the Head Porter, are to be trusted."

"Can we leave her with the laundry whilst we work out how to sort out the bigger problem?"

"I think so, Excellency, although not for too long."

---

[105] Grand Duke Michael Alexandrovich of Russia (1878-1918).

"Well, at least until I've raided Rothschild's." But, before I needed to do so, later that morning Ivan had a brainwave.

"Excellency," Ivan said as we lunched on stale rye bread and black tea, "we have overlooked something."

"What's that?"

"Your half-sister, Princess Lieven, is a British subject."

"What of it?"

"The British Ambassador can demand her release by the authorities and, whilst that is being arranged, insist on access to her."

"But what about Dimitri and Anastasia – not to mention Tatiana in the basement? They're all Russians by birth."

"One step at a time, Excellency, and remember the proverb I told you."

"Whilst there's life there's hope. Yes, I remember. Well, I'd better get myself around to the Embassy and see old Buchanan."

A couple of hours later I was seated in our Ambassador's comfortable study.

"I'm sorry that I can't offer you anything other than tea, Brother Speedicut," Buchanan said as he parked me in a deep armchair on one side of the blazing hearth, "but the last diplomatic bag brought only documents. How are you faring at the Europe?"

"It's pretty grim," I replied, "but I'd hoped we'd be out of here before much longer. However, there's been a development which I simply can't ignore."

"Can I be of assistance?" Over the next ten minutes I told him about my Lieven relations and the predicament they faced. "I see," he said when I'd finished, "well, I can certainly make representation to whichever bunch of thugs has taken up residence in the Winter Palace since this morning's events, but I'm not confident that anyone will be listening. Kerensky might have helped but he's gone. This fellow Lenin seems to think that we are the enemy and, before too long, that may well be the case.

"I will, however, at the very least try to find out where your kith and kin are being held and what is planned for them. I will also lodge a formal request for the release of your half-sister and her daughter, who is of course British by descent." Whilst pleased that he could request the release of all but Dimitri, I must have looked somewhat disappointed, for he added: "… And I can do something positive about your other niece - Tatiana, is it? Disguise her as your Russian servant and bring her here after dark. It's not the Ritz, but until such time as we can arrange some British papers for her, she'll be more comfortable and a lot safer here than in a hotel laundry basket."

"That very decent of you, Brother Buchanan," I said, as I got up to leave.

"Not at all," he replied, waving his hand in a dismissive gesture, "if one can't help a Brother in need, then what's the point of the Brotherhood?"

"What indeed? Well, anyway, thank you very much." I took his paw and gave it a squeeze. I was about to head for the door when there was a faint tap upon it.

"Enter," said Buchanan. A rather mousey looking diplomatic clerk poked his head around the oak and stuck out his hand in which was a buff envelope.

"Coded signal for you, Your Excellency," he said and then disappeared closing the door behind him.

"Thank you, Vassal. Hold hard a moment, Speedicut," the Ambassador said as he took the telegram, "you never know…" He prised open the flimsy, strode over to his desk, opened a drawer with a key and pulled out an anonymous looking book. "Ah, ha… yes… well, it was just as well you stayed, Brother Speedicut. This is from the Great Boanerges. He asks me to locate you and send you back to London as quickly as it can be arranged. It seems that the Brotherhood has an urgent need for you, although the signal is silent as to its purpose."

"But what about my family?" I asked, whilst inwardly heaving a sigh of considerable relief.

"You must take your niece with you; I'll arrange for her to have papers that identify her as a British citizen travelling as your maid – no, better still, the English wife of your Russian valet. For the others, I'm afraid you'll have to leave them in my hands. If I can get them out of the Reds' clutches, I'll send them back to you as soon as can be arranged. If not…" He left the rest of the sentence unspoken, but it was clear that their prospects would not be good if he did not succeed.

CHAPTER TWENTY-THREE: OUT OF THE BASKET

In the event, my exit from Russia with Ivan and Tatiana was – under the chaotic revolutionary circumstances – pretty straightforward. The Embassy motor collected us from the hotel and took us to the Finland Station where we boarded a train for Helsinki. The Baltic was still firmly held by the Boche Navy but we risked the short trip to Stockholm on a neutral fishing boat and from there took the train to Oslo where, after a week's extremely dull wait, we boarded a British destroyer headed home to Scapa Flow. A few days after that, and thanks to a telegram I sent to Mount Street (and another to the Connaught Hotel reserving a room for Tatiana), we were met at King's Cross by Fahran and Atash.

"Welcome home, huzoor," they cried in unison as I stepped down onto the platform. "We have a surprise for you."

"And I have one for you – I think it is a long time since you have seen Colonel Speedicut's grand-daughter and my half-niece, Princess Tatiana Lieven." They both gave the girl deep oriental bows and their eyes were gleaming with tears as each silently took her extended hand.

"But where are Prince Dimitri, Princess Dorothea and Princess Anastasia, huzoor? Why are they not with you?" asked Atash. This time tears welled up in Tatiana's eyes.

"I'm afraid that they are under arrest in Russia, Atash, along with many members of the aristocracy and the Imperial Family. The British Ambassador is doing his best to free them but has not yet succeeded."

"But we must rescue them, huzoor!" exclaimed Fahran.

"All in good time, Fahran," I replied somewhat warily as I headed in the direction of the Daimler. Of course, I had no intention of ever setting foot again in Russia and, instead, as I told Atash and Fahran, trusted to British diplomacy to extract my father's family. "Now what's this surprise you mentioned?"

"We have taken the liberty of organising a dinner party to mark your return, huzoor," said Fahran, whilst Atash steered the big motor out of the station, "Lord Tertius is back on leave from France as is Sir Philip Sassoon, so – with the help of Mr Ivan's catering business – we have arranged for them to join you, and Princess Tatiana of course, for dinner this evening at your apartment."

"But I haven't got anything to wear," wailed my half-niece beside me, "other than my jewels," she added clutching her neck, "and my hair is not fit to be seen."

As she'd hardly spoken a word since she'd emerged from the hotel's laundry basket, a condition I'd ascribed to melancholia at having to abandon her family, this outburst came as something of a shock. Concerns about her appearance seemed to have restored her voice and driven out any sadness she felt about leaving her mother, father and twin sister behind in Russia.

"Ivan," I said to my valet, who was squashed in the front of the motor between my two Afghans, "can you use your contacts to find Princess Tatiana a lady's maid and to rebuild her wardrobe – at my expense, of course?"

"Certainly, Excellency, leave it to me. With the help of the Nehemiah…"

We deposited Ivan and my half-niece in Carlos Place and then drove on the short distance to my flat, where I spent the rest of the morning sorting through a small mountain of correspondence which had accumulated in my extended absence. I was about half-way through it when I came to an envelope with a Wrexham postmark. For some reason, perhaps the knowledge that my father's family house was near there, I felt a sense of foreboding at its contents. I slit it open and read:

Vanderpump, Wellbelove, Wellesley-Smith & Co
3 Town Hill, Wrexham, North Wales

16th October 1917

Charles Speedicut Esq MC
4 Mount Street
London W

Sir

In re: the Estate of the late Lady Charlotte-Georgina Speedicut

We write following the recent sad demise of our client, Lady Charlotte-Georgina Speedicut of The Dower House, Acton Park, Wrexham, & 6 Stratton Street, London W, and in connection with her testamentary heirs, Princess Dorothea-Charlotte Lieven, née Speedicut, and the Princesses Anastasia and Tatiana Lieven all of whom we believe to be resident in Russia.

Owing to the exigencies of the war, and the revolutionary situation in that sad country, we have been unable to establish communications with Lady Charlotte-Georgina's said heirs and, in pursuit of that purpose, we contacted the late Colonel Sir Jasper Speedicut's lawyers in London. They have informed us, for reasons which they did not disclose, that you may be in communication with the Lieven family. If, Sir, that is the case, we would be most grateful if you could assist us in this matter.

We have the honour to be,

Sir,

Your most obedient Servants,

Vanderpump, Wellbelove, Wellesley-Smith & Co

This letter clearly called for a swift response so I picked up my pen and wrote the lawyers an update in which I explained the situation and added that Tatiana was now in London and 'under my protection'. That would, I hoped, ensure that my half-niece's living expenses would be taken care of by her grand-mother's estate, although I was happy in the meantime to cover her immediate needs. I was less happy about adding to her woes with the news that 'granny had popped her clogs' and I decided that, unless she raised the subject herself, I would hold off doing so until I'd heard back from the Wrexham lawyers.

Several hours and another twenty letters later, I was lounging in my drawing room in front of a merry fire, clad in a previously unworn velvet smoking jacket of an elaborate design, awaiting the arrival of my guests. Ivan had returned earlier with the news that Tatiana was much happier following a visit to a couturier somewhere off Bond Street and the acquisition of a temporary maid, thanks to the concierge at her hotel. Tertius was the first to arrive, dressed in khaki.

"Am I incorrectly dressed?" I asked him as I realised that, perhaps, I too should have worn uniform.

"Not at all, my dear chap, although when you dine out it would be a good idea to drag on your Shiners' kit – you don't want some damned harpy hurling white feathers at you, now do you?"

"To be honest, Tertius, I feel a bit of a fraud in uniform. After all, I've haven't seen any service in the trenches."

"Perhaps not," he said, "but from what I've heard you earned your MC fair and square in Mespot, or wherever it was you were making sand castles, to say nothing of your secret squirrelling in Russia – about which I want to hear a lot more over dinner."

"That may have to wait until another time, Tertius. You see, I managed to bring out my half-niece, Tatiana, and she's joining us for dinner. However, the rest of her family are under arrest in St Petersburg and their prospects don't look good. So, I thought we'd try and stay off the subject of Russia this evening; Tatiana's gloomy enough company as it is and I don't want her to put a complete damper on the evening."

"How old is she?"

"A couple of years older than you."

"And what does she look like – not you, I hope," he added with a laugh.

"To be perfectly honest I'm not sure. The first time I met her, at the Yusupovs' a year or so ago, she was unremarkable. I didn't see her again until I rescued her in St Petersburg last month, since when she's been dressed like a peasant so it's been difficult to tell."

"Not very appealing, then?"

"I'm afraid not. She's also been virtually catatonic since she appeared at my hotel. So, I'm afraid that, as a result, we may be in for a bit of a dull evening…" Before I could add that, in any event, Tertius would soon have the opportunity to judge for himself, Fahran appeared in the doorway.

"Sir Philip Sassoon," he intoned. Philip slid into the room, gave Tertius one of his most dazzling smiles and a limp hand shake, then he took my outstretched paw and held it for what seemed like an age.

"*Mon cher, Charles, bienvenu à Londres*" he lisped, "and looking so well despite your adventures *en Russie*, which *malheureusement* are not yet at an end for you or any of us for that matter – but that can wait until tomorrow. Tonight, we celebrate your return, *n'est pas*, Lord Tertius, and we forget *les horreurs de la Flandre*." What on earth did any of that presage, I wondered gloomily in the knowledge that I had been recalled for an urgent although unspecified purpose?

"Princess Tatiana Lieven," Fahran announced.

The apparition who wafted past him drove all such thoughts from my mind and reduced my guests to silence: Tatiana was virtually unrecognisable.

Thanks to the efforts of Madame Paquin and a good French maid,[106] she was dressed in what looked like an exotic costume from one of Diaghilev's oriental ballets. Her silk dungarees were gathered in at the waist and held by two thin shoulder straps that left her nearly naked from chin to cleavage –and her hair had been sculpted into the latest fashion and was secured by a diamond-studded bandeau. In addition to the sparklers around her brow, Tatiana had diamonds hanging from her earlobes and around her throat and wrists: I knew that they were the only things of any worth which she'd managed to bring out of Russia, concealed in the hem of her peasant smock.

"Philip, Tertius – may I present my half-niece, Princess Tatiana Lieven?" I managed to say after the immediate shock had worn off. "Tatiana – Lord Tertius Beaujambe and Sir Philip Sassoon."

Philip gave Tatiana an appraising glance – actually, I think it was her jewels and frock rather than her body which he was evaluating. Tertius, on the other hand, was practically dribbling at the sight of her finely chiselled face not to mention her bare shoulders, well sculpted cleavage and shapely ankles. As a result, a very jolly evening ensued. Shortly before midnight, Tatiana said that she had to return to her hotel and Tertius offered to escort her there. Philip hung back, as I thought he might, and settled back into his chair as I poured him another Armagnac.

"I said that our business could wait until tomorrow, *Charles*, and I don't want to spoil a splendid evening, but perhaps I should tell you what I have planned for you – *en France*." My face must have assumed a woebegone expression for he added quickly, "*mais pas à la Flandre – à Paris*."

"Paris? What's going on there that needs my attention?"

"*Notre petit Prince de Galles* has formed a most unsuitable entanglement *amoureuse* with a lady of your acquaintance."[107]

---

[106] Jeanne Paquin (1869-1956), an *avant garde* French couturier who had branches in Paris, London, Buenos Aires & Madrid. Leon Bakst, who created the costumes for the Diaghilev ballet, *Scheherazade*, was one of her designers.

[107] HRH The Prince of Wales, later HM King Edward VIII (1894-1972).

"Who?"

"Miss Marguerite Meller."

"Not the tart who I persuaded to get the truth out of old Mata Hari in return for membership of the Brotherhood?"

"The very same."

"But if she's a member of the Brotherhood, surely you can just tell her to climb off the Prince and find another cock to suck?"

"*Charles! Quel crudité...*"

"But it's nothing less than the truth."

"*Vraiement et tu as raison, mon petit*, if she was a member of the Brotherhood, but she is not."

"But I thought…"

"She had served her usefulness to us and I saw no reason to induct her. Anyway, *c'est trop tard maintenant.*"

"So why are we so bothered?"

"It is because of her particular skill *avec ses lèvres* that she has made such a conquest of the Prince."

"Why?" I said out of idle curiosity although, as my prick had been on the receiving end of Miss Meller's mouth, I was reasonably sure that I knew the answer.

"Because…" he paused. Philip was clearly having second thoughts on the subject of royal indiscretions, "because… *le Prince à un petit problème – un très petit problème…*" Ho, ho, I thought, it's not a question of pleasure preferred but of necessity.

"You mean his dick's too small for fucking?" Philip looked pained at this but nodded nonetheless.

"How do you know?"

"Brother Dawson is the Physician-in-Ordinary to the Royal Family."[108]

"I see. Well, he should know. And the only way the Prince can get his end away is by being sucked off?" Philip looked as though he was being forced to chew on a very sharp lemon but nodded again. "I see, but what's the problem with that? He may be a Prince, but even a Prince is entitled to some pleasure before he has to walk down the aisle with some beefy Protestant Princess with fat thighs and a bristling moustache?"

"That *is* the problem, *chèr Charles*. There are concerns that if the Prince can only be satisfied in the manner you have so robustly described – a technique which is unknown to any lady of breeding – that he will insist in contracting *une marriage* with someone unfit to wear the crown of a Queen Consort. Not only that, but there would be no prospect of him fathering children…"

"There's always a turkey baster…"

"*Charles!* Such methods are wholly unknown to the Royal Family."

"Well, there's always the warming pan trick."

"We no longer live in the *Moyen Âges, Charles*, besides which it is for that reason the Home Secretary has to be present at the *accouchement*."

"So, you want me to bimble over to Paris, drag Miss Meller's mouth off the Prince of Wales's tiny *bijoux de famille* and ensure that she never darkens his doorstep again?"

"*Tu as raison.*"

---

[108] Dr Bertrand Dawson CB (1864-1945), later 1st Baron Dawson of Penn GCVO KCB KCMG.

"And for that you dragged me back from Russia – for which, incidentally, I'm very grateful."

"Yes."

"Then what? Time in the trenches?"

"I think not, *Charles*. I do have something in mind for you but it can wait until you are back from Paris."

"So, when do you want me to go?"

"The Prince has returned from Paris to spend Christmas with his family and won't return to his duties until the New Year. Meanwhile, you now have the unexpected *responsibilité* of your niece and need time to get her settled. I could, of course, send you to Paris almost immediately so that you can deal with Madam Meller before the Prince returns *mais* I – and others - think it would be better if you were to join the Prince's personal staff."

"In what capacity?"

"As an Extra Equerry – an appointment your father held with both King Edward VII, when he was *Prince de Galles*, and his eldest son, The Duke of Clarence. From that position of closeness to the Prince you can not only warn-off our *poule de luxe* but also ensure that the Prince doesn't stray back in her direction. You will report to St James's Palace on 5th January to take up your duties."

It could have been worse and it left me time to sort out Tatiana, although from the attention Tertius had paid her over dinner it was likely that I would be getting in some practice for the Paris job before ever donning the aiguillettes of an Equerry. On that subject, Tatiana that is, I didn't have long to wait. The following morning Tertius was around at my flat begging my permission to 'pay court' to Tatiana, as he rather quaintly put it, and in the evening post I received a letter from the Wrexham lawyers:

Vanderpump, Wellbelove, Wellesley-Smith & Co
3 Town Hill, Wrexham, North Wales

11th December 1917

Charles Speedicut Esq MC
4 Mount Street
London W

Sir

In re: the Estate of the late Lady Charlotte-Georgina Speedicut

We thank you for your letter of the 10th inst and the information contained therein.

As the Trustees of the late Lady Charlotte-Georgina Speedicut's estate, we are authorised to provide Princess Tatiana with sufficient income to maintain her in an appropriate style, pending the settlement of her late grand-mother's affairs and we will be writing to her at the Connaught Hotel accordingly. In the meantime, please advise us of any expenses which you have incurred on Princess Tatiana's behalf and we will arrange for you to be reimbursed instanta.

We have the honour to be,

Sir,

Your most obedient Servants,

Vanderpump, Wellbelove, Wellesley-Smith & Co

This letter left me with no choice but to be the bearer of sad tidings, albeit ones with a gilt lining, so the following morning I strolled the short distance from my flat to the Connaught and sent up my card. Fifteen minutes had scarcely passed before Tatiana appeared in the hotel's small sitting room off the entrance hall, wreathed in furs and scent.

Vanderpump & Co were probably in for a shock when I submitted my expenses claim, I thought as I took in her extravagantly sable-trimmed and sand-coloured ensemble, cut *à la militaire*: if she had been dressed to kill two nights earlier, now she was dressed for multiple murder. No wonder Tertius was smitten.

"Uncle Charles, how lovely to see you," she purred as she lowered herself into a seat opposite mine. "Lord Tertius will be here soon – he's giving me luncheon at the Ritz - but I'm glad you've called-in as there was something I wanted to ask you."

"Yes?"

"I know that Grandmamma Speedicut has been unwell since dear Grandpapa died, but I thought I should really get in touch with her now that I am in England. She is, after all, the only person I know here, except you, of course," she added with a smile.

"Actually," I replied, feeling damnably awkward, "it was about your grandmother that I'm here. You see…" How was I to put this? "You see, it would appear that she has, err, gone."

"Gone where?"

"To, err, join my father."

"But, how *could* she?" cried Tatiana looking positively shocked. "She's only been widowed for two years - and at her age…"

"No, Tatiana, I think you have misunderstood me. She has gone to join your grandfather."

"But I thought you said…" Then a look of comprehension came over her face. "Oh, how silly of me. I quite forgot. So, she has died?"

"Yes – I'm afraid so." Tatiana reached into her tiny handbag and extracted a face-edged handkerchief, with which she delicately dabbed the corner of one eye. "She was a great age, you know, and hadn't been able to speak or move since my father – your grandfather - died."

"I know," she said as she started to sob gently, "but she was all that I have left in England…"

"I'm not sure that's right," I said leaning forward and patting the hand that wasn't clutching the now somewhat moist snot rag. "I believe my father - your grandfather - had a sister and she probably had children, so you've certainly got Speedicut cousins."

"They're rather common," Tatiana sniffed, "their father was a stockbroker and dear Mama would never have anything to do with them.

"Well, I'm sure there are heaps of Whitehall cousins for you to contact."

"I don't think so," she replied, "Mama forbade us to speak of the present Duke – I don't know why – but I do know that he doesn't have any children and Mama is his only living relative. Indeed, if he dies before her, Mama will inherit the Dukedom."[109]

"I see," I said at this sudden revelation of – to me at least – previously unknown family history. "Well, buck up. It seems that your grandmother left her entire estate to you, your mother and your sister. I don't know what's it's worth but…"

"How do you know all this, Uncle Charles?" I explained. "So, the lawyers will be writing to me?" I confirmed the fact. "And I will have some money of my own?" I confirmed that too and she brightened considerably. "Perhaps you and I could visit her grave once I have all the details? At the very least I would like to place a wreath – ah, here's Lord Tertius…"

---

[109] Editor's Note: Readers of *The Speedicut Papers* will know that Lady Charlotte-Georgina's elder sister, Lady Charlotte-Elizabeth FitzCharles, had eloped with a music hall singer called Sidney Hadfield and given birth to a son, Charles Hadfield. In 1910, and following the deaths in quick succession of all the prior male heirs, Hadfield inherited the Dukedom which, uniquely for an English ducal title, could pass through the female as well as the male line.

CHAPTER TWENTY-FOUR: ON & OFF THE JOB

In the days that followed, Tertius and Tatiana became virtually inseparable. In the absence of any positive news from Russia, any concerns that I might have had about keeping her in good spirits proved to be unnecessary; and the looming problems of a tear-stained Christmas were solved by Lady Frodsham who, at Tertius's insistence, invited Tatiana and me to spend the holiday with them.

With Atash at the wheel, and with Fahran next to him, Tatiana and I motored up to Cheshire. When we arrived at the lodge and the headlamps illuminated the long, straight drive to the hump-backed bridge, I think that my trusty Afghan chauffeur was tempted to repeat Tertius's dash down the drive. But a cautionary word from me ensured that we arrived at the front portico in one piece. Such was the pace of entertainment laid on by our hosts, from a ball on Christmas Eve to the New Year's Day Meet of the Frodsham Hounds, that, by the time we left, I was more than ready for a long stay in a Parisian bed.

However, before that restful eventuality, on New Year's Eve I was having a bath prior to changing for the evening entertainment, when Tertius bimbled into my bathroom, sat on the edge of the bath, ran his fingers idly through the soapy water and then, whilst fondling my recently somewhat under-used wedding tackle, asked my permission to propose to Tatiana. Seeing no reason to refuse – I've always been broad-minded – a few minutes and some further sub-aquatic fumbling later I gave my consent. Their engagement was announced by a beaming Lord Frodsham (who knew a good thing when he saw it) as the long case clock in the hall of Frodsham Splendens chimed the arrival of 1918 to the assembled throng of local landowners.

Following the news that my half-niece was to be united to one of the most eligible (and dissolute) bachelors in England, I was free to fret about the upcoming challenge as to how I was to sunder the highly undesirable union of The Prince of Wales and Paris's premier suction pump. But first I had to join his Staff. It was with a heavy heart that on 4th January I headed south to St James's Palace after bidding farewell to the Beaujambes and Tatiana. There, the following morning whilst Atash waited for me in the motor parked in Pall Mall, I reported to the Prince's Principal Equerry, a monocled Grenadier aristocrat by the name of Lord Claud Hamilton,[110] who was to brief me on my role as an Extra Equerry. At least, I thought that was the purpose of the meeting…

"Ah, Speedicut. Take a seat and listen carefully," he said pointing to an uncomfortable looking chair in front of his desk. I did as instructed. "Your temporary appointment to His Royal Highness's Staff is probably the most important assignment of your life. It is no exaggeration to say that the future of the Monarchy depends on your ability to regularise the Prince's private life." So, no pressure then, I mused to myself as I wondered when he would tell me of my daily duties.

"But," he went on, "it must be done without his knowledge and it is vital that the termination of this most unsuitable liaison appears to be on the lady's part. Were the Prince to find out that it had been engineered for his own good the consequences could be almost as disastrous as a continuation of his romance. Do I make myself clear?" Somewhat dazed at this unexpected turn of events, I said that he did.

"Good. So how do you plan to bring it about?"

As this was not what I had expected would be the subject of the briefing, I had not taken the opportunity of discussing the assignment with the Mount Street team and so I hadn't got a clue. Instead of answering, I stroked my chin, stared out of the window in a brave attempt to look considered whilst my brain churned. Then I tried a diversion.

"I believe, sir, that I have been assigned to the Prince's Staff because I know the lady in question." The courtier's eyebrows headed for the ceiling. "That is to say," I added quickly, "that I have had business dealings with her in the past." I laid a heavy emphasis on the word 'business'.

---

[110] Captain Lord Claud Hamilton MVO DSO (1889-1975).

"So I understand - and it is for that reason that Sir Philip Sassoon has persuaded me that, despite your youth, you are the man for the job and that your discretion is guaranteed. But I repeat: how are you going to set about the task and ensure that there are no unfortunate consequences?" Christ, what was I going to say? I decided to play for time.

"I can't give you a considered answer to that question, sir, until I have been able to assess the situation on the ground."

"I see," he said, "but you must at the least have a plan to recover the letters." 'The letters', what letters? Philip hadn't said anything about any amorous royal scribblings. My dismay must have shown on my face for he added: "Ah, I see that you are unaware of the fact that your task includes recovering His Royal Highness's correspondence with the lady." I nodded. "Well, it does. In fact, the recovery of the letters is quite as important as the termination of the relationship."

"What resources will there be to help me achieve this?" I asked, in a desperate attempt to put the courtier on the back foot.

"Resources? If, by that, you mean money then the answer will depend on the quantum required - but there can *never* be any question of the Household having submitted to blackmail. Is that *clearly* understood?" I nodded again and assumed a wise look. "But first you have to arrange for the permanent separation of the Prince and the lady - and I remain concerned, Speedicut, that you do not appear to have a plan."

"I think you may have misunderstood me, sir," I said in a desperate bid to maintain my credibility, "I do have a plan." I didn't. "But it's execution will depend on the attitude of Miss Meller - and I can't know that until I have seen her."

"Hmm." Hamilton looked anything but convinced and I was certain that he was about to terminate my attachment before it had even started. As the alternative, despite what Philip had said, was almost certainly a posting to hell, otherwise known as the Western Front, my mind went into overdrive.

"Very well, sir," I said, "I can see that I will have to show you my hand. I didn't want to do so as it is a delicate matter and I was concerned that my strategy might shock you." He sat up at this and screwed his monocle tighter into his eye socket.

"I know from my past dealings with the lady that Miss Meller has a certain *tendresse* for me." That was a barefaced lie. "And I intend to play on my youth to lure her out of the Prince's bed and into mine."

As a shock tactic, this grossly indelicate and utterly undeliverable announcement worked better than I could ever have hoped: the monocle sprang out of the Grenadier's face and a look of profound shock, accompanied by prolonged harrumphing, replaced it. When, at last, he'd recovered his composure and his eye glass he gave me a rather fishy stare through it.

"Do you mean to tell me that Miss Meller will be willing to exchange the privilege of a liaison with the Heir to the Throne with, you will forgive me Speedicut but it is a plain fact, a gentleman of, err, somewhat uncertain antecedents?"

"My antecedents may be, as you so delicately put it, sir, 'uncertain' but there is no uncertainty about my advantage in another department. I'm sure that you would prefer that I didn't go into details."

"No, indeed," he blustered, "let's just hope that you are right. The future of the nation hangs on your 'advantage'."

The picture that immediately formed in my mind of Britannia dangling from the end of my erect cock was so ludicrous that I couldn't help laughing. It was a bad move which brought me a stern rebuke from the crusty courtier for 'making light of a serious matter of State'. In an effort, I presumed, to steer the conversation onto less risqué ground, he at last briefed me on my duties which, so it emerged, were no more onerous than being on hand to take the Prince's hat and cane whenever it was my turn on the royal duty roster. As there were a bevy of other Equerries, it seemed probable that I would have plenty of off-duty time to track down the Prince's popsy and persuade her, by whatever means were necessary, to use her tongue to lick another lolly and to hand over the incriminating letters in return for lolly of an altogether different type.

Two days later the Prince's entourage boarded the boat train for Paris and, eight hours after that, we settled the tiny royal into the Ritz whilst we stowed our bags in the altogether less luxurious Hotel Westminster around the corner in the rue de la Paix. The plan was that David, as Miss Meller's squeeze was known by his family to his pretty face and behind his narrow back by his Staff, was to spend a few days in the capital of the Frogs. Whilst there he would be 'visiting senior members of our political allies', for which read having his dick sucked by Miss Meller as often as official business allowed, before touring British and Empire regiments behind the front line. By the time the boat train pulled into the Gare du Nord I was no closer to finding a solution to my tasks and neither Atash nor Fahran were any help, although whilst his brother unpacked my uniforms Atash did suggest that we could always fall back on his father's answer to all problematic situations.

"He was fond of saying, huzoor, that the simplest answer was to slit the person's throat. I have brought his knife with me, should that be necessary."

"Let's hope to God not," I said with some feeling.

I was still mulling over the issue later that evening as I strolled into the lobby of the Ritz to start my first stag 'in waiting'. I was passing the concierge's desk when I heard someone call my name. I turned and saw a handsome fellow of about my own age in an exotic uniform topped by a red tarboosh. He looked not unlike a younger version of Philip Sassoon and it was that thought which triggered my memory.

"Ali Fahmy?" I said walking over to him with my hand extended.

"The very same," he said with a broad grin.

"How very clever of you to have recognised me after two, or is it three, years?"

"I never forget a face," he said, "particularly not one like yours."

"So, what brings you to Paris?" I asked, ignoring the suggestive compliment but pleased nonetheless.

"I'm attached to the French General Staff where I'm acting as an interpreter – and you?"

"I'm officially here as an Equerry to The Prince of Wales but, in reality, I'm on a mission for Philip Sassoon to part the Prince from Miss Meller and recover some embarrassing letters he's written to her."

"Miss who?" asked Ali.

"Surely you remember – the French tart who we discussed over dinner the first time I met you."

"Oh, you mean Marguerite Laurient."

"Laurient?"

"It's her married name – although marriage hasn't stopped her from plying her trade as the twentieth-century's answer to La Belle Otero."[111]

"How do you know this?"

"Because we are, as they say, acquainted."

"I thought that girls weren't your style."

"They're not really, although 'any port in a storm' as you English say. Besides which she has a technique that is *impeccable*."

---

[111] Carolina Otero (1868-1965).

"So, would your 'acquaintance' with the lady stretch to introducing me? I frankly haven't got a clue where to start on what I very much fear will prove to be an impossible mission."

"I certainly would be able to introduce you - and I might even have an idea that could deliver to you the result you seek."

"God, I do hope so, Ali."

"What time do you come off duty this evening?"

"Once my employer has gone to bed."

"As he spent most of this afternoon with Marguerite, that shouldn't be too late. Shall we meet back here at midnight and I'll take you around to her hotel?"

I agreed that I would, although I still had no plan - other than Atash's knife - for completing my task for the Brotherhood and the Royal Household. In my experience, however, solutions to difficult situations often present themselves if you put yourself in the way of them. So, it was to be with Marguerite Meller, although the utterly disgraceful story about how it happened is worth the telling.

For those of my readers who are familiar with the City of Sin will know - which should be most of you, thanks to cheap packaged holidays by Thomas Cook whose impecunious clients now clutter up airports and make travel a pain rather than a pleasure for those of us who can afford a full fare - Paris is divided into districts which define their inhabitants. The fact that Monsieur Gitanes lives in the area bounded by the rue de Rivoli, the place de la Concorde and the Opera tells one that he is well-heeled and probably from a good family; the *nouveaux riches* invariably live around the Bois de Boulogne. Madam Gauloises defines her morality immediately if she confesses to living in Montmartre or Montparnasse - and her profession if she admits to living in Pigalle. By contrast, the penniless young bourgeois male who lives in the same area is almost certainly an artist or a poet. Loafers of both sexes, with more money than morality, invariably live on the Left Bank around the church of St Germain and within easy reach of a clutch of cafes, said by the guide books to be the haunts of the intelligentsia: in recent years, this has been a mistaken claim, as the savants have fled their absinthe dispensaries to escape the gawpers pointed in their direction by Mr Cook. As for 'professional ladies', the *grands horizontales* invariably have expensive apartments in the place Vendôme and the *poules de luxe* tend to conduct their business in the better class of hotels between the Palais Royal and the top end of the Champs Elysees; their less successful or still upwardly mobile sisters have to make do with a *maison de passe*, a temporary room over a cheap cafe or the wall of a reeking backstreet. When I'd last met her, Marguerite had already progressed as far as a room in the St James & Albany Hotel, chosen I suspect because - with two entrances - it was convenient for someone with more than one runner in the Marital Hurdle Stakes.

Later that evening, wrapped up against the January night air, I strode and Ali rather unexpectedly waddled past Napoleon's bronze-sheathed erection in the direction of the rue du Faubourg St Honoré. As we did so he told me that, despite the fact that she was now married, Marguerite had progressed to a suite in the Bristol. This was, of course, the penultimate stop for Miss Meller before arriving at an all-expenses-paid first floor apartment in the *place* we were crossing, along with a discreet lady's maid to manage her affairs.

The fact that Marguerite's suite at the Bristol was at the back of the hotel, rather than the more fashionable front, indicated that her horizontal trajectory had yet to climax or that HRH was being kept on short commons by his parsimonious parents. Either way, her rooms on the second floor were comfortable, the floral displays impressive, the fizz seemingly on tap and the bed large enough to accommodate simultaneously more than one priapic Prince of the Blood Royal.

As Ali tapped on the door to her suite I did, however, have a nagging worry: as a result of our last meeting, poor old Mata Hari had ended up being shot at dawn. Whilst it was certain that Marguerite would not have forgotten her enforced role in this gross miscarriage of justice, nor that the

Brotherhood had denied her a promised reward, would she hold a grudge against me in consequence? And, if she did, would that prevent me from successfully completing my assignment? When at last Marguerite opened the door I immediately noted that she was dressed for bed and was plainly surprised to see me. It was also apparent that Ali had not forewarned her that I was in the party but, as she glared at us, he whispered to me that I should just follow his lead.

"What do *you* want?" she demanded haughtily of me in French before even greeting Ali.

It was not a promising start, although she made no attempt to slam the door in our faces. In fact, she opened it a little wider and then retreated into the sitting room where, without another word, she lowered herself onto a *chaise longe* on one side of a welcoming fire. Here she reclined with her legs partly splayed and her cleavage fully revealed as her satin dressing gown parted. It wasn't much of an invitation to enter the suite - or anything else for that matter - but nor was it a demand for us to fuck off.

"I thought you were expecting us," said Ali rather shyly from the door.

"You, yes - him, not," she said giving me the sort of look I imagine she must have reserved for rabid dogs.

"Can we come in?" Ali asked.

"I suppose so," she said without much enthusiasm, "and one of you can pour me a glass of champagne whilst you're about it."

Ali gave me a wink, which I'm sure did not pass un-noticed by Marguerite and, whilst I parked myself in a chair on the other side of the fire, he busied himself with an unopened magnum of fizz on a well-stocked sideboard.

"So, what brings you to Paris, Mr Speedicut?" she demanded as she jiggled a wedge-heeled slipper balanced on the end of her foot nearest to the fire. I decided to take the heifer by the horns in an all-or-nothing bid to progress my mission.

"You do."

"Why?" she asked suspiciously, "so that I can do your dirty work for you again?"

"Not at all," I said with a measure of truth.

"Why then?" But before I could answer, Ali broke in.

"Because I told Charlie that I needed him to help me with that challenge I gave you the other day." What challenge, I wondered? Ali hadn't mentioned anything about a challenge: it was me who had that problem.

"So, you came all the way to Paris just for that?" she sneered. As I hadn't a clue what either of them were talking about I decided to head her off in the direction of my problem.

"That - and my job as one of His Royal Highness's Equerries." Her eyes narrowed at this.

"He didn't mention you when I saw him earlier."

"Well he wouldn't, would he? I'm only a glorified valet."

She didn't respond to this but her eyes softened a little as she took a long pull on her glass and drained it. Ali got up from his chair, collected the magnum from the sideboard then interposed himself between me and Marguerite whilst he slowly filled her glass. I couldn't see what she was up to whilst this was going on but the next thing I did see was Ali's evening dress trousers slipping down to his ankles, followed by a splashing sort of sound and a sharp intake of breath from our hostess.

I couldn't be sure but I guessed that Marguerite had flipped out the Gyppo's dick and was using it as a swizzle-stick. In this I was not entirely correct as I discovered when Ali used his free hand to wave me forward into the action. I rose and crossed the carpet to the *chaise longe* where I found Marguerite's lips and one hand attached to the tip of Ali's enormous, quivering member, whilst with the other she was clutching firmly onto a large diamond bracelet which encircled his *bijoux de famille*. Ah ha, I thought, that accounts for Ali's earlier waddle and Miss M's recent hyper-ventilation. Then, as I watched, with all the skill of a circus performer she managed to ingest Ali's quivering prick right up to the ring of sparklers, a trick that many professional sword swallowers would have applauded vigorously.

"In a minute, Charlie," Ali gasped, "it will be your turn, so get it out and let's see if Marguerite can win the first part of my challenge." What, dear reader, would you have done in the circumstances? I didn't hesitate for an instant and in less time than it takes to tell I had my own equipment out of my flies and ready for action.

In the minutes that followed, Marguerite serviced us alternately and together. Quite how she achieved the latter without gagging I don't know, but it was under the circumstances a considerable accomplishment - as was her ability repeatedly to bring us almost to the point of no return without allowing us to flood her cleavage.

"So far so good," said Ali as, for the umpteenth time, the Prince's paramour ingested both of our rods at the same time, "now let's see if you can win the bracelet outright."

Without a word, Marguerite rose and headed off in the direction of what turned out to be her bedroom. Without a backward glance, she shed her dressing gown and nightdress, then threw herself, stark naked, onto the bed. Ali was already stripping for action, so I followed suit. It soon emerged from what followed that the second half of Ali's challenge involved Marguerite being penetrated simultaneously front and rear, a feat which – after a bit of manoeuvring - we achieved by sandwiching her prone form between us on the bed. Because of his size, Ali had assigned me Marguerite's back door but, nonetheless, maintaining the connection proved to be quite difficult. I had just mastered the trick of swaying together and was about to suggest that we might try it on our knees when there was a blinding flash and a loud pop.

CHAPTER TWENTY-FIVE: END GAME

Marguerite screamed and leapt off the bed, nearly taking Ali's and my overexcited manhoods with her, grabbed her dressing gown and stormed off in search of the photographer. The room to the bedroom and the corridor were open, full of acrid smoke but of a man with a camera there was no sign. Whilst my Egyptian friend and I got dressed, Marguerite sat fuming and muttering.

"It was that damned husband of mine," she growled.

"How can you be so certain?" asked Ali.

"He's been behaving most unreasonably recently. He seems to think that just because we're married that I can't have a life of my own." As I thought it wouldn't improve matters, I refrained from saying that his attitude seemed perfectly reasonable to me,

"But you can't be sure," Ali continued.

"Well, who else could it be? The next thing I'll be served with divorce papers citing you two as co-respondents and, once that gets out, it will be all over with David."

"I'm sure that it won't come to that," said Ali, "Charlie has some very powerful friends and I'm sure that he can arrange for this to be hushed up, can't you, Charlie?" I assumed that Ali was referring to the Brotherhood.

"I'll see what I can do," I said, "but I can't do anything until your husband makes the first move. As soon as he does, leave a message for me at the Westminster. In the meantime, Ali," I said turning to my friend, "we should get the hell out of here."

"I agree," said Ali. "Marguerite, I think it would be wise if we didn't see one another until Charlie can sort out this mess - although I would like to finish what we started this evening..."

"Absolutely not," I said, dragging the randy sod to his feet. "It's time we were both tucked up in our own beds not making matters worse in Marguerite's. If her husband's got any sense, he'll have paid off the hotel staff to give evidence: so, the less time we spend here the better."

"He's right," said Marguerite, looking a little wistful nonetheless, "you should go - and don't forget to leave the bracelet. I won our bet four-square - and I may need it." She left the rest of the sentence unfinished, but it was clear what she meant.

"Come and get it then," said Ali as he started to unbutton his flies once again.

The upshot was that, whilst I watched, Marguerite completed what she had started an hour previously. I was not included in her exertions, which was a pity for she was an expert, but I consoled myself with the thought that I might be able to finish my own business with Ali once we got back to my hotel. We did, but that was not the best part of the evening. I was lying back on the pillow with Ali beside me when he started to laugh.

"I wasn't that bad, was I?" I asked with some consternation.

"*Au contraire, mon brave*, you were better than I expected."

"So why are you laughing?"

"At the delicious irony of the evening."

"What on earth do you mean?"

"So, you haven't yet worked it out?"

"Worked what out?"

"That I have not only engineered a situation which is going to allow you to complete your assignment but that, in so doing, we have just had a five-star fuck - and all for the price of a second-hand diamond bracelet."

"You mean that you arranged the whole thing: the sex and the photographer?"

"Yes," he said looking smug.

"But why?"

"'A friend in need' and all that."

"Well, I'm damned grateful, Ali, but you must at the very least allow me to pay you for the photographer and the bracelet. I can recover the costs from the Household."

"I wouldn't hear of it, old chap. It was a trifle to pay for such an evening. But - if you insist on making a small contribution - then I'll roll over and you can once again show me your gratitude..."

The following morning, we met, as we'd agreed before he left for his own hotel, for a late breakfast at the Cafe des Deux Magots on the Left Bank to plan the successful completion of my task for the Brotherhood. Ali arrived carrying a large manila envelope.

"What have you got there?" I asked him as he lowered himself into a wicker chair opposite mine. He handed me the package with a grin.

"The evidence - and don't wave it around or we'll be mobbed or arrested."

Cautiously, I opened the envelope and, without pulling out the photograph, peeked in. I could see enough to know that I was handling high explosive.

"What are we going to do with it?"

"I've been giving that some thought," he replied. "It seems to me that it would be dangerous to rely on Marguerite's belief that this is her husband's doing. She's bound to see him at some point and that will raise some very awkward questions. No, I think that the best thing to do would be to launch our attack from a wholly different quarter."

"What did you have in mind?"

"In my experience, it's always a good idea to stick as close to the truth as possible. To that end we should draft a letter that will appear to have been written by HRH's Principal Equerry, in which we will state that unless Marguerite breaks with the Prince and returns his letters the photograph will be sent to her husband - and *Le Monde*."

"But they'd never publish it."

"Of course not, we all know that, but Marguerite will shit herself at the thought of that photo lying in a file in *Le Monde*'s offices and the leverage it will give the editor over her."

"But why should she care?"

"If she was just a common tart, she wouldn't. But she undoubtedly still has ambitions to play La Pompadour with your future King and that would be fatally compromised if she had to kiss him and then tell all to *Le Monde*."

"Could it work?"

"It can't fail. She'll have to break with the Prince - for now - and send his letters to the Palace: they'll both be surprised, but no one will ask any questions and if you aren't in next year's Birthday Honours I'll eat my fez."

"But what's in it for you, Ali?"

"The solution to my own problem."

"What's that?"

"Like all Egyptians of my age and class I'm coming under considerable family pressure to get married. Frankly, I can't think of anything worse that having to live with one or more of my fellow countrywomen and as for having to service them regularly, it doesn't bear thinking about. But if

I was to marry Marguerite I would at least be certain that the after-hours entertainment will be up to scratch."

"Why would she agree to marry you, even if she did ditch her current husband - and what makes you think that you wouldn't have to share her with half of Cairo Society and the Prince of Wales?"

"The answers to your questions are easy: I will offer her money - lots of money - and a title. She has a much better chance of being a grand lady if she marries me than if she tries to snag the real thing. I may only be a Bey but that won't stop her from calling herself a Princess. As for her infidelity: once we are living in Cairo and Alexandria she will for the most part be confined to the women's quarters and so won't have the opportunity. Of course, if she ever found out about all this I'm sure she'd shoot me!" And one day she did find out, but that's a story for later in this tale.

In the meantime, Ali's plan went almost without a hitch. I say 'almost' because, although Marguerite packed her bags and announced that she had decided to pass the rest of the winter in the sun (the sun of Egypt, you won't be surprised to learn), there was no sign of the diminutively-equipped Prince's letters as I learnt from Hamilton, who summoned me to his temporary office at our Embassy, situated somewhat appropriately adjacent to the recent scene of our debauch. I was expecting, at the very least, an effusive thank you and the promise of an honour.

"It would seem, Speedicut, that the first part of your assignment proved easier than any of us expected," he sneered. I was about to ask him if he had ever tried simultaneous-two-way penetration whilst being photographed in the act, but I thought better of it and made a dismissive gesture with my hand which implied that it was all in a day's work.

"As to the letters," he went on, "they are still in the lady's possession and, as such, pose a real and present danger to His Royal Highness." I said nothing. "So, what do you propose to do in order to recover them?"

Because I had no intention of doing anything further and, indeed, had agreed with Ali that he would arrange for their recovery once Marguerite had become Mrs Fahmy, I decided that a diversionary tactic was required.

"Miss Meller is on her way to Egypt," I said, "so there's not much that I can do - unless you issue me with a First Class return ticket for Cairo and book me a suite at Shepheard's." The colour rose dangerously in the courtier's pink cheeks but, before he could say anything, I continued: "and whilst you are about it, I would be grateful for payment – as promised - of my not inconsiderable expenses to date."

I thought he would have apoplexy at this and, for a moment, he seemed lost for words. At last he recovered and his tone was, to my surprise, faintly emollient which should have put me on my guard.

"I will, of course, arrange for you to be reimbursed and, on reflection, I don't think it will be necessary for you to follow the lady to the East. I will entrust the recovery of the letters to another department," for which read the Secret Service, I thought, "and - once I have your written undertaking that you will respect the confidentiality of this matter - I can release you from royal service."

I assured him that I would sign anything he put in front of me and the next moment I was signing a paper that was supposed to seal my lips on the subject of The Prince of Wales's carnal indiscretions.

"Thank you," he continued once I'd handed the document back to him, "I can now arrange…" Here comes the CVO, I thought, "for your immediate posting to your regiment." At first, I was sure I had misheard him. "The Tenth are, I believe," he went on, as my jaw headed towards my flies, "in reserve, but have recently deployed an infantry Company in the front line." I could scarcely believe what I was hearing, "… and I know that your Commanding Officer is keen to deploy your military talents with the new dismounted unit."

I was sure that the Tenth were completely unaware of my existence, so how could I have been singled out for this duty? It was a death sentence and, at that thought, the penny dropped: my silence on the subject of the Prince's indiscretions was to be doubly guaranteed by a German bullet. What could I say? Then, as the mud and blood of Flanders nearly closed over my head, I had a brainwave.

"Is Sir Philip Sassoon aware of this?" I asked with as much composure as I could muster. "When I last spoke to him, he mentioned that he had another assignment for me once I'd cleared up your mess." A look of extreme distaste flitted across the courtier's features.

"Sir Philip? I'm not sure what *locus* he has in this matter - besides which, he is far too busy with the C-in-C to be troubled with the posting of a line cavalry subaltern." That's all you know, I thought. "But we will, of course, be speaking to him about you," he ended with a nasty gleam in his eye. Well, in the absence of a gong, congratulating the GB on my performance wouldn't go amiss, I added to myself.

Ten minutes later I was back at the reception desk of the Westminster where I sent a telegram to Philip at GHQ. The following morning, I got an answer:

AWAIT MY ARRIVAL TOMORROW STOP ACQUIRE CIVILIAN WINTER AND SUMMER WEAR STOP GB

My relief that I was to be spared the prospect of certain death in the trenches was replaced by anxiety at Philip's instruction to equip myself for St Moritz and Cap Ferrat. Where could he be sending me? Clearly, it wasn't back to the Land of Sand in pursuit of the Meller letters, as I would have required only one half of the new wardrobe, and the same held true of the trenches in the unlikely event that the Palace had over-ruled Philip on the subject of my next posting. I decided to share the problem with the Khazis, who had been distinctly under-employed whilst I had been using my principal asset in the service of King and Country.

"It is a good question, huzoor," said Atash somewhat unhelpfully.

"It could indicate that Sir Philip has more than one destination in mind, huzoor," said Fahran.

"I agree, but where? I won't need a fur-lined overcoat in Egypt and I won't need swimming trunks on the Western Front."

"Perhaps it's not a military task, huzoor," said Atash, who seemed to have upped his game.

"But, with a war on, what else could it be?"

"There is a war in East Africa, huzoor," said Fahran.

"But if that's where he's sending me, why would I need winter clothes?"

"It can be cold on Mount Kilimanjaro, huzoor," said Atash. I didn't answer that suggestion.

"Maybe he has news of the burra memsahib, huzoor, and is going to get you to rescue her," he continued, looking a bit shamefaced. I knew that springing my relations from durance vile in Russia was high on my staff's agenda, but it wasn't high on mine.

"Possibly, but that still doesn't explain why I need summer clothes. The last we heard of them, my half-sister and her family were being held in St Petersburg."

"They could have been moved to the Crimea where some of the Imperial family are being held," said Fahran, "and it can be warm there at this time of year."

"So why then would Sir Philip tell me to invest in an overcoat – it's hardly likely that he would want me to travel there from the north, which is now under the control of the Reds. The obvious route to the Crimea is via Persia."

"Or from the east with the White Russian forces," said Fahran, who seemed to be well informed about events in Russia, "that would account for the need for the two different types of clothes."

"But the last I heard of the Whites," I said, dimly recalling a newspaper article I'd read the previous week, "they were headed for Moscow not the Crimea." And so, the debate wore on until the point where we found we were going around in circles. "Alright," I said at last, "we'll just have to wait until tomorrow and, in the meantime, go shopping."

And that is what we did, although I drew the line at the floppy hat, cotton drill suit and mosquito netting which Atash, who was obviously trying to keep my mind on Africa, said I should acquire. It was just as well that I did.

"Are you packed and ready, *mon chèr*," asked Philip when he arrived at my suite the day after our shopping expedition.

"Ye-es," I said, "although it would have been helpful to have known my destination." Philip ignored this reproach.

"*Sa Majesté* is most grateful for the way in which you ended *l'affaire* Meller."

"How does he know?"

"Brother Stamfordham telephoned me at GHQ to say so."[112]

"How did he know?"

"It seems that Claud Hamilton telephoned him *avec les bonnes nouvelles*." I wondered what else he'd said: in all probability, a recommendation that I be sent to the trenches as a reward. "He was most complimentary and said that the King now relies on you for the next *affaire*."

"Is the King in the Brotherhood?" I asked in disbelief.

---

[112] The Rt Hon the Lord Stamfordham GCB GCIE GCVO KCSI KCMG ISO PC (1849-1931), Private Secretary to King George V (1910-1931).

"*Certainement non, Charles,*" said Philip, "but, as you know, his Private Secretary is."

"I see," I said, "but Hamilton said – despite what The King has said – that I'd been released from royal service."

"So you have been - but not from that of the Brotherhood - unless, that is, you are keen to join *ton regiment*, a sentiment I would applaud *avec regret*."

"Not really," I said somewhat cautiously for, if The King was involved, the alternative was probably even more unappealing. "So, what does he want me to do? Rescue my half-sister?"

"*Malheureusement non, mon chèr Charles,*" he said with a look of real concern on his face, "I am afraid that *la famille Lieven* will have to wait." Thank God for that, I thought. It was the briefest of respites for Philip went on: "The King now regrets bowing to his government's refusal to offer *sanctuaire à sa tante et ses cousins* and has told Stamfordham that *la famille impériale* must be rescued."

"But if Lloyd George won't agree,[113] surely that's a pipe dream?"

"This is a *family* matter," said Philip somewhat enigmatically.

"So, you want me to go to the Crimea and collect the Dowager Empress. Is that all?" I sighed in relief. "Why then do I need winter clothes?"

"Because it is not just the Dowager Empress *et sa fille* who you are to bring out."

"What?" I asked in horror, "who else?"

"You are to facilitate the escape from Russia of as many members of *la famille impériale* as are rescued by the Whites - and to ensure *leur passage sûr vers la Crimée*, where a British warship will be waiting to take them to safety and exile in Canada."

---

[113] The Rt Hon David Lloyd George (1863-1945), Prime Minister.

"Where are the Whites at the moment?"

"In Siberia, heading west towards Tobolsk where the Tsar and his family are being held."

"But surely the Reds will move the family if they think that Tobolsk is going to fall to the Whites?"

"Unless you were able to rescue them *before* the Whites get to the Tsar."

"You're not serious, are you?" I asked in disbelief, as the trenches started to take on the appeal of the Côte d'Azur in a mild winter.

"Ça dépend."

"On what?"

But before he could reply, Fahran entered.

"Sir Philip," he said giving my Nemesis a deep bow, "there is an urgent telephone call for you at reception."

"Wait here," said Philip, "I will be back as quickly as I can." Half an hour later Fahran returned without Philip but with a message.

"Sir Philip has been recalled to GHQ, huzoor, but he said that we were to return to London and await his further instructions there."

Once back at Mount Street I didn't have long to wait for a telegram which, despite its reassuring contents, was to launch me on the most dangerous mission of my life up to that date:

> CHANGE OF PLAN STOP RESCUE OF DOWAGER EMPRESS NOW PRIORITY STOP DETAILED ITINERARY ETC TO FOLLOW STOP GB

...

Printed in Great Britain
by Amazon